The Passer

∞

Robin Christophersen

Book Cover Design by Jason Bradley-Krauss at
House of Krauss Graphic Design

ISBN-13: 9781493589630
ISBN-10: 1493589636
Library of Congress Control Number: 2013920520
CreateSpace Independent Publishing Platform
North Charleston, South Carolina

-To Jonathan and Karen for their time and talents
-To Brenda and Sam V for their enthusiasm
-To Roy for his unending love and support, and for making this journey possible

The quotes noted at the beginning of each chapter are from the following plays by William Shakespeare and are listed below in the order in which they were performed by the Alexandria Shakespeare Festival during their summer season.

Romeo and Juliet
A Midsummer Night's Dream
Hamlet

Prologue

∞

"Jeremy?"

Eleanor's voice melded with the thunder as it rumbled through the room. No answer. The wind was building outside, rushing through the trees, growing louder and louder until a tremendous force shook the entire house. Another crash sounded from the kitchen.

"Jeremy!"

No response.

Damn.

She threw off the covers, grabbing her cell phone from the night stand. The tavern had closed more than two hours ago. He should have been home by now. As she rushed through the family room and into the kitchen, she could see both deck doors rotating violently on their hinges, water pouring through the open doorway. She was certain that she had locked up before she went to bed.

It occurred to her, while she slid across the wet kitchen floor, that Jeremy had not answered his phone because it was nearly impossible to get a cellular signal inside his restaurant. No one could ever get their mobile to work in that building, and it was a well-known fact in the tiny community of River Mist, that if you wished to be less accessible to the instant access world, you went to Jeremy's Tavern. However, there was always the restaurant landline, which she dialed while she secured the first of the heavy deck doors. She was forwarded to the answering machine. Now her only choices were to either call the sheriff's office or go looking for Jeremy herself.

Grabbing her raincoat and boots from the laundry room, she figured she could be driving down the mountainside towards downtown River Mist within two minutes. As she started for the foyer she realized she had neglected to secure the second deck door and returned to the kitchen. Her hand had nearly grasped the long metal handle when she caught the outline of a large, dark object moving across the deck. She froze, watching from the corner of her eye as the four-legged creature made another pass inches from where she was standing.

Her mind raced. It was too late to secure the door. Either she remained in place and hoped the bear wandered off or make a run for it. The decision was made for her when another rush of wind barreled through the kitchen, sending the door slamming against the wall and the bear bounding into the house. Now, both her heart and mind raced as she sprinted toward her bedroom door.

Jeremy had insisted that she keep his shotgun next to the bed- especially when he was working late- but in all the years that they lived in this house not once did she ever have to use it. Now, as she grabbed the heavy weapon and steadied it against her trembling body, she wondered if she even remembered how it worked. The bear approached, grunting. She backed away from the doorway, her heart pounding wildly as the bear's shadow grew larger against the hallway wall. Placing a shaking finger against the trigger, she took a deep breath and aimed at the looming figure.

Then the bear stopped, its shadow growing smaller and smaller until it completely disappeared. She waited for several moments before inching her way forward. Pausing at the door, she listened for any movement in the family room, surprised when she heard the sound of footsteps on the stone floor. Her gun aimed and ready, she turned the corner into the hallway and found him standing in the kitchen.

"Jeremy, don't move. There's a bear in the house."

Eleanor crept into the middle of the large family room, scanning across the front sitting area, into the entryway and up the stairwell leading to the second level. There was no movement in the loft overlooking the kitchen, and both of the guest bedroom doors were closed. She followed the staircase back down and towards the dark doorway that led to the laundry room. That was when she noticed the line of muddy paw prints trailing across the kitchen floor, ending at the puddle of water that had formed around Jeremy's feet. She looked up at his face and saw the blood streaming down his neck, saturating the front of his light-blue Jeremy's Tavern T-shirt.

"Oh my God, what happened to you?"

She started towards him but he backed away, signaling for her to stop.

"Are you kidding? You're bleeding like crazy. I need to get you to a hospital."

Jeremy shook his head as he moved towards the open deck door. Suddenly she knew what he was up to and could not believe she had allowed this to happen to her again.

"Dammit Garrison, you either stay here and we talk, or you leave and *never* come back. Do you hear me?"

Her threat apparently registered, because he stopped and locked his piercing blue gaze on her. Immediately she regretted her harsh words.

"I'm sorry. I didn't mean to say that. Please don't go."

As usual he stood silent, his glassy stare ripping her heart into pieces. She took a tentative step forward, hoping this time he would allow her to approach him. He continued to back away.

"I'm begging you. Please don't leave me."

He hovered near the doorway and Eleanor thought that surely this time he would give in to her plea, but it was not to be. He met her eyes for a brief moment before vanishing through the doorway. By the time she ran onto the deck he had passed his workshop and was nearing the woods, his familiar silhouette fading into the darkness. Lightening rippled across the treetops and she saw the bear slowly lumbering along the perimeter of trees that rimmed their property.

Shotgun in hand, she started after him. She was nearing his workshop when she noticed a shimmering light deep within the woods. At first it appeared as a tiny sparkle, twinkling like a distant star. But, then it began to grow larger, and she realized that whatever it was, it was rapidly approaching the backyard heading directly towards her.

She spun around, sprinting across the yard and onto the deck. She had nearly reached the kitchen door when a brilliant flash of light overtook her, sending a jolt of electricity shooting through her limbs.

When she opened her eyes, she was lying on the deck, looking up at an apparition floating over her. She could not make out any details of its face or form, other than its crystalline blue eyes and golden beams of hair. It was beautiful to behold, and as the white creature met her gaze, exhilaration and terror swept through her simultaneously. She was convinced that she had been struck dead by a bolt of lightning, and an angel had come to retrieve her.

Then the radiant being reached towards her and Eleanor extended her arm. Their fingers intertwined, and her body lifted off of the deck as her mind exploded with a rush of thoughts and images, thousands and thousands of them blasting through her veins. They filled her up at such a rapid speed she could barely hold onto a one, and she gave herself over to the white creature as a monstrous roar rattled the earth.

Help him believe.

Eleanor's eyes shot open as her body jolted awake.

"Jeremy!"

His name echoed through her bedroom.

The dreams had returned.

ACT I

Awakening

Chapter One

Sleep dwell upon thine eyes, peace in thy breast!
Would I were sleep and peace, so sweet to rest!

∞

Eleanor remembered the first time Jeremy spoke those words to her, on that fateful day at Julliard when they first met. He entered the rehearsal space with Alex Leesman, the director and head of the drama division, who promptly escorted the ruggedly handsome actor to a large table where the cast of *Romeo and Juliet* had assembled. A hush fell over the room as Alex pointed his West Coast protégé to an empty seat directly across from her.

"I thought it best you two get acquainted before we commence," Dr. Leesman instructed before assuming his position at the head of the table.

Jeremy introduced himself as *your Romeo*, flashing an irresistible grin as he extended a bronze arm across the table. Eleanor swore she heard a collective sigh emanate from the entire cast. When it was her turn to reciprocate she could barely form the words.

"Eleanor Bouchard...Juliet."

During the entire first rehearsal she was unable to take her gaze off of him. He was entrancing: piercing blue eyes, golden tousled waves, and an incredibly sweet smile. By the time they reached the balcony scene she had to fight to keep her mind focused on her lines and off his hypnotic good looks. She could not tell if Leesman was grimacing or smirking when she delivered Juliet's famous quote, trembling from head to toe:

"Good night, good night! Parting is such sweet sorrow

That I shall say good night till it be morrow."

Never had she been so thankful to have a rehearsal come to an end. Embarrassed by her complete lack of decorum she bolted for the nearest exit, only to have him chase after her and ask her out for a drink. She politely declined his offer as she escaped through the doorway, but he persisted, following her down the hallway and out the front entrance into a warm September afternoon. Finally, tired of the pursuit, he grabbed her arm. To this day she still shuddered to think of that moment when she felt his touch. She turned to look at him, swearing she had met him before.

A few hours and glasses of wine later, she learned that he had lived in Northern California his entire life, most recently in San Francisco where he had met Dr. Leesman. Alex had been spending summers in The Bay Area developing a regional Shakespeare festival, and had directed Jeremy in several productions. After a few years of prodding, Leesman convinced Jeremy to audition at Julliard, and now at the age of 24 he was just beginning his college career.

Eleanor shared with him that she was in her final year at Julliard and was planning to attend graduate school at either Yale or Pace. He told her that he was single with no attachments back home, and she begrudgingly relayed to him her recent, rather painful break-up from another actor who was living in New York.

Jeremy burst into laughter.

"What's so funny?" Eleanor asked.

He continued to laugh, explaining that he knew the actor to whom she was referring and that the break-up had been mentioned in the Los Angeles Times. Then, seeming to realize he had embarrassed her, he apologized for his rudeness.

"That's all right," she said. "We're still friends. We just didn't work as a couple."

At that point he ceased laughing, and inquired as to whether or not there was a chance they might reconcile. When she told him no that it was most certainly over, he leaned in, expressing his relief. Though she savored the moment when his lips met hers and her body turned to mush, she could not ignore the warning in her head: *stop, before this goes too far.* But, as they paid their bill and found the nearest exit, she told herself this would be a good thing, a chance to forget her current sadness for a while.

That night…

It still unnerved her to think she had ever been that incredibly horny or brave. Within the week she was hooked on the talented actor from Northern California, and by the end of the run of *Romeo and Juliet* her world had been turned upside down. She fell in love and she fell hard.

Sixteen years ago….it passed by so fast.

Kneeling, she cleared a spot for her vase of yellow roses, his favorite. She had not seen this many flowers since the funeral: dozens of arrangements surrounded the headstone, creating an eclectic show of colors that spread well beyond his plot. Everyone remembered, but then again, how could they forget? Jeremy was an institution in this town, a local boy who had gone off to pursue his dreams in the big city and then returned because he could not imagine calling anywhere else home. She had never met a person in River Mist who did not know him or had not heard of him, and from the display of flowers dwarfing his gravesite, she imagined that there were many thinking about Jeremy today.

Tiny flakes of white began to fall. Shivering, she leaned forward and wiped the icy droplets from the inscription. A few years ago, after they had survived a rough time in their relationship, Jeremy had told her he wanted the quote from *Romeo and Juliet* inscribed on his gravestone. At the time she shrugged it off as a sentimental reaction to their near breakup, but when he died she discovered the request was in his will, so she was bound to honor it. She touched her fingers to her lips and placed them against the cold stone.

"I shall forget, to have thee still stand there,
Rememb'ring how I love thy company."

A series of beeps jolted her from her reverie. She turned to discover Jeremy's closest friend, Jared Adams, disappearing down the hillside with a phone pressed to his ear. Realizing her private mourning had ended, she said a final goodbye before walking to the edge of the gravesite. At the bottom of the hill she found the scruffy detective, cigarette in hand, pacing as he talked. She signaled for him to join her.

Jared finished his call and jogged up to the gravesite, taking a puff from his cigarette before flicking it to the ground. His dark, thick hair was highlighted with specks of snow.

"Sorry, I didn't mean to disturb you. There is some issue with an abandoned car nearby. So, how are you?" Jared said.

"Let's just say I'll be glad when this day is over. Where have you been? I haven't seen you at the restaurant in a while."

"I know. It's been crazy lately. And with Jeremy gone, I really don't have a legitimate excuse to hang out there all the time. If you know what I mean."

"Well," she said. "I think everyone would expect to see you today."

"Yeah, I guess. Damn, that's a lot of flowers."

"Amazing, isn't it? I can't believe it's been a year already."

Jared grew quiet as he approached the headstone. Kneeling among the sea of flowers, he pulled a small object from his coat pocket, studying it. As he placed it next to her vase of roses she saw that it was a ring, somewhat worn, with an unusual marking on top.

"What is that?" she said.

"A memento from our San Francisco years. I thought it was lost, but I found it a few days ago in a mover's box."

"You do realize it's been six years since you moved back."

"What can I say? I'm still unpacking."

"What's the history behind it?"

"That's between Jeremy and me." Jared winked as he stood, brushing the snow from his black trench coat.

"All right, I guess I won't pry. Besides, San Francisco was before my time." She glanced at the gravestone and was reminded of a question she wanted to ask. "Weren't you called in for Jeremy's accident?"

"Yes." He pulled a crumbled cigarette pack from his pocket. "Do you mind?"

"No. I know this is going to sound strange, but I have a few questions and I was hoping you could answer them."

"Sure. What do you want to know?"

"Well, first off, when you found Jeremy was he inside the car?"

Jared lit his cigarette and inhaled before answering. "No. We found him several feet away. Apparently he had been thrown out on impact."

4

"He wasn't wearing his seat belt?"

"No."

"That doesn't sound like him. In fact, he was always on me about buckling up before I even started the engine."

"Believe me," he said. "I saw his body and there was no way he was wearing a seatbelt."

His voice was cold, and when she met his eyes he immediately looked away.

"I never saw him after the accident, only after the undertaker had fixed him up. Do you remember the extent of his injuries, especially around his head?"

"Eleanor, where is this going?"

"I just want to know what happened to him, that's all. Where on his head was he injured?"

Jared shifted his gaze towards Jeremy's grave, slowly inhaling his cigarette. He seemed to be thinking through his next response. "He sustained one major blow to the back of the head."

"Just one?" she said.

"For God's sake Eleanor, his head smashed against a boulder, completely crushing the back of his skull. The coroner said that's what killed him."

"Do you know if he suffered at all?"

"He probably died instantaneously. Why are you asking about this now? Has something happened?"

"You have to promise me you won't get upset."

"Just tell me what it is," he said.

"I had a dream about Jeremy last night. Or, I guess it was early this morning."

Jared's eyes narrowed. "Was it like the other ones?"

"Yes. Except for the very end, and I'm not entirely sure what that was about. But when I woke up this morning, I realized I had no idea how Jeremy had been injured. I just knew that he had died in the crash."

A round of beeps sounded from Jared's coat pocket and he retrieved his cell phone. "Dammit. Sorry, I have to go."

"Is it that abandoned car you mentioned earlier?"

"Yes. It looks like we have a little problem. Come walk with me."

As they hurried down the hill, Eleanor's eyes fell on the several dozen gravestones that populated the small cemetery. Only a few families were buried here; old families that had been in River Mist since its inception. All of Jeremy's family was here, and someday if she chose to, she would join them, forever looking out across the vast expanse of valley below.

When they arrived at Jared's car they quickly embraced.

"Thanks for answering my questions," she said. "I know it probably sounds odd, but I feel better knowing what happened to him. Oh, and for the record, I'm not worried about the dream."

Jared threw down his cigarette, crushing it with his foot. "Look, everybody is expecting it to be a tough day for you. I'm not worried either, but it sounds like this dream was different?"

"It was. It ended the same, with Jeremy disappearing, but then there was this thing that came to me and…"

Another round of beeps fired off and Jared shook his head as he placed his phone to his ear. She gave a short wave and turned for her car.

Driving down the mountainside towards downtown River Mist, Eleanor was reminded of why she loved it here more than any other place she had ever been. At this early morning hour, as she entered the final curve before descending into the foothills of Birch Mountain, she was met with a glorious merging of heaven and earth. She pulled into an overlook and as she watched the final moments of the sunrise illuminating the woodlands below, she was reminded of how incredibly beautiful, even on a wintry day, her little corner of the world could be. Like Jeremy, she could not imagine living anywhere else, and like Jeremy she would always call River Mist home.

Jared ended his call just as Eleanor's blue Forester left the parking lot. He rolled down his window and lit another cigarette, his mind churning.

For a moment, I thought she knew.

Chapter Two

Now cracks a noble heart. Good night, sweet prince,
And flights of angels sing thee to thy rest.

The actor who played Horatio had just delivered his lines to the slain Hamlet when Daniel Archer caught several voices murmuring backstage. Daniel had died, as he had for the past several performances, facing stage left, close enough to view the commotion stirring in the wings. When he opened his eyes, he did not expect to find his personal assistant, Trevor Kincaid, a NYPD officer, and the stage manager engaging in an intense conversation. Soon their voices were silenced by the rapid pounding in his chest.

When the curtain fell everything seemed to shift into slow motion. The actors hovering on stage stopped moving as the somber trio approached him. It was the distressed look on his assistant's face that made his heart race, and when Trevor took his arm, relaying that his wife, Katharine, had been in a serious accident, Daniel's senses left him. He remembered several hands reaching for him, leading him offstage; mouths were moving, but he could not hear.

He vaguely remembered the ride in the police cruiser as Trevor explained that the power had gone out in his apartment building and that Katharine was found unconscious at the bottom of the stairs. When they arrived at the hospital the local news had already assembled, but he barely registered the blur of cameras as he was rushed through the emergency room doors.

By the time the surgeon met with him, his entire body was numb. The doctor relayed the severity of Katharine's head trauma and the concern that there was bleeding inside her brain. Other injuries were discussed, but Daniel lost track of them. The doctor firmly gripped his shoulder, checking for his understanding. When Daniel assured him that he comprehended the seriousness of Katharine's condition, he was allowed to enter her room. Trevor and he spent a sleepless night at her side.

By early morning her condition had deteriorated, requiring emergency surgery to relieve a confirmed subdural hematoma. An hour later she had a seizure on the operating table; her heart stopped beating, and Katharine Monroe was pronounced dead.

As the surgeon delivered the news Daniel's world fell silent. He recalled steadying Trevor as they were ushered into an operating room. The various machines that had been attached to her during surgery had been rolled away and Katharine lay on a table, a sheet pulled up to her shoulders and a surgical cap on her head.

Gone were her flowing golden locks and rosy complexion; her long, thin face bore several bruises and her lips were swollen and blue. Her eyes were closed, but he could still picture them in his mind: large, luminous, crystal blue, encircled by a dark rim. Day or night, her eyes would sparkle like sunlight on the water, entrancing and at times unnerving, much like Katharine herself.

Trevor only lasted a few moments before he broke into tears. He kissed Katharine on the forehead and told Daniel he would wait for him outside.

Alone, Daniel approached the table and placed his hand against her colorless skin. Less than 15 hours earlier he was brushing his lips against her check, a hasty kiss goodbye as he passed her on the way out the front door. She followed after him into the hallway, watching him as he rushed down the stairs. How was he to know that the brief moment he took to look up and wave would be the last time he would see her alive?

A hand on his shoulder pulled him from his dark thoughts and back into the living room of his in-laws. He lifted his head to find Trevor placing a steaming cup of coffee and a manila folder in front of him.

"How long have I been sitting here?" Daniel said.

"For about an hour now. I wouldn't have bothered you, except I received a text from Mr. Monroe's driver that they are on the way. Also, Michael faxed over the press release for you to review, which is in that folder in front of you. Your lawyer said to check your e-mail for a message regarding a discussion you had with him earlier this morning. And Father Jessup from St. Francis is coming over later to help with the funeral arrangements."

Daniel buried his face in his hands, groaning.

"I know," Trevor said. "That's why I scheduled the meeting for this afternoon when Mr. and Mrs. Monroe are here."

Daniel sank back into the living room couch as Trevor placed a container of toothpicks next to his cup. He felt mildly irritated with his young assistant's gesture, but when he glanced down at his half-chewed fingernails he flipped open the top and put one in his mouth.

"So, you might as well give me the bad news now," Daniel said.

"Well, it's been on all the major news networks since early this morning. Also, the media is now camped out in front of your apartment building. I imagine it won't be long before they work their way uptown."

"Paparazzi?"

"Yes. Both Monroe Industries and Michael have been inundated with calls all morning. I've received a few as well, mostly from your friends."

"Mostly Kate's, I'm sure."

"I did speak with Dr. Leesman," Trevor said.

"Alex called? What did he say?"

"Well, actually, he was trying to get hold of Michael, but he did tell me that he's planning on attending the funeral and hoped he could see you while he was here."

Daniel quickly retrieved his iPhone and started paging through his messages. "I don't understand why he didn't just call my cell."

"I imagine he didn't want to bother you."

"Are you sure he didn't say anything else?" Trevor shook his head. "What about the police?"

"Still at the apartment I'm afraid," Trevor said. "Have you heard back from the officer who visited you at the hospital this morning?"

"Damn, I forgot about him. No, I haven't. Where the hell did I put that card?"

"It's in your leather jacket. I'll get it for you," Trevor said.

"OK, but can you call Michael first and…"

"He's actually coming over shortly to discuss your replacement for the show. Oh, and the Monroes' cook has arrived. Can I get you something to eat?"

"How long before they get here?"

"Ten minutes. Daniel, I really think you should eat something before …"

"Before what? Just get the bourbon from the bar, OK?"

Daniel checked his e-mail, locating his lawyer's message. When Trevor returned, he snatched the bottle from his hand, pouring a generous shot into his coffee cup.

"Are you sure that's a good idea?" Trevor said.

Daniel held his iPhone in front of Trevor so he could read the message from Hank Stevenson titled RE: Amelia Adoption. He watched Trevor's expression turn grim.

"Oh Daniel, I'm so sorry. I know this is the last thing that you need right now."

"Tell me about it." He drank a large gulp from his cup and glanced over at Trevor. "You know, I think you're the one who needs to eat. You're looking more peaked than usual."

"You're just trying to get rid of me."

"Yep, so I suggest you go." Daniel poured another shot of bourbon in his cup while his lanky assistant continued to hover over him. "Now!"

Trevor left without further argument and the apartment grew quiet. Uneasy with the silence, he left the comfort of the soft leather couch and barreled across the spacious living room, throwing open the balcony door. Once he stepped out into the cold March air the sound of the busy traffic gave him solace. Closing the heavy ornate doors behind him, he settled into a lounge chair that had been covered for the winter.

Looking out over Central Park he recalled the first time he visited this apartment. Katharine and he had recently met while making a movie together and their relationship had progressed enough that it was time to meet her family. He could still remember the shock he felt when he walked through the front door and stood in the massive foyer.

Oh my God! I could easily fit five of my apartments into this place. I knew Kate came from money, but I had no idea.

After a tour of the 12,000 square foot penthouse, Daniel learned that it had been in the Monroe family since 1940, when Katharine's grandfather, Phillip Monroe, Sr. purchased the building. Her father inherited the apartment during the 1970s when he became CEO of Monroe Industries. It would be Katharine's home until they were married.

Ten years ago…

The balcony doors flew open and Amelia Monroe appeared. She ran to him, throwing her arms around his neck. He pulled her close, her wet cheeks rubbing against his face, wondering how he could possibly console his daughter when he was unable to feel anything. She tightened her hold around his neck.

"Don't worry Daddy. I'm good."

Amelia had always been a precocious child, but her comment still gave him pause. He pulled away so he could look at her. "Honey, it's all right for you to be upset."

"I don't want you to worry about me."

He cradled her grown-up face in his hands, wiping the tears from her cold, red cheeks. "I'm your Dad, baby girl. I'm supposed to worry about you and love you. And I do love you, very, very much."

"I love you, too, Daddy."

He pulled her onto his lap, her head resting against his chest. Closing his eyes, he focused on the sound of her breathing, wishing he could hide out here with her forever. His hope was short lived when he heard someone walk onto the balcony.

"She didn't sleep at all last night."

Daniel opened his eyes to find Katharine's father standing over him, wearing his winter coat and gloves.

"Phillip."

"Hello son. You look terrible." The elegantly dressed patriarch patted Daniel's face, smiling.

"Were you able to make it over to the hospital?" Daniel said.

"We were. Only Christine and I saw her, of course." Phillip sat next to him, whispering. "I just spoke to Trevor. He told me that the police stopped by the hospital this morning? Did they have anything to say about the accident?"

"Honestly, I hardly remember the conversation, but the officer said he would call me sometime today."

Phillip nodded as he stroked Amelia's long, blond hair. For a moment his calm faded as his pale eyes rimmed with tears. Then he stood, walking to the edge of the balcony, his silver hair shimmering against his gray cashmere coat.

"I remember the first time I saw this apartment. I was struck by the magnificent view. Christine was all about the kitchen, of course, but for me it was this. Katharine was almost Amelia's age when we moved here, and she used to love to sit with me and gaze at the skyline. It moves by so quickly. So, so quickly." He retrieved a handkerchief from his pocket and wiped his eyes. After a few moments he regained his composure and turned to Daniel. "I am going to say this now, while we have a few moments alone."

Daniel felt a lump form in his throat.

"Amelia loves you, and to her and to our family you are her father. Even Christine can't deny that. However, as you already know, my wife believes she should have Amelia. I am not entirely clear as to her reasons. Though I am sure losing her only child is mostly driving it. But, I am here to tell you that I won't support her in a custody fight and that I believe Amelia belongs with you. It's what Katharine would have wanted and I know it's what Amelia wants."

"Does Christine know this?"

"Yes. I told her before we left Toronto. She hasn't spoken to me since."

"I'm sorry Phillip. I don't want to do this, believe me."

"I've been down this road with Christine before. I understand how to handle her, but I also acknowledge that she is suffering greatly, which brings me to a request. I know how you two are son, and I am asking you to avoid any altercations with her these next few days. I will ask her to do the same. Can you agree to this?"

Daniel nodded.

"Good. Well, now that is out of the way, I guess we should head inside. It's quite cold out here. Do you need any help?" He pointed to Amelia.

"Nope, I'm good." With one swift movement Daniel swung his legs over the side of the lounge chair and stood. Amelia barely stirred.

"Good God, man. No wonder they hire you for those action movies."

"I'm still benefiting from my last role. The personal trainer was amazing. But don't tell Amelia. She thinks I have some sort of super-human strength."

Phillip held open the balcony door for Daniel as he entered the living room, and head-on into a livid Christine Monroe.

"I wondered where you two were." Christine said. "Have you been out there this whole time?" She placed the back of her manicured hand against Amelia's face. "For heaven's sake Daniel she's freezing cold. I'll take her."

Christine carted his daughter away before he could say a word. Phillip gripped his arm.

"Just let it go, son. I'll have a talk with her."

Phillip left just as Trevor entered the living room, bearing a fresh cup of coffee. His assistant gave him a studied look before setting down the cup and pulling out his laptop.

"Do you have a hotel preference?" Trevor asked.

Daniel shook his head as he poured the bourbon into his cup. As usual Trevor was one step ahead of him. Several minutes later Trevor said there were suites available at the Four Seasons through the weekend. He was about to call the hotel when Phillip came marching towards them.

"Do not book that reservation young man. Daniel and Amelia are staying here."

"I appreciate the offer Phillip, but I can't," Daniel said.

"It wasn't an offer. This is your home too, and there is absolutely no reason why you should stay anywhere else."

"You want me to avoid a meltdown with Christine? This is how I plan to deal with it."

"I told you to leave Christine to me and I have taken care of it. Listen to me son. We need to be a family right now. We have a funeral to plan and a growing media frenzy to deal with. Not to mention the fact we haven't been able to reach Charles."

"Why? What's going on with Lourdes?"

"Nothing as of yet, but the point I'm trying to make is that the next few days are going to be very difficult, and it would be best for all of us if we dealt with it together. We can't accomplish that if you and Amelia are hiding out in some hotel."

Daniel sat silent while he considered Phillip's argument. "OK we'll stay. But I swear if Christine starts in about anything, I'm out of here."

"She won't. She gave me her word. You should take it easy, son. You look like you are about to implode." Phillip turned to Trevor. "I'm sorry, my boy. I didn't mean to ignore you. I'm afraid I'm not myself today."

Trevor stood and the two men embraced. Daniel's normally reserved assistant rarely showed any outward display of affection, but with Phillip Monroe he always made an exception. Phillip would not allow anything less, for he had always treated Trevor as part of the family.

"Why don't you boys join me in the kitchen?" Phillip said. "You both look like you could use some sustenance. Daniel, are you all right? Your forehead is sweating."

"I think I just need some air."

Daniel stood, his head buzzing. As he started towards the balcony, his cell phone rang and it was David Chen, the officer who had visited him that morning at the hospital. He listened as Chen shared an update regarding the status of his apartment. Then he heard something that stopped him in his tracks.

"What the hell do you mean you can't release her yet?"

As he listened to Chen explain why the autopsy was taking longer than anticipated, an image of Katharine lying on a metal table flashed into his mind. There was a lone coroner leaning over her, his scalpel placed just over her heart. Nausea swept through him and he picked up his pace towards the door.

"Yes, I'm still here."

Daniel tried to shake the image from his mind, but now he saw the scalpel pierce her pale, white skin and glide down her chest. A stream of blood oozed from the incision, moving between her breasts, down the length of her long torso. He could not understand why the police needed to keep her a few more days. The officer attempted to explain, but the buzz that had started in his head had now moved through his entire body and he was forced to end the call.

Drenched in sweat, he leaned his head against the door, his phone slipping from his hand. His eyes closed, and as his legs gave away he felt a cold metal surface smack against his forehead before he fell into the darkness.

Chapter Three

What's in a name? That which we call a rose
By any other word would smell as sweet.

Last summer, when Eleanor sold a majority interest in the restaurant to Ben and Mikayla Garrison, they had discussed renaming it. Mikayla was for it of course; Ben was not quite ready to shed his brother's name, and Eleanor absolutely refused to discuss it. She argued that in the eyes of the tight-knit River Mist community the restaurant was still seen as Jeremy's, and to change the name so soon after his passing seemed disrespectful. So, the name remained, and a year later the Jeremy's Tavern sign continued to illuminate the handful of businesses that populated downtown River Mist with its loud neon flashes of purple and teal.

Travel mug in hand, Eleanor ended her musing over the sign and entered the coffee shop. Inside, the Garrison family was busy handling an unusually large Saturday morning crowd. Mikayla gave Eleanor a quizzical look as she approached the front counter.

"Good mornin' darlin', you want the usual?" Mikayla said.

"Make it a triple, please."

"Sure thing. Just leave your mug and I'll join you momentarily."

"Are you sure you don't need any help?" Eleanor scanned the back area which was brimming over with dirty coffee mugs.

"No, we're good. Take a seat and relax."

Mikayla gave her a look that indicated she wanted to talk, and Eleanor set down her travel mug. She then said hello to the rest of the family. Sarah and Sam, the Garrison twins, barely nodded as they poured coffee and pulled pastries from the front case.

Ben Garrison dried his hands on his apron as he came around the counter to greet her. "Don't worry about them. They're just having texting withdrawal. How ya holding up?"

"All right, I guess. I just came from the cemetery."

"Yeah, Mikayla and I are heading over later." Ben removed his glasses, rubbing his eyes. "So you still all right that we didn't go ahead with a memorial service?"

"Of course, I wasn't up to it and Jeremy wouldn't have wanted it anyway."

"Yeah, my baby brother wasn't much on ceremony."

Ben folded his arms, moving in close. The inevitable lecture was coming and she found herself suddenly fixating on the large eagle tattoo that covered the entire right side of his neck.

"Look," he said. "All I want you to know is that no matter what happens, you'll always be a part of the Garrison family. Don't ever forget that, you hear me?"

"I promise I won't. Are you all right?"

"Yeah. I'm just tired. Those crazy storms kept me up last night. Well, I should get back to work. See you tonight for dinner, right?"

Eleanor nodded as Mikayla approached them.

"Here's your drink honey. Let's have a seat."

Ben walked behind the counter while Mikayla nudged Eleanor towards the front of the café. They settled in on a small couch that cradled one side of an enclosed gas lit fireplace. Mikayla set a cup of cappuccino on the table in front of them and collapsed.

"So I take it with the triple latte you didn't sleep either?" she said with tired brown eyes.

"I'm afraid so. Is Ben all right? He seems unusually distraught?"

"Oh, he just woke up in his usual foul mood this morning. Don't worry about it. Why are you here? I thought you'd be off today?"

"We're meeting this morning to finalize the Shakespeare festival."

"That's wonderful darlin'," Mikayla said as she patted Eleanor's knee. "I was hoping you'd get back to the theater thing this year. Not that I didn't appreciate your help last summer at the restaurant. Heaven knows we couldn't have done it without you, but I think it is time for you to do something nice for yourself."

"It was just too soon last summer to be thinking about creating theatrical productions. My heart wasn't in it. But, all that's behind me now and I'm ready to move on."

"That's good honey, because there's something I need to discuss with you." Mikayla laid a soft brown hand over hers.

"Is anything wrong?"

"Well, not so much wrong, but…"

"Oh no, I just forgot. I'm supposed to meet Kyle at the university at 8:30."

"Honey it's almost 8:00. You'll never make it to the coast by then."

"I know, but I have to go. If he arrives at my office before I get there, well, believe me it won't be good."

"I don't understand?"

Eleanor grabbed her travel mug and purse. "I'll explain later. What about the coffee?"

"It's on me today. Isn't Kyle that musician friend of yours from LA, the one who was here last spring?"

"Oh yes." She kissed Mikayla on the cheek and started for the door. "By the way, I saw Jared at the cemetery this morning. He told me to say hello."

Mikayla's face lit up. "I know. He stopped in here for a minute and got a coffee to go. I guess there's some problem down the road. He promised to come by the restaurant soon."

"Good. Oh, what did you want to talk about?"

"It can wait till tonight. We'll see you at the restaurant for dinner, right?"

"Of course, where else would I be?"

Six miles into her drive to Edmond, traffic on Route 6 came to a complete stop. As Eleanor left a message on Kyle's cell, a helicopter passed overhead, slowing as it disappeared around the curve in the road. Traffic crept around the rocky bend approaching Turner's Pass, which marked the halfway point around Birch Mountain.

Drumming her fingers against the steering wheel, she wondered if Ben's sour disposition had anything to do with Jared's visit. The two men usually got along, despite Jared and Mikayla's history, but she also knew Ben was a man who kept his true feelings locked deep inside him, just like his brother. She shuddered to think what would happen if Mikayla and Ben split up. Her relationship with them and the restaurant were the last vestiges of her former life, and if they were ever to leave her, then Jeremy would be lost to her forever.

Finally, her car cleared the bend, revealing the cause for the traffic jam. Along the south side of the road, were a dozen Alexandria County Sherriff's Department cruisers parked with their lights flashing. Hovering above was the same helicopter that had passed over her a few minutes earlier, and now she could see that it was from Channel 10 , one of the local stations in Edmond. In the middle of the sea of red and blue lights was a white SUV, cordoned off with yellow tape. Several deputies were slowly moving through the area, searching the ground and surrounding woods.

Obviously, the abandoned car situation had grown beyond a little problem.

A thick mist had settled over the area and Eleanor struggled to locate Jared. Finally, she found him standing next to the white SUV with Eric Garrison, Jeremy and Ben's cousin and the head of the River Mist Sheriff's Station.

As she slowly inched forward, she continued to watch Jared and Eric as they interacted with a pair of men who were examining the SUV. Suddenly, she saw a dark object quickly filling her peripheral vision and snapped her head forward. She had missed a stopped minivan just a few feet in front of her and was forced to slam on her breaks, sending her tires screeching across the wet pavement as she swerved to avoid hitting the vehicle. Her Subaru came to a hard stop as it hit a ditch, sending her body slamming against the steering wheel. She was only there for a moment before someone threw open the door.

"Eleanor, are you all right?"

Jared's voice was in her ear as he placed his hand on her back. Then she heard Eric next, instructing her not to move until they were certain she was not injured. She held up her hand, waving them off and pushed away from the steering wheel.

"Hey cuz, you know you almost hit that car back there," Eric said.

"I know, Eric. I wasn't paying attention. I'm sorry if I gave you gentlemen a scare, but I'm all right and I'll just be going now."

"Not without some help you won't," Eric said as he motioned for her to exit the car.

Reluctantly she stepped out and moved up the hill away from her vehicle. She watched as Eric rolled her Subaru back and forth, while Jared pushed from behind. Eventually her eyes wandered over to the white SUV. A prickling sensation moved down her spine and she knew she had stood here before, looking across the highway at the very spot where the SUV was parked. She turned around, her eyes moving up the hillside to the northern woods. She focused on the perimeter, continuing down the long line of trees. An uneasy feeling came over her.

"Eleanor," Jared appeared next to her. "Did you hear me? We got your car out."

"What happened here?" she said.

"I can't tell you that right now, but I promise you it will be on the news within the next few hours."

Eleanor turned towards the direction of the northern woods. She could feel a tension rising inside, her body urging her to flee this place. Suddenly she felt warm and sweaty, and her heart was racing like she had been running. Something was wrong and she felt the need to escape, now.

"Eleanor!"

She saw a dark-haired woman running along the hillside and into the woods. Eleanor followed. The woman was moving fast, her body straining against a steep uphill climb. Suddenly there was a man's voice calling out. Someone was following the woman; Eleanor could hear the sound of fallen branches snapping behind her. The woman picked up her pace, sprinting upwards into a blinding light.

When the vision ended, she found herself kneeling on the wet ground with Jared. "What happened? Why are you out of breath?"

"Are you kidding? I came after you when you took off for the woods. What's going on with you?" Eric Garrison yelled at them, asking if they were all right. Jared waved him off and then locked eyes with her. "Eleanor, what just happened here?"

"I have no idea, but I need to get up. My pants are wet," she said.

When they arrived at her car Jared held the door open while she slipped in, securing her seatbelt. She thanked both men and put the car in gear.

"Wait," Jared leaned in. "Are you sure you should be driving over to the coast today?"

"I'm fine."

"Then promise you'll call me when you get to work."

"I said I was fine, so please stop looking at me that way."

"What way is that?"

"You know exactly what I mean," she said. "I have to go. I'm incredibly late."

Jared lit a cigarette as he watched Eleanor drive away. Eric joined him, folding his arms.

"You know she used to be nuts, don't you?"

"I'm aware of her troubles last year," Jared said.

"Troubles my ass, she completely flipped her lid. Holed up for over a month in her house and it took a half-dozen people to get her out of there."

"She came out of it all right."

"I guess, but what was all that nonsense just a minute ago? Where was she going?"

"She wasn't going anywhere," Jared said. "We both thought we saw something moving in the woods, but we were wrong. Come on. Let's get this damn search started."

They crossed Route 6 and one of Eric's deputies came to them with a new development. A few minutes later Jared was signaling for two of his men to follow him.

As he walked to his car Jared recalled a conversation he had with Jeremy shortly before he died. They were having lunch at the tavern, discussing plans to celebrate Eleanor's completion of her doctorate, when his friend suddenly grew solemn. Jeremy then told him that Eleanor was special and not just to him. He asked Jared to watch over her if anything should happen to him. She would need friends she could trust.

Jared took a drag from his cigarette before dropping it to the ground. As he watched it smolder in the snow his thoughts turned to that moment on the hill when Eleanor touched him, and he wondered if this is what Jeremy meant.

Chapter Four

O, yet defend me, friends. I am but hurt.

Daniel fell limp across the stage. He closed his eyes, as he did every night and waited for the play to end. Suddenly, there were muffled voices surrounding him, calling his name.

Did I nod off?

Several hands were now on him, shaking him, urging him to wake. He struggled against the heaviness, unable to lift his eyelids more than part way before closing again.

"Daniel, can you hear me?"

Katharine was probably at the theater already, most likely waiting for him in his dressing room. If they found out that he had fallen asleep on stage he would never hear the end of it.

I have to get up now.

A cool cloth pressed against his forehead helped him to force open his eyes. Surprisingly, Trevor's face came into focus. He tried to push himself up on his forearms, but a firm hand forced him back down.

"Don't move son, you're bleeding."

Phillip Monroe pressed the cloth firmly to his forehead while a pillow was placed beneath his head. The presence of his father-in-law now had him thoroughly confused. Had he forgotten that Phillip and Trevor were planning to attend his performance tonight?

"Daniel, do you know where you are?"

A booming voice filled the room and his agent, Michael Portman, came into view. Daniel's eyes slowly travelled over the faces of the three men surrounding him and suddenly his present circumstances came rushing back. "What happened?"

"You fell against the door when you passed out and cut open your forehead. How are you feeling?" Phillip said.

"It hurts like hell."

"I can see why. You have a nasty gash. Who is your doctor? Does he make house calls?"

"Are you kidding me? Someone help me up."

"Not until the bleeding has stopped. I'm going to call my doctor."

Phillip left, and his agent moved over him, frowning. "I don't know. This looks deep. I think you need to go to the emergency room."

"No way," Daniel said. "I'll see Phillip's doctor, but no hospitals, not today."

"You may not have a choice. You might need a plastic surgeon. We can't risk mucking up that handsome face of yours."

"Yeah right," Daniel said. "I don't think handsome is a word people use to describe me. Do you mind? I'd like to get off the floor now."

Trevor and Michael pulled him to his feet and led him to the couch. Trevor placed a glass of water in his shaking hands and motioned for him to drink.

"So what's up with the police and your apartment?" Michael said.

Daniel was silent for several moments as he recalled his earlier phone conversation. "I don't know, but the officer told me that they need more time. He said he would call later."

"Well, it doesn't look good having all those cops there, especially with the media surrounding your place. You need some answers my friend, and I think you should have your lawyer contact this guy."

"The police are just trying to figure out what happened to Kate."

"I understand that, but it won't be long before the media starts conjecturing over it. Look, you are about to sign a lucrative movie deal and if word gets out that the police are camping out in your apartment, I guarantee you it will hinder negotiations. We're going to have to address this with the press release before it spins out of control."

"What the hell are you talking about…before what spins out of control?"

"Daniel, need I remind you that you still have that incident with that asshole photographer hanging over your head?"

"We settled that out of court."

"Yes, but you know how the media is. Once they get wind that anything is amiss with Katharine's death, they'll drag out that scumbag Marco along with every other public blow-up you've ever had, and not just the ones with the paparazzi."

"That was a long time ago. No one remembers that."

"Doesn't matter, the police got called in. Someone is bound to dig that up."

"It was an argument, and I never touched her. You know that. I'm not that kind of man."

"I know, but you've had more than your share of run-ins with the paparazzi and you're known to be a hothead. Look, as your agent and your friend, I'm telling you, you've got to be careful these next few days. Let your lawyer work on the police. I'll take care of the media. I'm telling you to please stay away from *everyone* and keep your temper in check."

Trevor, who had been hovering near by, handed Daniel a toothpick before leaving to go find Phillip. Daniel was silent as he grabbed the bourbon bottle off the table and filled his empty coffee cup. Michael sat next to him, leaning in.

"Listen, I'm sorry for all that, and at a time like this it shouldn't be about the money, but there is twenty million on the table right now."

"Not to mention your fee."

"Of course, why else would I put up with your crap? Speaking of which, maybe you should lay off the booze. You know what it does to you."

"I'm sure no one would blame me for wanting a drink today."

"Then have a glass of wine or a beer, but not that stuff. You need to keep a clear head, and you should avoid any contact with Charles Lourdes over the next few days if you can."

"I don't have to worry about that. I guess no one can find the son-of-a-bitch."

"Why? Where is he?"

"Don't know, and I really don't give a damn," Daniel said.

"He's the CEO of Monroe Industries. If he's missing, that will affect your situation as well. What happens if that scuffle between the two of you suddenly surfaces? Then we'd really be in a shit storm with your contract."

"He accosted my wife."

"No one cares whether or not he is a lech Daniel. It would just be another smear on your reputation that you can't afford right now. Is that what you want? Do you really want to send the biggest deal of your career down the toilet because you couldn't keep your cool? I didn't think so. You stay away from Lourdes, and if anyone questions you about him, you say nothing disparaging. Just smile and walk away."

"Has your brain always worked like this?"

"I used to be a lawyer, remember? Anyway, I'm supposed to think ahead, which reminds me. We found an actor to finish the last four shows of *Hamlet* for you."

"That's right. Trevor told me. Did you get Peterson?"

"No, actually he's performing in London right now. We got Leesman."

"Alex? Is that why he was trying to reach you?"

"Yes. He called early this morning and offered to help. I've talked it over with the director, and he's good with it if you are. So, what do you think?"

"I think it's amazing. Alex is my friend and he's the best there is. I just can't believe he's doing this. He swore he'd never come back to New York."

"Well, he is for you, and if you're fine with it, we'll fly him in tomorrow."

"I'm OK with it. Thanks, this is a big relief."

"Thank Leesman for popping out of nowhere. Oh, and he would like to meet with you while he's here, if you're up to it."

"Of course I'll see him," Daniel said.

"I'll have Trevor work it out. Look, unfortunately, I need to go. Is there anything I can do, besides tracking down a plastic surgeon that makes house calls?"

"No, I'll be all right. I think the bleeding stopped."

"Yeah, the cut doesn't look that bad now." Michael placed a hand on his knee "I'm so sorry. She was an amazing woman and I can't imagine what you must be feeling."

"Thanks for taking care of everything."

"It's Trevor you should be thanking, that boy's a saint. I just make you lots of money and keep you out of trouble, but I wouldn't have it any other way. Call me if you need anything and try to get some sleep, you look like hell."

Michael left. Exhausted, Daniel closed his eyes and attempted to rest, but soon his thoughts drifted to Alex Leesman and his impending visit. He had not seen his mentor in more than a year when they were in San Francisco together. He had done everything in his power to forget that night. Now all he could do was think of *her*.

Phillip was ending a call when Trevor found him in his office. "How is Daniel?"

"He's better," Trevor said. "But someone needs to look at that cut."

"Well, as luck would have it, Dr. Fitzgerald has a light schedule this afternoon and should be here within the hour. Come on in and have a seat."

Phillip crossed the room to a set of chairs that were near a window overlooking Central Park. Trevor joined him and they sat gazing out at the heavenly view. After a few moments Phillip cleared his throat.

"Katharine never had much use for this office, but every so often she would come here and sit on the floor so she could look out at the park. Eventually I rearranged the room and placed these two chairs here. Sometimes I would be working at my desk, and I would look over at her, reading a book or just looking out the window. It would always bring me joy, just seeing her sit, quiet and thoughtful. After she moved out she rarely came back here, yet I had grown so accustomed to looking across the room at her, that I didn't have the heart to move the chairs. Now, I'm not sure if I could bear to ever look this way again."

Phillip rubbed his eyes and Trevor laid a comforting hand on his arm. "I'm not sure what I can do to ease your suffering, but I will say this. When I started working for Daniel seven years ago I had only been in New York a short time. I didn't have any friends and both my parents had recently passed away. When Katharine discovered this about me she took me in, so to speak, and made me feel like I was part of her family. She treated me like a brother and helped me through a lonely time in my life. I will never forget her kindness, and I will always feel honored to have known her."

"Thank you, son, she had a very generous heart as we all well know." Phillip took his handkerchief from his pocket, blotting his face.

"Yes Sir. She has a beautiful soul." Trevor paused a moment to take in the view of the park. "If you don't mind Mr. Monroe, I'll go check on Daniel."

"Trevor."

"Yes Sir?"

"What you just said about Katharine, what did you mean by that?"

"Exactly what I said. She has a beautiful soul."

"So, you believe in some sort of afterlife then?"

Trevor started to answer but was interrupted by a voice echoing through the hallway. He turned to find Christine Monroe marching towards him with a look of consternation on her face. She brushed past him, grabbing the remote off the table. Phillip joined her in front of the television and Trevor stood silent as they watched a news alert flash across the screen.

Our affiliate in Edmond, California has just confirmed with the Alexandria County Sherriff's Office that a white Lexus SUV, belonging to supermodel Monica Bellaso, was found 35 miles inland near the quaint resort town of River Mist. It is believed that Ms. Bellaso was vacationing in the area. However, at this time her whereabouts are unknown. The sheriff's office has launched a search of the surrounding area.

Mr. and Mrs. Monroe were silent for several moments before she recommended that he call the authorities. Phillip agreed and went to his desk.

"Why is the discovery of Ms. Bellaso's car requiring you to call the police?" Trevor said.

"Because Charles Lourdes has been in Los Angeles supposedly visiting with this woman and no one has been able to reach him since yesterday afternoon." Phillip turned his attention to his call, asking his administrative assistant to locate the general counsel for Monroe Industries.

"Charles Lourdes is missing?" Trevor asked.

"Lourdes has been seeing Monica Bellaso?" Everyone turned as Daniel entered the office and stood in front of the television. "How long has this been going on?"

"We're not sure," Christine said. "Do you know her?"

"Of course I do. She was Katharine's friend," Daniel said.

"Since when?" Christine Monroe's eyes narrowed as she approached Daniel.

"For a few years now. I can't remember how they met, probably some fundraiser, but they became friends and visited each other regularly. I think she even stayed at our place once."

Christine continued pummeling Daniel with questions about her daughter's relationship with the now missing super- model until Trevor's voice rose above the din, directing everyone's attention to the newscast. Phillip hung up the phone, joining the group and they stood silent, staring at the updates streaming across the screen.

"Good God, what the devil is going on?" Phillip said.

Alongside the coverage of the abandoned SUV was a report that a nearby home had been vandalized. Footage from a local station's helicopter showed a trail of blood leading from the front door to the driveway and what appeared to be a set of luggage scattered across the front yard. The sheriff's office was investigating if the two incidents were related.

Chapter Five

'Tis in my memory locked,
And you yourself shall keep the key of it.

Eleanor was still shaking from the incident with Jared when she turned into the university parking lot. Immediately she spotted Kyle Fiorelli leaning against the trunk of his BMW, his arms folded and his signature black sunglasses perched on his nose. As she zoomed towards him he gave a quick wave. He looked like a model posing for a clothing ad. She grabbed her tote and took a few calming breaths before she opened the door.

"I am so sorry I'm late."

Kyle moved to greet her and she did everything within her power to stop the trembling that had consumed her body. They hugged, and he immediately pulled away, studying her face.

"You went to the cemetery this morning, didn't you?" Kyle said.

"Yes, I'm sorry. I know you wanted to come with me, but I needed some time alone."

"Ah, now I know why you forgot our appointment."

"I did not. How could I when we've been talking about this for months. I just didn't remember that I was supposed to meet you here."

The events of the morning flashed through her mind till she landed on the moment with Jared on that snow-covered hill. Her entire body shuddered.

"What is wrong with you? Did something happen?" Kyle said.

"I'm just cold. I can't believe this weather."

Kyle took her arm. "So are you late because the roads were bad?"

"No, there was some abandoned car on Route Six that held up traffic. In fact one of the TV stations was there and it's probably already on the news."

"You must be referring to Monica Bellaso. I just got a text on that." Kyle pulled out his phone and showed her the message.

"No kidding, that was her car?" Eleanor pondered the oddity of having a famous celebrity that near to her home before she questioned Kyle on receiving text alerts about supermodels.

"I'm signed up for all kinds of news," he said. "Besides, I'm in the business. I have to keep up with these sorts of things."

"Did you know her?"

"God no, I may work in the movie industry, but I don't travel in *those circles.*"

"Let's get inside and see what Nina knows. She always checks out the news websites."

"Wait," Kyle stopped, halting Eleanor's march toward the front door. "So that's why you told me to wait out here for you? Nina doesn't know I'm here, does she?"

Eleanor's shoulders slumped forward as her gaze fell to the ground. She felt like a coward, but she could never find the right time to tell Nina that Kyle would be staying in Edmond for the next five months.

"No, she doesn't. Nor does she know that all of us will be working together. I'm sorry, but it seems anytime I mention your name, she gets… well… she gets angry. Seriously, I will never understand what happened between the two of you at Jeremy's fortieth birthday. I can see why you would be mad with me for attempting to hook you up, but really, after two years wouldn't you think you could call a truce?"

Kyle sighed. "Nothing happened at Jeremy's party. We just didn't hit it off. She thought I was obnoxious, and I thought she was weird and very rude. I still think that."

"She's my best friend."

"I know, but that doesn't change the fact that she's a complete loon. Really, what is up with the glasses and gloves?"

"It's just her way."

"She wears them all the time."

"I'll be the first to admit she is eccentric, but if you tried to get to know her, you'd see that she's a lot of fun."

Kyle shifted his gaze past her shoulder. She found herself studying the sharp angles of his face, his long, elegant nose and thin, perfectly shaped lips. He was by far the most attractive person she had ever encountered. Yet in all the years they had been friends, she had never known him to be in a relationship. She always found this odd because he was as accomplished a flirt as he was a musician, yet he simply did not date. He never revealed his reasons for his monastic behavior and on the few occasions when she tried to broach the subject, he would make some clever remark and quickly dismiss her. After a while she gave up asking.

"Don't worry. I'll figure it out." He turned towards the door offering her his arm.

"So, do you know where you'll be staying yet?" she said.

"No. Alex made the arrangements, so I guess I'll find out after our meeting. How about we have lunch today?"

"Sure, but I think we should invite Nina. Don't roll your eyes at me. You just said you'll figure it out. Well, here's your chance to do that."

Kyle shook his head in resignation as he held open the lobby door. They were ascending the stairs to the second level when Alex Leesman appeared in the hallway. His expression was somber, and after exchanging a hug with his cousin Kyle, he put his arm around Eleanor and asked her to join him in his office before the meeting started.

Eleanor was very young when she met Daniel Archer, barely 20 years old and completely awestruck by his commanding presence. He was 31 and the guest director of Julliard's spring production of *Hamlet*. Once the show had opened and Daniel's official duties as director had ended, he asked her out. She was amazed that anyone of his stature would want to date a woman that could not order a glass of wine at a restaurant. But her age did not matter to him, and they embarked on a tumultuous relationship that would endure for the next 18 months.

She tried to return her focus to the festival meeting, but her thoughts drifted again.

Daniel's wife is dead.

Almost a year and a half had passed since she last saw him. Alex and she had been in San Francisco attending a stage director's workshop where Alex was a guest speaker. As planned, Daniel joined them on the last day and the three friends went out to dinner.

When they returned to the hotel, Alex excused himself, retiring to his room for the evening. Daniel and Eleanor were not quite ready to call it a night, so they slipped into the lounge, hopeful they could have a drink without being disturbed. That proved to be wishful thinking. As soon as they had their first sip of wine a fan approached Daniel for an autograph. Within a few minutes more people appeared, then cameras starting flashing, and before long it became impossible to have any kind of conversation. Frustrated with the situation, Daniel suggested that they take refuge in his suite. She agreed. He ordered some wine for the room and a sympathetic waiter helped them steal away through a back exit.

"Eleanor?"

A gentle voice pulled her from her thoughts, and she realized Alex Leesman was patting her arm. She looked around at the empty conference room and realized the meeting had ended.

"I am so sorry. I'm not myself today," she said.

"Clearly, I can see that. You barely spoke the entire time. Are you all right?"

"Yes. I didn't get much sleep last night and the news about Daniel is such a shock."

"I'm sorry I told you beforehand, but I didn't want you to hear about it on the news."

"I know and I appreciate that." She stood up, gathering her things.

"Eleanor, wait."

She gazed down at her longtime mentor and friend and met his pale-blue gaze. She had known him for almost 20 years and except for his graying hair, his appearance had hardly changed. He still had a distinguished face, with round haunting eyes, high cheekbones, a large prominent nose and thin lips. He reminded her of Daniel, much shorter of course, and when Alex and Daniel were together they looked as if they were father and son.

He motioned for her to sit and held her hand, signaling that a serious discussion was about to commence. Knowing the inevitable question would come next she decided to initiate the conversation.

"Alex, I'm fine, and despite my behavior during the meeting, I'm very excited about the summer season."

"So, you're managing all right with the anniversary?"

"Yes. I still miss him, but I'm all right. There are no issues like last year. I promise."

He took a moment to study her face, before smiling. "Well, that's good to hear, because there's something I would like to discuss with you."

He leaned forward, gripping her hand, and she wondered if he was about to fire her. "How would you feel about performing this summer?"

She let out an abrupt laugh. "What? Alex, I haven't acted in two years."

"True, but what does that have to do with taking on a role?"

"Please, you can't be serious."

"Of course I am. Why else would I be asking you?"

"Well, for one thing we've established a reputation for high-quality productions and I don't think I should use the festival to brush up on my acting skills."

"Your acting skills are perfectly fine. You're just afraid to get back on the stage again."

"I'm directing *Romeo and Juliet*."

"I don't see why you can't do both. You're a seasoned professional. Now stop this nonsense and let's talk about the roles I would like you to consider."

"I'm not ready for this."

"I think you are more than ready and I also believe that getting back on that stage will help you find your way to happiness again, or at least get you out of this melancholy state that you have so fondly embraced over the past year. Now, I'm not saying that you should cease mourning Jeremy's death—you'll do that when the time is right. But I do think you should channel some of that energy into an endeavor that brings you joy. It would be wonderful to see you on that stage again and you can't tell me you haven't missed it."

Eleanor twirled a strand of hair around her finger. "So, what are you thinking?"

"Titania... of course."

"What else?"

"Gertrude."

"Oh, that would be fun. It's been a while since I died on stage. So, which one are you leaning towards?"

"Actually, I was thinking that you could do both."

"Are you joking? How would I do that *and* direct a show?"

"Really, how many times have you done Titania? That was a rhetorical question. And Gertrude would not be that difficult to pick up."

"Who do you have in mind to play across from me?"

"I'm working on that."

"Alex, we've always made the casting decisions together. Well, except for last year."

"Sorry, I have dibs on this one, but I'm thinking that whomever I cast as Oberon will also play King Claudius. Ah, I see I've piqued your interest now."

"Yes, you most certainly have."

"Good, then maybe I can get you to pay better attention in our meetings going forward."

Eleanor smacked his arm as they gathered up their belongings and left the conference room. She had an uneasy feeling about Alex's secrecy. It was not in his nature to play games.

"When are you leaving for New York?" she said.

"I fly out in the morning. Should I tell Daniel that you said hello?"

"Yes, and I have something I would like you to give to him. I can bring it by later, if that's all right."

Alex smiled. "Of course, I'll be here the rest of the day."

When Eleanor entered her office, Nina St. John was sitting at her desk, her feet propped up, reading the news on her laptop. She glanced up momentarily at Eleanor, her green eyes glowing beneath her rose-colored glasses. It did not take a doctorate degree to figure out that her friend of nearly 22 years was supremely mad at her.

"You knew he was going to be here, didn't you?" Nina said.

Eleanor sat in a chair next to Nina's desk. "I just couldn't find the right time or the right way to tell you. Then before I knew it the day was here and of course it was today of all days. I'm really, really sorry."

"What I don't get is why Leesman hired him. There's plenty of talent right here that could compose music for the festival."

"True, but having someone with Kyle's credentials helps ticket sales. He's very talented, and I feel honored that he has joined us."

"I never said he didn't have talent. He's just flashy and full of himself."

"If you would just try to get to know him you'd see he's a nice guy. Look, he's going to be here through the summer and the three of us are going to be…well, we're going to be a team. So, you need to be prepared for that. And look at the bright side, he loves wine and clothes, just like you. Think about it. You would finally have someone around that enjoys shopping."

"Remind me again how you know him?" Nina grumbled.

"Stop it. You know we met at Julliard."

"Yeah, and I keep trying to forget."

"You don't have to be his best friend, just try to be civil. Please, do this for me. Before you know it the summer will be over and we'll take our trip to Napa."

"Can Josephine come?" Nina said.

"Yes, if she's back in the states by then."

"*And* this time we go shopping in San Francisco."

Eleanor sank back in her chair and shook her head. "All right, but if I agree to that, then you have to come out to lunch with Kyle and me today."

"What?"

"Kyle asked, and I think it would be a good way to smooth things out between the two of you before we start work next week."

"Whatever."

Nina resumed her reading while Eleanor returned to her desk. Her eyes fell on the top drawer and her thoughts wandered back to Daniel and that night in San Francisco.

Daniel's hotel suite at The Ritz-Carlton turned out to be the size of a small apartment, divided into a nice sized living room with a small kitchen and a bedroom that was separated by french-style glass doors. A few minutes after they arrived, room service delivered the wine he had ordered. Daniel turned on the television and they settled in, resuming their conversation.

At first, everything was fine. They chatted about their families, her work at the university, his movie career, occasionally tuning in to catch the sport scores. They finished a delicious bottle of Pinot Noir and opened another-just two old friends enjoying each other's company. She was having a lovely time.

Then the mood shifted.

She was not sure what prompted it, most likely the second bottle of wine, but Daniel started reminiscing about Julliard. She could still recall the uneasy feeling in her stomach when he said those words: *Do you remember when?*

Talking about their past was a dangerous topic for them, because it always led to their time together as a couple-how they met, their first date, how long they were together, and so on. At first the conversation would be tolerable, but eventually it would turn sour as they went down the inevitable path of discussing their breakup, her subsequent relationship with Jeremy and her move to California. That was when the evening started to get ugly.

She tried desperately to change the subject, but he refused to let it go. She recalled watching in disbelief as he worked himself into a frenzy, pacing the room, arms flying through the air as he attempted to dissect the final days of their failed relationship.

Then the conversation took a truly bitter turn.

"I will never understand what possessed you to give up an acting career just to follow Leesman out to the hinterland," Daniel said.

"I didn't give up acting. What do you call what I'm doing now?"

"You know what the hell I'm talking about. You gave up a promising career, one that would have made you famous a long time ago."

"I never wanted that. Yes, maybe if I had stayed in New York I would have remained on Broadway, but I'm not like you. I can't live your kind of life."

"What the hell is that supposed to mean?" Daniel said.

"You're comfortable with your fame, and though I know you've had a few problems here and there, you still seem to like it. I on the other hand, could never be comfortable with it."

"Are you saying if we had stayed together you wouldn't have tolerated my lifestyle?"

"I'm just saying I like my quiet life. I teach and I'm still able to perform as much as I did in New York."

"Really Ellie, like your little Shakespeare in the sticks gig compares to Broadway. You were good, damn good, and you let some stupid mountain man convince you to give all that up because he couldn't handle your success."

Initially, she sat their wondering how an expensive bottle of red wine could cause him to be that cruel, but shock eventually overwhelmed that thought, followed rapidly by outrage and tears. Too stunned to say anything, she grabbed her purse and ran for the door.

The next few moments she recalled were like scenes from a movie. He rushed after her attempting to apologize, but she kept going. He tried to stop her, but she pushed him away. As she approached the door, he threw himself in front of her, begging her to listen to him. That was when she stood back and slapped him across the face. Finally she had enough anger seething inside her that she could speak.

"What the hell is wrong with you? Haven't you humiliated me enough? Don't you see all I want is to walk out that door while I still have my dignity intact? Let go of me now!"

Kyle Fiorelli waltzed through her office doorway, interrupting her thoughts.

"Are you ready? I was thinking we could go to Jasper's." His statement solicited a groan from Nina. "I take it Ms. St. John, that you aren't a fan of sushi?"

Nina's emerald eyes locked on Kyle, her black brows furrowing. Eleanor sprang from her seat, determined to avoid a confrontation in the office.

"Actually, Nina loves sushi, it's just that we were at Jasper's this past weekend, but I don't see why we can't go again. I'll just get my coat and purse."

Nina rolled her eyes, tossing her laptop on the desk. Eleanor caught a glimpse of Nina's computer screen and noticed she was on a news website.

"Is there anything new with the Monica Bellaso story?" Eleanor said.

"I guess some guy named Charles Lourdes was with her and is missing too. Your detective friend is mentioned," Nina said.

Kyle moved next to her and they stared at a picture of Jared Adams addressing a group of deputies.

"So how is the morose investigator these days?" Kyle said.

"The same. Wait Nina. Is that a picture of Monica Bellaso? Can you make it bigger?"

Nina clicked on the picture and the screen filled with the image of the brown eyed beauty. Eleanor began to experience the same sensation she felt with Jared on the hill. Her heart was racing and suddenly she felt overheated. She snatched up a magazine lying on Nina's desk and fanned herself.

Kyle produced a handkerchief from his pocket, dabbing her forehead. "What's going on with you? You're sweating like crazy. When's the last time you ate?"

She stared at Monica Bellaso's picture, unable to answer his question. "We should go."

An hour later they emerged from Jasper's restaurant. Nina was the first to part, and Eleanor watched Kyle's expression turn sullen as she sped away in her powder-blue Beetle.

"Lunch was nice, wasn't it?" She took his arm as they stepped into the parking lot.

"It was fine," Kyle said. "I thought we were fairly civil to each other."

"Sure, if you consider no eye contact or conversation as the definition of civil. I don't know about you, but I'm exhausted from doing all the talking."

"At least you ate. Though I noticed you left your carryout container on the table."

Eleanor stopped, facing him. "All right, let's get this out of the way right now. I eat, all the time as a-matter-of-fact, and I just had a physical at which I was told I'm perfectly healthy."

"You still look too thin to me, especially for your height. You don't need to be like some of the fashion models I know."

"Fashion isn't even a part of my vocabulary, and I thought you said you didn't travel in those kinds of circles."

"Well, I just meant I don't rub elbows with the likes of Ms. Bellaso, but I still know plenty of anorexic females who look like they're near death."

"Are you saying that I look like I'm dying?"

"No, I most certainly am not. You're my friend and I'm just expressing my concern for your well-being and this is the last I'll say on the subject." Kyle held up his hands, signaling he was done and they resumed walking. "Dad asked me to say hello."

"He has managed to stay clear of Edmond the past year."

"He's been swamped since Dr. Livingston passed. It wasn't until recently that he was able to get all her patients transferred to other colleagues. And there is the psychologist thing."

"What do you mean?" she said.

"Well, he just felt it would make you uncomfortable if he came up here with everything that was going on. He didn't want you to think he might try and, you know, counsel you."

"I didn't even think about that. You should tell him not to worry and to come visit."

"I'll see what I can do. So, are we on for lunch again tomorrow?"

"Absolutely, I plan on dining with you every day while you're in Edmond. We haven't spent this much time together since Julliard."

"I know. It will be like old times."

"Yes, except for Jeremy."

"Well, that goes without saying, but don't forget I was in your life at least a year before your Romeo arrived. We had our own memories before he swept you away."

"True, and if I remember correctly most of them were of me trying to help *you* from getting expelled from school."

Kyle sighed. "Ah yes, you had to bring that up."

"You started it my friend."

He was silent for the rest of their walk. When they arrived at her car he leaned against it, staring across the parking lot. Eleanor touched his arm.

"Are you thinking about Jeremy too?" she said.

"What? Oh… yes…of course. I need to pay my respects."

"You should wait till the weather improves. Travelling back and forth today could be a problem. Besides, don't you need to locate your apartment?"

"That's right. I forgot about that," Kyle said. "So, how are you doing today, really?"

"I was wondering when you would get around to asking me."

"Sorry, I tried to hold off for as long as I could."

"And since you always seem to know when I'm not being completely honest with you, I'll tell you the truth. It's a year later and there isn't a moment that passes that I don't think of him. He's always with me, no matter who I'm with or what I do. I still miss him very much."

"It makes sense. You were together a long time."

"Yes, but it's not like last spring. This time *I know* he's gone."

Kyle nodded, wrapping his arms around her. They hugged for several moments and then he opened her car door. As she slid into the front seat she met his luminous brown eyes.

"Why don't you come out to River Mist tonight and stay with me?" she said. "I'm having dinner with Ben and Mikayla. I'm sure they would love to see you."

He seemed to consider her proposal for a moment, but then he shook his head. "Thank you, but I really should get settled in. Also, I've got the movers coming tomorrow morning with my sound equipment, which reminds me I need to call and give them my address."

"All right, I understand, but if you change your mind, it would be lovely to have you."

He leaned into the car. For a moment she thought their lips might touch, but instead he kissed her on the forehead.

Kyle watched Eleanor drive away, wondering if he had it in him to spend the next several months in this place. Wearily, he got into his car and opened the envelope that Alex had given him. He removed the contents, scanning the apartment information. When he got to the address he shot up in his seat.

"Oh, please tell me that isn't so."

He put the car in gear, his tires screeching as he turned onto the bayside road. He drove through downtown Edmond, passing several trendy shops and restaurants until he came to a row of charming yellow and white town-houses. Slowly he drove to the last unit, checking the address before pulling into the driveway. He turned off the ignition and took a deep breath.

Really Alex, this was the best you could do?

With a heavy heart he walked to the front porch. He was just about to insert the key into the lock when a car pulled into the driveway next door. He waited until he heard the door close before he turned to face his new neighbor. Nina was expressionless, her short black hair blowing across her pale skin. She was a stone-cold little thing, all wrapped up in a designer clothing bow. If it had been anyone else he would have told her how chic she looked in her brown suede coat and boots, but he did not dare. She started for the front door, stopping at the landing.

"I didn't do this," she said.

"I realize that."

She disappeared into her townhouse, the door slamming behind her. Kyle turned the key, wondering if it was too late to take Eleanor up on her offer.

❈❀❈

Eleanor returned to her office and sat at her desk for several minutes, staring at the top drawer. Eventually she opened it, and behind the pens, paperclips and various other items, she located the letter that had been tucked away for the past year and a half.

She picked up the envelope, running her fingers over the edges. The handwriting on the front had faded, her name barely legible, but it still evoked the same anxious response as it had the first time she saw it. Carefully she lifted the flap, removing the contents. Her eyes wandered over The Ritz-Carlton logo and down to the words he had scribbled.

Ellie,

I am so sorry.

- D

She selected her favorite pen and wrote. When she was finished she sealed the envelope and placed it in her purse.

Chapter Six

My words fly up, my thoughts remain below.
Words without thoughts never to heaven go.

∞

As the limousine drove past St. Francis, Daniel grimaced at the enormous crowd gathered around the church. He loved Katharine and he wanted to honor her, but he wished the Monroes had heeded his request for a private service. This was the last place he wanted to be right now.

The long black car turned the corner, travelling towards the back entrance of the church. Daniel turned his attention to inside the limousine, glancing at Christine Monroe who was sitting across from him. He had barely exchanged two words with her since Sunday afternoon, and now she was avoiding his gaze as she eyed Amelia with her icy stare. He knew that once the funeral was over it would only be a matter of time before Christine launched her attack. The thought of dragging Amelia through a custody suit made him sick.

He looked over at Phillip who was on his cell phone. That seemed to be the norm lately; if he was not speaking with one of the company's lawyers than it was with someone from the board of directors of Monroe Industries. Since Charles Lourdes disappeared, the board of the multi-national consumer product company was putting pressure on Philip to step into the leadership role until the crisis was under control.

He gazed down at Amelia who was leaning against him, listening to *Wicked* on her iPod. Three days ago she put the earphones on and stopped talking to everyone. Initially, he was alarmed with her behavior, but then he came to realize her self-imposed isolation was her way of dealing with the steady stream of strangers that had invaded the Monroes' apartment over the past week. He attempted to arrange for a few of her school friends to visit, but she was not interested. Instead, she spent her days listening to her beloved musicals, shutting out the world around her.

His thoughts turned inward. Planning for the funeral had been tiring. Though the Monroes took the helm on the arrangements, there were still many decisions to be made regarding the memorial service. Katharine was a well-known supporter of several arts and women's organizations in New York and for years her generosity and fundraising prowess had touched many lives. From the moment her death was announced, hundreds of calls poured in from her friends and fellow philanthropists who wanted to contribute to the service. The offers were too numerous to include everyone. They spent the next two days considering each request, returning calls, scheduling performers, and speakers, and determining the program.

Yesterday, as Christine finalized arrangements with the staff at St. Francis, she believed they had woven together a worthy service for Katharine.

Daniel's interaction with the police was just as wearisome. Each day he received an update as to the status of the apartment and the autopsy, and each day he was told they were still gathering information. Katharine's body was finally released Wednesday morning and the apartment yesterday afternoon. The police had made arrangements to meet with the family at 2:00 today to give their report.

The limousine approached the back entrance of St. Francis where dozens of reporters and cameras were waiting. Bodyguards that had been hired by Monroe Industries, as well as NYPD officers, formed a line between the crowd and the limousine.

Daniel firmly gripped Amelia's hand. "Whatever happens baby girl, don't let go."

Amelia nodded, turning up the music on her iPod.

"Here we go," Phillip said glumly.

The doors of the limo flew open and the bodyguards encircled the family, moving them towards the door. The size of the crowd amazed him. He had certainly experienced the constant annoyance of paparazzi stalking him outside a restaurant, but nothing like the throngs that were now closing in on them. Flashes of light came from every direction while reporters screamed out questions, mainly regarding the disappearance of Charles Lourdes and Monica Bellaso. As they inched towards the doors, he kept his head down, focusing on Amelia.

Once the family was safely inside, they were greeted by Father Thomas Lorentz, the pastor of the church, who escorted them to a private room. Daniel heard music and realized it was coming from Amelia's earphones.

"You can turn that down now honey," he said.

"I think perhaps it's time that you put that thing away, Amelia," Christine said.

Daniel felt the hair rising on the back of his neck as he turned to face his mother-in-law. "I think she is fine for now, as long as the volume is down."

"And I think that it is disrespectful," Christine fired back.

Amelia removed her earphones and stuffed the player into her pocket

"Thank you," Christine said. "Why don't we visit the ladies room before the service starts?"

Daniel watched them exit the room and suddenly he had a vision of his hands wrapped around Christine's neck. His daydream was interrupted when his lawyer, Hank Stevenson, approached.

"Zach Walker is here," Hank whispered.

"Are you joking? What the hell is he doing here?"

"He called me early this morning to ensure he could get into the funeral and to arrange for some time with you." Hank took Daniel's arm, leading him to a quiet corner of the room.

"Did he mention the adoption papers?" Daniel said.

"No, he didn't mention that nor would he say what he wanted to discuss. He just said that it was important that he speak with you."

"Well this is unexpected. Months of silence and now he surfaces."

"I don't want you to worry about this," Hank said.

"Are you kidding? I have moved right past worry and straight into panic."

"Listen to me. Katharine stated in her will that you are to have full custody of Amelia and with Phillip's support we'll fend off Christine."

"So why should I agree to talk with him then?"

"Because on the birth certificate he is listed as Amelia's father, and even though I believe he absolutely has no interest in her, he still could make it difficult for you. Speak with him and see what he has to say. It would be better to have him on your side than against you."

Daniel looked out the window as he contemplated his answer. "I guess I'll see him."

"Good. I'll arrange for a few minutes after the service. See you out there."

Hank left, and Daniel walked over to a nearby window. The late morning sun had not yet reached the back of the church and the gardens below looked cold and bleak in the shadows of the building. He found no comfort in this place and struggled over how he would make it through the next few hours.

His thoughts returned to Zach Walker. Daniel could not help but think that his presence here was not a good sign. Several months ago Katharine and he had approached Walker about Daniel officially adopting Amelia. Initially, Zach agreed to cooperate, but after they sent on the paperwork for him to sign, they did not hear from him again. They attempted several times to contact him, but he never returned their calls or e-mails, and all registered mail came back as undeliverable. Finally, Katharine hired a private detective to find Walker, and that was when they learned that he had moved out of his Los Angeles home and it was up for sale.

No one seemed to know where to find him and it was as if he had vanished into thin air. Now, the day of Katharine's funeral he decided to make an appearance.

Father Lorentz entered the room and prepared the family for the service. He led them in prayer and then escorted them down a long hallway to a large set of ornate doors. When they swung open the sounds of instruments echoed through the corridor. As the family continued through the doorway, he could see that a small chamber orchestra was set up in front on the opposite side of the church, between the first row of pews and the steps that ascended to the altar. They passed several marble pillars on their left, and as the sanctuary came into full view Daniel turned, looking out into the congregation. What he saw took his breath away.

Hundreds of people, maybe more than a thousand filled the pews. He saw where folding chairs had been set up in the back and side isles to accommodate the overflow, and beyond that people were standing as far back as he could see. He knew that Katharine's philanthropic work had impacted many lives, but he had no idea as to the magnitude.

For two hours, those who had been fortunate enough to know Katharine Monroe honored her with glorious music and beautiful words. With each person that spoke, Daniel discovered something new about her, and through their words he continued to see her life unfold. Musicians from everywhere shared their amazing gifts and offered up their remembrances through the music of Beethoven, Chopin, Debussy, Fauré and Mozart. In every piece of music, in every spoken word, he could feel Katharine's presence, and he did not want it to end. But the service did end and after Father Lorentz said his final blessing Phillip walked to the podium.

"I speak on behalf of the Monroe and Archer families. Katharine was taken from us. She left this world before we had a chance to say goodbye. I cannot pretend that this loss has not been devastating to all of us. It has filled us with great sorrow and it will take time for us to heal from this painful wound. However, as I look at all of you who have come today to honor Katharine with your wonderful stories and exceptional music, I am reminded that she led a full and remarkable life, and that she was very much loved. Our family takes great comfort in that knowledge, and we thank all of you from the bottom of our hearts."

A heavy silence followed. Phillip returned to his seat, pulled a handkerchief from his pocket and pressed it to his eyes. Christine bowed her head, sobbing. Amelia rested against Daniel's arm, her tears soaking through his jacket sleeve. The whole church echoed with the sounds of tears. Everyone seemed to be crying. Everyone was crying, except for him.

The conductor of the chamber orchestra stood and raised his baton for the final piece: Samuel Barber's *Adagio*. It was Katharine's favorite. Daniel had not heard it in a while, but he recognized its haunting opening immediately.

The strings began quietly and with each new phrase grew and receded like ocean waves beating on the sand. The sorrowful melody continued to build and build until it reached a mournful crescendo, and when it seemed to cry out at its most desperate moment, the music soared and lifted upward, releasing its suffering into the heavens. Then, having given up their sorrow, the strings descended back to earth and slowly gave way to peaceful slumber.

When the music ended no one stirred. Several moments passed before the mourners began to stand, and a soft murmur of voices filled the church.

Hank appeared next to Daniel, whispering. "I'm going to get Walker. Are you ready?"

"Let me get Amelia out of here first."

Hank left as Daniel explained the situation to Phillip Monroe. Moments later Christine was guiding Amelia away from the sanctuary. Daniel's heart sank as he watched his daughter's eyes meet his. Katharine and he had told Amelia about Walker, but because the infamous rocker had absolutely no interest in knowing her, the two had never met. He felt terrible sending Amelia away, but this was not the time or place for a first encounter.

"Hello Daniel."

The low, gravelly voice made him cringe. He turned to face the weather worn musician, who had an attractive woman on his arm.

"Hello Zach. How are you?"

"I can't complain. I'd like you to meet Angie."

The woman shook hands with Daniel and then told Walker she would be waiting in the back. Walker watched the thin, blond woman as she left.

"She saved my life. I wouldn't be here right now if it wasn't for her." He turned towards the front of the sanctuary, staring at the altar. "Man, I haven't been in a church for a long time. I forgot how beautiful they could be. The mosaics in here are amazing."

"Zach, why are you here?"

"Sorry. I guess I should get to it. Do you mind if we sit? These old bones ain't what they used to be." Walker shuffled to the front pew, plopping down. He waited for Daniel to join him before starting.

"First, I have to apologize for not answering your messages. Several months ago I relapsed. Actually, I was in bad shape when you guys came to me about Amelia. Not too long after that I met Angie and she convinced me to get help. The first thing I did was shut down party central, which meant leaving my house and putting it up for sale. I moved in with Angie and right after that I went into rehab. I just got out a few weeks ago."

"We had no idea you were in trouble. Why didn't you let us know?"

"No one knew except Angie and my agent. My career couldn't take another setback and I was desperate to get clean. We told everyone I was leaving town and taking time off to write."

"But, you could have at least returned one phone call."

"I know. I sorta shut down. Then Angie started checking my e-mails and pressured me to call you. I kept blowing her off, but she kept at me. Then that private detective showed up."

"What?" Daniel said.

"Yeah, Angie found him snooping around the house one day. When she threatened to call the police he told her why he was there. She gave him her number and asked him to give it to Kate. The next day Angie and Kate talked and when I got out of rehab we made arrangements."

"Arrangements for what?"

"For Kate and me to meet."

Daniel was dumbfounded. He tried to speak, but he could not form any words.

"That's my reason for talking to you," Walker said. "I've been in town since last Friday. I met Kate at the apartment and signed the papers. I wasn't sure if she told you yet, because she said it was a surprise. I'm guessing from the look on your face that you didn't know."

"I haven't been back to the apartment since before Kate's accident."

"I'm sorry man. This is really weird having to tell you all this."

"You have no idea," Daniel said.

"I should get going. Your lawyer has my number if you need anything."

"What time were you at the apartment?"

"I think I got there about 6:30 and stayed about forty-five minutes. Why?"

"You were probably the last person to see her alive."

"God, you're probably right," Walker said. "Hell, now I feel awful."

"Why do you say that?"

"Well, I wanted to stay with her until the power came back on in the building, but she made me leave."

"Sounds like Kate. She was always headstrong."

"Yeah, she was. I gotta go. We fly out in a few hours." Walker stood.

"Look, I know it took a lot for you to come here today. Thank you for that, and for signing the papers."

"It's the way it should be. You're her real dad. Take care, man."

They shook hands. Walker sauntered down the aisle towards the front entrance, his long gray ponytail swaying. Daniel would never understand what possessed Katharine to date a known drug addict who was old enough to be her father, let alone have a child with him.

"Well, what happened?" Hank asked as he approached.

"It appears that I can move ahead with the adoption." Daniel loosened his necktie and undid the top button of his shirt.

"That's good news."

"Yeah, I guess so."

"You guess?" Hank said. "Why do you say that? Is something wrong?"

"It appears my wife was good at keeping secrets."

Daniel relayed his story as the two men left the sanctuary. Hank was surprised but viewed the situation as a positive turn of events. He cautioned Daniel not to read too much into Katharine's actions and to be thankful that they had another defense against Christine Monroe's custody pursuit.

They pushed open the ornate double doors leading into the back hallway and saw Alex Leesman talking with Phillip Monroe. Daniel called out to his old friend and picked up his pace as he walked towards him. The two men shared in a powerful hug before pulling away to survey each other.

"God it's good to see you," Daniel said. "I still can't believe you're doing this for me. I heard the show is going well."

"I believe so," Alex said. "The service was very beautiful. You honored Katharine well."

"Thanks, but Phillip and Christine deserve all the credit. Can we give you a lift over to the apartment? There's plenty of room in the limo."

"Thank you, but I have a car waiting and I need to stop by my hotel first. Perhaps you would like to ride with me?"

"I wish I could, but I've got Amelia, and I need to keep a low profile. You go on and I'll see you there."

Daniel and Alex started to shake hands, but Phillip stopped them, taking both men by the arm and guiding them towards the exit. He instructed

Daniel to go on with Alex and that he would see to Amelia. A few moments later they were safely inside Alex's limo heading uptown.

"Where are you staying?" Daniel asked.

"I am at the Four Seasons."

"Good. They have my favorite bourbon at *The Bar.*"

Chapter Seven

My fault is past. But, O, what form of prayer
Can serve my turn? "Forgive me my foul murder"?

The vehicle came to a hard stop, slamming him against the dashboard. Unbearable pain shot through his body as he gasped for air. He attempted to push away with his shoulder, but a powerful arm shoved him back as the driver reached across to open the door. With one thrust, he tumbled onto a cold, wet surface, and then he heard the sound of tires screeching. He wasn't sure if he was dying. His lips were numb, he could no longer feel his extremities and he was shaking with fever. How he ended up in this condition was incomprehensible to him. Suddenly, there were voices around him. He felt something press against his neck and his blindfold was removed. A rush of light brought more pain, followed by darkness, and then silence.

❧

Eleanor had just returned to her office from teaching a class, when she felt a sharp pain in her chest. It hurt for several moments and she had to sit down in order to breathe. Then she had an overwhelming sense that someone close to her was in trouble. Without thinking she pulled out her phone and called her mother, her sister Josephine, and all her friends. She left messages for those she could not reach. However, when she came to Daniel's name she stopped.

Since she learned about his wife's death, she had come close to calling him several times. By now Alex had delivered her message. Even if Daniel had not read the card at least he knew she was thinking of him. As her thumb hovered over his name, she wondered how he would react to seeing her number flash across his phone. Would he take her call or would he let it go to voicemail? She decided that she was not ready to know the answer to that question yet and returned the phone to her purse.

The uneasiness intensified and like the moment with Jared on the hill, her heart was pounding as if she had been running a race. She shot up from her seat, pacing the room, perplexed by her sudden distress. Why was she feeling this way? Why now, after a year of feeling nothing?

Alex Leesman had fondly referred to it as her melancholy state, but in all honesty she did not feel melancholy at all. The truth was she did not feel anything. She was numb inside, and the emptiness- as she liked to call it- had been with her since the day Jeremy died.

But now, her palms and chest were sweating, and she concluded that she must be having some sort of anxiety attack. Perhaps her reconnection with Daniel was the cause. She did not know, but whatever it was, it felt real. Unable to shake it off, she grabbed her purse and coat and bolted for her car.

As she drove towards town, her thoughts jettisoned back to that night in San Francisco and the moment when she slapped Daniel's face. He was so stunned by her action that it took him a moment before he released his grip on her arms, allowing her to leave. However, by the time her hand touched the doorknob her emotions got the best of her, and she leaned against the door, sobbing.

He let her cry for a few moments before he laid his hands on her shoulders. At first his touch made her flinch, but when he kissed the top of her head her anger subsided.

"I don't understand you," she said. "Why can't you just leave our past where it belongs?"

"I'm sorry Ellie. I'm just dealing with some issues right now."

A tear fell on her bare shoulder, followed by several more. She turned to him, unable to recall the last time she saw him cry.

"What's wrong with you?" she said. "Has something happened?"

"I don't want to talk about it right now. Are you still angry with me?"

"Yes, but I forgive you."

She attempted to wipe the tears from his face, but he grasped her hands, kissing each one, before resting his forehead against hers. His breath was warm against her skin, and she closed her eyes, wondering what it would feel like to kiss him again.

A blue Nissan barreling through a red light sent Eleanor's thoughts rushing back to the present. She slammed on her brakes to avoid the car and watched in amazement as it turned north onto the 101, cutting across four lanes of traffic. A car horn sounded behind her and she realized she had stopped in the middle of the intersection. Still shaking from the near collision, she decided to get off the main road, and turned right onto Morgan Street, which ran along the south side of Edmond Memorial Hospital.

It was then she felt her anxiety increase exponentially, and she looked towards the building as she passed the emergency room. Several people were running towards the entrance and a crowd had already formed. She was not sure what compelled her to stop, but a few moments later she was rushing across the hospital parking lot to join the group of onlookers.

❀❀❀

Detective Jared Adams eyed the cold plate of food in front of him and pushed it away. He was exhausted. It was Friday morning and his department had been working on the Bellaso case around-the-clock since her abandoned car was discovered on Route 6.

"Doesn't look very appetizing, does it?"

Jared looked up to find his dark-haired beauty behind the counter holding a coffee pot.

"Hey Sunshine," he said.

"Hey Shug, want me to order you something else?" Mikayla said.

"That's all right. I'm too tired to eat, but I will definitely have some more coffee."

"You don't have to sugar coat it honey. I know the food is bad. We lost our best cook last week and our temporary chef isn't working out very well."

Her sweet southern smile had left her completely, and she looked truly distressed. She filled his cup and was about to take his plate when he grabbed her hand.

"What's going on Mik?" he asked.

"You don't want to know."

"Come on, this is me you're talking to. Let's have it."

She let out a long sigh and placed the coffee pot on the back warmer. A moment later she was sitting on the bar stool next to him. "Look honey, the only reason I'm divulging this is because we finally told Eleanor this past weekend."

"Oh God, is it the restaurant?"

She lowered her head, nodding. "The recession hit us pretty hard this past year and we're just not doing enough volume to sustain the business. Unless we have a successful summer season, it looks like we're going to have to close by the end of the year."

"Is there anything I can do?"

"Help me find a new chef that won't scare off what few customers we have left."

"Actually, I think I can help you there. My cousin Jonah might be looking for a job."

"Jonah?" she said. "I thought he was the chef at that new restaurant over on the coast?"

"Yes, but I heard he's not all that happy there, something about creative differences."

"Well, we certainly are not as fancy as what Jonah is accustomed to, but what the heck. Have him call me."

She picked up a business card off of the cash register, laying it next to his coffee cup.

"You do know I already have your number." He reached for the card, momentarily allowing his fingers to rest on top of hers.

"It's been nice having you in here this week," she said. "How's the investigation going?"

"Very frustrating, the only pleasant part has been my morning visits here."

Just then, Eric Garrison sat down on the bar stool next to Jared, placing his hat on the counter. "Hey there Mikayla, how's it going?"

"Good morning Cuz, something to eat?"

"Who's cooking?"

"Ben," she said drily.

"I'll pass. Just give me some coffee."

Mikayla waltzed around the bar and grabbed the pot and a cup. She leaned towards Eric as she poured. "Listen, I just told Jared about the restaurant, so you don't have to worry about letting it slip. And guess what? He may have a chef for us."

"Let's hope so," Eric said. "I don't think you can survive much longer with Ben's cooking. Hell, you may not even make it to the tourist season."

"Shhh, before someone overhears you," she said. "I'll leave you two to chat. Jared, tell your cousin to give me a call as soon as possible."

She gave him a wink and Jared followed her sway as she disappeared into the kitchen.

"I don't get you two," Eric said as he blew on his coffee.

"There is nothing to get. We've just known each other a long time."

"And after twenty years you're still not over her."

"Well, if your cousin Jeremy hadn't introduced her to Ben we wouldn't be having this conversation now would we?"

"There is no way in hell she ever would have married you."

"Well, maybe not in this lifetime," Jared said. "Let's get down to business."

"Look, I know it's a long shot, but I'm going to expand the search today to the west side of Birch Mountain."

"Eric, I can't imagine why Bellaso would travel that far from her car. I still think someone planted that scarf up there on Wilkins Road just to throw us off."

"I agree, but with this crazy weather it's been impossible to track anything and I'm running out of options. What's going on with the break-in?"

"We interviewed the rental agency manager that oversees the house. Bellaso has been using it exclusively for the past two years. The actual owner of the property is Bellaso's lawyer in LA. We finally made contact with her, but she is out of town on business and can't get here until tomorrow."

"Damn celebrities," Eric said. "They should stay downstream where they belong."

"Well, don't share that sentiment at the next press conference. I don't think Ms. Bellaso's manager or fans would appreciate it. Speaking of which, we got one later today. Hopefully we'll have something to report. God, I really could use a body about now, preferably a live one."

"You know if there are bodies out there somewhere, animals have probably gotten to them by now." Eric pulled out his wallet, throwing a few bills on the counter.

"Yes, I know. I was thinking we keep searching through tomorrow and then reassess."

"Agree. You ready to go? I need to make a call and I can't get any reception in here."

Eric placed his hat on his head and marched towards the door. Jared looked around for Mikayla, but she was nowhere to be found. He followed Eric and within seconds of passing through the front door both their cell phones went off.

"This is Adams. What?" Jared put his hand over his phone asking Eric to wait. "Yeah, I'm still here. I'm heading back now. And Tommy, get a blood sample if you can." Jared ended his call, turning to Eric. "Someone just got dumped in the hospital parking lot in Edmond. He's badly beaten, no identification, but Tommy says it looks like it might be Charles Lourdes."

"Well, you'll be happy to know I just got a call about an abandoned car five miles east of here. It's a rental with a wallet lying on the front seat."

"This day is suddenly looking brighter my friend."

"Sounds like it," Eric said. "I'll give you a call after I have a look."

Jared lit a cigarette while he watched Garrison drive away. He slid onto the front seat of his car and was about to close the door when Mikayla appeared with a carryout coffee.

"I thought you might want one for the road," she said.

"Thanks. I'll make sure Jonah calls you today, and don't worry about the restaurant. I'm sure between all of us we can figure something out."

"All of us? What does that mean?"

"Jeremy was my best friend and so is Eleanor. I know how important this place is to her."

"I get that honey, but I'm not so sure how Ben would feel about you getting involved."

"What are you talking about?" he said. "Ben and I get along just fine."

"Yes, but he hasn't been himself lately."

"What's up Mik? Has something happened between you two?"

Mikayla's dark brown eyes glistened momentarily. "Nah, you know how he gets sometimes, all quiet and grumpy. Jeremy's anniversary was really tough for him."

"Speaking of that, have you talked to Eleanor at all this week? I left her several messages but she hasn't returned them."

"I haven't seen her since we had dinner Saturday night. She's probably staying on the coast this week since her guy friend is in from LA."

"You mean Kyle Fiorelli? He's here?"

"Well yeah honey, since Saturday. What's wrong? You look worried?"

"No, I'm just surprised. Usually I know when he's coming to town. I should go."

"Oh, I almost forgot your coffee." Mikayla leaned into the car, setting the cup in the holder. "It's been really nice talking with you." She placed her hand over his, and for a moment he felt nothing except the gentle caress of her thumb.

"Thanks Mik."

"Take care Shug, and I'll see you soon."

She waved as he drove away, and he realized that his heart was beating so hard in his chest that he could feel the pounding in his ears. After all this time she still had that effect on him, and he knew that she always would.

❊❊

Eleanor had just returned to her car when she saw Jared rush across the hospital parking lot. She quickly slid down into the driver's seat, watching from her rearview mirror as he entered the emergency room. Confident she had escaped his notice she started the car and put it in gear.

As she drove away, she realized she could not avoid him for much longer. He had left her several messages since their strange encounter last Saturday, and she had not responded, knowing very well what he wanted. Something had passed between them on that hillside. She knew it, and obviously Jared did too. And although she had spent the past week assuring herself that what happened was nothing more than a reaction to the anniversary of Jeremy's death, in her heart she knew that was not true.

Her cell phone vibrated in her purse. She did not bother to check it. Most likely Jared had talked to Detective Tommy Reyes and learned that she had been at the hospital. Reyes had arrived shortly after she joined the crowd, and recognized her among the onlookers. When he asked why she was there, she explained her near collision with the blue Nissan, and then he requested that she remain with the other witnesses so he could take her statement.

Her phone went off again.

This is nuts. Just get it over with and talk to him.

She pulled off the road to take the call, and took a deep breath before retrieving the phone from her bag. She glanced at the caller name and her pulse soared.

Oh my God.

Her entire body was shaking as she answered.

"Hello?"

"Ellie?"

"Daniel…"

❇❇❇

When Jared arrived at the hospital he was met by his lead investigator, Tommy Reyes. They flashed their badges at the security guard and the two detectives flew through a pair of double doors and into the main corridor of the emergency room at Edmond Memorial. As they approached the nurse's station, Dr. Gwendolyn Keats glanced up from her chart and smiled.

"Why hello there Detective Sergeant Adams," she said. "Tommy said you'd be here."

"Good to see you Gwen. So what's the condition of our guy?"

"Right to business I see. All right, our John Doe has a bullet wound to the shoulder. However, it has already been removed. Crudely, I might add. There are still some fragments left and as a result he has a serious infection. Also, he's been badly beaten, his shoulder is broken, he has a stab wound to the stomach and has lost a lot of blood. He is not in good shape. We just ran a CT scan and found serious internal injuries that are going to require surgery. I can address the clean-up of the gunshot and knife wounds, but we are not equipped to deal with the other issues. So, we are going to stabilize him and fly him down to San Francisco."

"Is he conscious?" Jared asked.

"No, and I don't think he will be any time soon. Oh, and there's something else you should know. When they brought him in here, he was bound with heavy metal chains around his wrists and legs. It looked like they had been on there for several days."

"It's amazing he's still alive."

"Tell me about it. Tommy said that this man might be Charles Lourdes."

"We think so, which is why we'll need to have someone from my team travel down to San Francisco with him."

"We'll make the arrangements for you. Also, I'll make sure we secure the bullet fragments that we remove from him."

"You're too good to me Gwen."

"I know. Don't be such a stranger, all right?" Dr. Keats winked as she walked away.

Jared glanced over at Tommy Reyes who gave him a curious look. "Don't ask. So what do you have for me?"

Reyes referenced his note pad. He informed Jared there were six witnesses who saw the dark blue Nissan pull up to the emergency room entrance where Lourdes was dumped, and one witness who was nearly hit when the car left the parking lot. Jared was shocked when he learned it was Eleanor. Then Reyes proceeded to review the accounts of the incident.

"The driver was wearing a ski mask, black gloves and black leather jacket. Our witnesses described the person as having a large frame and broad shoulders. No one saw any other passengers. The car exited south onto Morgan Street, and then travelled east across the main highway and took the Route 6 exit."

"I don't get it," Jared said. "He's chained up for days, nearly beaten to death and then left in a public place where there are witnesses. His captors were intending to kill him, but then changed their minds. And where is Bellaso? How long had Lourdes been dating her?"

"About a month," Reyes said.

"And who was he with before that?"

"There hasn't been anyone that we could find. The last time he was seen in public with a woman was ten years ago, when he first became CEO of Monroe Industries. He attended an event with Katharine Monroe, but there is no indication they were dating."

Jared's phone lit up with a call from Eric Garrison, and he learned that the abandoned car was a dark blue Nissan Altima that had been rented by Charles Lourdes on Friday.

"Sounds like that's our vehicle," Jared said. "Can you see any blood?"

"Not yet," Eric said. "But it reeks of bleach. Also, there are tire tracks running alongside the car. It looks like whoever left the car had a ride out of here. We're going to check the surrounding homes and see if anyone saw something. I have to get going. We have a search party starting at 11:00. Deputy Vargas has the area secured until you can get here."

Jared ended the call, informing Reyes about the abandoned rental car. Then he went to examine the area where Lourdes had been discovered. Outside, he found his evidence technician, Chad Richardson, taking photographs. He lit a cigarette and walked the perimeter around the area that had been sectioned off.

His thoughts turned to Eleanor. He was amazed that she had been in the area when Lourdes surfaced and even more amazed that she had stopped to join the onlookers. As he pondered this highly unlikely coincidence, he pulled out his phone to call her. Suddenly, he heard music playing, and he turned to Richardson who had a perplexed look on his face.

"Where's that coming from?" Jared said.

The music continued to play and Jared scanned the area until he located the source: a cell phone lying on the ground between two bushes. He leaned in examining the caller ID.

"What the hell. Chad, I need gloves, now!" Richardson slapped a pair in his hand and he snatched up the phone. "I believe I'm going to take this call."

Jared hit answer and held up the phone to his ear.

Chapter Eight

My lord, I have remembrances of yours
That I have longèd long to redeliver.

When Daniel entered the Monroes' penthouse from his visit with Leesman, he took the stairs to the upper level and went directly to his bedroom. Closing the door behind him, he grabbed a bottle of bourbon that was sitting on his nightstand and walked over to a settee that was positioned near the window. From his coat pocket he produced the envelope that Alex had given him an hour earlier. He could not stop his hand from shaking as he studied the faded Ritz-Carlton logo, unsure if he wanted to read the message inside.

His meeting with Alex had been a good one, though he probably had consumed one too many bourbons on an empty stomach and was starting to feel drowsy. It was a relief to get away from the madness for a while and talk about something other than funeral arrangements and autopsies. He confided to Leesman about his inability to cry at Katharine's funeral, and Alex told him it would probably be some time before he felt normal again.

"Believe me, this past year with Eleanor has taught me a lot about the grieving process."

"So, how is she?" Daniel said.

"The first six months were very tough for her. She had to take a leave of absence from the university and missed the entire summer season. There was a brief span of time when she scared the hell out of us, but eventually she got better."

"And now?"

"I would say we almost have our Eleanor back. She's returning to the festival and she is directing one of the shows. I'm also trying to convince her to take on a role, though she's fighting me on that one."

"Let me guess," Daniel said. "She thinks she's been away from acting for too long and feels she isn't good enough."

"You know our Dr. Bouchard all too well," Alex chuckled.

"That's right, she was working on her doctorate the last time I saw her."

"So, how long has it been since you spoke with her?"

"It's been a while. Not since San Francisco."

Alex reached over the bar and placed his hand on Daniel's arm. "I was wondering what happened after you called me that night. Did you ever apologize to her?"

"I left a note. She never responded."

Alex removed an item from his coat pocket and placed it in front of Daniel "Well then, perhaps this is what you've been waiting for."

Daniel's thoughts returned to the cream colored stationary that was now stained from his sweaty hands. His mildly inebriated mind floated back to that night in San Francisco and his heated exchange with Eleanor in his hotel room.

He still was not sure as to the exact moment when the argument started, but what he did remember was her reaction when he wanted to reminisce about the first time that they met. For some reason, recalling that day at Julliard solicited a groan from Eleanor.

"What was that for?" he said. "Are you ashamed of our past?"

"Of course not, but every time we talk about our early years it never ends well."

"That's bullshit. We've talked about our past plenty of times and I don't remember there being any issues. You just don't like discussing it because it reminds you of what you gave up."

"What I gave up?" she said. "What's that supposed to mean?"

"You know damn well. You gave up on us Ellie."

"Are you kidding me? You booted me out of your life and your apartment and told me to never come back."

"Yeah, maybe I did. OK, I'll take the blame for that one."

"Daniel, this is not about blame. Please, can we talk about something else?"

The argument further deteriorated from there, until somewhere along the line he said something disparaging about her work with the Shakespeare festival that made him instantly regret his words. He had never seen such a mortified look on her face, and as she raced to the door he had to take several long strides to catch up with her.

He attempted to apologize, but she ignored his pleas, refusing to look at him. Finally, he was forced to plant himself in front of her, and she walloped him across the face. He was so shocked by her actions that he released his grip and stepped aside. She yelled some nonsense about him humiliating her, and as he massaged his cheek she continued for the door. A minute later she started crying, and that was when he knew he had really screwed up.

When he went to console her, it was not his intent to kiss her, but the minute he rested his head against her forehead and his eyes fell on her lips, he knew he was sunk. At first he was discouraged by her unresponsiveness, but when she did not resist him either, he took that as a sign to continue. And he did, working his way down her neck to that one place he knew would drive her mad. She responded and he carried her to the couch.

She made no attempt to stop him as he undid her blouse and kissed her breasts. She even helped to remove his shirt as his hands moved beneath her skirt. He knew their bodies were rapidly approaching the point of no return and neither one of them were putting on the brakes. Obviously this was going to happen, consequences be damned.

Still, he asked her if she wanted to proceed. When she nodded, he slipped off her panties while she unzipped his jeans. He pushed her skirt away, and he was nearly inside her when he found himself staring into her sorrowful sea-green eyes. He was not sure who stopped first, Eleanor or him, but suddenly their movements ceased.

It was only a matter of seconds before she wiggled out from beneath him and quickly moved to the opposite end of the couch. She sat silent,

ing straight ahead at the television. He rolled over on his back, contemplating what he should do next, when she grabbed her purse and rushed by
him. This time he did not attempt to stop her, sighing with relief when he
heard the door shut.

The next hour was hell. He paced the suite trying to decide if he should
call her or just knock on her door. If he called her and she did not answer,
what would he do? If he went to her room and she let him in, how would
he handle it? Eventually, he gave up on deciding for himself and woke Alex
from his slumber to ask his advice.

Two hours later he checked out of the hotel and left a note at the front
desk- with a sizeable tip- instructing to have it delivered to Eleanor's room.
He then spent the next few hours sulking in the VIP lounge at the airport
while he waited for his pilot to arrive.

Daniel returned his thoughts to his present situation and brought the
bourbon bottle to his lips. The lump in his throat burned as he opened the
envelope, removing the contents. He had misplaced his reading glasses, but
eventually he located his original message. Just below his handwriting he
found her words to him.

I'm sorry too.

Please forgive me.

-E

He closed his eyes, pressing the note against his chest.

Thank you!

Incredibly relieved, he pulled out his phone, punching in her number.
He was just intoxicated enough to endure the nervousness that was rapidly
spreading throughout his entire body. It took two tries, but when he heard
her soothing alto voice, his heart swelled up inside him.

"Ellie?"

"Daniel…how are you?"

"Not so sure right now." He took another drink from the bottle.

"That was a stupid question. I'm sorry."

"No, don't say that. Hey, are you good to talk?"

"Yes, I'm in the car, but I just pulled over."

"Thanks for the flowers. I saw them at the wake. They were very nice."

"You're welcome," she said.

"And, ah…well I got your note. I'm looking at it right now."

"I'm sorry I waited this long to respond to you."

"It's all right. I understand. Listen, I need to ask you something."

He decided he needed another drink before he continued, and as he emptied the bourbon bottle he caught a reflection in the window. He had no idea how long she had been standing there, but when he turned to find Amelia glaring at him, he choked, spewing liquor everywhere.

"Shit."

The word left his lips before he could suppress it, and he quickly wiped the liquid from his mouth and phone. "I have to go. I'll call you later." He stood up, and then sat down again when the room started to spin.

"What's wrong Daddy?" Amelia said.

"Nothing, I'm just a little tired, that's all."

"Who was that?"

"A friend of mine…what's going on baby girl, is something wrong?"

Amelia searched his eyes and frowned. "Have you been drinking again? You have very messy thoughts in your head."

"What?"

"Why are you sad about your friend?"

"What friend?"

"The one who wrote the note." She pointed to the envelope that had dropped on the floor.

"What are you talking about?"

Amelia picked up the letter, handing it to him. "You feel bad because you hurt her."

Daniel's chest tightened and he took the note from her, stuffing it back into his suit pocket. "That's enough Amelia."

"You like her very much," she said.

"I said that's enough."

"Who is Eleanor?"

"How do you know about Ellie?"

Amelia stood silent, her crystal blue eyes glistening. "I saw her name on the envelope."

Suddenly she burst into tears. Mortified, Daniel pulled her into his lap, holding her close. "I'm sorry baby girl, I'm so sorry. I didn't mean to raise my voice. Daddy's just not feeling very well right now."

"Is everything all right?"

Christine Monroe's deep monotone voice sent a chill down his spine, and when he looked up he found her looming in the doorway.

"Is there something you want?" he said

She marched across the room and picked up the empty bourbon bottle off the floor. "Are you drunk?"

He had to think about that for a moment. He did not feel drunk, but he was certainly having difficulty keeping her in focus. He decided that given Amelia's presence there, it was just best to say no.

Christine's eyes narrowed. "That's good, because right now the police are waiting for you in the sitting room."

Daniel tried to stand, swaying as he attempted to steady himself. He sat down again, resting his head in his hands.

"Amelia," Christine said. "Go get Trevor now, and tell him to bring up some coffee."

Amelia left and Christine disappeared into the bathroom, emerging with a wet washcloth and a towel. She handed him the cloth and gestured for him to wipe his face. He obeyed and then she tossed the towel in his lap.

"I promised Phillip I would keep my distance from you until we got past this tragedy that has descended on our family, but given your current condition you have left me no choice. I understand that you are not yourself at the moment, but that doesn't excuse the behavior I just observed between my granddaughter and you."

"Christine, you need to put a cork in it right now."

"Listen young man, I may not be your mother, God rest her soul, but I am still a person in this family who should garner your respect. We're all suffering here, every one of us. You need to get a grip on yourself now, because downstairs are two rather serious looking people who are quite anxious to speak with us."

Daniel buried his face in his hands and at that moment he truly felt he had it within him to punch his mother-in-law in the face. Just then Trevor entered the room.

"Pour as much coffee down him as you can and see to it he's presentable and downstairs as soon as possible." Christine said as she stormed away.

Miraculously, Daniel emerged from the bedroom five minutes later, donning a clean shirt, fresh breath and a slightly less inebriated posture. He managed to descend the staircase without any major mishaps and proceeded towards the sitting room. Amelia appeared at his side, clenching his hand and they moved towards the center of the room where a darkly clad couple stood talking with Phillip and Christine Monroe. As he approached the group, the woman glanced at him, flashing a curt smile. She stepped forward, extending her hand to him.

"Mr. Archer, I'm Detective Sheila Bellows and this is my partner Detective David Chen."

He shared a firm handshake with Bellows before Chen stepped forward, gushing. "It's a real pleasure to meet you sir. I absolutely loved your last movie."

Bellows cleared her throat and Chen stepped back.

"I'm sorry, who are you again?" Daniel said.

"Detective Sheila Bellows. Detective Chen and I are the lead investigators on your wife's case."

"Chen…yes, we spoke earlier this week. I didn't realize you were a detective, and what do you mean by case?"

"Mr. Archer, that's why we're here, but I need to ask if this is still a good time. Do you have guests?"

Phillip Monroe interjected. "We have a few people who joined us after the funeral, but we should be fine for now."

"Then, if you wouldn't mind, I think it is best that we speak with the three of you, *alone*."

Bellows glanced down at Amelia and Daniel could feel his daughter's grip tightening around his fingers. Suddenly, she broke away and approached the attractive female detective.

"You don't think my mommy's fall was an accident."

Bellows stood motionless, one eyebrow lifted. "We just need to talk to your father and grandparents for a few minutes."

"You think someone hurt her," Amelia said.

Daniel moved in, gripping Amelia's shoulders. "That's enough honey. Go with Trevor and wait for us in the living room."

Trevor moved in, attempting to take Amelia's hand, but she refused to budge. "Why would someone want to hurt Mommy?"

Bellows was expressionless. "I'm very sorry about your mother, but I'm not able to answer that question."

Amelia started to speak again, but stopped. She sighed, and then glanced briefly at Christine before allowing Trevor to escort her from the room. Daniel exchanged blank stares with the two detectives. He had absolutely no explanation for Amelia's behavior and was at a complete loss for words.

Phillip brought the room to attention as he asked everyone to sit. Bellows leaned forward with her hands folded in her lap and cleared her throat.

"Mr. Archer, I want to apologize for upsetting your daughter. However, it appears she is very perceptive and must have sensed we have concerns regarding your wife's accident."

Daniel had to let the words register in his head before he responded. "Excuse me?"

Bellows cleared her throat again and locked eyes with him. "Mr. Archer, after thoroughly investigating the apartment and reviewing the results of Ms. Monroe's autopsy, we have found evidence that suggests that your wife's fall was not an accident."

"What kind of evidence?" Daniel said.

"Sir, unfortunately at this time I cannot share the exact details with you. However, I can tell you that the most serious of Ms. Monroe's head injuries were not caused by her fall. We believe someone attacked your wife, someone who knew exactly where to strike her in order to cause a specific type of damage."

Daniel could not speak. His pulse was racing and his heart felt like it was about to burst. Phillip grasped his arm and asked Bellows to continue.

"Aside from the severity of the injuries, the power had gone out in the building which we now believe was intentional. Also, the upstairs office had been disrupted, though we will admit it was very subtle and took us some time to confirm. We believe her attacker was looking for something on her computer before she was pushed down the stairs."

"Pushed?" Daniel stuttered. "Who the hell would do that?"

"That's what we need to figure out Mr. Archer. There were no signs of forced entry, which suggests that her attacker had access to the apartment, or Ms. Monroe knew the person and let them in. I'm sorry sir, but we have officially moved into a homicide investigation."

Daniel collapsed into his chair as Detective Chen stepped in, explaining that they had already started working with the building security on establishing visitors that evening as well as reviewing the security tapes. They also would need to establish the family's whereabouts that evening.

"You mean alibis?" Daniel choked.

"Mr. Archer, no one is suspected at this time. However, we do need to speak with you and anyone who would have had access to your apartment. Also sir, do you recognize this man?" Bellows pulled out a photo from her bag and handed it to him.

"Yes I do. That's Zach Walker, and he was probably the last person to see Kate alive."

Daniel explained his encounter with Walker earlier that morning and Christine flew into a rage, demanding to know why he had not mentioned it before. An argument ensued and Phillip had to step in, commanding them to lower their voices. Christine returned to her seat, fuming, and Daniel explained to the detectives that Zach Walker was Amelia's biological father.

"Do you know if Mr. Walker is still in New York?" Bellows asked.

"He said he was flying out today. My lawyer has his contact information if you need it. I think you spoke with Hank before."

Detective Chen pulled out his phone and stepped into the foyer.

"Mr. Archer," Bellows said. "There's one more thing for now. Did your wife have a cell phone?"

"Yeah, but I'm not sure where it is."

"That's all right sir. If you could give us the number and carrier we will request her call history. It will help us with the investigation."

"Wait, I think I might have it after all. They gave me an envelope at the hospital." Daniel started to stand but Phillip stopped him.

"Son, are you sure you want to do that? Shouldn't we just have the detective acquire the records with a warrant?"

"Why? You just heard the woman, she thinks someone murdered Kate. If it will help track down who did this, then I say hand it over."

Daniel struggled to stand and Phillip steadied him. "You stay here. I'll get it."

Phillip left the room. Christine stood, smoothing the creases in her skirt and announced she was going to check on Amelia. She gave Bellows a silent nod, ignoring Daniel as she exited the room. He realized that he would not last another 24 hours with his mother-in-law and decided that he would leave first thing in the morning. Detective Chen appeared, informing Bellows that he had acquired Zach Walker's information and was now trying his cell. Philip returned, handing him a large envelope with Katharine's name on it.

"Mr. Archer, if you wouldn't mind, it would be better for the investigation if you handed that over to us," Bellows said.

Daniel ignored her request, unfastening the flap and emptying the contents onto the coffee table. What he discovered sent a shudder through his body. Among Katherine's belongings were her sapphire wedding ring, a heart-shaped pendant, a pair of diamond earrings and her iPhone. There were several missed calls appearing on the front screen.

"Two calls just came within the last hour, and they're both from Monica's phone." Daniel stared at the screen and highlighted the last entry. "Maybe she's been found."

"Mr. Archer, please don't," Bellows said.

Daniel hit call and his heart raced as he waited to connect. The phone rang several times, and he was about to give up when a raspy voice answered.

"Hello. This is Detective Jared Adams with the Alexandria County Sherriff's Office. Who is this?"

"Daniel Archer. I guess since you have Monica's phone that means you've found her?"

"I'm sorry, Mr. Archer, but Ms. Bellaso is still missing. We found this phone a few moments ago when it started ringing. Sir, are you calling from Katharine Monroe's phone?"

"Yes, I am. If Monica is still missing, then who just called her?" Daniel then learned from the California detective that Charles Lourdes had been found alive, but had sustained life-threatening injuries. "You still haven't answered my question. Who made these calls from Monica's phone?"

"Mr. Archer, I honestly don't know. We just found the phone in a hospital parking lot. I'm sorry sir, but I have to go."

Daniel ended the call and within a few seconds Phillip's cell phone rang and he left the room. Since the detective on the other end had not been very helpful, he decided to page through Katherine's received call list. Bellows moved into the seat next to him.

"What is it Mr. Archer?"

"Katharine got a call from Monica at 7:30 Friday evening. Katharine tried to call Monica back at 7:35….and again at 7:40. Nothing after that until these two calls came through a few minutes ago. Monica was probably the last person to speak to her, and now she's missing and her phone just turned up in a hospital parking lot in California."

"It's probably the same town where Ms. Bellaso's vehicle was found." Bellows leafed through her notepad. "River Mist."

Daniel's heart raced. He had not thought about it till the detective spoke the words. *Why would Monica be in River Mist, unless…*

"Eleanor."

"Eleanor?" Bellows said.

"They didn't even know each other, but Kate must have figured it out."

"Figured out what Mr. Archer? Who is Eleanor?"

Daniel leaned towards Bellows and whispered. "Eleanor Bouchard was my first wife."

❊

When Christine found Amelia, she was sitting at the kitchen counter eating a sandwich and chatting with their cook, Camille. Immediately her granddaughter turned quiet as she sat next to her. Camille gave Christine a thoughtful look while she poured her a cup of coffee.

"I think I will go check on the food. Can I get you anything Mrs. Monroe?"

Christine cringed. She hated it when Camille addressed her formerly, but in this case she knew it was spoken intentionally. "I'm fine, thank you."

She watched as her cook of 40 years passed through the swinging door into the formal dining room, allowing her the privacy she needed to confront her granddaughter. Amelia turned to her with an exceptionally defiant look and jumped off the stool. She grabbed her sandwich and went over to the kitchen table.

"We need to talk. Your behavior was unacceptable." Christine took a drink of coffee while she waited for Amelia's response. When none was forthcoming, she picked up her cup and joined her granddaughter. "This is a serious matter, young lady. Outbursts like the one you just demonstrated in front of that detective are not only irresponsible they're dangerous."

Amelia continued her silence as she took a bite of her peanut butter and jelly sandwich.

-Fine, you don't want to talk? Then we'll do it your way. Christine sat down at the table and continued her silent conversation with Amelia.

-You need to stop listening into people's thoughts, unless it is an emergency. It's impolite and quite frankly, all it will do is cause you unnecessary pain.

-You're not my mother.

-No, but your mother is not here Amelia, and I'm the only one qualified right now to guide you in your abilities. Come child, you must know all I want to do is to help you.

-Only my daddy can tell me what to do.

-Don't test me. You know I have the power to stop you, so don't force me to do that. I want you to develop your powers. I want you to get stronger.

-Are you going to take me away from Daddy?

-I will do whatever is necessary to protect you, and if that means having you come live with your grandfather and I while your abilities mature, then so be it. You must realize that your father is not equipped to help you and if you keep blurting out every thought you hear, you're going to put him and even your grandfather and I in harm's way.

-Why would that police woman want to hurt Daddy?

-It's not that she would intentionally hurt him, but that she would question how it is you know so much about your mother's death. She would want to know where you got your information.

-I don't know what happened to Mommy. That's what the police woman thinks.

-Which is why you need to stay out of her head, and you need to learn how to control your gifts. Let me help you with that, please.

-If I let you help me, can I stay with Daddy?

-I can't answer that question right now, but I promise you I'll think about it.

Amelia looked up at her with wounded eyes and then pushed her plate aside. She shot up, exiting through the side door that emptied out into the foyer. Christine followed Amelia's trail of angry thoughts as she ascended the stairs to her bedroom, slammed the door and turned on her music.

The dining room door swung open and Camille appeared at her side holding the coffee pot. She topped off Christine's cup and laid a comforting hand on her shoulder.

"She's a powerful one, isn't she?"

"Oh God Camille, I don't know if I have it in me to do this again."

"There is nothing wrong with asking for help."

"Yes, I guess so, but what if the answer is no?"

"There's only one way to find out."

Chapter Nine

My ears have yet not drunk a hundred words
Of thy tongue's uttering, yet I know the sound.

Jared sat at the bar nursing his drink while he observed Eleanor and her friends eating dinner. He was tired and in a lousy mood, and wanted nothing more than to be home watching the NCAA semi-finals. But after a week of Eleanor ignoring his calls and messages, hunting her down at her favorite Friday night haunt was the only way he was going to make contact with her.

The trio had been at the restaurant for nearly two hours and they were now working their way through a fourth bottle of wine. Eleanor and Kyle Fiorelli were clearly drunk, as was demonstrated by her increasing inability to keep her eyes open and his growing flirtation with the female server, the wine steward, and a handful of other women that had congregated around the table. The only person that appeared to be sober was Nina St. John, who sat silent and stone- faced while Eleanor and Kyle jabbered away.

Finally, the waiter brought the bill and Jared made his move. Nina was the first to see him approach. She glanced up at him through her rose-colored eyeglasses and cracked the only smile that he had seen from her all evening. Eleanor must have noticed Nina's reaction, because she suddenly swung around to face him, her eyes widening. Despite his highly irritated mood, the last thing Jared wanted to do was to cause a scene, so he immediately took control of the situation and turned to Fiorelli.

"Kyle, it's been a long time, how are you?"

One thing Jared knew he could always count on was Fiorelli's ability to act perfectly normal and charming under any circumstances. The tall, Italian born composer stood, extending his hand as he teetered over Jared.

"I'm fine Adams. Still honoring your Friday night ritual of vodka and steak?"

"Yes, as a matter-of-fact. Never had much of a taste for the wine thing, which by the way I noticed you have been enjoying quite a lot tonight. Can I assume that you're not driving?"

Fiorelli grinned. "Ah, Adams, leave it to you to be the ever-watchful eye. No, we are not driving. We walked here from Ms. St. John's abode."

"Good, and Eleanor I hope you're planning on spending the night in Edmond."

Eleanor, who had remained silent during the exchange with Fiorelli, turned her back to him and downed her glass of wine. "Of course, I don't want to end up like Jeremy now, do I?"

The table was silent.

"Ellie, that's not what I meant," Jared said.

"Don't call me Ellie. Nobody gets to call me that name, ever again." Eleanor lowered her head, biting her lip. "I really should go now."

She shot up out of her seat, grabbing her coat. Kyle followed her, leaving Nina and Jared alone.

"She's been a little crazy lately," Nina said.

"How crazy?"

"Nothing like last year, but something is going on."

Nina darted out of the restaurant, leaving Jared to wonder if he should run after Eleanor and convince her to have coffee with him. He was contemplating this thought when he looked down and saw a handbag on the floor next to her seat. Seconds later he was flying through the front doors of The Wine Bistro, calling out her name. Eleanor turned, recognizing the black object tucked under his arm and stumbled towards him.

"Thank you, I can't believe I left it," she said.

"Not so fast. Why haven't you returned my calls?"

"Please Jared, give me my purse. I'm drunk and I need to go home."

"No, not until you tell me what is going on. I'm concerned about you."

Eleanor moved in, whispering. "This is exactly what I was trying to avoid. I know what you're thinking my friend, and there is nothing wrong with me. I feel fine, so stop worrying."

"Well, I'm not fine. I know something happened to me on that hillside and I want to talk about it. I saw her Eleanor, and I know you saw her too."

Since Jeremy died, it was difficult for him to gauge Eleanor's mood. She had gone from what he considered a fairly happy person to someone who rarely displayed any emotion. For the longest time he blamed it on the anti-depressants she was taking for the better part of last year, but she had been off her medication since November. Now he did not know what lurked behind her empty, expressionless stares.

Finally, she invited him back to Nina's townhouse for espresso and asked for her purse. As he handed it to her she leaned into him, resting her hand on his chest.

Everything went black.

He saw a tall, dark-haired woman, dressed in a cream colored jacket and boots, rushing up a steep hill. She had a long, silver object in her hand and as she climbed towards the sunlight, he could see that it was a knife. In the distance he could hear a man calling her name. Her speed increased as she disappeared into the sunlight. Then he experienced a feeling of weightlessness, before the pull of gravity took hold.

When he opened his eyes he was lying on his back, looking at Fiorelli. Jared pushed himself up on his elbows and glanced over at Eleanor who was on the ground next to him. "What the hell happened?"

"I don't know," Fiorelli grinned. "The two of you were talking and then you tumbled to the ground. I guess we're not the only ones who had too much to drink tonight."

When they arrived at Nina's townhouse, Eleanor went directly upstairs to her bedroom, instructing Jared to bring her espresso when it was ready. Nina went back to the kitchen and Fiorelli flopped down on the stairs, donning a curious look.

"Why are you here Adams?"

"I was about to ask you the same thing. I understand you're gracing us with your presence for the next several months."

"I've been hired by the university to teach and compose music for the summer festival."

"I see. So you're going to leave your glamorous life down in LA and get paid a fraction of what you normally make just to hang out up here with us boring, small town folk."

"I wouldn't say that it's boring. There's been a lot of excitement around here lately."

"Yes, funny how you showed up just when it all started."

"Are you implying something Detective?"

"Only that you have incredible timing."

Kyle shrugged his shoulders. "It's the anniversary of Jeremy's death. I'm here to support Eleanor."

"I'll be sure to make a note of that."

Nina appeared bearing two espresso cups and Jared took both, heading up the stairs. She started back towards the kitchen, leaving Kyle to wonder if he should leave now and avoid any further unpleasantness.

"I'm making yours next," Nina said. "If you want it, you'll have to come and get it."

When he arrived in the kitchen she was busy making his drink and he sat at the island, watching her work. He focused on the tiny white gloves she was wearing and wondered if she had to buy them in the children's department. Without thinking, he moved in for a closer look, and she stepped away from the espresso machine.

"Sorry." He stopped his advance and leaned against the counter. After a few moments of silence she resumed her task. "So, how long have you owned the townhouse where I'm staying?"

"Thirty-five years."

"How is that? I thought you were only in your early thirties."

"My family owns it along with the rest."

"The rest of what?" he said.

"The townhouses that are on this block…they own them."

"They own all ten? That has to be worth a few million."

Nina finished his espresso and placed it on the counter. "My family likes to invest in real estate. I'm sure your big fancy home cost a few million, and it doesn't generate revenue. Do you think you'll want another? I don't want to have to clean the machine twice."

"I'm good. So is your family from this area?"

"No."

Kyle sipped his drink while she worked in silence. After a few minutes of waiting for her to elaborate, he continued. "So where are they from?"

"Is this necessary?"

"What's wrong? I'm just trying to break the ice and get to know you a little better."

"Why?"

"Because, we're going to be spending the next several months working together and I promised Eleanor I would try to get along. This is my attempt at that."

"I see. How's that working for you?"

"So far it's giving me a tremendous headache."

"Same here, maybe you should stop."

"You and I are her oldest friends. Don't you think we should give this a try? That's what she wants from us, right?"

At that moment there was a scream from above, followed by a loud thud. Nina shot past him like a rush of wind and he followed, struggling to keep pace. They flew up the stairs and into Eleanor's bedroom, landing in the middle of a terrifying scene which had Adams lying on the floor bleeding and Eleanor wielding a large dagger.

"What the hell happened?" Kyle said.

"We were talking, and suddenly she turned on me, like I was attacking her," Adams groaned. "I tried to reason with her, but she kept coming at me with that thing."

"Where did she get the knife?" Kyle said.

"From the closet, there's a shitload of weapons in there," Adams said.

Kyle turned to Nina, who gave him a defensive look.

"It's my stage combat equipment. I need to store it somewhere," she said.

"It's a guest bedroom," Kyle said.

"Will you two shut the hell up and keep an eye on her." Adams yelled. "She's in some sort of trance, and she has no idea what she's doing. And don't make any sudden movements. That seems to set her off."

Kyle nodded, slowly moving towards Eleanor who had positioned herself in front of the open deck door. Her weapon was extended and the long white sheers covering the glass were blowing alongside her, occasionally enveloping her entire body. At that moment he was reminded of a particularly haunting performance of *Lucia di Lammermoor* that he had seen in Milan, where the heroine, dressed entirely in white, sang herself into madness on a stage filled with mist. Suddenly, he had an uneasy feeling about Eleanor's close proximity to the open door and he took a step forward. She vanished onto the balcony.

Nina took off, sailing across the room in a single bound. He rushed after her, and when he flew onto the deck he found Eleanor backed up against the railing. He started towards her but stopped when she lunged at him with the knife.

"All right mia cara, just take it easy. It's me, Kyle, your friend."

She jabbed the dagger in his direction, hissing. "Soon you will pay for your sins."

Her hollow tone surprised him and he froze, unsure what to do next.

"Fiorelli," Nina whispered. "I have an idea. Give me thirty seconds." She vanished down the deck steps that led to the lower level.

"Where are you going?" he cried.

Suddenly, a dense fog consumed the entire balcony and the air was filled with a thick, pungent scent. Eleanor screamed and Kyle staggered in the direction of her voice. When he came upon her he discovered she had thrown her leg over the railing. He grabbed her arm, attempting to pull her back, but she swung at him with the knife, forcing him to release his grip.

"You don't get it, do you?" she yelled. "This was meant to be."

"For the love of God Eleanor, wake-up," Kyle yelled.

In a single movement she swung her other leg over the railing and leaned forward. Kyle latched on to her hand as she let go, and for a moment she dangled there, her wild eyes fixed on his. Then the fog grew thicker, obscuring his view of her face. He felt her fingers slip from his grasp and a crushing pain bore down on his chest as he collapsed, gasping for air.

He laid on the deck, waiting for a scream or the thud on the ground below, but neither happened. Instead, when he was able to breathe again, he rolled over on his side to discover Eleanor lying next to him coughing. Then he looked up and saw Nina standing a few feet away. She was no longer wearing her glasses, and her short black hair was disheveled. She inched forward, her emerald eyes fixed on him.

"Are you OK?" she said.

"I think so."

"Take care of her. I'll check on the detective."

Nina left and Kyle turned to Eleanor whose eyes were now open. He brushed her red hair away from her face and saw that his hand was shaking. Eventually when they recovered enough to stand, he helped her back into the house, where they found Nina reassembling the bedroom and Adams struggling to dress his wound. Eleanor went to assist him, but stopped when Adams threw up his hand.

"Maybe it would be better if someone else helped. I'm not so sure physical contact with you is a good thing right now," Adams said.

Eleanor nodded in agreement and stepped away. Kyle moved in, surveying the gash in his chest.

"I don't know Adams. I think you're going to need stiches."

"I've had worse."

"I'll say. That's quite a collection of scars you've got there."

"Just put the damn patch on, so I can have a smoke."

Kyle did as he was told and then the group moved down to the kitchen where Nina made tea. Adams returned from the deck, smelling of cigarettes, and everyone sat at the island, staring into their cups.

"So, are we just going to sit here and not talk about this?" Adams said.

"What's there to talk about?" Eleanor said. "Isn't it obvious? It's happening again."

"Eleanor, don't do that"

"Why deny it? I need help and we all know it. I'm going to call Dr. Stevens first thing tomorrow and get an emergency appointment."

"This is not like last spring," Adams said.

"You're right, it isn't. It's worse, much worse. I'm having visions of a woman I've never met. I just stabbed you in the chest and tried to jump off the balcony. I'm going insane."

"No, you're not."

"Jared, stop placating me. I know I'm crazy. I was crazy last year and don't tell me I wasn't because I know what people said about me. I saw the stares and I heard the whispers when all of you thought I wasn't listening. I knew I was in trouble and I should have checked into the hospital back then, like Dr. Stevens wanted me to."

"Dammit Eleanor, will you please just stop." Kyle's angry tone surprised even himself, and he took a deep breath before he continued. "You've just come off a traumatic week with Jeremy's anniversary, you've been drinking all night and you're tired. I think that you should just go to bed, get some sleep, and then we can deal with this in the morning."

"*We...* what exactly does that mean?" Eleanor said.

"All of us that are present now in this room. We're in this together."

"No, *we* are not dealing with this. I am. I'm going to get the help I need, the help I should have had last year."

"I agree with Fiorelli," Adams interjected. "You need to sleep on it before you make any rash decisions."

"No amount of sleep is going to change what happened here tonight. Look at you. You belong in an emergency room right now. And why aren't you going? Because you'll have to explain to them how your friend went nuts and stabbed you with a stage knife. Jared, look at me. Look at me! Because of me, both of us could have died tonight. I was completely out of control and we both know it."

"Yeah, I'll give you that, you were out of control, but you're not the only one who saw the face of that woman. I saw her too and I'm sure as hell not checking myself into any psych ward tomorrow." Adams stood, wincing as he pulled on his leather jacket. "I'm going home to crash. I'll stop by in the morning. Promise me you won't do anything until we talk."

"Promise me first that if your wound gets any worse you'll go to the hospital." Eleanor said.

"Don't worry. I got a doctor friend that owes me a few favors. Look, just do what Fiorelli said and sleep on it, preferably not in the same bedroom with the weapons." He stuck a cigarette in his mouth and left.

Eleanor turned to Nina, who had been silent the entire time and apologized for destroying her home. Nina listened, expressionless, and then informed Eleanor that she would move the combat equipment first thing in the morning. In the meantime, Eleanor could sleep in the second guest bedroom at the end of the hall. Eleanor then turned to Kyle and thanked him for saving her life. She embraced him and hurried from the kitchen, leaving him alone with Nina.

"You go ahead," Kyle said. "I'll clean up here and then let myself out."

"I don't think she should be alone tonight," Nina said.

"I agree."

"It can't be me. You have to do it."

"All right I will, but I want to ask you something. What happened tonight with Eleanor, after you left?"

"What do you mean?"

"Well, I'm positive she jumped off the railing, or at least I think she did. I couldn't tell with that damn fog."

"She never jumped. You pulled her off. I did the fog. I have a huge theatrical machine downstairs. I thought if I confused her you'd have a better chance of nabbing her."

"Well it worked, but I'm still not entirely sure how she ended up on the deck."

Nina moved in front of him, her emerald eyes glistening. "You saved her. That's all that matters."

She lingered for a moment, her tiny porcelain face arched towards his, and he found himself mesmerized by her childlike features. Then she slowly backed away, disappearing into the dark hallway. He had no idea what she was thinking or feeling, only what he observed about her, and it was obvious that she was very protective of Eleanor.

He cleaned up the dishes before heading upstairs. When he entered Eleanor's bedroom, she was asleep. Carefully he removed his shoes and fully clothed lay next to her. As he watched her slumber, he thought about what he would say to her tomorrow. Then he closed his eyes and hoped that someday soon their relationship would finally be allowed to move beyond its current restraints. How he longed for that day when he could share everything with her.

Chapter Ten

She is so conjunctive to my life and soul,
That, as the star moves not but in his sphere,
I could not but by her.

Daniel turned his key in the deadbolt lock as Amelia pushed open the door, and they were met with the smell of pine and lemon. Trevor had assured him that any evidence of Katharine's accident had been removed and it was safe for him to return.

It was his first time in the apartment since Katharine died. He had hoped to come alone, but when he tried to slip out of the Monroes' penthouse earlier that morning, he was met at the door by his determined daughter. Her bag was packed, her coat was on and her arms were crossed in front of her. She had barely talked to him since the incident with the detectives, and he didn't have the heart to deny her anything. So he let her join him and they spent a silent ride in the limousine down to the Flatiron District.

Amelia rolled her suitcase across the large entryway into the main room, stopping near the foot of the stairs. Daniel put his hand on her shoulder, coaxing her upward.

"Go on. I'll be up soon."

Slowly she climbed the staircase, her pink roller bag banging against each step along the way. He considered asking her to pick it up, but decided against it. She disappeared into her bedroom and slammed the door.

Sighing, he knelt down to examine a large reddish area on the floor. The small rug had been removed, but it was evident that Katharine's blood had seeped through the carpet, staining the wood beneath it. He wondered if there was a way to remove it, or if they should just buy another rug to cover it up. This was probably what captured Amelia's attention, he thought. He should have made her stay at the penthouse.

He stood, scanning the spacious living room. It was a quiet Saturday morning. A soft gray light filled the loft, the sun a few hours away from pouring in through the southern windows. Daniel loved the mid-morning. If it were a weekday he would just be getting up, Amelia would be at school, and Katharine would be attending a meeting, leaving him alone with his pot of coffee and his paper. He would sit in his favorite chair, a nicely worn brown leather chaise, reading and watching the last bit of morning news.

Occasionally, Katharine would be home when he woke, and after some friendly persuasion would return with him to bed. In their early years, they never made it back to the bedroom, which proved to be an issue when Trevor started working for him. After a few embarrassing encounters, his assistant announced himself when he entered the apartment and they did their best to keep their lovemaking behind closed doors.

That seemed so long ago now. The last few years their playfulness had slowed a bit. Katharine was fully immersed in her philanthropy work, his movie career kicked into overdrive, and Amelia became the center of their lives. There was always some function to run to, a movie to make, a recital to attend, dozens of obligations weighing them down, making it easy to roll over at night and let the passion slide. They had allowed the pressures of life to distract them, pulling them away from the intimacy that defined them as a couple. They joked about it recently, promising each other that once everything settled down they would take a much needed vacation.

How quickly it all changes…

The sound of the door latch engaging pulled him from his thoughts. Trevor entered carrying several bags of groceries and Daniel followed his assistant into the kitchen.

"How's the apartment look?" Trevor said.

"Fine so far. We just got here a few minutes ago. Amelia's upstairs in her room." Daniel eyed the bag of coffee beans as Trevor placed it on the counter. He picked it up and pulled out the coffee grinder. "I'll get started on this."

"Give me a moment and I can do it."

"What, you don't think I know how to make a pot of coffee?"

"How is Amelia doing?"

"She's still upset with me. I don't know Trev, maybe I need to get her some help. Someone she can talk to."

"Perhaps, but it has only been a few days since Katharine died. She probably just needs some time to adjust."

"Yeah, we'll see. So what all did you get at the store?"

"Just a few basics for now: milk, orange juice, eggs, Amelia's favorite cereal. Later on I'll get a list together and do a full run."

"I should go with you. I need to learn how to do these things."

"You can get a service for that, or you can just let me do it. Katharine had me pick up groceries all the time."

"I know. I think sometimes you worked more for her than you did me."

"Hardly, but there were times it was just too difficult for her to be out in public. I liked to help out whenever I could."

Daniel forgot how his fame affected Katharine's everyday life. She never complained or wished for it to be different. She just accepted it and took it in stride. They retained a limousine and a driver, they had his private plane, and she donned all sorts of disguises on Amelia and her, so that they could lead as normal a life as possible. And when she was spotted, whether it was the paparazzi or an enthusiastic fan, she was always very eloquent, gracious and polite. She believed that was the price to be paid for their success and the best course of action was to face it head on, with grace and dignity. Daniel did not share in his wife's tolerance of the media and frequently had to be counseled to walk away before his temper got the best of him.

"I guess we can figure the grocery thing out later. Right now I need a cup of coffee." Daniel pulled open the top of the machine to insert a filter and realized he had no clue how to measure the grounds. Thankfully, the intercom buzzer rang, and he handed the scoop to Trevor.

When he heard the front desk announce Christine Monroe's presence in the lobby, all the energy in his body drained out of him. Was there no escaping this woman? He leaned his head against the wall and reluctantly told the guard to send her up. When she arrived he opened the door and was met with the usual cool greeting that she bestowed upon him. There was no hug, just a slight nod as she entered.

"I came to see how Amelia was doing."

Slowly, she removed her camel leather gloves and hat and handed them to him. Then she unbuttoned her matching cashmere coat and waited for him to remove it. Daniel threw her ensemble on a nearby chair.

"Certainly you have a closet for that?" she said.

"Yeah, but I'm sure you won't be here that long. Amelia is in her room."

Daniel returned to the kitchen, accepting a cup of coffee from Trevor before sitting at the kitchen table to read his newspaper. Much to his disappointment, Christine followed, sitting across from him. Trevor started to leave.

"Hold on a minute," Daniel said. "Bring that bowl back. Amelia needs to eat down here."

"Go ahead Trevor," Christine said. "Daniel and I need a few moments alone."

Daniel laid down his newspaper, locking eyes with her. "Stay right there Trevor."

"We need to talk," she said.

"Not without our lawyers present."

Trevor darted out of the kitchen, cereal bowl in hand.

Christine leaned into him. "She's my granddaughter and I have every right to be concerned about her."

"Why are you questioning my ability to take care of Amelia? When have I ever given you any reason to doubt my love for her?"

"You haven't. Will you please lower your voice?"

Daniel slammed his hand on the table and stood. "I will not. You started this, remember? What the hell is wrong with you? Kate gave me custody of Amelia. It's in her will. She wants her to be with me."

"I know that, which is why I want to talk to you."

"And why would you want to take her away from the only father that she has known? Why are you so hell bent on tearing us apart?"

"Daniel, will you please shut up."

Daniel was silent. Not only was he stunned by her loud, piercing tone, he was shocked to find her grasping both his arms. Christine was equally surprised and quickly released him.

"I came here to tell you that I have no intention of filing a custody suit."

He leaned back and let her words sink in. "OK... what brought this on?"

Christine cleared her throat. "I came to the realization that a battle within the family would only serve to hurt Amelia, and despite what you may think about me, I'm not completely heartless. Besides, the only reason I considered fighting for custody is because I don't want to lose access to her."

"What would make you think that? I have no intention of keeping her from anyone. As far as I'm concerned, you, me, Phillip, we're her family. Nothing has changed there."

"Everything has changed I'm afraid."

Christine rarely displayed any outward emotion, so when she began to cry, Daniel could not help but reach over and take her hand. "I'm so sorry."

"So am I," she said. "Would you mind bringing me a tissue? I saw a box in the hallway."

When he returned she had poured herself a cup of coffee and was seated at the table. He placed the tissues in front of her and she plucked one from the box.

"I spoke with Phillip this morning. Charles is out of danger. They were able to repair the internal injuries, though he's still unconscious."

"How's Phillip holding up?" he said.

"He is his usual stalwart self. He's decided to assume the CEO position for now."

"Oh God, isn't there someone else who can do it?"

"Phillip is the only one who can step in right now and instantly calm the waters. The senior team runs the daily operations and I'm sure that Victor will assume more responsibility."

"Who's that?"

"Victor Naumov. He's the COO. He's very good. Daniel, until this situation with Charles is cleared up the police will be looking at everything. I know how you feel about him, so you need to be prepared. If any questions should come your way, you have to remember that Phillip has an entire organization to protect."

"So are you telling me I need to keep my trap shut?"

"I'm just saying that if the subject of Charles comes up that you refrain from commenting on it. Now, if you don't mind I'm going to go visit with Amelia, and then I'll be on my way."

"Look, since you're here, there is something I would like to discuss with you." Before he could speak the buzzer rang. Daniel shuffled into the hallway, pressing the intercom, and learned that Detective Bellows was at the front desk. Christine appeared next to him.

"Were you expecting her?" she whispered.

"No, though she did mention yesterday she might be following up on a few things. But, I thought she would call first."

"Obviously not, you should answer." She pointed to the intercom. "I'll keep Amelia in her room. We can't afford another outburst like yesterday."

Christine rushed up the stairs and for once he was grateful for her presence.

When Daniel opened the door to find Zach Walker standing next to Detective Bellows, he knew the aging rocker's presence could not be a good sign. Bleary eyed, Walker shuffled into the hallway, followed by Bellows with her black briefcase in tow. Bellows thanked Daniel for allowing them into his apartment and explained that she had some questions regarding Walker's visit with Katharine and if it would be all right for them to take a look at the office.

"Go ahead, he said. "I guess you already know where it is."

Bellows started up the stairs as Walker lingered in the hallway, noticeably swaying.

"Do you have any coffee man? I could really use some right now." Zach nodded his head towards the kitchen. "Hey Detective Sheila, do you mind?"

Bellows told him to meet her in the office and continued up the stairs while Walker sauntered into the kitchen. Daniel followed, baffled by his nonchalant demeanor.

"What the hell is going on?" Daniel said.

"I told you man. I really need some coffee. Where are the cups?"

Daniel pulled a mug from the cabinet, smacking it on the counter. "That's not what I meant. Have you been arrested?"

"What? No man, why would you think that?" Walker said.

"Why? Because that detective up there thinks that Kate's death was a homicide and you just spent the last twenty-four hours at the police station."

"Yeah, I spent the day with that tight-ass bitch, thanks to you, but she didn't arrest me. Thankfully, your security guard at the front desk remembered Kate and me in the lobby Friday night. I totally forgot she walked me down to say goodbye."

"Sorry about that, but I had no choice," Daniel said.

"Right, thank God Angie was with me or I would have had to find a lawyer."

"Is that the woman I met yesterday at the funeral? She's your lawyer?"

"Yep, and now she's back home dealing with her own mess." Zach lowered his voice. "I shouldn't tell you this man, but Monica Bellaso is her client and that's Angie's house she was staying at before she went missing. When Detective Sheila found out, I thought she was going to arrest us both. But Angie took a lie detector test and then a cop went with her to California."

"You're kidding me. I wonder if Kate knew that your girlfriend was Monica's lawyer."

"I don't know man, but Monica's the one who hooked me up with Angie. A few months ago I ran into Monica at a party and I told her about my legal problems and she asked Angie to help me. Angie came over to my place a few days later for a meeting, and boom, the sparks flew. A week later I moved into her house and then on to the rehab center. Anyway, Angie is really freaking out right now and I hope Detective Sheila lets me go today so I can be with her."

"Why does Angie have property in River Mist?"

"It belonged to her folks. She got it when they died. I think she rents it out mostly. I should get going. Thanks for the coffee man."

Daniel walked with him as they ascended the stairs.

"So is the little lady here?" Zach said.

"Amelia? Yeah, she's in her bedroom. Her grandmother is making sure she stays put until Bellows is gone."

"I saw her at the funeral. She looks just like Kate. God, it must really suck for her right now. You too man."

"Zach, not that I think this is the right time, but you know the door is always open."

"I can't man. I'm barely hanging on myself, and if it wasn't for Angie, I probably would be dead. Believe me the munchkin is better off without me."

When they arrived at the office door Daniel found Detective Bellows talking with Trevor. She turned to them, her eyes narrowing.

"I'm glad you joined us Mr. Archer. I have some questions for you as well."

Daniel sighed and followed Zach into the office, closing the door.

Amelia confronted Christine the moment she entered the bedroom. "That police woman is here."

"I know," Christine said.

"Is Daddy in trouble?"

"No Amelia, she's just doing her job, which is why you need to stay away from her. We can't have another incident like yesterday. Do you understand me?"

"Do I have to move in with you?"

"Really Amelia, I know you were listening in. You may not be able to penetrate my thoughts, but I know you heard your father's."

"Sorry. He's very loud sometimes."

Christine smiled. "Yes, I know, but you're going to have to try harder. So, if you already know that I'm not going to make you live with me, why are you still so cross?"

Amelia went over to her bed and flopped down. "Do you know who Eleanor is?"

"No dear, who is she?"

"Daddy was talking to her on the phone yesterday. He likes her very much."

"She could be a friend."

"Daddy doesn't have any friends."

"Yes, that's true."

"He likes Eleanor the same way he likes Mommy."

Just then Amelia's attention shifted towards the office next door and she jumped off the bed. Christine grabbed her arm, pulling her back.

"But it's him. He's here!" Amelia said.

"I don't care, that detective is also next door."

"But he's leaving, Nana."

Amelia slipped from her grasp and bolted for the door. Christine tried to stop her, but her granddaughter proved to be the quicker of the two. By the time she made it to the hallway Amelia had planted herself outside the office and was there to greet an unsuspecting Walker. Surprisingly, he smiled and held out his hand.

"Well hey there little lady, how you doin'?"

Christine grasped her granddaughter by the shoulders, silently begging her to behave. Amelia politely introduced herself and Walker reciprocated.

"If you'll excuse us, we were just heading to the kitchen." Christine took Amelia's hand and quickly led her down the steps. She was thankful for her granddaughter's sudden obedience but was wise enough to know it would not last. They arrived at the bottom landing where she quickly pushed Amelia into the kitchen. There was a brief conversation in the hallway. Then she heard the front door open and Bellows and Walker were gone.

Christine watched Amelia rush to the window that overlooked the front entrance to the building. She felt sympathy for her granddaughter, but at the same time she was relieved that Walker had left without incident. Despite Katharine and Daniel's attempts to include him in Amelia's life, Walker had never shown any interest, other than signing her birth certificate and offering financial assistance. So Christine was surprised when she heard the front door open and felt his presence in the apartment again. Amelia sensed him as well, and by the time Walker entered the kitchen with Daniel, Amelia was there to greet him.

Daniel knelt down in front of Amelia. "Honey, there's something that Zach and I would like to discuss with you."

Daniel escorted Amelia into the living room, and for the next ten minutes Christine listened in on their conversation. When she had heard enough, she retrieved her coat and left without saying goodbye. Trevor took notice of her departure and followed after her, asking if he could help. She thanked him for his offer and told him that she needed to be alone. Trevor waited at the curb while her driver opened her door. She decided then, that despite his loyalty to Daniel, he was a good boy who also cared deeply for Amelia.

It was not until the car had pulled away that Christine let the tears flow from her eyes. Katharine was gone, and there was nothing that she could do to bring her back. All she had left of her daughter was Amelia, and despite Daniel's promise that she would never lose access to her granddaughter, the wheels were already in motion to separate them. Walker was the first step in that process, and another more mysterious threat was looming on the horizon.

Eleanor Bouchard.

Chapter Eleven

Is there no pity sitting in the clouds
That sees into the bottom of my grief?

Eleanor sat at the kitchen island staring at the text message she had just received from Daniel. He apologized for abruptly ending their call yesterday and promised he would contact her soon. She tossed the phone aside, rubbing her eyes.

What am I doing?

Nina placed a plate of over-easy eggs and bacon in front of Eleanor. She sighed. It was the perfect hangover breakfast.

"More coffee?" Nina said.

"Please."

"So what's this stuff at the end of his message?"

"You mean the *X O?*" Eleanor caught Nina's perplexed expression and realized her friend was serious. She explained the meaning and Nina shrugged her shoulders.

"So, why is he bothering you all of a sudden?"

"I asked Alex to give him a message from me and now he's responding."

"You know what they say about him. He's not a nice person."

"Don't believe all that celebrity gossip. He's a good guy. He just has a bit of a temper and occasionally he gets into a scuffle with a photographer that gets too close to him."

"What about Fiorelli and him at The Academy Awards? I read they got into a fight."

"It wasn't a fight, and I wouldn't bring that up around Kyle. He's a little sensitive about that subject."

"What subject is that?" Kyle breezed into the kitchen. "What are we talking about?"

"Your blow-up with Daniel Archer last year," Nina said.

"Yes, that was just a bit of a misunderstanding, and I'm sure whatever you read about it was greatly exaggerated."

"So Archer didn't throw a glass of Champagne in your face?"

Kyle locked eyes with Nina. "Yes, he did. But then he walked away, and that was it."

Kyle and Nina were silent as they stared intently at each other. Then Nina jumped off her seat, assembled a plate of food and placed it in front of him. She left, and they heard the lower level door open and close.

"What in God's name is down there?" Kyle said.

"Describing it wouldn't do it justice. You have to see it to believe it."

"I doubt very much that will ever happen, and I'm not sure I would want it to either."

"Really Kyle, she's perfectly harmless."

"The woman keeps weapons in her closet. I wouldn't call that harmless."

"You know very well those are theatrical weapons, and that Nina has been kind enough to allow the university to use them free of charge. I admit she can be insensitive, and I'm sorry that she probed you about Daniel. But you have to know that she doesn't mean anything by it."

Kyle drank his coffee, staring out onto the deck. She studied his sullen expression, trying to recall exactly when it was that Nina had morphed into an incredibly anti-social being.

Eleanor thought back to their early years, when her father's niece from his first marriage came to live with them. Nina was a quiet, reserved girl, but she certainly allowed people to touch her. In fact, Nina craved physical interaction, soliciting hugs and kisses whenever possible, as if she had been starved of it her entire childhood. Her college years were not much different. Nina and Eleanor's younger sister, Josephine, lived together while they attended school in Boston, and Eleanor recalled all sorts of sisterly affection among them.

It was not until later, when Nina moved to San Francisco to attend graduate school that she started to change. It was subtle at first, so subtle Eleanor did not notice that Nina had stopped kissing her on the cheek when they would greet each other. Then their hugs became less and less frequent until they ceased entirely. Next to go was the shaking of hands and not long after that the white gloves appeared. By the time Nina had accepted her position at Alexandria University, she no longer had any physical contact with people or animals.

When Eleanor asked Nina why she did not want to be touched, Nina just shrugged her shoulders and said that was not her way anymore.

Eleanor's attention returned to Kyle, who was now staring at his plate of food. "What is up with you my friend? You seem depressed."

"I'm just a little tired, that's all."

"Is that because I toss and turn in bed?"

"Ah yes…about that," Kyle said.

"No need to explain. Nina already told me she asked you to stay with me, but it only serves to validate the point I was making last night. Even you two are worried enough that you're afraid to let me sleep alone."

"I am concerned, but not because I think you're crazy. On the contrary, I believe something extraordinary happened to you last night and that you should explore it before you run off and have yourself committed. Adams will be here shortly. Let's see what he thinks. He seems to be as much a part of this as you."

At 10:00 Jared arrived, looking like he had not slept. Nina surfaced from her lower level grotto and the group travelled upstairs to the guest bedroom where they discussed in detail the events of the previous evening. An hour later, they returned to the kitchen for more coffee and continued their conversation while Jared leaned in the open doorway, smoking.

"We need to discuss what's going to happen next," Jared said.

"What else is there to do?" Eleanor said. "I agreed to not call Dr. Stevens."

"That's not what I mean. You saw her face, and so did I. We both know the woman in the vision is Monica Bellaso."

"All right, so it's her. I'm not sure what I'm supposed to do about it."

"I think she is trying to tell us where she is. I want you to come out to Birch Mountain tomorrow and help me find her."

Eleanor was speechless. What she considered a terrifying hallucination was suddenly having real life implications. Nina shot up from her seat and marched towards Jared, shocking everyone with her impassioned tone.

"No way Adams, you saw how she was last night. She had no control over her actions."

"I know, but if anything happens to her, I'll be there. Fiorelli can come along too."

"She stabbed you, remember?" Nina said. "You weren't much help after that."

"True, but Fiorelli kept her from jumping off the balcony."

Nina spun around, facing Eleanor. "I think this is a lousy idea."

"I agree with you. But, at the same time I have to think that if I do this the visions will stop, and all this madness will end."

"Visions?" Nina said. "Are you saying you've had more than one?"

"I'm afraid so. Jared, I'll do it, but can Nina come with us?"

"Sorry, but I can't do that. I'm going to have a tough enough time explaining your presence to Eric Garrison, let alone one of your friends. Look, I don't care who comes with you, but I have to limit it to one person. You choose."

Nina turned to Jared, her fist clenched. "Fiorelli can go, but I'm warning you Detective Adams. If anything happens to Eleanor, I'll come after you with more than just a stage knife."

Chapter Twelve

I have a faint cold fear thrills through my veins
That almost freezes up the heat of life.

Kyle completed the curve around Turner's Pass and the barely visible forms of Jared and Eric Garrison came into view. They parked behind Jared's Toyota and Eleanor peered up into the southern woods. The tall spindly trees appeared as shadowy figures in the gray mist.

"This weather is impossible," Kyle said. "You can't even see the road. Maybe we should wait until the fog lifts."

"O, here will I set up my everlasting rest and shake the yoke of inauspicious stars from this world-wearied flesh," Eleanor said.

"That sounds rather morbid."

"Sorry, I've been reading *Romeo and Juliet* in preparation for the festival."

"I wish I had your memory for quotes. It certainly comes in handy at a time like this."

"I'm sure if you were writing music for this moment you would find a way to capture this eeriness. Perhaps something haunting, like the score from your last movie."

"You liked that, did you?"

"Yes, I listen to it all the time."

"Well, as fate would have it, I'm scoring one of Archer's movies."

"Interesting, I didn't think you did action films."

"I heard this one is very different. So, I wasn't in the mood to ask you this yesterday, but why were you talking about Archer? Have you been in contact with him?"

"Yes. His wife just died and I wanted him to know I was thinking of him."

"I see, just like he did for you when Jeremy died."

"Kyle, I don't want to do this. I know how you feel about him."

"It's not a matter of how I feel. It's how he treated you. I was there to pick up the pieces after he cast you aside."

"That was a long time ago, and it doesn't matter anymore."

A rap on the passenger side window made her jump and Jared opened the car door. "We need to get going. Garrison is about to bust a vein. So are we good with our story?"

"Yes, let's get this over with," Eleanor groaned.

Jared led them to Eric who was standing with his arms folded, next to an area cordoned off with yellow tape. She could already tell by his sour expression he was not pleased to see her.

"So cuz, Adams tells me that you might have seen Bellaso's SUV last weekend."

"Yes. I knew when I was here on Saturday, that I had seen the car somewhere before. It didn't dawn on me until a few days ago that I had driven by it on Friday afternoon."

"And you think you might have seen the Bellaso woman too?"

"Well, I thought I might have seen her running west on Route Six. I'm not sure."

"That's why she's here Eric," Jared said. "We're just trying to see if we can jog her memory. Why don't we get started?"

Eric proceeded to brief Eleanor. He began with the abandoned vehicle and how it had been found with the driver's side door open and the keys still in the ignition. There were no personal belongings other than the registration and driver's manual in the glove compartment. Eleanor walked around the perimeter of the area where the white SUV had sat, unsure as to what she was supposed to be experiencing. Eric went on to explain that footprints had been discovered, leading from the SUV up through the southern woods and trailing off at Wilkins road, about a quarter mile up Birch Mountain. A red silk scarf had been found on the south side of the road and Eric believed Monica might have eventually moved west."

Eleanor retraced the path that Eric had described, taking several steps up the hillside before she stopped. Immediately she sensed something was not right with his report. She turned around, walking down the hill past the yellow tape, and stood looking east. "Monica was never here."

"But her car was here and there are footprints leading up the hillside," Eric said.

"Someone else was driving her car."

"How do you know that?" Eric snapped.

Jared placed a hand on Eric's shoulder. "Let's just take it easy for a moment. Eleanor, tell me everything that you can see."

She took a deep breath and closed her eyes. "Monica came from a house...somewhere near by... from the east."

"That's probably the property where we found her purse and bags," Jared said.

"I see it. It has dark green siding, and there is a large deck in front with a gravel drive."

Garrison stormed towards them and Jared silenced him before asking Eleanor to continue.

"She's running from the house onto the front deck, someone is chasing her, and...and she has a knife in her hand. It's a big one, like a chef's knife. Now, she's jumping over the railing onto the ground. It's snowing. She's running ...wait...she dropped her cell phone, but she can't go back. Now she's running into the woods. It's slippery and she keeps losing her footing."

Eric emitted some explicative and threw up his hands, walking away. Eleanor continued.

"The sun is high overhead. Monica's approaching the road, and now she's on Route Six." Eleanor opened her eyes and pointed east. "She came out somewhere along there and..."

"What happened?" Jared said.

"She crossed the road."

Eleanor and Jared darted across Route 6 and walked up the hill to the exact spot where they had stood the previous Saturday.

"This was it," Eleanor said. "This is where she stood when she saw them driving her car. They were travelling east when they pulled over."

"You keep saying they. Who was in her car?"

"There are two men, but I can't make out their faces. Jared, given what's transpired between you and me over the past week, I imagine you can see this with me." Eleanor held out her hand.

Jared peered across the road at Eric and Kyle and then turned to Eleanor. "What the hell. If we actually find Bellaso today Garrison is going to totally freak. Look, before I do this, do you have any sharp objects on you that I need to be aware of?"

"Just put your cigarette out and let's get this over with."

Jared flicked his butt into the snow. "We really need to stop meeting like this."

After he joined hands with Eleanor, Jared was jettisoned into the vision. He saw the two men leave Monica's SUV and cross Route 6. Then the vision ended, and he found himself on his knees, watching Eleanor sprint up the hill. She was already entering the woods by the time he was able to stand. Eric Garrison jumped in his cruiser while Kyle sprinted across the road after her. His cell phone rang as he started up the hill.

"Where is she?" Eric shouted.

"She just disappeared into the northern woods."

"What the hell Adams, there's nothing up there but a ridge and a dry riverbed. In half a mile she'll hit a two hundred foot drop."

"Fiorelli just entered the woods and I'm not far behind."

"I'm coming up on Gambier Road," Eric said. "I can take that till I hit the ridge and see if I can stop her on foot. Where the hell is she going anyway?"

Jared ended the call without answering Eric's question. He did not know exactly where Eleanor was heading, but he had a hunch that the search for Monica Bellaso would be over soon.

Eleanor could see Monica watching the two men leave her car and head towards her. Monica took off up the hillside, running along the perimeter of trees before heading into the woods. She could hear one of the men yelling for her in the distance, and she picked up speed, sprinting uphill until she reached the top of the ridge. Suddenly, she stopped. One of the men was now just a few feet away.

"Monica, why are you doing this?"

"Why are you here?" she yelled.

"Katharine asked me to help you. She said you were in trouble."

"You're lying. She didn't know I would be here."

"Yes she did. She told me where to find you."

A second, considerably larger man appeared and Monica slowly turned around to face him. Eleanor saw that Monica was wearing a chain with a key around her neck.

"Come on you monster. You know I've been waiting for this day. Soon you will pay for your sins. All of you will pay for your sins." She took a step towards the large, blond man and produced a knife from underneath her jacket. Defiant, Monica dared him to make a move.

The other man came into view, approaching Monica. "I'm begging you. Don't do this."

"You don't get it, do you?" she said. "This was meant to be."

"What was meant to be?"

"All of this…me, him, and you. This was meant to happen, Charles. Soon The Passer will come, and our world will be changed forever."

"What are you talking about?"

Charles moved closer and Monica pointed her knife towards him. "I'm warning you. I'll take you with me if I have to."

Then the blond giant made a run for Monica. Charles yelled, leaping towards her, trying to pull her away from the edge of the ridge. She stabbed Charles, and he fell to his knees. Then the giant grabbed hold of Monica and she latched onto his shirt. For a moment it appeared that both of them would go over the side, but the giant was able to loosen Monica's grip on his shirt, pushing her away. He stumbled backwards as Monica sailed out into the mist. Eleanor ran after her and watched as Monica floated, weightless, her arms flowing out from her sides. Then Eleanor felt a tremendous force pulling on her, lifting her off her feet and sending her soaring downward.

When she opened her eyes she was on her back with Eric Garrison on top of her. "What the hell Eleanor, you almost fell off that cliff."

Kyle approached, and Eric yelled for him to stay with her while he returned to the top of the ridge. Jared appeared next, out of breath.

"Damn Eleanor, I didn't know you could run that fast. I saw Eric tackle you. Are you hurt?"

"No, I don't think so," she said.

"Let's get you up then."

She took Jared's hand and something that felt like an electrical shock blasted through her limbs. Everything went dark and the entire vision flashed through her mind in a high-speed fury of images and sound. In an instant she relived every moment of Monica's ordeal and when she emerged she found Jared lying on his side, red-faced and clenching his chest. Kyle rolled him on his back and was about to administer CPR when Jared held up his hand, signally that he was fine.

The sound of gunshot fire sent their heads turning towards the ridge. Garrison announced that he had found something, and the trio scrambled to their feet, rushing to join him. A thick layer of mist had settled over the riverbed and it took a few moments before Eric located a body lying at the bottom. Two large, dark objects were moving around it.

"Damn bears," Eric grumbled. "Cover your ears." He fired two rounds, and the animals took off running towards the east. "I'm going to call this in."

Eric left. Eleanor and Jared stood silent for several moments, staring into the mist.

"I saw what happened to her Eleanor. I saw all of it," Jared whispered.

"I'd really like to hug you right now, but I'm afraid to touch you."

Jared laughed and held out his hand. She took a deep breath, slowly wrapping her fingers around his. When there was no reaction they shared in a mutual sigh of relief. He put his arm around her.

"Thank God you didn't get hurt," Jared said. "I should probably go talk to Garrison. I can't imagine what's going through his mind right now."

"What did Monica mean by *The Passer will come?*"

"I don't know."

"That man, Charles, tried to save her and she wouldn't let him."

"It sounded like Monica didn't trust him either. Listen to me. We don't know anything yet, not till you and I sit down and talk through it. However, that isn't going to happen right now because I have damage control to tend to, so here's what we are going to do." Jared lit a cigarette. "You will not talk to anyone, or answer any questions unless they come from me or Garrison. Also, we need to keep what you and I just saw between us. We witnessed a murder and we don't need to be dragging Fiorelli or Nina or anyone else into it. Do you understand me?"

"Yes, but what happens if they ask?" she said.

"Then you tell them I told you to not talk about it. If Fiorelli has a problem with that then he can come to me. Speaking of which, you should go check on him. He doesn't look so good. And tell him to keep his mouth shut. I'll go deal with Garrison. Wish me luck."

It took two hours before the emergency equipment and technicians arrived. The teams split up. One secured the riverbed while the other scoured the hillside. Amazingly, the body had been untouched by the bears. After the photographs were taken and the evidence collected, the body was placed in an ambulance bound for the coroner's office in Edmond. Then Eric Garrison officially ended the search for Monica Bellaso.

As the sun set on Birch Mountain, Jared no longer required Eleanor's presence and pulled her aside. "I'm going to have one of the deputies take Fiorelli and you back to his car. I'm probably going to be here for a while, so I need to know if you're good with our story?"

"Yes. I came here to show you what I saw. Then we went into the woods while Eric drove down to the nearest side road and searched from the west. Eric found the body."

"Good. That's all we'll say for now and tomorrow we'll figure out how to handle the rest." They hugged before he handed her off to the deputy.

Kyle was silent during the ride to her house. She was the first to speak when they reached her front door.

"Would you like to come in for a glass of wine?" Eleanor said

"No. If I start drinking I'll never make it to the coast. I wish you would come back and stay at Nina's."

"I'd rather be here tonight. But I promise I'll stay in Edmond tomorrow and we'll have dinner. You should go before it gets dark." She kissed him on the cheek and started for the door.

"Eleanor, wait." He slipped his arms around her waist. "I hope you know how happy I am that I'm here with you. I'm looking forward to our time together."

"So am I. Now go on. I'm fine."

"I know you are, but before I take off I just want to make sure that you and I are fine."

Kyle was silent as he looked intently at her and for the first time since she had known him, he seemed to struggle with his words. Suddenly she realized why he was so tongue tied. "If this is about the reason why I asked you to come to Edmond, then please stop worrying. I know that is not what we're about."

For a moment she thought she registered disappointment in his eyes, but then a faint smile crossed his lips and he nodded.

"All right then, enough said. I will be on my way. Please, get some rest and call me if you need anything. Oh, and could you make sure you contact Nina and tell her you're all right. I prefer not to have to face her wrath when I return."

✖✖

Kyle had only driven a few miles when his cell phone sounded. After several rings he eventually pulled over and took the call. He flinched slightly when he heard the heavily-accented voice on the other end.

"Has it begun?"

"Yes," Kyle said. "She has awakened."

It took a few moments before the caller responded. "Then this is a joyous time for us all. Good work, son."

The call ended and Kyle continued driving towards the coast. Ahead the sun was low in the horizon, casting a red hue on the surrounding foothills. Soon it would be dark. He pressed his foot to the gas pedal, increasing his speed.

He was not feeling joyous at all.

✖✖

Before Eleanor phoned Nina, she poured herself an ample glass of red wine and drew a hot bath. Then, for the next hour she soaked in the tub, relaying as much as she could about how they found Monica's body and assuring her best friend that she was unharmed.

It was 8:00 before she thought about food and by then she was too exhausted to cook. She scrounged up some grapes, olives, and cheese from the refrigerator and stood at her kitchen island eating until her stomach stopped growling. There was no reason to get on the scale tonight. She knew by the fit of her jeans that she had lost weight.

An hour later she sat in bed reading *Romeo and Juliet*. In a few weeks she would begin rehearsals. She looked forward to getting back to her old routine, once again enjoying the passions that had eluded her the past year. She wished she could leap ahead to late April when hopefully all the drama of the past week would be far behind her. But at this moment she could not shake the vision of Monica from her thoughts.

She tossed her script aside and picked up her phone as she left the bed. On the way to her office she contemplated another glass of wine but decided against it. Travelling up the stairs to the loft, she sat at her desk and brought up Google Search on her laptop. Entering the words *The Passer* she was presented with 110 million results, of which the first several pages were about football and a movie called *The Passerby*. She frowned. Obviously it was going to take some digging to uncover the meaning of Monica's warning.

As she began to amend her search her cell phone lit-up. Given the late hour she was surprised by the caller ID. Her first inclination was to let it go to voicemail, but she knew if she did not answer he would just keep calling.

"Hello Daniel."

"Oh, you sound mad," he said.

"No, I'm not. I'm just tired and I was about to fall asleep. You're up late."

"Yeah I know. There's a lot of craziness going on here right now. The police are starting to question the entire family. It's turning into a real mess."

"Mess… what do you mean?"

"Don't you keep up with the news? Kate's accident has been ruled a homicide. They think someone broke into the apartment and attacked her."

"When did this happen?"

"Someone let it leak out earlier today and the police were forced to make a statement. Then the Monroes and I had to make a statement, and it has been sheer hell since. You should see the number of news vans that are parked outside my place. Amelia and I haven't been able to leave all day, and now with Monica's announcement it's really going nuts."

"You mean Monica Bellaso? How does that affect you?"

"What the hell Ellie, do you live in a bubble out there? It's all over the news that they found Monica and that she and Kate were friends. Not to mention the mess with Lourdes."

"Charles Lourdes was the man that was found on Friday. He was with Monica."

"Well at least you're up to speed on that."

"Daniel, what's that noise I'm hearing? Are you biting your nails?"

"Yes, dammit…I can't help it. I'm about to explode."

Eleanor sighed. "Look, I'm sorry. I've been away from any sort of TV and internet all day. Would you like to talk?"

He moaned, and then she heard a clinking noise followed by the sound of liquid pouring.

"Bourbon?" she said.

"Yes."

"Are you drunk?"

"No, but I'm sure as hell working on it. Listen, I didn't call you to discuss my drinking habits. I need to talk to you about something very important."

Eleanor took a deep breath. Now she wished she had a drink.

"First off," he said. "I'm sorry about hanging up the other day. My daughter came into the room and I had to talk with her. Right after that the cops showed up and I couldn't get back to you."

"No problem. I understand."

"All right, second thing, and I don't want you to answer right away. I just want you to think about it first before you say anything. And keep an open mind. Can you do that?"

"I'm listening."

"OK, here it goes. Alex and I had a talk the other day. I'll spare you all the boring details, but long story short, he offered me a job with the festival. And if you're OK with it, then I'm coming to Edmond this summer. So what do you think?"

He paused to take a drink.

"Ellie, are you still there?"

Entr'acte

∞

Before he opened his eyes, he had sensed the two powerful beings looming nearby. He gripped the side railing. If necessary he could use it as a weapon.

"That won't be necessary. We come in peace."

Two men in black emerged from the shadows and stood at the foot of his hospital bed. "I am William Toulouse and this is my brother Claude. Perhaps you have heard of us?"

He did not speak. He had no idea who they were and he did not care.

"Sir, we share in your suffering and like you we seek answers. We wish to help you."

His hand tightened around the bed railing, dislodging one side. The two men immediately sensed his warning.

"As you wish, but we know you search for the meaning of The Passer. Soon you will need our help."

The elderly man laid a business card on the bed and the brothers vanished from his room. He relaxed his grip, resting his head against the pillow. Although he had regained much of his strength, he still tired easily, leaving him vulnerable to the forces around him. He needed time to heal, and to mourn, but mostly he needed time to think.

Lourdes picked up the thick white card, holding it close to his face. His vision was still blurred, but he was able to make out the raised symbol on the front. After a few moments, he realized where he had seen it before.

Katharine. What have you done?

ACT II

Transformation

Chapter Thirteen

O cursèd spite,
That ever I was born to set it right!

Detective Sheila Bellows stood in front of a large white board, scanning the evidence that had been collected to date in the Katharine Monroe murder case.

Dead ends everywhere.

Four weeks into the investigation and they were still without a solid suspect or a motive. The leads were minimal and the pressure to solve the high profile case was mounting. Detective Chen appeared with two coffee cups and a large manila envelope.

"Good news," Chen said. "We finally got the last two years of billing statements from Fenton Electronics and it looks like our electrician had a few odd jobs that were loosely documented."

Chen secured four invoices on the board. Bellows leaned forward, examining the barely legible handwriting.

"There's no name, only an address on Fifty-Seventh Street. How did they know who to bill?"

"They didn't," Chen said. "Take a look at what's written at the bottom."

"They paid in cash?"

"Correct. First invoice was two years ago in March, and the final one June of last year. We checked Fenton's bank statements and the cash deposits into his checking account started around the time of the first job."

"So, Fenton was working with someone as far back as two years ago."

Bellows leaned against her desk, staring at the picture of Gus Fenton, the now deceased electrician who responded to the power outage problem the night of Katharine Monroe's attack. For the two weeks leading up to the murder, he supervised a substantial re-wiring of Monroe's building and was on call the night the electricity faltered. He arrived an hour after the outage was reported, around 7:00. It took him approximately an hour to make the necessary repairs and by 8:00 the electricity was fully restored. Thirty minutes later Katharine Monroe was discovered when a security guard made a sweep of the building and found her apartment door open.

The next morning, Bellows and Chen visited Fenton Electronics and discovered that Gus had been the victim of a hit and run accident. When they caught up with the detective who was handling the case, they learned that after Fenton left Katharine Monroe's building he returned to Queens, stopping at a bar he frequented. The police report stated that around 11:00 the bartender saw Fenton go outside for a smoke, where he struck up a conversation with an unidentified man. Afterwards, he came back into the bar and drank until midnight, at which point he paid his tab and left. Seconds later the bartender heard a loud thud and rushed outside to find Fenton lying in the middle of the street. He was pronounced dead on arrival at the hospital.

As they dug into Gus Fenton's past, they learned that he was the nephew of the owner, Albert Fenton, and had been employed with the company for 10 years. He had never missed a day of work and in his uncle's opinion, was the best electrician on the payroll. He was single, lived in a small apartment in Queens, and was described by his neighbors as a quiet man that kept to himself. He was also a heavy gambler and had racked up a lot of debt. Whoever paid Fenton to ensure the electricity would be out in Monroe's building knew this about him.

"Morgan is checking on the Fifty-Seventh Street address this morning," Chen said.

"Any updates from surveillance on Archer's building?"

"Nothing unusual to report. You know, he leaves for California in a few weeks."

"I can't believe he's leaving town and of all places he's ending up where Monica Bellaso was murdered. How is that possible?"

"The Alexandria Shakespeare Festival is a big deal. Did you see the New York Times article last year?"

"Can't say that I did, but he's not going there because of the festival. He's going there to hide."

"Can you blame him? The media is pretty much stalking him and his daughter daily."

"I get that, but it still looks bad. He's lucky he isn't a person of interest or he wouldn't be going anywhere. All right, let's move on. What about our friends on the eighth floor?"

Bellows eyes wandered over the various names on the board before landing on Anna and Daphne Lutsenko, the occupants of the top floor apartment in Archer's building.

Once the immediate family, including Archer's assistant, Trevor Kincaid, were ruled out as suspects, Bellows and her team took a closer look at Katharine Monroe's neighbors. As there were only 15 tenants in the building, it did not take long to work through the interviews and background checks. That effort turned up no significant leads; however, the Lutsenkos had proven to be a challenge.

Bellows tapped her fingers against the desk.

"Ivan Milin."

Ivan Milin was Anna Lutsenko's estranged son from her first marriage and the owner of record for the apartment. The property was purchased two years ago through a trust set up in Milin's name, and was managed by a local law firm who saw to Anna and her daughter Daphne's needs. Daphne Lutsenko claimed she had never met her half-brother, and as far as she knew, her mother had not seen her son in over 30 years. All of their travel arrangements to the states had been handled through lawyers acting on Milin's behalf. A search for Ivan Milin had not produced any results that could be tied back to Anna Lutsenko.

Next was the mother, Anna Lutsenko, who spoke very little English and had been diagnosed with advanced dementia. Her socialite daughter,

Daphne, had managed to restrict access to her mother, requiring interviews to be scheduled in advance, and only when Daphne could be present. Finally, after several failed attempts to meet with the two women, Bellows obtained a warrant that forced Anna and Daphne to appear at the precinct for questioning. That was when Victor Naumov interceded.

Naumov, the soft-spoken COO of Monroe Industries, had been dating Daphne Lutsenko for the past year. Distracted with his increased responsibilities at the company, he was unaware of his girlfriend's issues with the police and was shocked to learn about the warrant. Anxious to avoid any negative press, he ordered Daphne to cooperate fully with the investigation and told Bellows to call him personally if any other problems arose.

"No change to report with the Lutsenkos, "Chen said. "The same caretaker is watching the mother during the day. Victor Naumov has cut back on his overnight stays though."

"If he knew what was good for him he would dump that bimbo before she causes him real problems. She was in the building when Monroe was attacked, and I'm certain she is not telling us everything she knows about Ivan Milin."

Her eyes wandered back to the board and landed on Zach Walker. Despite the fact that the front desk security guard had witnessed Katharine Monroe escorting Walker to the front door the night of her attack, the biological father of Amelia Monroe was still a person of interest. He had spent nearly an hour with Monroe in her apartment and was possibly the last person to see her alive. But, more importantly, he was the boyfriend of Angie Miller.

Bellows sighed.

Veronica Angelina Miller had been responsible for arranging the meeting between Walker and Monroe and had also been inside the apartment for a brief period to serve as a witness for the adoption papers. She left after dispatching her duties; anxious to get to Barney's in Soho before the store closed. When Bellows asked if Ms. Miller could prove her whereabouts, Angie produced the bag with receipt, showing that the purchase for the $4000 purse was made at 7:45 that evening. The next day when they questioned the sales person who assisted Angie, she remembered her distinctly as the beautiful blond woman who purchased a *The Row* handbag.

However, Angie Miller had another more ominous connection to the case. She was the owner of the River Mist vacation home where Bellaso was staying. Miller, who had inherited the property from her parents, rarely used the home and had allowed Bellaso to rent it exclusively when she took the supermodel on as a client. According to Angie, Bellaso was fond of the area because she could stay there without being easily recognized. After interviewing Monica's agent and her business manager, Angie's claim was substantiated.

Bellows frowned. Unlike Daphne Lutsenko, Angie Miller was a nice person who gave a damn about the case. She had willingly submitted to a lie detector test, turned over every piece of information she could regarding her client, ensured that Zach Walker returned all phone calls from Chen and her, and even attempted to provide a little investigative help. Bellows smiled as she recalled the e-mail she received from Angie one day, containing the name and address of Monica's closest friend in Italy. The Italian born model, whose mother had died in childbirth and father was unknown, had no family in the U.S., and any insight into her past, even if only from a high school chum, was greatly appreciated.

Bellows liked Angie Miller, and if the circumstances had been different, she probably would have been friends with her. But Angie was still a person of interest.

She finished her coffee as her thoughts turned to Charles Lourdes. Her stomach soured. "What's the latest? Is he still due back in New York this week?"

"Yes," Chen said. "I spoke with Detective Reyes from the Alexandria County Sheriff's Office. Lourdes is on track to be released from the hospital mid-week and then he will enter a rehab facility here."

"That reminds me. I need to contact Detective Dreary this morning."

Chen laughed. "Be careful. You may accidently call him that someday."

"I can't help it. Every time I talk to him he sounds depressed, not to mention he always has bad news."

"He just has news you don't want to hear. By the way, did you look him up online yet? He's got a pretty impressive resume."

"Well, yeah, when he was in San Francisco, but now he's just wasting away in Granolaville."

"The town is called Edmond and he runs the show up there."

"Whatever," Bellows said. "He's just as clueless as we are. He has no idea who was up there on that hill with Bellaso and Lourdes, or who dumped Lourdes in that hospital parking lot."

"Well, it's not exactly his fault that Lourdes has been comatose the past four weeks."

"Like any of us buys his amnesia story. He was tortured and nearly died. You think he would want us to find the people who did that to him. He's hiding something."

"Is something wrong?" Chen said. "You seem down this morning?"

"I'm fine. Look, if you're going for more coffee can you get me a double?"

Chen left, and Bellows sank into her desk chair, staring at the board.

Dead ends everywhere.

She picked up the receiver and punched in a number. It took several rings before a raspy voice answered on the other end.

"Hey it's Bellows. What? Oh, sorry, I keep forgetting about the time difference. I can call back later if you like. Are you sure? So listen, I talked to my boss earlier, and he wants us to make an official announcement. Yeah, I know it sucks, but the pressure is on. Look, we just have to bite the bullet on this one and say what we already believe. Katharine Monroe and Monica Bellaso's murders are connected."

Chapter Fourteen

It is my lady! O, it is my love!
O, that she knew she were!

∞

Nina leaned against her Volkswagen Beetle, watching Eleanor pace the parking lot of the Edmond Airport. She could not tell if her best friend's nervousness was a result of opening night jitters or that Daniel Archer was due to arrive at any moment.

Eleanor stopped and turned to her. "Are you certain my attire looks all right?"

Nina nodded her head in affirmation, but behind her large black sunglasses she was expressing her true response. Earlier that morning she had spent two painful hours helping Eleanor select an outfit from the handful of tunic tops and black leggings she had brought from her River Mist home. Fashion completely eluded her friend, which was why Nina was determined to take Eleanor shopping to buy a dress for the opening night festivities.

Eleanor's cell phone beeped and she stopped pacing, staring intently at the screen. "The plane just landed." She took a deep breath. "I guess we should go."

Nina decided that Daniel Archer was most definitely the reason for Eleanor's anxious state, and when he breezed through the terminal doors into the airport parking lot, she knew exactly why. *Whoa.* She had seen pictures of the imposing actor online, but nothing could prepare her for the real thing. This guy was big, not only in height but in his overall physical appearance. When he threw his arms around Eleanor he towered over her, which was saying something since her friend was considered a tall woman. But what really got Nina's attention were his arms. She had never seen muscles that pronounced, and as he lifted Eleanor off her feet he absolutely dwarfed her with his imposing physique.

Eventually Eleanor introduced them and Archer glanced down at her, flashing a perfectly white smile. She noticed he did not attempt to shake her hand.

"It's nice to finally meet you," he said. "Thanks for putting us up this summer. I hope we're not too much trouble for you."

His loud bass voice caught the attention of a few onlookers that stopped and pointed.

"Where are your travelling companions?" Eleanor said.

"They're still on the plane. Amelia fell asleep and Trevor stayed back while I came to meet you. We just need to drive over to where the private planes are and pick them up."

Nina grimaced as Archer flung his mighty arm around Eleanor's shoulders and pulled her next to him. Despite Eleanor's assertions that this mammoth person was not the temperamental hothead the media portrayed him to be, Nina still had her concerns. She eyed him cautiously as his hand slid down Eleanor's back and around her waist. Eleanor did not reciprocate, keeping her arms folded in front of her.

They drove to the opposite side of the airport where a lone hanger sat and waited outside the security gate. Soon, a large covered golf cart emerged from the building, carrying a thin blond-haired girl, an equally thin brunette man and several black suitcases. As the cart drew near, the gate slid open and the young girl leapt off. Archer easily scooped her up with one arm.

"Ladies, I would like you to meet Amelia Monroe."

Silence followed as Eleanor and Amelia stared at each other with wide eyes. There was no movement for several moments and then the girl surprised everyone by lunging forward, forcing Archer to release her so she could grasp on to Eleanor's neck. The pair gazed at each other, and Nina felt a prickly sensation forming on her scalp.

Archer cleared his throat. "I guess I don't have to worry about you two getting along."

Eleanor woke from her daze. "Sorry. Amelia, it's wonderful to finally meet you. Let me introduce you to my best friend. This is Nina St. John."

Eleanor turned so that Amelia's crystal blue gaze was now fixed on her. Nina's hair felt like it was on fire. The child said hello and then saw her convertible.

"Is that yours?" Amelia said.

Nina nodded. She was not sure how the child knew it was her car, but she told the girl she could ride with her. Daniel agreed and Amelia leapt from Eleanor's arms.

"Just make sure she has her seatbelt on. She's never ridden in the front seat before," he said.

Nina turned towards her vehicle, rolling her eyes. *Never driven in the front seat…private planes…strange little girl…what have you gotten yourself into Eleanor?*

After both cars were loaded up with luggage, Trevor joined Amelia in Nina's convertible while Daniel rode with Eleanor. As they drove towards downtown Edmond, Daniel rolled down the window, taking in an enormous breath.

"God, the weather here is spectacular," he said.

"Yes, though we've had a strange year with all the rain and snow inland, and when the mist rolls in it can cover everything. But overall it is quite beautiful."

"How hot does it get?"

"Usually no more than the upper seventies, that's why during the summer everyone likes to go inland. In River Mist, it can get over a hundred degrees on some days."

"Ah yes, your dream home in the mountains, I hope I get to see it while I'm here."

"Of course you will. I plan on taking Amelia and you out there next weekend."

"That's great." He placed his hand on her leg. "It's good to finally be here."

"You look wonderful. Have you been working out?"

He roared with laughter. "I was wondering if you would say anything. Usually you don't pay attention to that sort of thing."

"That's not entirely true. But come on, look at you...you look..."

"What?" He squeezed her knee.

"You look good. Let's just leave it at that."

He winked. "You look good too. So how big is this town anyway?"

"Edmond has a population around twenty-six thousand, though it swells to about thirty-eight thousand during the school year. River Mist, where my home is located, is very small. Only about a thousand of us there, though it can get pretty busy during the tourist season."

"Oh God Ellie, you're talking to a man that lives with eight million other people. It's like no man's land up here."

"I know. That's why I love it, but it has its drawbacks, like anywhere else I guess."

"Like what, too much incredible scenery and clean air?"

"No, it's just a very small community and it's hard to keep things private around here."

"Yeah, well, try having the camera vultures following your every move or people always printing absurd lies about you."

"Speaking of which, I imagine that the media is not going to ignore you all summer just because you're hiding out here in the hinterland, as you like to call it."

"Sorry for that, but you do sort of live out in the sticks."

"Regardless, you should know that we're sold out for *A Midsummer's Night's Dream* and *Hamlet* is getting close."

"Wait till they see my acting. They might change their minds."

"I'm trying to make a point. Maybe you should reconsider having a body-guard. Even if the paparazzi don't show up, there are still going to be lots of people wanting your autograph."

"Like how many people?"

"Well, the large theater seats a thousand. So you do the math."

"You're kidding. You've got that many people around here that like Shakespeare?"

"They come from all over California, Oregon, Washington and Canada. We even have folks who come from New York. It's quite a reputable program."

"I know. I read last summer's write-up in The New York Times. I noticed they only interviewed Alex for the article."

"I was on sabbatical last summer."

"Yeah, look, I have no problem with the autograph thing, so let's just wait and see what happens, OK?"

Daniel returned his gaze out the window and they continued their ride in silence, his hand still resting on her knee.

When they arrived at Nina's townhouse it was bustling with activity. Several of Eleanor's student actors were milling around outside, setting up for the celebration that would take place after the show. Lights were strung everywhere, and one of Nina's student set designers had constructed a water fountain in the shape of the famous star-crossed lovers, which was now sitting in the front yard. Eleanor pulled in the driveway and Daniel's mouth dropped open.

"Damn. You guys take your cast parties seriously."

Trevor opened Daniel's door, and the six foot six actor emerged. Eleanor noted the sudden lull in activity, followed by several hushed voices, and then one of the female students made a run for him. Before she knew it, almost everyone in the front yard had dropped what they were doing and were surrounding Daniel, shaking his hand as they pummeled him with questions. Eleanor popped the hatch of her Subaru, and Trevor joined her, helping to remove the suitcases.

"Is it always like this?" she said.

"Yes, though, it's usually a lot less friendly crowd."

Eleanor, Trevor and Nina hauled in the luggage while Daniel remained outside with the young actors. Nina showed Amelia to her room and Eleanor took Trevor next door where she introduced him to Kyle Fiorelli. The two men seemed to hit it off as they carried Trevor's suitcases upstairs, and by the time she left they were in the kitchen enjoying a bottle of wine.

Eventually, the townhouse emptied of the student helpers and Daniel and Amelia retired to their rooms. Eleanor took advantage of the down time and went into Nina's bedroom, which was now her room for the summer, to nap. She was about to nod off when the door opened.

"You asleep?"

Before she could answer, Daniel crawled into bed next to her, lying on his side.

"God, it's so good to be here with you," he said. "I know we've been Skyping the past few weeks, but it's just not the same as seeing you in person."

"How's Amelia doing? Is she settled in?"

"She's fine. I made her take a nap. You two sure hit it off right away."

"She seems to like Nina as well."

"I can see why. Nina looks like a kid herself. What is it she does again?"

"She heads up all of production: set design, costumes, lighting, everything."

"Wow, that's a big job," he said. "And was that Armani she was wearing?"

"I have no idea. That reminds me, I want to thank you for not shaking her hand."

"Yeah, I tried to explain to Amelia about the touching thing, but I can't promise she won't forget. She's only six you know. So those white gloves were a part of her outfit?"

"I'm afraid not. Nina wears them constantly, along with the glasses."

"Does she just have some sort of condition?"

"No. It's just her way. After a while you'll get used to it."

Daniel lay on his back with his hands behind his head, sighing. She realized her nap was not going to happen and she sat up, swinging her legs off the bed.

"Hey, where are you going?" he said.

"I have a lot to do before we head over to the theater."

"Is something wrong, you seem nervous?"

"I do?" she said.

"Yeah, you do. Look, if having Amelia and me here is too much I need to know now, so I can make other arrangements."

"No, everything is fine. I'm glad you're here."

Daniel smiled. "That's a relief. I was worried you were having second thoughts. So what do you think about all this crap with Lourdes? Can you believe he took off like that?"

"What do you mean? I thought he was on a leave of absence from Monroe Industries."

"Well, that's what the papers say, but remember what I told you. He tried to resign and the board wouldn't let him. They're too worried it would hurt their damn stock price. Now he's disappeared and nobody knows where the hell he is."

"He's been through a horrific ordeal. I'm sure he's just gone somewhere to recuperate."

"The guy is a major sleazebag and his amnesia story is bullshit. I still can't believe Monica got involved with him. She was Kate's friend. You think she would have known."

"Known what?"

"Eh, it's a long story and I don't want to get in to it right now."

The door opened and Amelia entered the room, yawning. She informed them that Nina was looking for Eleanor and that it was time to go into town to run their errands. Then she giggled, and said that Nina intended to buy Eleanor a dress.

Daniel laughed. "No way, now this is something I gotta see. Come on Amelia, we're going with them."

"Oh no you don't," Eleanor said. "I don't have time for this nonsense. I have a play opening tonight."

"Ah come on Ellie, where's your sense of adventure. Besides, you don't have to be at the theater for four hours." He placed his hand on Eleanor's back, pushing her through the doorway.

※※

Eleanor finished addressing the cast and crew of *Romeo and Juliet*, and after a hearty round of applause she left with Nina, heading for their seats. She passed a mirror along the way, catching a glimpse of her new black dress. "I look entirely too dressed up. I can't believe you convinced me to wear heels."

"It's opening night. The big guy is here, plus lots of people will be taking pictures."

"Your ensemble is impressive. I didn't know they could get that many colors into one dress. And where did you find the fuchsia sandals to match?"

"I'm impressed that you even know that this color is fuchsia."

Eleanor rolled her eyes as they climbed the stairs.

"So why are we sitting in the box?" Nina asked.

Eleanor explained that Daniel had bought it so they would have a good seat for the show, but she also figured he wanted it for the privacy. Nina mused that it would be unfortunate to have to sit behind him and Eleanor heartily agreed. They arrived outside the box just as the warning lights flashed. Eleanor took a deep breath. She was not nervous or even anxious, but there was a vague feeling of uncertainty moving through her.

Nina's brow furrowed. "Stop worrying. It's a great show. The actors are good, the costumes and sets are awesome. Even that music Fiorelli wrote is all right."

"It's more than all right, his music is beautiful."

"Whatever. I noticed he wasn't hanging around the house as usual."

"I'm sure he's just trying to avoid Daniel."

"So I take it the big guy knows that Fiorelli is here all summer?"

"Yes," Eleanor said. "And he's not too happy about it either."

"Who is?"

"Nina, why won't you tell me what happened between Kyle and you? Did he say something at Jeremy's birthday party that upset you?"

"Why does he need to be here? We were doing just fine without him."

The theater lights flashed again and Daniel came bounding through the curtains. "There you are Ellie. I don't think they're going to start until they see you in your seat."

Nina glared at her before disappearing through the curtains.

"Is something wrong with her?" he asked.

"No, just a little opening night jitters."

"There's no reason to be nervous. It's going to be fine. By the way, you look beautiful. You should wear a dress more often." He whispered in her ear. "You're doing that hair thing."

She really was not nervous at all, but a feeling of anticipation was now swelling inside her. She stopped the twisting motion of her right hand, releasing the strand of hair from around her index finger. "Sorry."

"Don't be. It reminds me of the old days." He kissed her forehead. "Break a leg, kiddo."

The show went as Eleanor had hoped. The acting was solid and there were no major technical malfunctions. The curtain call came, the audience rose to their feet, and she could see two of the regional theater critics darting out before the aisles filled with people. Nina left to check on final preparations for the cast party while Eleanor led the remainder of the group backstage to congratulate the cast and crew.

Daniel stood patiently by her side the entire time, shaking hands and chatting away like he had known these people forever. He was gracious and charming- two characteristics she usually did not equate with him- and by the time she finished speaking with everyone she could tell he had won them over. As they left backstage she had to comment on his performance.

"Where did you learn to work a crowd like that?"

"Years of attending fundraisers. You just learn to smile and turn on the charm. Though tonight, I meant every word I said. The show was great Ellie. You should be very proud."

Eleanor thanked him as she pushed open the side door that led to the parking lot, walking into a sea of flashing lights. "Oh, my God!" Someone grabbed her, yanking her back inside. The door shut and it took a moment for her to realize that Daniel was griping her shoulders. "What was that? There must have been two hundred people out there and they were yelling your name."

"Is there another way out of here where we won't be seen?" he said.

Eventually one of Nina's students pulled a van into the loading dock, and using a few pieces of stage scenery, they were able to hide Daniel and Amelia from view. Eleanor and Trevor managed to steal out the back entrance, retrieving Eleanor's Subaru without notice. However, Trevor spent the entire ride watching for any cars that might have followed them.

When they arrived at the townhouse the party was well underway. Eleanor went directly to the kitchen and found Daniel at the island pouring Champagne. He handed her a glass, and she emptied the contents in one swallow.

"Is Amelia all right?" she said.

"She's fine. She's outside with some of the actors."

Eleanor walked onto the deck, peering down into the backyard. She spotted Amelia who was dancing with several members of the cast and waved until she caught her attention. Daniel appeared with two more glasses of Champagne.

"She's a very good dancer," Eleanor said.

"I know. You should hear her sing. Look, I'm really sorry about what happened tonight."

"How did anyone know you would be here? You're not even in the show."

"I don't know, but I feel bad for the cast. It should have been their big night."

"It's not your fault, obviously, but I think you need to reconsider the whole autograph thing. You could be signing for an hour or more each night. Do you really want to do that?"

"No, but if I don't sign at all that will piss people off. I guarantee you."

She returned to the kitchen in search of a bottle. "We're going to have to figure out something. Maybe we announce that you'll sign for a limited time each night, or arrange for one all-day session. What does your contract say? Can you even sign autographs while you're with us?"

"Give me a break. I signed the same contract as everyone else."

"Really, your agent allowed that?"

"Yeah, why not, it's not like I'm making any money off of this."

"Daniel, don't say that too loud. A lot of these people count on the festival for income."

"No, you don't understand. I'm doing this for nothing. I told Leesman to take my pay and put it into the program."

Daniel grabbed the Champagne bottle before it completely slipped from her hand. She sat down on a barstool, dumbfounded.

"I don't know whether to feel pleased or offended by that look on your face," he said.

"I'm really not sure what to say. I guess thank you would be in order, but right now that sounds awfully lame to me."

Daniel moved in, filling their glasses. "Look, we'll figure out this mess with the autographs and the crowds, but can we just forget all that and celebrate your success. I have a feeling this is a partying crowd and I really need to have some fun right now."

The party ended at 2:00 AM and Daniel carried a sleeping Amelia upstairs while Eleanor and Nina collected the empty cans and bottles strewn throughout the house. She was surprised when she found Trevor in the backyard smoking, while he conversed with Nina's set designer, Frank Bishop. Trevor shot up, quickly crushing his cigarette in a nearby ashtray.

"Here, let me help you." He took the bin from her and started to clear the table.

"Trevor, that's all right. You stay and enjoy yourself. I'm sure you don't have that many opportunities to relax." She attempted to take back the container and he gave her a curious look.

"When did you leave New York?" he said.

"Ten years ago, why do you ask?"

"I feel like we have met before, but I came to the city long after you left."

"Well, maybe I just remind you of someone."

"Yes, I'm sure that is it. Please, let me at least clear up the backyard for you."

She allowed him to continue and returned to the upper deck. The music switched to a familiar guitar piece and Daniel appeared, slipping his arms around her waist.

"What is this song? It's beautiful," he said.

"It's called *Cavatina*. It's from *The Deer Hunter* and it's one of my favorites." Eleanor pulled away, gathering several beer bottles from a nearby table.

"Do you remember how to waltz?"

"I suppose."

"Then dump that stuff and let's dance."

"It's late and we still have this mess to clean up."

"Screw it, we can do it later. Come on, dance with me, unless you forgot how."

Eleanor entered the kitchen, depositing the bottles on the counter top. "Are you going to be like this all summer?"

He moved in front of her, placing his right hand against the middle of her back and offering his left hand. "Like what, a demanding son-of-a-bitch who expects your full attention?"

"Yes, like that." Eleanor placed her hand in his and they took off.

"Oh, I don't know. I considered going easy on you, but I thought why bother. You already know what I'm like and you still let me come here."

"What was I thinking?"

"I don't know, but I'm so thankful you said yes."

"You know, I don't remember saying that exactly."

"But you didn't say no either."

As they flowed through the living room in a lilting circle, she recalled their beginning, before all the arguments, misunderstandings and conflicting aspirations tore them apart. She decided in that moment, as he swept her through the open doorway and onto the front porch, that she would make the effort this summer to forget their stormy past and forge more pleasant memories. She closed her eyes, losing herself in their dreamy dance, unaware that anything was wrong until Daniel broke their embrace.

"What the hell? Marco? I don't believe it."

Daniel stormed towards a black car parked across the street while Eleanor latched onto his arm. He tried to fend her off, but she persisted, knowing very well his history with this man. Tired of her interference, he grabbed her shoulders, demanding that she release him. Then a flash went off and they turned to find Marco pointing his camera at them.

Eleanor met Daniel's eyes and she swore she felt his anger shoot right through her. She released his shirt, allowing him to go after Marco. Trevor rushed past her yelling at Daniel to stop, while she stood there hoping that Marco's camera would end up in several pieces on the ground. Nina appeared alongside her, and the two women folded their arms, watching with interest as Daniel leaned into the bald, portly man.

In the distance she could see the flashing lights of an approaching deputy cruiser.

Chapter Fifteen

*And thy fair virtue's force perforce doth move me
On the first view to say, to swear, I love thee.*

"What are you doing?"

Eleanor glanced up from her script for *A Midsummer Night's Dream*. "I'm just studying my lines for our show. How did you sleep?"

"Good." Amelia crawled onto the bench next to her. "Will I have lines too?"

"Yes, as well as singing and dancing, which reminds me. Your father tells me you have a beautiful voice. If we can get Mr. Fiorelli to write you a song for the show, would you sing?"

"That would be fun," Amelia yawned.

"Are you sure you got enough sleep? It's tough getting used to the time difference."

Amelia nodded, studying her face. "What color are your eyes?"

"Blue or green, it depends on what I'm wearing. Right now they're probably bloodshot."

"They look like the ocean."

"Well now, that's very poetic. Let me see, I would say your eyes look like diamonds sparkling in the sunlight. They're very beautiful. By the way, I meant to tell you yesterday, I really like your necklace. It's quite unique. Is this a key to something?"

"Mommy gave it to me. She said it's the key to her heart."

Eleanor's throat tightened. "Oh... well, it's very lovely."

"Does your mommy have red hair?"

"No, she is blond, just like you. My father had red hair, which I was lucky enough to inherit, along with his pale skin."

"Zach has blond hair."

"Zach...oh, you mean Mr. Walker. Yes, your father told me you two met recently. So what is he like?"

"He's nice. He's coming to see me in the show. Will your daddy and mommy come to see you?"

"No. My father passed away many years ago and my mother really doesn't like the theater very much. I have a sister, Josephine, who would love to come, but she's living in Paris right now and won't be able to visit until October."

"What is passed away?"

"That is another way of saying someone has died."

"My mommy passed away."

"I know honey. I'm so sorry. I never met your mother, but I've read about her, and I know she was an extraordinary woman who helped a lot of people."

"You're like Mommy."

"Really, you think so? I find that hard to believe. From what I read about your mother, she was a very glamorous and worldly person."

"What does that mean?"

"Worldly? Well, it means sophisticated, refined, or world-wise. Your mother travelled all over the world whereas I've only been to a handful of places in the U.S., and once I visited Europe."

"Were you with Daddy?"

Eleanor froze. "I'm sorry. What did you just say?"

Amelia moved into her lap. "You went to that place with Daddy, right?"

"Do you mean Europe?"

Amelia nodded her head, her eyes narrowing. "What's a honeymoon?"

Before Eleanor could answer, Daniel lumbered into the kitchen and poured a cup of coffee. Amelia looked at him, gasping.

"Daddy, what happened to your face?"

Daniel took a long drink before answering. "Well baby girl, you remember Mr. Marco from last summer?"

"Is that the man you accidently punched?"

"Yeah sweetie, that's him. He showed up after you went to bed, but instead of Daddy hitting him, he hit me. Now he's in the county jail and I filed a restraining order against him."

"What's that?"

"It's a legal thing I can use to keep the moron away from me. We won't be seeing him again. Though the bad news is, since he knows I'm here it won't be long before the other vultures show up." Daniel sat at the kitchen table, studying them. "So what are you two lovely ladies up to this morning? Looks like you're still getting along."

Eleanor stood. "Actually, I was just about to make breakfast. How do eggs, bacon and pancakes sound?"

She received a unified yes and went to the refrigerator to gather up her ingredients. Amelia appeared next to her, asking if she could help and Eleanor gladly assigned her the task of assembling the pancake mix. After starting a skillet of bacon, she sat Amelia on a barstool at the island. Daniel joined them, standing behind her as she supervised. Soon she could feel his warm breath on her neck, and she found it hard to focus on anything else except his arm brushing against her as he dipped his finger in the mix. She smacked his hand and for a moment their fingers intertwined. Suddenly she remembered the moment when they first met.

It was February of her sophomore year at Julliard and she had just finished her audition for *Hamlet*. She left the rehearsal room and heard his booming voice call out her name. When she turned, she found she had to look up in order to address him, something she rarely did with her fellow classmates. He introduced himself, complimenting her on her monologue, and as she shook his hand she was amazed at the strength of his grip.

Eleanor broke from her thoughts. Her heart was racing, and as she placed a griddle on the stove for the pancakes, she had to pause a moment to wipe the sweat from her forehead. Then she noticed that Daniel's arm was now wrapped around her waist, pressing against her rib cage. Quickly, she pulled away before asking him to set the table.

Soon they sat down to breakfast, complete with juice and salsa for their eggs. They had only taken a few bites when Amelia broke the silence.

"Daddy, are you going to marry Eleanor again?"

Daniel choked on his food while Eleanor froze in mid bite. It took an entire glass of orange juice to clear his throat before he could respond.

"Who told you that Ellie and I were married?"

"Nobody," Amelia said.

"Did you read that online somewhere?"

"No."

"Then how did you find out?"

Amelia shrugged her shoulders. Daniel started to question her again and Eleanor gripped his arm. He lowered his voice. "Honey, that was a long time ago, before I ever met your mom."

"Do you like Eleanor?"

"Well, of course I do. She's been my friend for many years. You know that."

Amelia turned to Eleanor. "Do you like Daddy?"

Eleanor nodded her head, unable to speak.

"Then you should get married."

A knock on the deck door saved them from responding to Amelia's comment, and Trevor entered with a sleepy-eyed Frank Bishop in tow. At the same time Nina emerged from her lower level apartment, announcing that she was going to the university to start constructing the fairy wings for the next show. Amelia's head shot up and she pleaded with Daniel to let her go with Nina. Happily he agreed, as long as Trevor accompanied her, and there was no more talk of marriage.

After breakfast the house emptied and Daniel disappeared upstairs. Eleanor sat on the living room couch with her script, unable to focus. Her mind replayed the bizarre exchange with Amelia. Obviously the child missed her mother very much, and Eleanor worried that Daniel had taken her away from her family and friends too soon. She began to think about what she would say to him about the incident when suddenly she felt sleepy from the meal. She rested her head on the back of the couch and soon her eyes fluttered close.

She was in a hospital bed and a doctor handed her a newborn baby. She held the child, kissing its forehead and then presented the infant to the man next to her. Someone with well-manicured hands took the baby while the doctor and nurses lifted her from the bed onto a gurney. Then she was moving down the hall and he was moving with her. She heard his soothing voice resonate through her body as he held her hand. They passed through a set of swinging doors into an operating room filled with people in surgical garb. Someone placed a mask over her face and everything went dark.

Her eyes popped open and she saw Daniel standing at the end of Nina's grand piano, staring intently at a small, flowery picture. He turned to her with a questioning look.

"Did you hear what I said? I noticed all the expensive art in this place. Does Nina come from money?"

It took a moment for her to shake off the dream. "Yes she does, but you wouldn't know to look at her family that they were rich."

"Why, what do they look like?" he said.

"Well, it's more the way they dress, very plain and almost archaic looking, especially her Aunt Mila. The only outfit I've ever seen her wear is a peasant blouse, a long skirt, and a cloak with a hood."

"They still make those things?"

"In a costume shop perhaps, anyway, they're a bit odd, and I need to warn you that they usually show up here unannounced."

"Well I'll have to make sure not to roam around the house naked then," Daniel winked.

"What are we going to do about Amelia?" she said.

Daniel walked over to the couch and plopped down, resting his head on her lap. "I still don't get how she found out. I've been upstairs the past half hour searching you and me on the internet to see if there is any mention of our marriage or annulment. I couldn't find a thing."

"You searched yourself on the internet?"

"Oh yeah, I do it all the time. By the way, the review of your show is out. It's very good."

"Thank you, "she said. "I saw it in the paper this morning, so back to Amelia."

"Look Ellie, there's something you need to know about her. She's different."

"How so?"

"She's very smart and picks up on everything. I can't seem to hide any-thing from her."

"She knew about our trip to Europe."

"Hmmm, the only thing I can figure is she overheard me telling Detective Bellows. But I don't remember talking about our honeymoon."

"You told the police we were married? Why? I've never told anyone, not even Jeremy."

"Yeah, I know," he said. "But right after Bellows told me about Kate, I wasn't thinking straight. I thought maybe she had figured out who you were and sent Monica to spy on you. I know it was stupid, but at the time I thought it was really weird that Monica was here of all places. Don't worry. Bellows won't tell anyone."

"Not unless she decides to tell Jared. I don't know, maybe it doesn't mat-ter anymore. I still don't understand why we hid it from everyone."

"I was trying to protect you."

"Protect me from what?" she said. "Our break-up still got attention. The only thing we were spared was the embarrassment of ending a three month marriage. We should just have a talk with Amelia, answer whatever questions she might have and be done with it. I'm going to make some tea. Would you like some?"

"Don't go yet. This is kinda nice, just you and me alone."

He took her hand, holding it to his chest. She noticed his unshaven face and when she commented on it he told her that Alex wanted him to grow his hair and beard for the shows. She questioned the necessity for facial hair and he gave her a devilish grin.

"What...you don't want to kiss me with a beard? Sorry, it's a sacrifice you'll make for the summer."

"Who says we will be doing any kissing?"

"We are playing a husband and wife in both shows. You think there would be some of that going on."

"Have you actually read *A Midsummer Night's Dream*?"

"Give me a break Ellie. You know I've played Oberon before."

"Then as you recall, we spend very little time on stage together and when we do we're arguing."

"Until the end when we make up. And in *Hamlet* we play newlyweds, so you think there would be some action there."

Eleanor leaned her head back, moaning. "Different subject please."

"Ok, who is playing Bottom?"

"What?"

"Who is the actor playing Bottom? He's spending all this time on stage with you."

"This is a joke, right?"

"No, it's not," he said. "Who is he?"

"His name is Kevin Mallard. I did *As You Like It* with him three years ago."

"Did he play Orlando?"

"No, he did not. He played Jacques."

"So he's probably an older guy, but should I still be concerned about him?"

"I don't like where this conversation is heading."

"I'm serious. What about the guy who played Orlando, is he around this summer?"

"*What, jealous Oberon?*" she said.

"Funny. I just want to know what I'm dealing with, that's all."

"I didn't realize when Alex asked you to play this role that he was type-casting." Eleanor moved off the couch causing Daniel's head to snap back.

"Ouch. It was just a joke Ellie."

She went into the kitchen and fired up the tea kettle, unloading the dishwasher while she waited for the water to boil. Daniel entered and she thrust a stack of brightly colored plates in his direction, pointing to the cabinet. She pulled out the silverware holder and smacked it down on the counter. She was not sure how it happened, but she definitely felt angry.

"The actor who played Orlando was Jeremy. It was the last show we did together."

She threw open the cutlery door, throwing each piece of silverware with such force that Daniel rushed over, stopping her hand. The water kettle hissed and she turned off the burner.

"Tea?" she said.

"Sure," he said.

Daniel took a seat at the counter, watching her assemble the cups and saucers. She held up a box of Earl Grey, he nodded, and a she joined him at the island. The anger had left her and now she felt anxious. *Very strange.* She glanced up at Daniel who was biting his nails.

"There's something you need to know about me. I haven't been with anyone since Jeremy died."

"Ellie, you don't have to …"

She held up her hand. "Just hear me out. I don't know how much Alex has told you about what happened last year, but after the accident I was not in a very good place. I took off from work and locked myself in my home for over a month. By the time Alex and Nina found me, I was completely out of it and for some time after that most everyone thought I wasn't going to make it." She took a sip of tea. "But, I made it past those wretched few months and I got better. By midsummer I was helping Ben and Mik with the tavern and in the fall I returned to work."

Daniel held her hand. "Look, I'm sorry for upsetting you. But I've been in a really shitty place lately, and if I joke with you, it's only because it feels so damn good."

"I understand. But you need to know that other than a few concerned hugs from my male friends, I've had no physical contact with men."

"None? Not even a kiss?"

"Nothing." She pulled her hand away.

"All right, I get it. It's not like I'm doing that great either. In fact I have a confession to make. I haven't cried since Kate died."

"Well, you never were much of a weeper."

"No, you don't get it," he said. "I didn't shed a tear the day she died, or at her funeral or any day since. I haven't cried at all. I've tried, but I just can't seem to bring myself to do it."

"Well, you're probably still in shock. It's barely been two months since she died."

"You probably think I'm nuts for coming out here so soon after, but I figured you of all people would understand what I'm going through."

"I do, but you need to know what you're dealing with, that's all."

"I get it. You've lost interest in sex."

"It was more than that," she said. "I lost interest in everything."

"Everything…meaning?"

"Just *everything*," she said.

"But you're OK now, right?"

"I'm better." Eleanor gathered up their empty tea cups. "I thought this morning I would take you on a tour of Edmond and then we could pick up Amelia and have lunch."

"Sure, that sounds great."

"I need to take care of something first. Why don't you get ready and I'll be right back."

"Where are you going?" he said.

"Next door, I'll only be a minute."

"Are you going to see Fiorelli?"

She had hoped to be out the front door by the time Daniel asked her that question, but his long stride outmatched hers and now his body was blocking the exit.

"I noticed he was MIA at the party," he said.

"Can you blame him? You did toss a drink in his face the last time you saw him."

"Listen, he was flirting with my wife and I didn't like it. And since we're on the subject, what's the story with him anyway? Why is he hanging out here this summer?"

"He's working for the festival, same as you."

"I get why I'm here, but you could have gotten anyone to write the music."

"Kyle has star power just like you," she said. "Obviously that attracts people to the shows as was demonstrated by last night's spectacle."

"Yeah, well Fiorelli's music is all right, but I wouldn't put him on the same level as me."

"No you're right. I wouldn't either. His ego is no match for yours."

Eleanor darted around him and was halfway across the front lawn when he caught up with her. She could feel her teeth clenching.

"All right, look that was a stupid thing to say," he said.

"We were having a nice time, and then you had to go down that road and spoil it."

"Can I help it if the guy makes me nuts? He openly flirted with my wife. What was I supposed to do, ignore that? Will you please stop?"

Eleanor spun around. "He touched Katharine on the arm and leaned into her. I don't think that constitutes flirting."

"Is that what he told you happened?"

"No, that's what I heard and read about the incident. Three different witnesses said the same thing. They also said that you overreacted to the situation."

"Oh yeah, well screw them, because Fiorelli wasn't talking to anyone else's wife or girlfriend that night. And it wasn't just some casual conversation. They talked for a half hour."

Before Eleanor opened her mouth, she glanced around to see if anyone was watching them. She really did not want to have another visit from the sheriff's office.

"Kyle is a known flirt and maybe he was paying too much attention to Katharine. I wouldn't know. I wasn't there. But, I do know he didn't mean anything by it, he never does. He may act like a Don Juan sometimes, but he's not."

"How do you know?" he said.

"I just do."

"He never came on to you?"

"You aren't listening to me. Kyle is not that way. He doesn't date women."

Her comment seemed to stop Daniel's mouth from moving. He stood there for a moment with his hands on his hips, staring straight ahead. "So … is he gay?"

"No, he's not gay, though that would explain why Trevor and he hit it off so well."

Daniel's eyes widened. "Trevor is gay?"

"Oh, please tell me you don't mean that. How many years has he been working for you?"

"Seven. But we never talk about that kind of stuff."

"Certainly you saw how Frank was flirting with him last night."

"Frank who?"

"Frank Bishop. The guy who showed up in our kitchen this morning with Trevor? The bleach-blond guy with the multiple earrings and tattoos?"

"Oh yeah, that guy. Wow … I totally missed that."

"Oh Danny, you really need to pay more attention to the people around you."

"Maybe, but it looks like you don't need to check on Fiorelli. He's leaving right now."

She swung around to discover Kyle backing his convertible onto the street, speeding away without even a wave. She started for the townhouse, worried that he had overheard their argument.

"Hey, you called me Danny. You haven't said that in years."

"I'm sorry about that, but I think I'm really angry with you right now."

"But you used to call me Danny when you weren't angry."

Eleanor threw open the door. "Wrong, the only other time I called you that name was when we were having angry sex."

Daniel paused in the open doorway while she pounded up the stairs. "Well, I guess I could live with that."

"Shut-up Danny, and close the door."

※❈※

Jared and Mikayla had just finished breakfast when Kyle Fiorelli flew into The Wine Bistro. The two men exchanged glances as Jared escorted Mikayla from the restaurant. She said goodbye at the front entrance, kissing him on the cheek. While he watched her drive away he lit a cigarette, considering if he should return inside to chat with Fiorelli. Since the day they found Monica Bellaso's body on Birch Mountain he had kept his distance from his former mentor's son; however, he was well aware of Fiorelli's activities. Eleanor and he had been inseparable since his arrival in Edmond, which made his solo appearance here an interesting one.

Inside Jared found Fiorelli at the bar hunched over a glass of wine. He sat next to him, ordering a cup of coffee.

"Starting a little early today, I see," Jared said.

"It's never too early for Prosecco."

"I guess some things never change."

Fiorelli turned to him, smiling. "I could say the same of you."

"Mik is dealing with a problem and she needed a friend's advice. I guess Eleanor is a little busy this morning and couldn't get away."

"Yes, she is."

"So that's why you're here sulking, Archer moving in on your territory already?"

"Please Adams, that's an insipid remark, even for you."

"What can I say? I'm just telling it like I see it."

"Not that it is any of your business, but my relationship with Eleanor is not of that nature. She is my friend, and I am concerned for her well-being."

"Do you think Archer poses some sort of threat to her?"

"No of course not. The man may be a jackass, but he is not malicious. I just would prefer that he wasn't here."

"Well, if you aren't interested in her romantically, and he's just some insensitive jerk that doesn't mean her any harm, then why are you so upset over their little spat in Ms. St. John's front yard?"

"That's right. I forgot you've been watching me. Really Adams, can your modest department afford such an extravagance?"

"The Bellaso case is getting a lot of attention. We have all sorts of help and resources available to us now. Maybe you've heard we've joined forces with the NYPD and just recently we have support from both the Los Angeles and San Francisco police departments. Everyone is just eager to help us solve this."

Fiorelli finished his drink and ordered another one. "All right, I'll bite. I understand why you would partner with the LA police, but why San Francisco?"

"It's interesting that you should ask that question, because as it turns out Katherine Monroe spent a great deal of time in San Francisco over the past several years. In fact, she made a trip in March, just a week before she died."

"That makes sense. Kate had a long history of fundraising for several organizations there. That's how I first met her, but you already know that, so what is the point of this conversation?"

"Bellaso was also in San Francisco in March, the same time as Monroe, but we don't know where either of them stayed. Monroe had a reservation at The Ritz, but she never checked in, and we've searched all the major hotels. They weren't registered at any of them. However, as we delved further, we found out that Monroe made a habit of avoiding hotels when she visited San Francisco, and we were able to determine at least two private residences that Monroe stayed at regularly. One home in Pacific Heights caught my attention. You would recognize the address."

"That is a family owned house that my father happens to be occupying," Fiorelli said. "Kate did an extensive amount of fundraising for my cousin Alex, so I would think she would have stayed there occasionally. But, I thought you just said you didn't know where Kate and Bellaso were on her last trip."

"That's right. They didn't stay at any of the private residences that Monroe frequented, including your father's home. In fact, I'm beginning to believe they didn't stay in San Francisco at all and that they were instead in River Mist."

"Why would Kate come all the way up here?"

"I've been asking that same question about Bellaso. And I don't think it was because she was enamored with her lawyer's vacation home. She was here for a reason, and I suspect it is the same reason you are here. Eleanor is somehow a part of this, isn't she? That's why she had the vision."

Fiorelli was silent as he finished his drink and paid his tab.

"I thought as much," Jared said. "Look, I don't give a damn about your way of life or your crazy beliefs. I have a murder to solve. If you or your father has information that will help with this case, then I need to know it now."

"It's more than just a way of life, Adams, and you know that. If we can help, we will."

As Jared watched Fiorelli walk away, he was reminded of why he left behind his life in San Francisco. But despite all his attempts to escape his past, it still managed to haunt him.

Secrets and lies. There was no escaping it.

Chapter Sixteen

Out of this wood do not desire to go:
Thou shalt remain here, whether thou wilt or no.

The door to Eleanor's house swung open and Amelia waltzed into the entry-way, her fairy wings floating behind her. "And then after you say your lines we sing and dance."

"That's right." Eleanor tossed a pile of mail on the foyer table as Amelia continued to twirl around the room.

Daniel entered carrying their bags and dropped them on the floor, groaning. "God that was a long ride once you turned off the main road. How many miles was it?"

"About three," Eleanor said. "It just takes a while because of the winding roads."

"How far up the mountain are we?"

"We're not at the very top, but we have a pretty good view."

He walked into the living room. "This is really nice. The fireplace is huge."

"I know. That's what Jeremy wanted. He laid that stone with his brother Ben."

"I did some carpentry work myself when I was young, but nothing like this."

"Well, you're way ahead of me. I can barely operate a power screwdriver. Jeremy tried to teach me a few things, but I could never seem to grasp any of it. After a while he gave up on me. Let me show you the deck, he built the entire thing himself."

Eleanor started towards the kitchen doors, but stopped when she realized that Daniel was gone. Sighing, she checked on Amelia, who was dancing in the front yard, and then went into her bedroom. She found him in the bathroom standing in the shower stall, biting his nails.

"The skylight is a nice touch and it's very spacious," he said.

"You should call Detective Bellows back and find out what she wants."

"I know. It's just that every time I talk to her, I learn something about my wife that I didn't know before. I still can't believe Kate made all those trips to California without me knowing. Some of them were while I was filming in LA. What does that tell you?"

"Every time Bellows finds something it always leads to Monica Bellaso. I'm sure that's what it is."

"Yeah, Kate and Monica were up to something, that's for sure. Look, I'll call her. Can we talk about something else?"

"Why don't I show you and Amelia to your rooms?"

She left the bathroom feeling anxious and exhausted. The past week had been challenging as she adjusted to Daniel's stormy temperament. After a year of feeling nothing, she was not use to such powerful emotions and she found herself easily overwhelmed by his anger. Her only moments of solace were when she was with Amelia. Despite having just lost her mother, the child seemed content when they were together, so Eleanor spent as much time with her as she could.

She passed through the living room summoning Amelia who was still in the front yard. Daniel followed, chewing his nails.

"You know," he said. "There's no way those wings will make it till dress rehearsal."

"That's why Nina made her two sets, so she would have one to play with."

Daniel picked up the bags and followed her up the stairs. At the landing they turned right and entered a rose-colored bedroom filled with blond oak furniture. Amelia burst into the room, nearly clipping her wings against the door. She squealed, throwing herself on the queen-size bed.

"You have your own bathroom and feel free to leave anything that you don't need in Edmond. We'll be here next weekend."

Eleanor's statement garnered another cry of delight and Amelia started to unpack. She turned to Daniel who was grinning. It was the first smile she had seen from him all week.

"This room is perfect," he said. "Pink is her favorite color."

"It's a bit sterile for a little girl, but maybe we can buy a few things to personalize it. Your room is next door."

Eleanor led him to a larger bedroom painted in jade with black trim. The king-size bed, dresser and other furniture were a dark mahogany, and a flat screen television was attached to the wall. Daniel wandered into the adjoining bathroom and his eyes lit up when he saw the sunken tub.

"Oh I know where I'm going to be later," he said.

"I'll let you get settled in and then we'll go into town and see the restaurant."

"Ellie, wait. I want to thank you and Nina for being so good to Amelia this past week. She's been really happy and I can't tell you what a relief that's been for me."

"She's a wonderful girl, Daniel. Katharine and you did a great job. Would you like me to close the door?"

Daniel nodded as he put his cell phone to his ear, and Eleanor pulled the door shut. Poking her head into Amelia's room, she could hear the child singing in the bathroom, and took advantage of the free moment to continue her search for The Passer.

As she sat at her desk, she pulled out a small notebook from her top drawer and referred to the list of searches she had performed to date. There had been several since her first attempt, which produced mostly football references. Upon her second try she focused on religious practices and eventually honed in on ancient religions. She then spent several weeks filtering out results that included the term *passer-by,* which eventually led her to researching the ancient Egyptians and the Celts. This endeavor went on for days, until she stumbled on the phrase *esoteric teachings.* She decided to scratch all her previous attempts and start fresh with this term.

From that point on it was an entirely different journey. Again, she had to weed out results with the words the *passer-by*, but soon she came upon a bio of a woman specializing in ancient religions and esoteric wisdom. Listed below her name she found the words *The Passer.* That was last Thursday, the day before Daniel arrived. She bookmarked the website, but had not the time to continue her research.

She opened a browser and clicked on the link for Dr. Helene Manning. Her heart sank when she saw the message appear, written in both German and English:

We are sorry, but our website is down for important updates. Please visit us again soon. To order from our bookstore, please contact us at the phone number or e-mail address below. For your convenience, we have included a download of our titles with a brief description.

At that moment Daniel surfaced from his bedroom with a toothpick in his mouth. Amelia emerged from her room as well, her fairy wings flapping behind her. Eleanor reluctantly closed her laptop, and they left for downtown River Mist.

✺✺

When she pulled into Jeremy's Tavern, she was concerned that she would not find a parking place. Ben had hired Jared's cousin, Jonah Adams, as the new chef and business had improved recently, though not enough to guarantee that the restaurant would survive past the summer. However, today's over-flowing parking lot was a positive sign.

As soon as they walked through the front door they were greeted by Mikayla, who quickly escorted them to a comfortable booth tucked away in the back corner. The bar and dining room were packed, and several heads turned as Daniel walked through the restaurant. Ben came out of the kitchen to say hello and Mikayla swooped in with water glasses and menus.

As they conversed with the Garrisons, someone approached the table, and when Eleanor turned she was surprised to see it was Jared. She introduced him to Daniel and then learned he was there to meet with Ben. The two men left for the back office and Mikayla slipped in next to her, bursting with news.

"Jared wants to invest in the restaurant."

"What?" Eleanor said. "He didn't say anything to me about this."

"It just happened. I told him a while back about the troubles we were having, which is why we have Jonah now, and I guess he's been thinking about it ever since. Isn't that great news! Now we have another investor and we can finally spruce things up around here."

"And Ben is all right with it?"

"Well yeah honey, he's back there talking with Jared now, so I think that should answer your question." Mikayla gave her a big grin. "Anyway, we can talk later. Y'all look hungry."

"Hold on a minute," Eleanor said. "Why do we need to spruce up the place, it looks fine the way it is?"

"Sweetie, it hasn't been touched in years, and besides, I think we need to update it a little so we can compete with some of those fancier places on the coast."

"That wasn't what Jeremy was trying to do here. He meant for it to be casual, like that old diner we used to eat at over by the university."

"But honey, look at our clientele over the past few years. They have money, and they want something a little nicer."

"Well, from what I can tell we're doing just fine with the new chef and I don't see why we have to make any changes right now. If you want to freshen up the paint that's fine, but I don't want to do any major renovations just yet."

Mikayla sat silent, tapping her fingers on the table. "Just think on it honey, and besides, we wouldn't do anything until after the tourist season ends. Now what can I get y'all to eat?"

Mikayla took their orders and glided back to the kitchen. Eleanor watched her, wondering what else was going on that she did not know about. She glanced at Daniel who was frowning.

"Why are you so afraid to make changes to the restaurant?" he said. "She's right. It could use some fixing up, probably a whole overhaul. It's a great space and you got all this traffic from the main road. I think it would be pretty exciting having a popular restaurant."

Eleanor shrugged her shoulders. "Yes, I guess so."

"I'm getting the impression that you don't want this place to succeed."

"That's not true. It's just if we change it too much, it won't be Jeremy's place anymore."

"Yeah, but from what you've told me, if business doesn't improve, there won't be any restaurant."

"The tavern did fine while Jeremy was alive. I don't see why we have to go and change the look just to attract business. Yes, the food needed to improve and it appears that it is has, so that should be enough."

"There must have been another reason why people came here, besides the food."

"Of course, they came to see Jeremy. Everyone knew him. He was the social epicenter of this town."

"OK, then let's give them *another* reason to come. When your friend brings my burger, tell her to take it over to the bar."

"Why, where are you going?" Eleanor said.

Amelia groaned, covering her face with her hands.

"See that couple over there?" Daniel pointed and waved to an elderly pair seated at the front of the restaurant. "They've been staring at us for the past twenty minutes. I'm going over there to say hi and sign an autograph. Then I'm going to sit at the bar and for the next half hour I'll sign anything that comes my way. I guarantee you once word gets out that I'm staying in the area and there's a possibility I might visit again, your business will boom." Daniel stood and walked over to chat with the astonished couple.

Eleanor said nothing when Mikayla brought Daniel's food. She just pointed towards the bar and told her to leave it there. A few minutes later Daniel sat down to his burger and fries, and in between bites he worked his way through the crowd that had swarmed around him.

※❈※

It was late afternoon when they returned home from their excursion through downtown River Mist. Daniel and Amelia helped Eleanor unload the groceries and then Amelia went up to her room to listen to music. Daniel, who was oddly energized by his autograph session, opened a bottle of rosé and located two glasses from a cabinet.

"Shall we?" he said, smiling.

Eleanor suggested they sit outside and she threw open the heavy double doors that led out to the backyard. His mouth fell open. He walked out onto the large, multi-level wood deck and took in the extraordinary vista. A large area around the back of the house had been cleared, allowing for a full view of the mountainside and surrounding foothills. As far as he could see there was only dark green and purple- no houses, no cars, no people- just miles, and miles of trees. Suddenly he felt uneasy in this strange and quiet place.

"Ellie, how close are your neighbors?"

"I guess about a half mile. So, what do you think?"

"It's beautiful." He handed her a glass of wine.

"It's funny," she said. "I didn't know about this house until the day I moved here. Jeremy had been back in California for about six months while I wrapped up my work in New York. The whole time I thought he had found a place in Edmond, he and his family were slaving away here."

"So what's that down there?" Daniel pointed to a small wood framed building that sat in the southeast corner of the property near the edge of the woods.

"That's Jeremy's workshop. I keep my gardening supplies in there, but mostly it's filled with his things." Eleanor walked down the stairs and stood in the middle of a large, barren area. "And right here I'm putting in an above ground pool."

"When are you planning on doing that?"

"Next year, so it's ready by summer. I've always wanted one and it will be nice when I have company."

"So if Amelia and I behave ourselves you'll invite us back to christen it?"

"Only if you promise to not sign any more autographs."

"Hey, don't be such a grouch. You'll thank me later." He took her hand, leading her to a double chaise lounge situated on the upper level of the deck. "I talked to Bellows."

"I know. Your nails are a mess. I wanted to say something earlier, but I figured you would tell me when you were ready."

"Yeah, don't know how ready I am, but here it goes. Right before I left for California I turned Kate's passport over to the police. I didn't think to look through it first, but it seems that she took several trips to Eastern

Europe that no one knew about. I guess they discovered the stamps when they were combing through it. Bellows questioned the Monroes and they didn't know anything, and there's no mention of the trips in The Monroe Foundation travel logs."

"Do they have any idea what she was doing there?"

"Not a clue. They even rechecked her credit card statements and cell phone records and couldn't find anything."

"Don't worry. I'm sure Bellows and Jared will figure it out."

"Yeah, I'm not so sure I want them to figure it out now. It's like she was living this mystery life that none of us knew about. Look, I don't want to talk about this anymore, it's too depressing. I noticed your fancy grill up there on the deck, any chance we can use it tonight?"

Eleanor sighed. "I don't know if there's gas in the tank. It hasn't been touched since Nina cooked on it last summer."

"Oh, you're breaking my heart. How can you let that fine piece of equipment sit idle?"

"That was Jeremy's thing, and after he died I didn't have the desire to learn how to use it."

"Well then, tonight I will give you a lesson and I promise after that, you'll want to cook every meal out here."

"So I guess I don't have the option of saying no."

"Nope," he said. "But it will be fun, I promise. Give us something we can do together."

"We've done plenty of things together this past week."

"Rehearsals maybe or hanging out with Amelia, but never just you and me. Hey, remember that summer we performed at Stratford?"

"How could I forget? We stayed in that large Victorian home where we pretty much alienated our fellow housemates. All of them thought we were highly unsociable."

"We had our reasons for not hanging out. It was a good time for us, don't you think? That production of *As You Like It* was amazing. Sometimes I got so caught up in you when you were on stage, that I forget where I was or what I was saying."

"And all this time I thought that was because you waited until the eleventh hour to learn your lines."

"You would remember that. Not all of us can memorize as quickly as you Dr. Bouchard."

"Daniel, you're a major procrastinator and you know it. You about drove me and the rest of the cast crazy with your ad libs. We didn't know what was going to come out of your mouth when you were on stage."

"So what, that was only during rehearsals. I was ready by opening night and if you search your memory banks, I believe I didn't screw up for the rest of the show."

"Well, I guess I have to admit you were all right for the run."

"I was better than all right, I was good, very good in fact."

"Yes, I know. I read the reviews. They loved you." Eleanor stared ahead into the woods.

"Yes they did and they loved our chemistry on stage. I guess it helped that we were having sex every chance we could get."

"Daniel, please…"

"What? Are you embarrassed by that? We were a couple at that time, who cares?"

"I know, but…"

"But what, don't you like reminiscing?"

"No I don't, because every time we talk about our past we end up saying or doing things to each other that we regret later."

"So that's what's been bothering you all week. I knew you were still angry about what happened in San Francisco. We need to talk about it."

"Not while Amelia is around." Eleanor swung her legs over the chair and stood.

"What are you talking about, she's upstairs. She can't hear us."

"Why do we have to revisit that night at all? Can't we just let it be?"

"I don't want it hanging over us the rest of the summer."

"It won't," she said. "I promise. I'm not angry about what happened. I take full responsibility for my actions and I completely understand why you never tried to contact me. We should just simply apologize to each other and be done with it."

"After I left you that night, I wasn't done with it. Not for a long, time."

"What do you mean?"

"Ellie, there's something I need to tell you. You better sit down for this."
She returned to her seat and he took a drink. "First off, you need to know
that when I saw you in San Francisco I was having problems with Kate."

"So that's what was bothering you. You could have told me. You know I
would have understood."

"Yeah, but I really wasn't in the mood that night to talk about my marital
problems. Anyway, I won't get into all the details right now, but our situation
was bad enough that when I left that October to film a movie, she pretty much
told me that she was going to take Amelia and move back in with her folks."

"Daniel, if I did anything to compromise your relationship with your
wife…"

He held up his hand "Before you say anything else, let me finish."

"Sorry, please go on."

"Anyway, I went to Canada for the film. The first few weeks of shooting
I was pretty miserable. I felt bad about how things were falling apart with
Kate, but at the same time I couldn't get you out of my head. I spent the
days feeling guilty about her and the nights tossing and turning over you and
I went crazy. Finally one day I woke up and realized it had to stop. Either I
had to contact you and tell you how I felt, or let go of it and get on with my
life. So I made a decision."

He paused to take another drink.

"I had it all worked out. I picked a day when I knew I would be home
early from shooting. I ordered room service, which included a bottle of bourbon, and I locked myself in for the night." He pointed to her glass. "I'd take
a drink now if I were you. You're going to need it. So there I was in the hotel.
It was about 8:00 in the evening in Canada and 5:00 here. I had dinner, and
after a few shots I made a call. I figured you were still at school and I could
talk to you before you went home."

"You tried to contact me?"

"Yep, I actually tried your cell several times, but I kept getting voice mail.
I'm surprised you didn't notice all the missed calls. Next I called your work
number, and I got voicemail there too. I didn't want to leave a message and
after a few more attempts I gave up and did something that only several shots
of booze would allow me to do. I called the restaurant and I got hold of…*him*."

"What?"

"I know it was completely stupid, but I was drunk by this point, and I had to know how you were doing."

"What did you say to Jeremy?"

"I made up some bullshit story that I lost your cell number and I was trying to get hold of you about something. We talked about the restaurant and finally I asked him how you were, and he said you were good, getting ready for a big fall production and that you were wrapping up your dissertation. We talked for a couple minutes and then the call ended. So, I take it from your reaction he never told you."

"No, he did not." Eleanor emptied the contents of her glass.

"There's more."

"Really…perhaps I'll have a refill."

Daniel picked up the bottle and filled both glasses. "I had decided that if I couldn't get hold of you on the phone, that I would come find you. And I did. I flew out early the next morning and I got here in time to get to the university before you arrived. I had the driver sit the limo in a far corner of the lot while we waited and about fifteen minutes later you arrived and parked near the front entrance. Then, I saw the passenger side door open."

"Jeremy."

"He jumped out and darted around the car so he could open the door for you. When you got out you gave him your keys, well, it was obvious that the two of you were doing just fine. After that, I told the driver to leave. As we passed by, you turned towards the parking lot. For a moment I thought you saw me and I had the driver slow down, but I realized you were just waving at him. We moved on and went directly to the airport. Thirty minutes later I was back on my plane heading for Canada."

Eleanor stared into her wine glass. "What happened after that?"

"I went back to finish my movie and then I returned home to Kate and mended things with her. Look, I know I should have called you when *he* died, but I didn't think you would talk to me. That's why I sent the flowers, so you'd know that I was thinking about you."

They sat silent for several moments, staring into the woods.

"I'm sorry for making a mess of everything," Daniel said.

"You didn't make a mess of everything. We did. You didn't force me to go to your room that night, or drink all that wine, or anything else for that matter. What I did, I did willingly. I was there because I wanted to be there. If anything, I should apologize to you."

"For what?"

"For leaving like I did, for never responding to your note, and especially for not saying goodbye to you in that hotel lobby when I had the chance. I had no business going to your room that night, and if I had shown some restraint, none of this would have ever happened."

"Oh, I don't know. I think that night I would have found a way to you somehow. I've missed you Ellie. I didn't realize how much until I saw you standing in that parking lot at the airport. I almost mowed some guy over trying to get through that door, and when I was finally able to hold you I thought my heart would burst open right there." He turned to her and saw that she had tears streaming down her face. "Why are you crying?"

"I'm not sure...but I think I might be sad."

"Me too."

Just then Amelia flew past them, heading for the woods. Eleanor's head snapped around.

"Oh my God... Amelia, stop!"

Eleanor sprang from the chaise lounge as Daniel turned towards the woods. He caught two dark objects moving in the distance. "What the hell! Amelia, get back here!"

"Hold on!" Eleanor raced into the house, emerging a few seconds later with a shotgun.

"What are you doing with that thing?" he said.

"I'm going to use it if I have to. I want you to stay back in case you need to call for help."

"No way in hell am I gonna let you go down there without me."

Eleanor spun around, her eyes determined. "Stay back. We can't afford to have both of us incapacitated."

"Incapacitated, are you shitting me?" Daniel pulled out his cell phone and watched as Eleanor marched towards the woods. He could now see two bears walking the perimeter of the property, sniffing the ground. As she drew closer, one of the creatures stopped and looked up.

The larger of the two bears began to step towards them and Eleanor pulled Amelia behind her before engaging the slide on her shot gun. Amelia threw her arms around Eleanor's waist, pleading with her not to harm the animals. Finally Daniel could not watch any longer and ran towards them, demanding that Amelia come to him. At that moment the large bear stopped its approach and released a menacing growl.

"Daniel, stay still," Eleanor ordered as she aimed her gun. "They've picked up on our scent."

"Should I call 911?"

"Just take Amelia and start for the house."

"Come on honey." Daniel reached for Amelia's shoulder and she jerked away. "This is serious. Those bears could hurt us."

Exasperated with his daughter's obstinate behavior, he scooped her up, turning towards the house. He had only taken a few steps before she began thrashing violently. Moments later she managed to slip through his arms, and took off running.

Eleanor fired off a warning shot and raced towards the woods, overtaking Amelia in only a few strides. She planted herself between his daughter and the growling creatures, aiming her gun. As Eleanor pulled the trigger Amelia let out a piercing scream that sent the hairs on his neck standing straight up. Then, the smaller bear roared and a terrifying silence followed as everyone froze. To Daniel's amazement the bears backed away, retreating into the woods. He ran to Amelia who was crying, and fell to his knees.

"Don't you ever do that again, do you hear me? Swear to me you'll never, ever pull a stunt like that again." He knew he should not be shaking her, but he wanted to make sure she understood his plea. Amelia nodded and buried her face against his chest, sobbing. He gathered her up and glanced over at Eleanor who still had her shotgun aimed at the woods.

"Ellie, you OK?"

Slowly, she lowered the gun to her side. "I don't think we should grill out tonight."

"Damn straight about that."

Chapter Seventeen

I pray thee, gentle mortal, sing again;
Mine ear is much enamoured of thy note.

Daniel finished his sound check, and then gave his daughter a kiss before leaving the stage. He hovered in the wings for a few moments, hoping that Eleanor would join him, and when she did not he made his way into the auditorium.

As he sat in the darkness, watching Eleanor assist Amelia with the placement of her ear mic, he tried to ignore the mounting frustration that was churning inside him. The past two weeks with her had been maddening. On the one hand, she was very sympathetic to his woes as his wife's murder investigation continued to unfold, yet when he tried to discuss anything else with her, she would immediately shut down and do everything she could to avoid him.

Compounding his frustration was the strong bond that had formed between Eleanor and Amelia. Ever since the incident with the bears they had become inseparable, spending nearly every waking *and* sleeping moment together. It gave him great joy to see Amelia happy again, but he was starting to grow weary of her constant presence at Eleanor's side.

Then there was Eleanor's relationship with Kyle Fiorelli, which the mere thought of her spending time with the self-assured composer made his blood boil. He did not care if she believed that they were *just friends*. He still did not trust the man, and it baffled him to no end how Eleanor refused to see Fiorelli for what he truly was: a womanizer and a cad.

Finally, his sour thoughts turned to Nina St. John and Eleanor's devotion to her oddball friend. It did not matter that Nina never touched anyone, or wore white gloves 24 hours a day, or rarely said a friendly word, because Eleanor would always come to her defense. It drove him crazy how Eleanor would go to extremes to justify Nina's bizarre behavior, but when pressed, she was unable to describe her feelings towards him. Yet, his misery did not end there. While his drama played out with Eleanor, another more disheartening plot was evolving with the murder investigation.

After the discovery of Katharine's mystery visits to Eastern Europe, Bellows and her team set out to determine the purpose of her trips. The first step was to construct a timeline using her passport, the foundation travel logs and any other information they could gather.

The initial trip took place nearly three years ago, while Katharine was working for the foundation in Berlin, Germany. During her visit she entered Moscow and disappeared. There were no credit card receipts, no calls from her international cell phone and no record of her staying at any of the major hotels. She spent three days in Russia before returning to Berlin and eventually flying home to New York.

The next trip occurred four months later and was identical in form. This time she visited The Ukraine, entering in Kiev. Again there were no credit card receipts, calls or hotel stays that the police could find. The same pattern continued for the remaining trips-twelve in all- with the final one occurring in November of last year, when she visited a country he had never heard of called Moldova.

As he sat there, biting at his fingers, he wondered how Kate could have done all this without anyone ever knowing, especially him. He was reluctantly coming to the realization that he really did not know his wife as well as he thought he did.

Trevor interrupted his thoughts as he sat next to him, bearing a container of toothpicks.

"It's about time. Where have you been?" Daniel said.

"Sorry, you were completely out and I had to make a run to the grocery store. I also picked up your favorite bourbon and left it in your bedroom."

"I hope you got two bottles this time."

"Yes, against my better judgment."

"Yeah, well I don't pay you for that."

"True," Trevor said. "You pay me to do your bidding, but you'll excuse me if on occasion I express my concern for your well-being. Speaking of which, I just spoke to Michael a few minutes ago and he said he's been trying to reach you all day."

"Yeah I know."

"Is something wrong?"

"Nope, just some last minute bullshit with the movie contract. I'll call him. So, what's going on with Fiorelli today? "

"He spent the morning in his studio. He did play some of his music from *Hamlet* for me. It's very good."

"Whatever. No mention of Ellie?"

"I really don't feel comfortable discussing Mr. Fiorelli in this way," Trevor said.

"Why, what do you care? You'll never see him again after this summer."

"Perhaps, but in general, I don't like talking about people behind their backs."

"Trev, all I want to know is what he says to you."

"No, you just want to know if Dr. Bouchard is the topic of conversation, which she isn't."

"OK, if Ellie never comes up, then what the hell does he talk about?"

"If you must know," Trevor said, "we usually chat about wine, music and travelling, that sort of thing. He's very enamored with San Francisco and he has even asked me if I would like to go down with him to meet his father."

"No shit, did you say yes?"

"Of course not, I'm here to work. Besides, I couldn't leave Amelia and you alone."

"What are you talking about?" Daniel said. "Amelia spends all her time with Ellie and as long as I got booze and toothpicks I'm fine. You haven't had a break in a while. You should go. I'll even let you borrow the plane."

"I appreciate that, but I believe Mr. Fiorelli wanted to drive down so he could stop in Napa first."

"Even better, that will take more time. Tell him you'll go. That's an order."

A spotlight appeared downstage center and Amelia moved into position as the music started. Eleanor disappeared into the wings and emerged through a side door leading into the auditorium. Daniel watched with curiosity as she hurried up the aisle and sat next to him.

"You two were up there for a while," Daniel said. "Anything wrong?"

"No, she's just a little nervous about her song." Eleanor sank down into her chair.

"She hardly talks to me anymore, so I'm kinda counting on you to let me know if there's anything going on with her."

"Can we not discuss this right now? She's about to perform."

"You won't talk to me when she is around, so I figure now is my only chance."

Eleanor turned to him, glaring. "I want to be able to tell Amelia that I heard her song and I would think you would want to do the same. Now will you please hush so I can listen?"

"All right, no need to bite my head off."

She rolled her eyes before returning her attention to the stage and he held his tongue for the duration of the song. When Amelia finished, a thunderous round of applause filled the theater as several of the cast members poured onto the stage to congratulate her. Eleanor shot up from her seat, starting for the aisle, and he grabbed her arm.

"Where are you going?"

"To congratulate Amelia," she said. "And then I have to try on my new costume."

"Why, what happened to the old one?"

"Apparently Alex didn't think it was exciting enough. Please let go of me."

"Why are you pissed off all of a sudden?"

"I could ask you the same question."

"How would you know how I'm feeling? You're never around me long enough to find out." His remark sent her bounding towards the stage, and he chomped down on his toothpick, biting it in half. He turned to Trevor whose brow was furrowed. "What?"

"I'm just curious as to why Dr. Bouchard is so upset? It seems out of character for her."

"Who knows? Getting her to talk about anything is like pulling teeth, unless it's about the boyfriend. Then she can go on for days. Whatever, I'm tired of this crap."

Daniel took off for the stage, chewing away at the fragments of toothpick in his mouth. By the time he reached Amelia, Eleanor had managed to once again slip away. He picked up his daughter, heading for the exit, and it was not until he was nearing the costume shop that he realized he had forgotten to compliment her performance. He stopped short of the doors and when he looked at Amelia she was smiling.

"It's all right Daddy. I know you liked my song."

His throat constricted. He did not deserve her. "Your singing was beautiful baby girl. I have a feeling you're going to steal the show."

When he entered the shop he found it bustling with students hunched over sewing machines and cutting tables. He located Nina who was standing outside the changing room, and just as he approached, Eleanor emerged through the curtains. His mouth dropped open.

Her former costume, which had been a billowy dress with layers of fabric, had been replaced with a skin tight, pale pink gown that shimmered when she moved. Nina motioned for Eleanor to turn and a hush fell over the room. Slowly, she rotated in a circle, and several gasps could be heard as her bare back came into view. One of the male students whistled and then a round of applause ensued. Eleanor looked like she was about to faint.

Daniel was speechless. He wandered over to her, touching the skirt of her dress with his chewed-up fingertips. "It's almost the color of your skin, and what is this fabric? It's like some sort of stretchy lace." He stood in front of her and saw that her cheeks were flush. "Ellie, what is the deal? You look incredible. Nobody is going to be able to keep their eyes off of you."

She stared into the mirror, silent. Her face and neck were now a bright red- a reaction he had not seen from her in years. After a while she gathered up her clothes, thanked Nina for the dress and left without saying a word to him. He stood there, still holding Amelia as he attempted to keep his frustration in check. Then his daughter suggested that he go after her. He agreed and left Amelia with Nina.

As he entered Eleanor's dressing room he took a deep breath before slamming the door. "What the hell is wrong with you?"

"Daniel, I can't do this right now. Please, just go."

"Not until you tell me what the hell is going on. Why are you so upset?"

"Why do you think? Look at me! I look like I'm naked."

"No you don't. You look…."

"What?" When he could not answer she sank into a chair next to the dressing table, burying her face in her arms. "I can't do this with you."

"Can't do what?"

"I can't perform like this. I'll never be able to concentrate."

"Why is that?"

Her head shot up. "Because of the way you're looking at me right now. The same way you've been looking at me for the past two weeks."

Daniel considered the many ways he could respond to her, but in the end he decided it was just best to go for it. "I didn't know I was being that obvious."

"Well, you are."

"I'm sorry."

"Why didn't you say something?"

"How could I after that whole bit about you not having sex in over a year. I would have scared the hell out of you. And it's not like I'm ready right this very minute. But I am thinking about it, a lot actually. So, now that you know do you want me to move out of Nina's?"

"What?"

"It's obvious I'm making you miserable. Maybe Amelia and I should just find a hotel for the rest of the summer."

"You're not going to move into a hotel."

"Well, I gotta stay somewhere and no way am I bunking next door with Fiorelli."

"Danny, stop it. I don't want you to move anywhere. I just need to figure this out."

"What's there to figure out? You either feel the same way as me or you don't, and based on the way you've been acting lately, I think we already know the answer to that question."

"Oh will you please give it a rest. I have no idea how I feel right now."

"You sound pissed off to me."

"That's because I'm feeling frustrated."

"Well, welcome to my world."

They sat in silence, Eleanor twirling her hair around her finger while he chewed on a fresh toothpick. Finally, he was tired of being angry at her and began to fixate on a more pleasant thought. She glanced at him, squinting, and he noticed her chest was a bright crimson. Suddenly, she shot up from her seat.

"What is going on with you?" he said.

"Nothing, we should probably get going. I'm sure Amelia is wondering where we are."

"Don't you ever miss it Ellie? And I'm not just talking about the sex, but just being close to someone?"

"I don't know. I haven't thought about it for so long, that I think I've forgotten what it feels like."

"Well, you must be thinking about it a little, because you're really red right now."

Eleanor glanced down at her chest, moaning. "Will you stop it? That is not helping me."

"OK, sorry. Let's try something else." He moved in front of her.

"What are you doing?"

"Just calm down and let me try this." He stretched his neck from side to side before clearing his throat. Eleanor rolled her eyes. "Do you mind. I'm trying to focus here."

She placed her hands in her lap, giving him her full attention. He took a deep breath and slowly exhaled.

"If I profane with my unworthiest hand this holy shrine, the gentle sin is this: my lips, two blushing pilgrims, ready stand to smooth that rough touch with a tender kiss."

Eleanor gasped. "You know that scene?"

"I played Romeo when I was young, before my body turned into this."

"I would have liked to have seen that. Please, go on."

"Well, I think Juliet's line is next," he said.

"Oh yes, let me see... Good pilgrim, you do wrong your hand too much, which mannerly devotion shows in this; for saints have hands that pilgrims' hands do touch, and palm to palm is holy palmers' kiss."

"Have not saints lips, and holy palmers too?"

"Ay, pilgrim, lips that they must use in prayer."

Daniel moved in front of her, his palms facing out. "O, then, dear saint, let lips do what hands do! They pray; grant thou, lest faith turn to despair."

She placed her hands against his. "Saints do not move, though grant for prayers' sake."

"Then move not while my prayer's effect I take. Thus from my lips, by thine my sin is purged." He kissed her and their fingers intertwined.

"How is it that you can remember all this," she whispered, "but you can't learn your lines for Oberon?"

"Shhhh, we're not finished yet," he said. "Keep going."

"Then have my lips the sin that they have took."

"Sin from my lips? O trespass sweetly urged! Give me my sin again." Daniel lingered in his kiss, long enough that a piece of toothpick passed into her mouth. Eleanor pulled away, smiling.

"You kiss by th' book." She grabbed a tissue, wiping her lips.

"Sorry about that. Look, I know my life is a mess right now, but that doesn't change how I feel about you. All I want is for us to be closer."

"Closer, meaning...?"

"Closer than we are now, that's for sure. But more like we were before."

"If you remember correctly, that did not work out so well."

"I know, but we're different people now. We're older and wiser...well, older for sure."

"I don't know if I'm ready for this," she said.

"Yeah, me neither, but I want to give it a try anyway. What do you say?"

She sighed, brushing the hair from his eyes. "What about Amelia? We need to consider how this is will affect her."

"Are you kidding? A few weeks ago she thought we should get married. I think she'll be just fine with us getting together. So what say you my Titania, my sweet queen?"

"Methinks you are an ass."

"Cute, I meant about us?"

"I promise to think about it, but on one condition." She scooped up her script off the makeup table, handing it to him. "That you learn your lines before opening night. If you start now, you just might make it."

Chapter Eighteen

Trip away, make no stay;
Meet me all by break of day.

Eleanor and Daniel Archer, along with a group of scantily clad people in fairy costumes, floated off the stage in a cloud of mist and twinkling lights. The audience applauded the disappearance, while one actor remained. Thankfully for Jared, the person did not speak for very long and the play finally ended.

After several rounds of bows, the curtain lowered, and the cast and crew broke out into an enthusiastic roar. Bottles of Champagne were opened as the actors congratulated one another. Archer grabbed Eleanor and gave her a lengthy kiss which solicited a raucous round of cheers. Meanwhile, Jared stood backstage, wishing he could step outside for a smoke. He, along with several deputies from the sheriff's office had been at the theater for the past two hours, preparing for the large crowds that were expected to form outside. As he waited he felt his cell phone vibrating in his jacket pocket and was surprised to see it was Mikayla.

"Hey Sunshine," he said.

"Hey Shug, what are you doing?"

"I'm at the theater making sure Eleanor and Archer don't get trampled on when they leave here. How's the restaurant?"

"We had a really good day today and when I left it looked like it was going to be another busy night."

"So where are you if you're not at Jeremy's?" he said.

"I'm on the coast having dinner with Mom. I was hoping we could meet later."

"I'll be here another hour or so, but I guess I could. What's going on? Is everything all right with Ben?"

"We can talk about it later Shug. I gotta go."

He felt uneasy as the call ended. This was the third time this month that Mikayla had sought his advice regarding her recent difficulties with her husband. He wanted to help, but it was becoming increasingly difficult to let her go after their long talks.

Finally, Eleanor and Archer left the stage. He quickly briefed them on what to expect when they exited the theater and then asked if he could speak with Eleanor about a business matter. When they entered her dressing room she hurried into the bathroom to change and emerged wearing a formfitting white dress.

"Wow. You look nice," he said.

She rolled her eyes. "Daniel got it for me. He likes me to wear dresses."

"So, we don't have much time. What's up with the message you left me."

Eleanor frowned. "Remember you told me to contact you if anything unusual happened."

"Did you have another vision of Monica?"

"Well, I wouldn't call them visions, more like dreams, and they aren't about Monica."

"Them? How many have you had?"

"Six, including the one last night."

"Just in the past week?" he said.

"No. The dreams started the day after Daniel arrived in Edmond. I should have told you earlier, but I really didn't think it was anything to be concerned about until yesterday."

"Why, what happened?"

"Perhaps I should start from the beginning. These dreams have been of a child, a little girl actually. The very first one took place on the day that she was born and they have progressed from there. In all of them I can see her, but I don't recognize where I am nor can I see the other people around me. But last night, the dream took place in my house in River Mist and Jeremy was there. He played with the little girl and held her. He seemed to know who she was."

"Who do you think the kid is?"

"The child has blue eyes and blond hair. It has to be Amelia. There is also another man that is in all of them, except the one with Jeremy. I can't see his face, but I can hear his voice. Look, I realize this has something to do with the fact that Daniel and Amelia are here. It's probably my mind trying to work through it all. But, what I find odd about these dreams is that they feel very real, as if I'm reliving something that has already happened to me."

"Like a memory."

"Yes, exactly like that. But they're not my memories."

"I wouldn't worry about it," he said. "You're probably right. It's just your way of dealing with Archer and the kid. Having them here is a big change in your life."

She stopped removing her makeup and turned to him. "You know how I've been since Jeremy died…emotionally I mean."

"Uh-huh…"

"Well, lately I've experienced feelings I haven't had in a long, time."

Jared leaned forward and took her hand in his. "You mean feelings for Archer? Well, that's good isn't it? I know I had my reservations about him at first, but he seems like an all right guy."

"That's not what I meant. Well… yes, I am experiencing feelings about him, but it's not what you're thinking."

"All right, now I'm confused. What the hell are you talking about?"

"Jared. What would you say if I told you that I can *feel* Daniel's emotions?"

"I would say that you've got my attention. Why do you think that?"

"It's simple, really. When I'm not with Daniel I feel nothing. I feel empty inside. But, when I'm with him I feel whatever emotion he is experiencing-happy, sad, angry, anxious-it doesn't matter. I feel them all."

Jared had to ponder her words for a moment before he could respond. "So how do you know it's only Archer? What about me right now? Can you sense anything?"

She shook her head. "Believe me, it's just Daniel. Once I figured out what was happening to me, I started to keep track of what I was feeling and when. Literally, the only way I can feel anything, is if I am with him. You have an odd expression. Am I making you uneasy?"

"Well no, but I don't know what to say. Have you talked to anyone else about this?"

"You're the only person I've told so far. I would like to discuss it with Kyle, but our relationship has been strained since Daniel arrived. They don't get along at all and I haven't been able to spend any time with him lately."

"Well, talk to Fiorelli if you can, but if anything else happens and I mean anything, let me know right away. Don't wait four weeks to tell me, all right?"

"Yes, I will. Oh, I almost forgot, there is one more thing. I finally found something on The Passer." She reached into her purse, producing a piece of paper.

"You're kidding me. You're still researching that? I thought you had given up."

"I almost did when I discovered that woman's website in Germany was down, but I went ahead and bought one of her books. It finally arrived a few days ago. You should see it. It's huge and it reads like a text book, but I skimmed through it and found this. It's estimated to be written around 1000 A.D. and is of Irish origin, probably Celtic. I realize it's a translation, but the words *The Passer* appear."

The Great Vessel will be awakened from great suffering and will come
Bearing the memories of the ancients and their wondrous gifts
The portal of the dead will open and the worlds will be united
The reign of The Passer will begin

"The author's name is Dr. Helene Manning," Eleanor said. "She runs an institute in Berlin that specializes in esoteric wisdom. Her website is back up now. I can send you the link to it if you like."

"Just write it down for me. So, this sounds sort of religious."

"It is. The book is focused on ancient mystical teachings and religious symbolism. According to Dr. Manning this is a prophecy of some kind. Most likely it's an excerpt from a much larger work. She doesn't explain the meaning of The Passer, but more that there was a group of people that believed in its existence."

"So, are you telling me that Bellaso was into some obscure ancient religion?" Jared said.

"It's possible. If you remember the vision, Monica said to Lourdes that all this was meant to be. That The Passer will come. This excerpt from Dr. Manning's book pretty much says the same thing. That the reign of The Passer will begin."

"But what does it mean other than something is awakening and the portal of the dead will open? Actually, it sounds a little creepy to me."

"I found it in a section of the book that dealt with reincarnation, so maybe it has something to do with that."

"Really… huh …" Jared's phone beeped several times. "Sorry. We gotta go. I appreciate you looking into this, but I'm not sure how this can help me right now."

"It seems to me that if we can figure out what The Passer means, we might discover the reason why that man came after Monica."

"I'm not so sure Eleanor. Lourdes didn't even know what the hell Bellaso was talking about. For all we know she could have believed in some religious mumbo jumbo that had nothing to do with why she was murdered."

Eleanor sighed. "All right, let me do some digging through the book and see what I can find. So, how is the investigation going?"

"Things are better with Detective Bellows, but she's struggling just like we are. We've got the CIA helping us now."

"Why is the CIA involved?" she said.

"Well, since Monroe spent a lot of time in Eastern Europe, we need some eyes and ears over there to help us figure out what she was doing. She was the master at covering her tracks."

"Yes, I know. Daniel reminds me of that daily. Most of the time he's angry, which means when I'm around him, I'm angry too."

"That can't be very pleasant," he said.

"It isn't. We fight a lot, but it's been great for the show."

✷✷

Amelia gripped her father's hand as the stage door flew open. They emerged onto the landing and were greeted with whistles and cheers as they descended down the steps that led to the parking lot. When they arrived they were surrounded by uniformed men and women who escorted them to a long row of tables.

The size of the crowd was overwhelming to Amelia, and it took every ounce of strength she could muster to block out the thousands of voices that were flooding her head. She did her best to maintain a smile as the long line of people filed by to ask for her father's autograph. To her surprise, both Eleanor and she had to sign several programs as well, and she wondered if this is what it would be like if she were to become famous someday. The idea of having to deal with all these thoughts and feelings, day after day, made her stomach queasy. Soon her defenses began to weaken and she was no longer able to block out the noise.

Trevor, who was standing next to her, whispered in her father's ear. Then Trevor took her hand and led her back into the building. Inside he guided her down a long corridor of dressing rooms, around the back hallway and into the costume shop. Thankfully, the large room was dark and void of human minds.

"Can I stay here until we go to the cast party?" she said.

"I don't see why not. I'll just text your father and let him know. It's all right Amelia. It happens to all of us," Trevor said, smiling.

"Not you."

"There have been plenty of times I've struggled with the noise. It's hard sometimes, especially when there are crowds like tonight."

"Some of those women were having mean thoughts about Daddy and Eleanor."

"You have to learn to tune it out little one. If you don't, you'll go mad."

"I'm worried about Eleanor."

Trevor sighed. "You know we can't do anything about that, not until she says something to us first."

"But she doesn't know what's happening to her."

"We don't know that."

"I do."

"Oh Amelia, have you not listened to a word of what your grandmother or I have said to you? You are not supposed to be listening in to people's thoughts unless it is an emergency."

"It is. She's scared and she thinks something is wrong with her."

"Well, that is troublesome. I have to admit that she is quite unusual."

"Why?

"Well, first off there is her age. Most of us come into our powers when we are young, usually around the age of eight.

"I was four," Amelia grinned.

"Yes, I know, and we're all suffering for that. Then there is the question of what she is exactly. I can't tell. She feels entirely different from anyone I've ever known. Also, I don't understand why no one is reaching out to her."

"You mean…"

"Don't say it, don't even think it. It's bad enough we're discussing Dr. Bouchard in this way."

"I want to help her."

"You can't little one. However, given the circumstances, I will talk to your grandmother and seek her advice. You know, since the moment I met her, she has seemed familiar to me." His cell phone beeped. "It's your dad. We need to go, but before we do I want your word that you will not interfere with Dr. Bouchard in any way."

"Oh pooh Trevor, you're no fun."

"My job is to keep you out of trouble, not to have fun. Now, do I have your word?"

Amelia reluctantly said yes and followed Trevor out of the costume shop, all the time with her fingers crossed behind her back.

Chapter Nineteen

I am a spirit of no common rate;
The summer still doth tend upon my state,
And I do love thee. Therefore go with me.

"Amelia, that's enough," Eleanor said. "Put the script down and finish your breakfast."

"But it's funny when you fall in love with Bottom."

"Yes, I know. I can see you grinning on stage every night during that scene. Please eat your eggs before they get cold."

"I'm not hungry," Amelia frowned, pushing her plate aside.

"It's all right honey. Your father is going to be fine."

"He's been on the phone a long time."

"I know. These calls with Detective Bellows always seem to take a while. Let's go outside."

They wandered onto the sprawling front porch, choosing to settle on a large wooden bench. Eleanor had watered the front gardens earlier that morning, and the flowers were glistening in the sunlight. For the longest time Amelia was silent, staring down at the ground as she dangled her legs.

"If it's too warm, we can go inside and watch TV," Eleanor said.

"I like it out here. It's pretty."

"I'm glad you think so, though I'm surprised you didn't want to stay in Edmond for the Fourth of July celebration."

"I like your house better."

"Yes, but I wonder how much that has to do with the bears."

Amelia grew still.

"I thought so," Eleanor said. "Honey, please do not go roaming near those woods. It's dangerous, and if your father catches you he most certainly will not let you come back here for the rest of the summer. I would hate for that to happen."

"Daddy doesn't understand," Amelia said.

"What doesn't he understand, honey?"

"He's not like us."

"What do you mean?"

Amelia started to speak, but stopped, emitting an exasperated sigh. The front door flew open, and Daniel appeared on the porch, bleary eyed. Amelia jumped off the bench and ran back into the house. They could hear her pounding up the stairs to the upper level.

"What's wrong with her?" Daniel said.

"I'm afraid she knew you were on the phone with Detective Bellows."

"Great." He closed the front door and started pacing. "What a mess. First off, Lourdes just surfaced a few days ago."

"Is he back in New York?"

"No, he's in Russia, which is ironic, because Bellows just discovered that Kate was there this past January *with him*. I guess some tourist who recognized Kate got a picture of Lourdes and her in Moscow during that time frame. The trip was completely buried. There aren't even any stamps in her passport. And the worst part is she did it while I was filming in Berlin. I remember when she came to visit me. It was a complete surprise. She stayed a few days and afterward I thought she went back to New York. Turns out I was just a damn pit stop."

"You don't think anything was going on, do you?"

"I don't know what to think anymore." Daniel stopped pacing and leaned against the railing chewing at his thumbnail. "You remember me telling you that Kate and I were having problems when I saw you in San Francisco? Well, it was because of Lourdes. The whole thing started about a month before I saw you. I was with Michael when it happened. You remember my agent, don't you?"

"Yes, of course. Michael was my agent too."

"That's right. Anyway, one night, Michael and I were getting off the elevator in my building and we saw Lourdes leaving the apartment. He took the stairs and when we got inside we found Kate in tears. Then she tells us that Lourdes had shown up unannounced with some crap story about needing to discuss something with the foundation. Long story short, he made a pass at her. Well, as you can imagine, I was ready to go after him right then, but Kate stopped me. Then she made both Michael and me swear to never tell anyone what happened."

"Not even her father?"

"Especially not Phillip, she didn't want to upset him or cause any problems for the company. I was furious. After Michael left, Kate and I got into a huge fight. I think I slept in the guest bedroom that night. The next morning when Lourdes arrived at his office, I was waiting for him."

"Oh God, what happened?"

"I gave him a bloody lip, that's all. He didn't even put up a fight and obviously he never reported it. After that he kept his distance from Kate. At least I thought he did. Looks like I was wrong." Daniel plopped down on the bench. "Bellows tells me that the woman who turned over the photo just wanted to help. Hopefully we can keep it out of the news for now. Phillip already knows, and he's working with his lawyers on how to handle it. Of course, Lourdes showing up in Russia all of a sudden isn't helping anything."

"Do they have any idea why he's over there?"

"Nope. I guess he hasn't contacted Phillip since he disappeared."

"Well, technically he is on a leave of absence," Eleanor said.

"You sound just like Phillip. What the hell is it going to take for everybody to see what a scumbag he is? He's lying about what he knows about Monica's death and now he's lied about his relationship with Kate. He told the police they hardly ever spoke. I guess that wasn't true."

"You should check on Amelia."

"Yeah I will. Once I calm down." He studied her face. "You look a little pale. Did you have breakfast?"

"Yes I did- yogurt and fruit."

"We should stop at the restaurant before we go canoeing and get something to eat."

"I have plenty of food packed for our trip. Speaking of which, I should pull the rest of our supplies together." She started to stand and he pulled her back.

"You look tired. I heard you roaming downstairs last night. Is it your insomnia again?"

"You know I've always been a light sleeper."

"You also used to sleepwalk. God, you used to scare the shit out of me when I would wake up and discover you were gone. Remember that time you managed to unlock the front door and take the elevator down to the lobby. I about had a heart attack when security called."

"No, I don't remember the episode. But what I do recall is that you barricaded our bedroom door at night, which I thought was rather extreme."

"It kept you from walking down Sixth Avenue naked."

"Well, I wouldn't worry anymore. I haven't done that in years."

"What, sleepwalking or sleeping in the nude?"

"May I go now?" she said.

"Not so fast." He pulled her to him. "I would like to kiss you first if that's OK."

She knew he would not wait for her to answer. His mouth was on hers, and before long he was working his way down her neck, forcing her to push him away. She started for the front door and he picked her up as he crossed the threshold.

"What are you doing?" she said.

"I'm going to help you get ready."

"No, you're not. Please go check on Amelia."

"I will, just as soon as we…" he stopped, his eyes widening. "What the hell?"

She looked out the kitchen door and saw Amelia outside on the deck, talking to a man who was standing in her backyard.

"Where's your gun?" he said.

"In my bedroom closet… why?"

He released her, taking off for her bedroom. She rushed towards the deck, and as she drew closer she immediately recognized his favorite T-shirt.

"Jeremy!"

By the time she threw open the doors, Jeremy was gone, and a large black bear was barreling across the yard. Daniel rushed onto the deck carrying her shotgun, and she stopped him from taking aim.

"It's all right. He's gone now." She went to Amelia, whose eyes were fixed on two dark figures that were moving among the trees. "It's all right honey. I don't think he meant any harm."

Amelia began to speak, but stopped as Daniel approached.

"We should go if we're going to make this canoe trip." Daniel handed Eleanor the shotgun and picked up Amelia. He was silent as he carried her into the house.

Inside her bedroom closet, Eleanor placed the gun on the back shelf, and gathered up the items she needed for their outing. She wandered into the room, tossing the supplies on the bed and looked out the window into the back yard.

I know I saw you. I'm sure of it.

Her eyes fell on the picture of Jeremy that was sitting on her nightstand. Picking it up, she ran her fingers over the glass and considered Amelia's reaction. The child did not appear to be frightened at all by the animal, and if anything she seemed frustrated that the bear ran away. Eleanor began to wonder if Amelia had seen Jeremy as well.

She sat on the bed, staring at his piercing blue eyes and thought about the significance of Jeremy appearing on this day. They had always spent this holiday in town watching the fireworks with Alex Leesman and his family. Then she thought about their last Fourth of July together and a chill came over her.

She turned Jeremy's picture over and unlatched the backside of the frame. Attached to the underside of the photo was a folded piece of paper. She removed it, glancing briefly at the grainy black and white image before refolding it and placing it in her purse. Someone entered the bedroom, and she turned to find Daniel staring into her closet.

"No way all these clothes are yours," he said.

"They aren't. Most of them are Jeremy's. The man loved his clothes."

Daniel disappeared into the closet and she quickly reassembled the picture frame, placing it back on the nightstand. He returned holding a garment bag.

"Is this your Ophelia costume?"

"Yes. Alex brought it with him when he left Julliard. I have my Juliet costume as well."

"Bet this still fits," he said.

"I highly doubt it," she said.

"There's only one way to find out."

A few minutes later she emerged from the bathroom wearing a white and hunter green gown. Daniel made her turn several times.

"God, you look the same as you did when you were twenty." He placed his hand against her back and began to dance with her. "I fell in love with you while you were wearing this dress."

"Is that so?"

"You walked out on that stage and opened your mouth to speak and I was sunk. You were so beautiful and talented. And yes I know you were too young for me, but I didn't care. After the opening night performance, the night of our first date, I about lost my mind. I'm sorry to say I did not hear a single word you said during dinner, because all I could think about was your perfect mouth and how it would feel to press my lips against yours."

Eleanor sighed. "God, you really know how to woo a girl, don't you?"

He kissed her. "Sorry about the gun, but that bear scared the crap out of me. Why do you think they keep coming back?"

"They've never been this close to the house before. They must sense we have food."

"Well at least Amelia minded me for once and stayed on the deck, but I told her from now on, one of us has to be with her when she wants to go outside. I still don't trust her to not run off and do something stupid."

"I imagine she doesn't get to see this sort of wildlife roaming the streets of New York."

"No, that's for sure." They continued dancing. "Do you ever miss it?"

"What?" she said.

"New York?"

"Occasionally."

"When does school start for you?"

"Classes begin the end of August."

Daniel stopped and held her face in his hands. He was nervous, which in turn made her nervous, and she was certain it had to do with what he was about to say.

"I want you to come back with me to New York after the season is over, for the Labor Day weekend, or longer if you can. You can stay with us. We have plenty of room and you won't have to fly commercial-private plane, both ways."

The question took her by surprise. She had not considered how her relationship with Daniel or Amelia would work past the summer, and before she could respond a high-pitched squeal sounded in the hallway. They turned to find Amelia running towards them with open arms. Daniel picked her up, and immediately she pleaded with Eleanor to say yes.

"What do you say, Ellie?" he said. "You're long overdue for a visit."

Leaning her head against Daniel's shoulder, Eleanor considered all the reasons why she should or should not go. But, when she met Amelia's crystalline gaze her decision was made for her.

"Yes. Yes, I'll come to New York."

❈❈

Kyle powered off his recording equipment and ascended the stairs to the main level. The townhouse was quiet. Trevor had opted to spend the holiday with his friend, Frank Bishop, instead of accepting Kyle's offer to travel down to San Francisco. Eleanor, along with Archer and his precocious child, was in River Mist and Nina had been gone since early morning, leaving him to spend the Fourth of July alone. He sauntered into the kitchen and opened a case of Pinot Noir that he had shipped up from Carneros. Then he went upstairs to take a leisurely shower before he went out for dinner.

It was a pleasant evening for a stroll through downtown Edmond. The temperature was warm and the streets were filled with people claiming their spots for the fireworks. Thankfully, all the restaurants were open to accommodate the influx of visitors and as Kyle wandered into The Wine Bistro, he found it humming with diners. He went directly to the bar, ordered a glass of wine and was surprised to discover Jared Adams at the other end nursing a beer.

"Care to join me?" Kyle said.

Adams glanced over, appearing to consider his offer as his eyes wandered across the crowded restaurant. Finally, he shrugged his shoulders, picked up his beer and sauntered over.

"So, why are you alone?" Adams said.

"I'm not alone now." Kyle emptied his glass and ordered another drink.

"If you're looking to get drunk, I'd try something a little stronger."

"Really, and what do you suggest?"

Jared smiled and motioned for the bartender.

A few vodka martinis later he was feeling pleasantly intoxicated and Adams seemed to be in a mood to talk. They ordered dinner and Kyle was able to convince the scrappy detective to sample a Bordeaux wine. The steward presented the bottle and after sampling the first pour Adams expressed his approval.

"There's hope for you yet," Kyle said.

"Believe me, I'll take a glass of vodka over this anytime, but I'll have to say for four hundred dollars, it's not bad."

"I really never understood what my father saw in you. Still sees in you."

"My irresistible charm I guess."

"No, I think we both know that's not it."

Adams emptied his glass. "Well, it doesn't really matter anymore. I haven't talked to him in a while."

"It was Christmas," Kyle said. "He went outside to make the call and was gone for thirty minutes. I recall this because I had to spend the entire time listening to Josephine and Eleanor arguing with their mother about whether or not they should sell their family home. It was mind numbing."

"How did you know he was calling me?"

"Because when he left the house he had a hopeful look in his eye, and when he returned it had been replaced with something melancholic. I guess he just can't give up on you."

"Then maybe you should tell him to stop wasting his time," Adams said.

"It's funny, but he and I have never discussed why you really left. I know the official explanation that was passed down, but he has never shared it with me personally."

"Now why do I find that hard to believe? You two have been together a long time. I would imagine you know everything."

"He's always been very guarded when it comes to you."

"There's no big secret to reveal. I discovered the truth about what was really going on inside that fortress of yours and after that I just couldn't stay."

"Our way is to protect and nurture our fellowship," Kyle said.

"Which is bullshit because I know your real purpose is to amass power and wealth."

"I admit we are a political organization first and foremost, but our members join us willingly and freely I might add. And as you can attest, they can leave us at any time."

"I'm not so sure about that."

"Really Adams, this paranoia of yours is so annoying. I saw how you checked out the room before you joined me."

"What about Jeremy?"

"What about him?"

"He tried to leave."

Kyle leaned over his glass, contemplating his next words very carefully. "Whatever happened to Garrison had nothing to do with us. We do not engage in that type of activity nor do we turn on our own."

"If that's true, then why haven't you tried to find out why his car went sailing off a two hundred foot cliff?"

"How do you know we haven't?"

"You're right. I don't know." Adams stood, retrieving his wallet.

"Garrison was a brother," Kyle said. "And we continue to treat him as one."

Adams nodded. "What about Eleanor?"

"I told you before. There is no need to be concerned."

"You're here. I have every reason to be concerned."

"It's not like that, Adams. Eleanor is …"

"What? Special? Tell me something I don't know."

Kyle polished off his drink and then asked for the bill. "Tell you what. Why don't you and I go outside and finish this conversation. I would love to have a cigarette."

"You're kidding. I didn't know you smoked."

"I don't. But I've been thinking about taking it up in this lifetime."

※※

It was dark when Kyle returned to the townhouse. As he entered the kitchen there was a distant boom and a vivid display of multi-colored streams lit up the sky. He grabbed the bottle of Pinot Noir he had opened earlier and stumbled out onto the deck.

His mood had improved considerably since his encounter with Adams. The conversation had gone better than he expected. And although Kyle did not share in his father's devotion to the sullen detective, he still enjoyed his company. Once he sobered up he would have to call his father with the good news.

Sleepy from his one too many martinis, he sat in a lounge chair and closed his eyes. The fireworks continued to sound and somewhere between the crackles and booms he heard Debussy's *Claire de Lune* playing in the distance. At first he thought it was an interesting choice to use for a Fourth of July celebration, but as he listened carefully, he realized the music was coming from next door.

His eyes shot open and he glanced over at Nina's backyard. The lower level light was on, the sliding glass door was open, and Nina was standing there watching the display. His first inclination was to call out to her, but he decided against it, instead opting to quietly observe her from his drunken perch. Suddenly she turned to him waving, and his body heated up.

"Would you like to watch over here?" She pointed towards her upper deck and then disappeared into the lower level of her townhouse. Grabbing the bottle of Pinot Noir, he tumbled down the stairs and into the backyard, passing through the rose-covered arbor connecting the two properties. He arrived on her deck just about the time she appeared with a bottle of wine and two glasses. His mouth dropped open when he saw the label.

"Where did you get that?" he said.

"France."

"I know where it comes from, how did you get it? That's an extremely limited production and very expensive."

"I have a wine cellar you know."

"Yes I heard. Are you sure you want to open it?"

"Why not, I have more."

Kyle watched with amazement as she opened the rare bottle of Burgundy and poured him a taste. He glanced up at her as he lifted the glass to his lips, and he could see the glow of the fireworks reflecting off her glasses.

"Is it OK?" she said.

Kyle choked. "Yes, it's quite fine."

She filled their glasses, decanting the remainder, and sat across from him.

"So what's the occasion?" he said.

"Who needs one to drink wine?"

"I mean what is the occasion for opening this extraordinary bottle?"

"I knew you would appreciate it, unlike Eleanor who doesn't care what I give her."

"I'm surprised that you didn't go with her to River Mist."

"I didn't feel like hanging out with Archer and his kid. Plus, it's boring."

"I take it you don't care much for the life of a small town."

"This place drives me nuts. I've tried to get Eleanor to move, but she won't go."

"You could always move without her?"

Nina looked up at the sky, sipping her wine.

"I heard the music that was playing earlier. It's one of my favorite pieces," he said.

"Do you know it?"

"Yes. I've performed it dozens of time when I was on the concert circuit."

"Where does your music come from?" she said.

"Do you mean creatively?"

"I mean the melodies. Where do they come from?"

"From inside my head, I suppose. I just hear things and write them down."

"What about Amelia's song?"

"Ah yes," he said. "That one has been floating around for a while. About two years ago I started to hear these unusual sounds. At first I wasn't sure what it was, it kept playing in my mind almost like background music. I tried to write it down a few times, but I could never quite capture it and then one day… it shot right through me, like a symphony. After that, the sounds were a part of me and when I agreed to write the music for the festival, I knew I had to find a way to express it. So tell me, do you like the song?"

"It reminds me of home."

"San Francisco?"

"No. My mother's home."

"Which is?"

"Far away." She turned her attention back to the fireworks.

"Well, if my music is a pleasant reminder then hopefully I earned the honor of sharing this incredible wine with you. By the way I love your outfit. Is that Versace?"

Nina glanced at him. "Why are you really here?"

"I could ask you the same question."

"I'm here because of Eleanor."

"So am I. Funny how we're both here for the same reason, yet Eleanor is not with us. Why is that? What does that say about you and me and our status in her life?"

Nina picked up the decanter and filled their glasses. He swore he saw a slight smile cross her lips.

"Are you hungry?" she said. "How about I fix us something to eat?"

✖✖✖

Jared sat on his deck nursing a glass of vodka while he watched the remnants of the fireworks linger in the air. For the past hour he had been mulling over his conversation with Fiorelli, trying to determine what prompted his sudden openness. He would like to think it was the numerous martinis they consumed, but Jared knew better. Fiorelli had planned for that discussion to happen, and he knew exactly what he was going to say and do, including the brilliant move of asking Jared if he could bum a smoke. Now the dilemma before Jared was how much of what Fiorelli told him tonight was he going to accept as the truth.

He lit a cigarette, peering out into the darkness.

First there was Jeremy Garrison's accident. Fiorelli admitted that his organization had considered it suspicious and that an investigation had been conducted. Finally, there was someone else who believed his best friend's truck had been purposely run of the road that night. Unfortunately, it was the same group of people Jared thought had been responsible for Jeremy's accident all along. Fiorelli told him that they were *in simpatico,* or whatever Italian word he used that Jared didn't understand, and that the organization would find out who did it and bring that person or persons to justice.

Then there was Eleanor. Fiorelli was not as forthcoming as he was with Jeremy, but he did confirm that he was there to watch over her.

"Is she one of you?" Jared asked.

"You mean one of us?" Fiorelli smiled as he inhaled his cigarette.

"I'm not like you."

"You're such a snob, Adams. Just because you prefer to throw caution to the wind doesn't make you that different. But the answer to your question is no. Eleanor is not like us. She is, as you said before, special."

"How special?"

Fiorelli dropped his cigarette to the ground, crushing it beneath his shiny brown loafer. "I'm afraid it has been a very long time since I smoked and I'm feeling a bit light headed. I should go."

"I don't get it. Why won't you tell her?" Jared said.

"We can't. Not until she is ready."

"Ready for what?"

For several moments Fiorelli seemed unsure how to respond. Then he met Jared's eyes, speaking in a solemn tone. "There is a message that Dad wanted me to give you when I thought the time was right. I think now would be appropriate. He wants you to know that he thinks of you as his friend and that the fellowship still considers you a brother. The door is *always* open."

"You know I'll never come back."

"Just as you know that I cannot answer your question."

Jared took a drag off his cigarette as he considered the many ways he could respond to Fiorelli. In the end he decided it was not worth it and turned away, heading towards home.

The smoke from the fireworks had finally cleared and Jared could see the stars twinkling above. He thought about Fiorelli's message and realized the sole purpose of their dialogue tonight was an attempt to lure him back into the fold. Fiorelli had shared just enough information to capture his attention, but not enough to help him with the Bellaso case. If he wanted answers then there was only one way to get them.

Crushing his cigarette into one of the several ashtrays littering the deck, Jared went into the kitchen and pulled a bottle of vodka out of the freezer. As he filled his glass he seriously contemplated whether or not he should call his former mentor. Then he shook his head, laughing. Fiorelli must be congratulating himself right now. He knew Jared would be tempted.

Secrets and Lies. There was no escaping it.

He took a long drink from his glass and pulled out his cell phone, his finger hovering over the speed dial key. Suddenly the screen lit up and he was shocked to see the caller's name.

"Mik, are you all right?" he said.

"Hey Shug, I'm outside your house."

"What?" He rushed over to the front window, checking for her Mercedes. "I see you. Come on up." When she entered, he saw that her eyes were swollen. "What happened to you?"

"Do you mind if I sit?" She did not wait for him to answer and flopped down on the couch, leaning forward on her knees. "I could use a drink. You know how I like it."

A few minutes later he returned with a vodka martini on the rocks with a twist, and placed it in her shaking hands. She took a few sips and then set the glass on the coffee table.

"Ben and I have separated."

"When, tonight?"

"No, last week, I should have said something when I saw you the other night, but the truth is I haven't told anyone yet. That's why I'm here. Ben's over at the house tonight with the kids and I told him I was going over to my mom's, which is a lie of course. I was thinking of sleeping in the car, and then I thought of you. The only reason I called was because I saw the kitchen light go on."

"How long have you been outside?"

"About an hour."

"God Mik I'm so sorry. Do you want to talk?"

"I just need to sleep first, and then yes I would like that. Can I crash on your couch?"

"You take the bed, I can sleep here."

"Seriously, I'm so tired it doesn't matter. I'll finish my drink and be asleep in no time."

"Let me get you a pillow at least." He returned a minute later with a pillow, blanket and an old T-shirt. He managed to scrounge up an extra toothbrush, which he set on the bathroom sink, and then he said good night.

As he lie awake thinking of her sleeping just a few feet away, he realized he had not hugged her. In fact he had not touched her at all. He hoped she was not upset by his coldness. This had become his defense mechanism over the years, the only way he could ensure he did not get both of them into trouble.

Then she appeared in his doorway, wearing his T-shirt that hit her about mid-thigh. She sat on the end of the bed, one leg resting near his foot, the other dangling. Slowly he sat up, his heart pounding in his chest, and he was reminded of why he left his former life behind. At that moment all thoughts of calling Fiorelli's father left him.

"I want to thank you for helping me through all this mess this past month," she said.

"Mik, you know I would do anything for you."

"Yeah I do honey, but I'm sure it hasn't been easy listening to all my problems with Ben, especially given our past."

"Has he told you why he wants to separate?"

"You know Ben. He doesn't like to talk about his feelings. Something happened to him after Jeremy died and he hasn't been the same since."

"Do you still love him?"

"Yes, I think so."

"Then you should try and work things out."

"I know, but he doesn't want to work things out, and I don't think I want to either."

Silence passed between them as she searched his eyes.

"What is it?" he said.

She crawled across the bed and sat next to him. "I've been thinking a lot about you lately, about us, and I realize that Ben leaving me is a good thing. We haven't been happy together for a long time, and I haven't been brave enough to admit it." She ran her fingers through his hair. "I still care for you Shug, and the truth is I've never really stopped."

"I don't want to start an affair with you," Jared said.

"Oh honey, who said anything about an affair?" She swung her leg over his body, straddling his hips, and pulled her T-shirt over her head.

Chapter Twenty

Be as thou wast wont to be;
See as thou wast wont to see.

Detective Sheila Bellows walked through the quaint terminal of the Alexandria airport, attempting to contain her smile. Though his back was turned to her, she immediately knew the man dressed in head to toe black, talking on his cell phone, was Detective Jared Adams. When he turned, she was surprised by his boyish face, despite his five o'clock shadow.

They shook hands and he guided her to the exit where a dark gray Camry pulled up to the curb. The trunk popped open and Adams took her suitcase while he opened the passenger side door. She got into the car and was greeted by a cheerful Hispanic man who introduced himself as Tommy Reyes. Adams slid into the back seat, rolling down the window. Bellows turned to him as he lit a cigarette.

"I can sit in back if you like," she said.

"No need, we're not going that far."

Detective Reyes drove to the middle of the lot and parked. Then he pulled out a camera with a telephoto lens and pointed it at the airport entrance.

"Do you mind if I ask what we're doing?" Bellows said.

"You didn't get my text? There's been a change of plans. Zach Walker is scheduled to arrive any minute and I want to see where he ends up. How was your trip?"

"Long. Do you realize what a pain-in-the-ass it is to get here?"

"Yeah, it's a bit remote," Jared said.

"I can't believe Archer hasn't gone nuts out here. He's lived in New York longer than me."

"I think he's happy that he can fly under the radar for now. Other than that moron photographer that showed up the night he arrived, no one has bothered him. I think our guy has arrived."

Bellows turned and recognized Walker's shaggy gray mane as he emerged from the airport with a limousine driver in tow. Two young women approached him while he waited for his luggage to be loaded, and soon he was signing autographs.

"Unbelievable. He's old enough to be their grandfather," Bellows said.

"As long as he's putting out music they want to hear, the kids don't care how old he is."

"What is really perplexing to me is how Katharine Monroe, an accomplished actress and patron of the classical arts ever intersected with Zach Walker at all, let alone procreate with him. It doesn't make a damn bit of sense to me."

"I'd have to agree with you on that one," Jared said as he flicked his cigarette out the window. "So is Lourdes still travelling through the Ukraine?"

"Yes, as far as we can tell. If he ends up in Moldova then it's official. He's following the same path as Katharine Monroe. However, we still have no clue what he is doing. He continues to keep one step ahead of the CIA. I did get some good news, though. Dirk, my contact at the CIA, told me they can get the security camera recordings from the hotel where Lourdes was staying last January. If we can get evidence that Lourdes and Monroe were staying together, then I'll be able to prove that he's been lying about his relationship with her."

"We have something to share as well," Adams said. "Go ahead Tommy. Show the detective what you've got."

Detective Reyes produced an envelope, removing several documents that turned out to be personnel records from a now defunct Canadian oil company. Upon examination she saw that they were for an Edward Xavier Lourdes, the father of Charles Lourdes. She scanned the work history and stopped when she got to the year 1967.

"Lourdes lived in Russia?" Bellows said.

"Yes, for four years," Reyes said. "His father was transferred there when Lourdes was seven years old. They lived in Moscow, but Edward Lourdes traveled throughout Russia for his work. We were able to get a copy of his entire file, which is mostly performance reviews, salary history and so on. However, there was also a report about an incident that occurred while they were living in Russia."

Detective Reyes went on to explain that in the summer of 1970, Edward Lourdes and his son Charles were on a fishing trip about 40 miles outside of Moscow, and during that trip the boat capsized. Charles nearly drowned. The report stated that the boy was incapacitated for quite some time, at least a year, and that he also suffered from amnesia. The family had to return to Canada earlier than planned so Charles could continue his rehabilitation.

"I don't understand," Bellows said. "Why is this even in his employment file?"

Reyes continued. "If you read through the report it appears that the local authorities had to get involved and there was some sort of investigation. The company had to send in a lawyer to help, but it doesn't list any details. Just that it happened."

Bellows examined the document. "The town where the accident occurred is called Dmitrov. I'll ask the CIA if they can look into what happened. Maybe they can find something that can help us."

"You know what I find fascinating about this discovery?" Reyes said. "In several interviews over the years, Lourdes has referenced this accident as profoundly changing his life. He's talked about it publicly, yet not once has he ever said that it happened in Russia."

Bellows nodded her head. "You know what I find ironic, is that he had amnesia before. What are the chances of that happening twice in a lifetime? This is good work gentlemen."

Adams flicked his cigarette out the window and announced that Walker was finally leaving. The limousine pulled away and Reyes followed, maintaining a casual distance. Bellows pulled a compact from her purse, quickly checking her lipstick and hair. She glanced at Adams from her mirror and thought that the pictures she had seen of him online did not do him justice.

Eleanor had just finished brushing Amelia's hair when the doorbell rang. The child bolted down the stairs, throwing open the front door to reveal Kyle Fiorelli. Groaning, she went into the living room and planted herself in front of the window. Eleanor motioned for Kyle to enter.

"Sorry, she's a little anxious right now. Zach was supposed to be here forty-five minutes ago. Thanks for coming over. Would you like some coffee?"

"Did Archer make it again?" Kyle said.

"Yes, I'm afraid so."

"Then I'll pass."

Amelia announced that Zach had arrived, and she bolted from the town-house. Eleanor and Kyle followed her to the limousine where the driver opened the back door, allowing her to hop in.

Walker laughed. "Well, I guess she's ready to go. Sorry I'm late. There was a little tie-up at the airport. You must be Eleanor."

They shook hands and then she introduced Kyle.

"Well, Miss Eleanor, not only are you beautiful, but you seem to attract some mighty fine men. You know, I think I might have worked on one of your soundtracks once, Mr. Fiorelli. It's hard to say anymore. My memory isn't what it used to be. So what time do I need to have the munchkin back?"

Eleanor gave him instructions to have Amelia home by 5:00 that evening and waited as the car drove away. A gray Camry that was parked across the street soon followed.

"Is that Jared's car?" Eleanor said.

Kyle shrugged his shoulders. "Let's walk into town for coffee, my treat. So, I noticed Trevor left early this morning. I'm assuming he's with Archer."

"Yes. Daniel had several errands to run before his workout, but really I think he didn't want to be present when Zach picked up Amelia. Despite his willingness to foster this reunion, he's not comfortable with it. But, it's important to Amelia and he would do anything for her."

"Well, despite our differences, I feel for the man. This business with Kate has to be taking its toll."

"You called her Kate?" Eleanor said.

"When I met her that's how she introduced herself. I guess I've always called her that."

"So how did you two meet?"

"After I graduated from Julliard I spent some time in San Francisco before I started my master's. I ended up assisting her with a fundraiser she was chairing for a local theater group."

"What was the company?"

"The Bay Area Shakespeare Festival. My cousin Alex was involved with them, which is how I got roped in."

"I remember that group. Jeremy used to perform with them, didn't he?"

"Well, he was already in New York by the time I got involved, but that's right. That's how Alex met him."

"Do you think Jeremy knew Katharine Monroe?"

"I don't know. Like I said, by the time I got involved he had been gone for a few years."

They arrived at the Main Street Coffeehouse and stood in line at the carryout window.

"What was Katharine like?" Eleanor said.

"She was beautiful and very generous to everyone around her. I don't think there was an unkind bone in that woman's body. Her mother is an entirely different story."

"You know Christine Monroe?"

"I had the misfortune of crossing her path a few times. She is not a pleasant person."

"Daniel has told me stories. She'll be here in a week and I have to say I'm very nervous about her visit."

"Oh I'm sure Christine will find you a breath of fresh air," Kyle said. "You're smart, highly educated, and from what I can tell her granddaughter adores you."

"But that's what worries me the most. Amelia and I have grown very close in a short amount of time, and I can't imagine she won't take exception to that."

"So is that why you've been roaming outside at night."

"How do you know about that?" Eleanor said.

"You forget I'm a night owl. Are you having trouble sleeping again?"

"A little, mostly I just like the quiet. It gives me time to think."

"Really, anything in particular if you don't mind me asking?"

"Well, there is one thing. Lately, I've started to wonder what it would be like to live somewhere else, besides here."

"What, are you finally thinking about joining your sister when she returns?"

"Not San Francisco, though it would be nice to be closer to Josephine. I was thinking more along the lines of Boston. I visited there several times when Josephine and Nina were in college, and I always loved that town. My aunt lives there and I could probably get a teaching position without too much difficulty."

"And it's not too far from New York."

"Yes, that's true."

"Eleanor, you've known the child for what- seven weeks? Are you really ready to move across the country for her?"

"I know. It's completely irrational, but I can't help it. I feel connected to her in a way I've never experienced before, not even with Jeremy. It's as if somehow we belong together."

"Does Archer know you feel this way?"

"He recognizes that she and I have grown very close, but he doesn't know about this. And I'm not going to tell him either, not until all this madness with Katharine is over."

"So how is it going with Archer?"

"Nothing has changed. He never talks about his wife unless it's in reference to the murder investigation. He's very angry and frustrated, but he tries to hide it so he won't upset Amelia. He's also full of pain, which he denies, but I know it's there."

"I'm sure you're very sympathetic. You understand his suffering."

"It's more than that Kyle. I know *exactly* how he feels, all the time."

They approached Nina's townhouse, and Eleanor saw her car pass by with Daniel behind the wheel. She closed her eyes as he pulled into the driveway.

"Don't worry," Kyle said. "He didn't hit anything. He's getting out of the car now and heading into the house. Trevor looks a little haggard though."

She opened her eyes in time to see Daniel glare at her before slamming Nina's front door.

"I'm sure that was for my benefit," Kyle said.

"He doesn't like you, and I don't know what to do about it."

"My work here will be done in a few weeks, and then we won't have to worry about that. So, I know he's filming in LA next, any chance of you coming down to visit while he's there? You could stay with me. Heaven knows I have plenty of room. Maybe Nina could come along. I'm sure she would have fun celebrity watching."

"So you're referring to her as Nina now," Eleanor said.

"That is her name."

"I've noticed you two chatting on occasion. Care to comment?"

"What can I say? Both of us seem to have a little more free time these days. I should go check on Trevor. He looked more peaked than usual, as do you by the way. Did you skip breakfast this morning?"

"Kyle, what I said earlier about Daniel, about knowing how he feels… there is something I need to tell you."

At that moment the front door to Nina's townhouse flew open, and Daniel leaned in the doorway, his arms crossed.

Kyle sighed. "It will have to wait, mia cara. That is my cue to exit stage right."

❈❈

Adams and Bellows sat at a front booth in The Bayside Cafe observing Zach Walker and Amelia Monroe in the guitar shop across the street. The aging rocker and his estranged daughter had spent the past hour examining several instruments and Jared was beginning to think that they would never leave.

"Good God, how many of those things is he going to have her play?" Bellows grumbled. "We'll have to order lunch if we stay here much longer."

"You know," Jared said. "I was thinking about what you said earlier about Katharine Monroe and Walker. It does seem strange that those two would ever cross paths."

"It's as if she purposely sought out the most undesirable person she could find. The guy was a known drug addict and had just come out of a long stint in rehab when she met him. Then she turns up pregnant within the first two months of the relationship. It makes no sense."

"It would if she was already pregnant."

"That's exactly why Walker ordered a paternity test. He thought for sure it was Archer's kid. Which is incredibly ironic, don't you think? It's like she had to get pregnant with someone else in order to get Archer's attention. That's another thing I don't understand. Of all the men in the world Monroe could have had, she picks that prima donna to marry."

"Archer's not that bad," Jared said. "Yes, he's a little rough around the edges and has a bit of a temper, but he appears to be very devoted to his daughter."

"So what's going on with him and Bouchard?"

"They all seem to be getting along well, including the girl."

"I find this relationship very intriguing," she said.

"Why, because they were married before, or that he is here so soon after his wife died?"

"Both. How did you know about the marriage, did Bouchard tell you?"

"Her boyfriend let it slip that he knew, which by the way needs to stay between you and me."

"You told me about him." Bellows pulled out a notepad from her bag. "Jeremy Garrison. He died in a car accident last year. You two were friends."

Jared leaned back in his chair. "Lifelong friends, until he died of course. Also, Eleanor loved him very much and she's still suffering over his death, which I suspect is why Archer is here. She is sympathetic to his pain. Make sure you make note of that too. Walker's ride is here."

A limo stopped in front of the guitar shop and the driver got out, rushing around to the opposite side of the car to open the door. Jared expected Walker and Amelia Monroe to emerge from the store, but instead a tan, blond woman took the driver's hand and stepped out onto the sidewalk. Immediately his cell phone went off. It was Reyes, and Jared gave him instructions to stay put. He signaled for the check.

"Did you know Angie Miller was going to be here?" Bellows said.

"No. She hasn't been back since we questioned her in early April, right after Bellaso went missing."

"Hopefully they aren't staying at her place."

"They won't. She turned over the keys to us. The house is ours until we're done with it."

The check was delivered to the table as Jared and Bellows watched Walker exit the guitar store. Amelia Monroe and Angie Miller followed after him, conversing.

"Now that's an eerie scene," Bellows said. "Probably the last two people to see Monroe before she was attacked, standing in the middle of nowhere with her kid."

Jared was silent as he considered her statement. In his mind they were not in the middle of nowhere. They were standing on ground zero, and the answer to solving both murders lay in the reason for Bellaso's visits to the area. Walker and Amelia Monroe entered the crosswalk, heading towards the restaurant.

"We should go before they see us," Jared said.

He escorted Bellows toward the back exit. They were nearly halfway across the restaurant when a piercing scream silenced the lunchtime crowd. All heads turned toward the front and Bellows took off running for the entrance while Jared called for help. As he raced to catch up, he saw a dark blue sedan barreling down on the crosswalk, sending Amelia Monroe and Zach Walker flying onto the pavement. Seconds later there was another scream and Angie Miller disappeared.

When Eleanor entered the townhouse Daniel took her hand, leading her to the kitchen. On the island was a bottle of Champagne chilling, and he poured two glasses, handing one to her.

"What are we celebrating?"

"We're alone for once," he said. "I take it Amelia got off OK?"

"Yes. Zach took her into to town. How was your workout?"

"Good, I guess. What were you and Fiorelli up to?"

"We went to get coffee."

"We have a full pot here you know." Daniel's eyes narrowed as he took a drink. "So, are we still going out for lunch?"

"Yes."

"Then I guess I should get cleaned up."

He topped off their glasses before leaving and she stood in the kitchen, alone, wondering what had just transpired between them. When she first entered the house she had clearly felt his anger, yet as he brushed by her on his way to the foyer his frustration had given away to resignation. It was not like Daniel to give up so easily. Something was going on.

By the time she entered her bedroom and saw the large, white box laying on her bed the emptiness inside her had returned. She removed the short mustard colored dress, and held it up. Jeremy would never have bought her anything like this- mainly because she showed no interest in clothes- but Daniel did not care. If he wanted to see her in a dress, he was going to buy it for her whether she wanted it or not. She pondered all the reasons why she should not wear it, but in the end she slipped out of her shorts and T-shirt and pulled the sleeveless sheath over her hips.

He was still in the shower when she entered his bedroom, and she wandered over to his nightstand, her eyes settling on a picture of Katharine Monroe. Immediately she was drawn to her crystal blue gaze.

She picked up the photo, focusing on the necklace Katharine was wearing. Recently, Amelia had been probing Daniel about the heart-shaped pendant. Apparently it was Katharine's favorite and Amelia wanted to know what happened to it. At first, Daniel told her he had no clue as to its whereabouts. That answer did not seem to satisfy Amelia and she kept at him, until one day, in a fit of exasperation, he told her the truth: her mother was wearing the necklace the day she died and it had been damaged. Amelia then asked if he could get the necklace fixed when they returned to New York. Daniel shook his head and told her it was broken beyond repair, and that he did not want to discuss it anymore.

The bathroom door opened and Daniel appeared, shirtless. "You found the dress I see." He took the picture frame and motioned for her to turn around. "You don't mind the open back?"

"Not at all, it's very pretty."

"And it's not too short?"

"It's fine," she said.

"Because, if you hate it we can just take it back and get something else."

"I said the dress is fine. Will you please put on a shirt so we can go to lunch?"

Her request did not produce the response she had hoped for, and he wrapped his arms around her waist, pressing her against his bare torso. His sullen mood was still with him.

"What is up with you?" she said. "You've been acting strange since you got home."

"How is it you look so young and I look so old?"

"Stop it. You know you're good looking."

"But I'm going to be fifty."

"Fifty is not that old. Besides, you're in better shape now than when you were thirty."

"Really...then how about we just skip lunch and see what kind of shape I'm in?"

She did not dare look into his eyes, and instead focused on his broad, well-defined, chest. She may have lost the ability to feel her own emotions, but she still had the sense to recognize that his body was extraordinary. She was numb, but she was not blind.

Still, when he laid her on the bed, the sensation of his magnificent form pressed against her was not enough to stir something inside. To make matters worse, she knew what it was like to be with Daniel. And although she did not consider herself an expert- as she had only slept with two men her entire life- she remembered that sex with him was very good. In fact, it was wonderful.

She stared up at the ceiling as his hands slid beneath her dress. Every muscle in her body tightened and she realized it was his tension moving over her. Closing her eyes, she let go of any inclination to fight against his emotions and allowed them to flow into her veins. His hands moved over her hips, removing her panties and she told herself she could do this, as long as she kept her focus entirely on him. She took a deep breath, preparing to unfasten his jeans, when he surprised her by kissing her inner thigh. Startled, she flinched, and he looked up.

"Is something wrong?" he said.

"It's just been... a while."

"You're kidding me. How long?"

"Not since you and me."

He studied her face for a moment before continuing. His mouth moved between her legs and she started to stress over how she was going to make this work. It was one thing if they made love, but this was an entirely different matter. Her heart clamped down, till she could hardly breathe and she was worried she was having another anxiety attack.

Then suddenly everything went dark and she found herself in the middle of a crosswalk with a dark blue car racing towards her.

"Amelia!"

Daniel's cellphone went off as her scream lingered in the air. She did not wait for him to tell her to get dressed. As his panic tore clear through her, she raced down the hallway and grabbed her purse. Seconds later they were in her Subaru speeding towards Edmond Memorial Hospital.

※※

Eleanor sat in her dressing room, examining the abrasions across Amelia's nose and cheek. "It's going to hurt, are you sure you want to do this?"

Amelia nodded and Eleanor applied several dots of cream foundation to her face. "I still can't believe this happened. Who is this man and why was he after Angie? There take a look. What do you think?"

"You made the bruises go away."

"For now, here let me do the rest." Eleanor located an eye pencil from her makeup case. "I didn't ask you earlier, but before the accident were you having a good visit with Zach?"

"He bought me a guitar."

"I know. Hopefully when his wrist heals he can teach you how to play."

"Zach is different," Amelia said.

"Yes, he's much different than your father, but once you get past the long hair and tattoos, I'm sure you'll find something you have in common. He loves music and singing just like you. Maybe you can start with that."

"He's not like me."

"That may be true, but he very much wants to be a part of your life and I hope you'll give him a chance. He did just save your life a few hours ago."

Amelia sighed. "Zach will never be like me."

Eleanor stopped applying Amelia's makeup and met her watery gaze. "Honey, what's wrong? Why are you crying? Did something happen between Zach and you?"

"I have to tell you something. Don't be mad."

Eleanor grabbed a tissue, catching the tears as they rolled down Amelia's cheek. "Why would I be mad at you? Honey, just tell me what it is."

"You're like me," Amelia sniffled. "We're the same."

"I'm not sure I understand. How are we the same?"

"I can feel things, just like you." Amelia laid her hand over Eleanor's heart. "I can feel when people are happy or sad, just like you do with Daddy."

Eleanor placed her hand over Amelia's and took a deep breath. She tried to respond but she could not.

"I can see things too," Amelia whispered. "I saw your friend at your house."

"My friend?"

"You have his picture in your bedroom."

"You mean Jeremy? You saw him?"

Amelia nodded. "Are you scared?"

Eleanor was silent while she processed Amelia's words. In the space of a moment her entire world had changed, and she realized she was not alone. Someone shared in her affliction. "Does this mean I'm not going crazy?"

"No silly. You're one of us. And soon Nana will come to help you."

"What do you mean? Who is Nana?"

At that moment she was filled with panic and her dressing room door flew open. Daniel towered in the doorway, clenching his cell phone. "The Monroes have changed their travel plans, and they're coming here tomorrow. You two better prepare yourselves."

He plopped down next to her, rubbing his eyes. Amelia moved alongside him, stroking his beard until his body relaxed. His panic vanished, and then he looked at his daughter, sighing.

"Thanks baby girl. You always know how to make Daddy feel better." He kissed her on the cheek and then left as abruptly as he came.

Amelia's crystalline eyes met hers, sending a shiver down Eleanor's spine. "Nana is Mrs. Monroe, isn't she?"

Amelia smiled. "Yes, and she will help you to be just like us."

Chapter Twenty One

Thou art as wise as thou art beautiful.

Jared leaned against his car smoking while he waited for Bellows to emerge from The Milton House Inn. His favorite Steely Dan song played, and he pulled his cell phone from his pant pocket.

"Hey Sunshine," he said.

"Hey Shug. Where are you?"

"Working. Are you still in bed?"

"Yes."

"What are you wearing?"

"The same thing I was wearing when you left me."

"That'll get me through the day. When are you heading back to River Mist?"

"I need to take off in about an hour. So, I'll see you at the restaurant later, right?"

"I don't know Mik, you sure about this? What if Ben suspects something?"

"Look Shug, Ben will suspect something if you don't show up. Besides, who cares? He's the one who asked for a divorce, not me."

"I know, but I don't want to rock the boat right now. Speaking of which, where does he think you spent the night?"

"It's none of his business, but if you must know I told him I was at my mother's. Come on honey, can I at least tell Eleanor about us?"

The front door of the inn flew open and Bellows emerged, dressed in a black suit with a folder tucked under her arm.

"Look, I gotta go. I'll talk to you later." Jared ended the call and flicked his cigarette to the ground. He darted around to the passenger side door to open it.

"Really Adams, I'm a cop, not your girlfriend."

"Sorry, habit of mine."

"Yeah, I guess not too many females on the force, huh?"

"There are a few deputies."

"Right, look, sorry I'm late. I was waiting on a call." Bellows slid onto the front seat. "Remember that building on Fifty-Seventh Street we had under surveillance, the one where Gus Fenton did several electrical jobs? We've been trying to get a tenant list for the past month and kept running into roadblocks. Finally we got something today, but it's not complete."

Jared started the car. "So, what's been the problem?"

"Someone high up is protecting that building, which is why I had to wait for my call this morning. My boss had to get the mayor's office involved. Believe me, it wasn't pleasant. I just hope I don't have to write my resignation letter when I get back."

"What are you talking about? Are you in trouble at work?"

"Not yet," she said. "But, if this case continues to go on like it has, I will be fired."

"I'm sure your chief knows how difficult it's been to investigate these murders."

"I wouldn't be so sure about that. I never had a case that was as screwed up as this."

Bellows folded her arms, turning her attention out the window. Sadly, Jared agreed with her. Their cases were entirely screwed up. Four months into the investigation and the only thing they really knew for certain was that Monroe and Bellaso had been involved in some sort of activity over in Eastern Europe that got them killed. They had no solid suspects, and even though they believed that Lourdes was withholding information, they did not have enough evidence to arrest him.

At that moment Jared wished he could share everything he knew about Bellaso's murder with Bellows. He wished he could tell her about the vision and the strange warning that Bellaso gave Lourdes. How he longed to express to someone his fear that Eleanor was connected to Bellaso's death, and that she might have been the reason Bellaso was in River Mist. But he knew he could not.

He turned to Bellows who was still staring out the window, fuming. He thought about reaching over and giving her an assuring pat on the arm, but he figured she would probably slap him. So he rolled down the window and had a cigarette instead.

When they arrived at Edmond Memorial Hospital they were met by Tommy Reyes, who informed them that Angie Miller had been cleared to be interviewed. However, their window of opportunity was short as the doctor who was treating Miller wanted to transport her to Los Angeles for neurological tests.

Jared and Bellows entered Miller's room and found Zach Walker lounging in a chair next to her bed.

"Hey guys. Angie baby, look who's here?" Walker said.

Miller slowly raised her lids. She glanced at Bellows before turning her sleepy gaze on Jared. "Zach told me everything you did for us. Thank you."

"Luckily we happened to be across the street at the time. You were supposed to let me know if you were in the area," Jared said.

"I'm sorry. It was a last minute decision to come here. I couldn't even get on the same flight with Zach." Angie's eyes fluttered closed for a moment and then opened again. "I'm afraid I'm having a hard time staying awake. We should get on with your questions."

"Of course," Jared said. "So far our description of the driver is a little spotty, since most of the witnesses on the street, including Ms. Monroe and Mr. Walker, only got a partial view. You were the closest to him when he tried to pull you into the car, and we're hoping you could provide us with more details."

"I can provide you with more than details," Angie said. "I know who he is. His name is Karl and he's the brother of my ex-husband."

Bellows stepped forward her eyes widening. "Angie, what are you talking about? You don't have a husband."

"Yes, I'm afraid I did," Miller said.

"But you never mentioned it before and he didn't show up on any of your background checks either."

"That's because we were married in Russia and we never made it official in the States. I'm sorry I didn't tell you, but I didn't think it was relevant."

Bellows started to speak, but suddenly stopped and signaled for Jared to continue.

"Ms. Miller, do you know where we can find Karl?" Jared said.

"No, I don't know where he is, but there's something you need to understand about him. He's very limited cognitively. I'm not even sure why he is still here. My ex-husband was his guardian, and I figured he would have taken him along when he left California."

"So, is Karl's last name Miller then?" Jared said.

Angie shook her head. "Miller is my maiden name. I never changed it when I married, and I'm assuming Karl had the same last name as my ex-husband, though I can't be certain. My ex-husband never shared that with me."

"All right," Jared said, rubbing his eyes. "What is your ex-husband's last name?"

Zach reached for Angie's hand. There was a long moment of silence while she appeared to struggle with her words.

"What is it Ms. Miller?" Jared said.

Angie looked at Zach, her eyes filled with tears. He encouraged her to go on, but she shook her head. "I can't. I swore I would never speak his name again."

"Ms. Miller. Karl almost killed Mr. Walker and attempted to kidnap you. We need your help finding him."

Bellows, who had been standing with her arms folded, approached the bed. She surprised everyone when she placed her hand on Miller's shoulder. "Tell us what is frightening you."

Angie looked up as the tears rolled down her face. Then she pulled back the bed sheet to reveal several round dark scars covering her legs. Jared and Reyes moved closer, examining what appeared to be dozens of cigarette burns.

"These aren't the worst," Angie said. "I can show you more if you like."

Bellows shook her head as she pulled the sheet back over Miller's legs. "I assume that your ex-husband did that to you?"

Angie nodded. "We've been divorced for six years now, but the last time I saw him was three years ago in LA."

"So the reason you didn't tell us about your ex-husband is because you're scared of him?" Bellows said.

"I wasn't always the most compliant partner, so a few years ago he found a more willing paramour and granted me a divorce. As part of the deal I swore to never talk about him or his profession, ever."

Bellows nodded. "Angie, I appreciate all that you have had to endure the past twenty-four hours, as well as whatever cruelty you suffered at the hands of this man, but we need your help."

Miller glanced over at Walker, squeezing his hand. "If I do this everything changes for us. He'll come after me and possibly you too."

Zach nodded, promising his support. Miller locked eyes with Bellows and Jared noticed that both women looked terrified.

"It's all right Angie," Bellows said. "Tell us his name."

"Anton. His name is Anton Milin."

Bellows patted Miller on the shoulder and left the room. Jared continued with his questioning, eventually convincing Miller to submit to a lie detector test. He left Reyes to make the arrangements and went in search of her doctor. As he approached the nurse's station he found Bellows speaking with the head of the emergency room, Dr. Gwendolyn Keats.

"Jared you old scoundrel," Dr. Keats winked. "Since when did the sheriff's office finally get with the modern world and hire a woman detective?"

"We didn't. Detective Bellows is visiting from the New York Police Department. Gwen, can you tell me why you want to transport Angie Miller down to LA? Is that necessary?"

"As usual it's straight to business. Yes it's necessary. I'm concerned about something that showed up on her CT scan, and I want a neurologist to take a closer look. I could send her to San Francisco, but I figured since she lived in LA that it would be better to take her there."

"Does she have a brain injury?" Jared said.

"Well, she has damage to her brain, but I don't think it's a result of the accident."

"What do you mean?"

"If you look at the scan there are several areas that are dark and inactive, as if she has had a stroke. However, she appears to be perfectly normal- no slurred speech or paralysis- and from what I can tell her memory is intact. It seems highly unusual to me and I want a specialist to look at her. Also there are two places on her skull that were fractured at one point. It looks to have happened several years ago. She's obviously been abused, and it appears it went on for quite some time."

"How long do we have before you transport her?" Jared said.

"Two hours. Should I make sure we have room for a few of your folks?"

"You know me too well, Gwen. Thanks for your help."

"No problem," Dr. Keats leaned in, whispering. "How's that injury of yours?"

Jared rubbed his eyes. Gwen was the doctor who had sewn up his wound after Eleanor stabbed him. She did not ask any questions and he spent the night. He told her he had recovered completely and took off for Miller's room with Bellows in tow.

"We can't let Angie go back to LA. It's too dangerous," Bellows said.

"Tommy is making arrangements with the LAPD to put them under surveillance."

"What about protection while she's in the hospital?"

Jared stopped in front of Miller's room. "We got authorization for our people to remain with her until other arrangements can be made. Someone will be with her at all times. Do you think you can have your contacts at the CIA run a check on Anton and Karl Milin?"

"That's why I left. My team is on it." She paused as she stared at him. "This changes everything. You do know that?"

He nodded, and for some unexplainable reason he suddenly had an urge to hug her. Thankfully, Reyes appeared in the doorway announcing they had found an address for Karl Milin.

"Holy shit," Jared said.

"What is it? Where is the address?" Bellows said.

"On the other side of downtown, we were parked in front of it yesterday after we followed Walker from the airport."

"You mean over where Archer and his daughter are staying?"

"Yes. The son-of-bitch has been living across the street."

※※

Eleanor stood on the deck outside the Monroes' hotel suite, looking down at the rocky cliffs of the Pacific Ocean. After meeting the stately couple at the airport, they had travelled three miles north to the village of Arlington, where Phillip had rented the top floor of a charming bed-and-breakfast. She heard the sliding glass door open behind her, and Daniel appeared bearing two glasses of sparkling.

"So, what do you think of them so far?" Daniel said.

"Mr. Monroe is very nice. I can't believe what he said about my outfit."

"I told you the dress looked great. What about Christine?"

"She's a lot friendlier than I had expected."

Daniel laughed. "I'll say. She damn near crushed you with that hug of hers. I don't know what it is, but these Monroe women have an immediate attraction to you. So I was thinking. Now that Amelia's grandparents are here, why don't we have her spend the night with them? Give us a chance to be alone."

The sliding glass door flew open and Amelia ran onto the deck. Moments later the Monroes emerged, followed by the owner who was pushing a small serving cart, boasting a bottle of sparkling-compliments of the house. While he poured, the grateful proprietor thanked Mr. Monroe for his business, and then Phillip offered up a toast. As their glasses touched, Eleanor met Christine's crystal blue gaze, and in that moment she felt the same inexplicable connection that she had shared with Amelia since her arrival in Edmond.

At lunch her feelings towards Christine intensified, making it difficult to concentrate on anything else. She did not realize until the server asked her if she wanted a carryout container that she had not touched her plate. When they left the restaurant, Daniel instructed Amelia to ride with the Monroes, and he escorted her to the passenger side door of her Subaru.

"What are you doing?" Eleanor said.

"You just drank your entire lunch and you're in no shape to drive. Give me your keys." He pulled out onto the main street heading towards Nina's townhouse. "Are you OK? You pounded down quite a few back there."

"I had no idea I was drinking that much. I guess I'm just nervous."

"Well, you shouldn't be. They obviously like you, so stop worrying." He reached for her hand. "So, you never had a chance to answer my question back at the hotel."

"I don't know Daniel. You and I are going to have the whole month of August to ourselves. Amelia is only going to be here for two more weeks and I would like to have as much time with her as possible."

"Fine, spend the days with her and the nights with me. You said you were going to give us a chance. So why not just start now."

"I know I did, but you've only been here seven weeks and everything is happening so fast. Don't you think we should slow things down a bit? Give ourselves more time."

"For what? I told you how I feel about you. I'm ready to move ahead."

She leaned against the window, closing her eyes.

"Come on Ellie, don't ignore me."

"I'm not. My head is pounding."

"Stop stalling and answer the question. Are you ready to move ahead or not?"

"I don't know," she said.

"What kind of answer is that?"

"The only one I can give right now. Can we please have this conversation when I feel better?"

"What the hell!"

Daniel slammed on the brakes, sending her head smacking against the window. She opened her eyes to discover that the street had been barricaded in front of Nina's townhouse and there were flashing lights everywhere. Detective Reyes approached the car, signaling for Daniel to roll down his window.

"Good afternoon Mr. Archer, Eleanor. Detective Adams asked that I escort you inside."

"What the hell is going on?" Daniel said.

"I'll let Detective Adams explain. If you two would come with me please, one of our men will see to the rest of your party."

Detective Reyes guided them past a swarm of deputies gathered in the front yard and into the townhouse where Jared was waiting in the living room. He approached them, shaking hands with Daniel before grasping Eleanor's arm.

"Are you all right?" Jared said. "You look a little pale."

"She's not feeling well," Daniel said. "What's going on out there?"

"Come with me. I'd like to talk with both of you before we bring in the Monroes."

Jared led them through the kitchen where Nina was talking with an attractive brunette woman dressed in a dark business suit. They went into the family room where Jared motioned for them to sit on the couch. As he placed a manila folder on the table in front of them, the brunette woman entered the room, and Eleanor was introduced to Detective Bellows.

"A few hours ago," Jared said, "Angie Miller identified the man who hit Amelia and Zach Walker. His name is Karl Milin, the brother of her former husband, Anton Milin. Now we haven't been able to find anything on Karl yet, but when we ran a trace on Anton, we discovered that he is the owner of the house across the street. As far as we can tell, Karl has been occupying the home since late March and prior to that it sat vacant for a year. No one has actually met Karl, as he comes and goes at night, but one of the neighbors did catch a glimpse of him a few months ago and described him as being a large man."

"He's been living here all this time?" Eleanor said.

"Yes, and from the evidence that we found, he was there for a reason." Jared opened up the folder, revealing several photos. "When we raided the house a few hours ago, we found it was empty except for a few pieces of furniture and these."

Eleanor leaned forward examining the pictures. "They're all of Daniel and me."

"There are a few with Amelia, but for the most part you're right. Now, you could argue that he's just some nut job that stalks celebrities, or he's being paid to take pictures of you two, but it doesn't explain why he went after Ms. Miller yesterday, as well as this." Jared nodded and Bellows handed him a large yellow envelope. He removed the contents, placing a single photo on the table. "I'm sorry Eleanor, but I had to tell Detective Bellows."

Her body went numb.

"I don't understand, what is this?" Daniel said.

"Mr. Archer, what I am about to tell you is known to only a few people. Until now Eleanor wasn't able to discuss this with anyone, mainly so we could assure her anonymity, and only this morning I shared this information with Detective Bellows."

Jared pointed to a picture of Eleanor and him standing at the location where Monica Bellaso's SUV was discovered. He then relayed the story that he had contrived in order to explain her involvement in the investigation. He described how she had been travelling home on Route 6 when she noticed a tall, dark-haired woman running alongside the woods on the opposite side of the road. She continued driving east for a quarter mile and came upon a white SUV parked on the south berm with its hazard lights blinking. She decided to pull over to see if the driver needed assistance.

"She saw a large man with blond hair in the driver's seat," Jared said. "He waved Eleanor on and she thought nothing of it. A few days later, after she had watched the Bellaso story on the news, she came to me about what she had seen. At first I wasn't sure how she could help the investigation, but as the search for Monica dragged on without results, we finally asked her to join us at the crime scene. It was then when we decided to expand our search to the north and later that afternoon we found the body."

Daniel sat silent as he stared at the picture of Jared and her. "So, Ellie is the only person who might be able to connect this man to Monica's murder?"

"Well, there is also Charles Lourdes," Jared said.

Daniel squeezed her hand and she felt nauseous.

"I don't get it," Daniel said. "If all this time he's been watching us from only a few yards away, then why did he wait until now to surface? And why go after Angie?"

"That's what we need to figure out," Jared said. "Starting today there will be twenty-four hour surveillance on this house. I'm also assigning a deputy to be with Eleanor and you at all times. You'll need to provide your schedule to us daily, keep your outside activities to a minimum and absolutely no visits to River Mist until we have a better understanding of the situation."

"And what situation would that be, Detective Adams?"

Everyone looked up as Phillip and Christine Monroe entered the room. Jared turned over the photos as Phillip took a seat across from Daniel.

"Help me to understand just what kind of trouble we're facing?" Phillip said.

As Eleanor listened to Jared recap the situation, Christine approached, handing her a coffee cup. She looked into Mrs. Monroe's crystalline eyes and realized they were identical to Amelia's. Daniel tugged on her arm, pulling her attention back to him.

"Ellie, did you hear that? Detective Adams thinks this lunatic isn't acting alone."

Jared went on to explain that Karl had limited cognitive abilities and that most likely he was taking instructions from his brother, Anton Milin.

"Excuse me, but I think I'm going to be sick."

Eleanor shot up from the couch and ran from the family room, barely making it to the hallway bathroom before she threw up. Moments later, Daniel and Mrs. Monroe entered arguing over whether or not Amelia should stay in Edmond. She moved to the sink, splashing cold water on her face. Suddenly, she felt a pair of tiny arms slip around her waist.

"Amelia, stop it, "Daniel said. "Ellie is sick. Go with your grandmother, now."

A yelling match ensued between father and daughter, and soon he was attempting to loosen Amelia's arms, causing her to burst into tears. Eleanor threw up her hand, silencing everyone. She dried her face and then held Amelia until her sobbing subsided.

"It will be all right. Now please do as your father asks, and I promise we'll talk later." Amelia released her, glaring at her father and grandmother before she stormed from the bathroom. Eleanor glanced at Daniel and Christine who had the same wounded look in their eyes. At that moment, she felt very odd about what had just happened and went upstairs to lie down.

A half hour later she was sitting in bed thinking of what she should say to Amelia when there was a knock on the door. Christine entered, carrying a glass of sparkling water.

"This should help settle your stomach."

"Thank you. Is Amelia all right?"

Christine sat on the edge of the bed, facing her. "Well, she would rather be with you, but Daniel convinced her that you need to rest."

"I'm sorry about what happened before. I'm afraid that Amelia and I have become rather attached to each other and it's going to be difficult for both of us when she leaves here."

"Well, I thought you handled the situation with Daniel rather well, though I would have to say that my granddaughter's feelings towards you far exceed a mere attachment. It's obvious that she cares a great deal for you, and I believe you feel the same towards her."

Eleanor nodded in agreement.

"Well then," Christine said, "if I were to separate the two of you now, I doubt Amelia would ever forgive me. Quite frankly, I would never forgive myself for abandoning you, especially in your current state. No use pretending anymore my dear. I know my granddaughter went against my wishes and told you about her abilities and subsequently mine as well, so you'll excuse me if I get right to the point. How long have you been struggling like this?"

"I guess... since Daniel and Amelia arrived. Why are you looking at me that way?"

"Is there no one here to help? No family member like you?"

"I don't think so. What's wrong with me?"

"Nothing is wrong with you, other than you're fighting against your abilities and it's making you sick."

"Can't I just make it stop?"

"No, this is who you are. You must accept it and learn to master the power that it can wield."

"I don't understand? What power are you talking about?"

"Surely, you don't think all this suffering is for naught?"

Christine touched her hand and the after effects of her alcohol laden lunch vanished. Her headache was gone and she no longer felt nauseous. She met Christine's crystalline gaze and was unable to respond.

"There is much you can learn about a person when absorbing their emotions," Christine said. "To understand a human being in this way is to know them better than they can know themselves. And when you have that knowledge you can use it to do miraculous things. If we remain in Edmond, please, let me help you."

"What about Amelia? Is it safe for her to be here?"

"The incident with Mr. Walker was unfortunate, but she was never in danger."

"But Amelia said Zach saved her life."

"And as far as everyone is concerned, that is exactly what happened. Our time together is about to end. Will you accept my offer?"

The door flew open and Amelia rushed in, announcing that Phillip had decided to remain in Edmond for the time being. A smile crossed Christine's lips.

"Well then, I will leave you to rest. Let's go Amelia. Feel better my dear and I'll see you tonight after the performance."

Eleanor made her decision before Christine reached the door. "My answer is yes. We can start tomorrow if you like."

Christine nodded, and took Amelia's hand, closing the door behind her. She then led her granddaughter into an adjacent bedroom where Trevor was waiting. The door shut and Christine folded her arms.

"Obviously you two were not exaggerating about Ms. Bouchard's condition. But, why did you not inform me of the others that are here? Did you really think I wouldn't notice? All right, let's start from the beginning. Tell me everything that you know so far."

Chapter Twenty Two

And sleep, that sometimes shuts up sorrow's eye,
Steal me awhile from mine own company.

The curtain fell on the final performance of *A Midsummer Night's Dream* and a round of cheers exploded on stage. Immediately there was a scurry of activity as the actors embraced each other and the crew prepared to strike the set. Daniel stood in the center of the chaos receiving handshakes and hugs from his fellow cast members while he watched in disbelief as Eleanor and Amelia rushed off stage without him.

When he was able to break away from the celebratory crowd, he made his way backstage and as anticipated he found Eleanor and Amelia conversing with the Monroes. As he neared the group he saw that Christine had her arm around Eleanor's waist, and the two women were posing for a picture. He took a deep breath, attempting to suppress his frustration. Thankfully, Amelia ran to greet him.

"Come on Daddy, Papa wants to take a picture of us in our costumes."

He scooped her up, kissing her on the cheek. "You sang beautifully honey."

"Eleanor said I made her cry."

"I saw that. I guess it's kind of sad having it all come to an end." He glanced over at Eleanor and Christine who were now hugging each other. "Though there are a few things I could do without."

"Do Nana and Papa have to watch me tonight?"

"Yes, for the millionth time. It's going to be a long, mind-numbing rehearsal for Ellie and me."

"You're still going to pick me up?"

"Yes, I told you we would, so just stop getting all worked up about it. What are you going to do when you have to leave here next week? You do realize that Ellie can't go with you, right?" Amelia was silent as she ran her fingers over his beard. "I know you like her a lot baby girl, so do I, but you have to get used to not having her around all the time."

"Why can't we live here with Eleanor?"

He laughed. "First off, this place is in the middle of nowhere. I can see visiting once in a while, but living here? I don't think so. Don't get me wrong, it's pretty and all, but it ain't New York and it doesn't have all the things that you and I love. Not to mention your grandmother would freak, although, the way she's attached herself to Ellie that might not be an issue."

"Eleanor could live with us."

Daniel met her eyes, smiling. "Now, there's a thought. She liked living in New York before, and she probably would have stayed if the boyfriend hadn't convinced her to go. You know, the more I think about it, we could use her visit to win her over, show her what she has been missing all these years. What do you think about that idea?"

"I like it."

"Good. Now all I have to do is plant the seed while we're still here."

"What's that mean?"

"Daddy needs to find a way to bring up the idea now, so she's thinking about it before we go to New York."

"I can help plant seeds."

"Yeah, I'm sure you could baby girl, but I think Daddy needs to handle this one, and for now we should just keep this our little secret OK? Now, let's see if we can pry Ellie away from your grandmother long enough to take this damn picture. I'm starving, and we have to be back here in less than two hours."

Surprisingly, it took very little effort for him to separate the two women, but as soon as the last camera flash had fired, Eleanor left his side, locking arms with Christine as they walked to the dressing rooms. Amelia scurried to catch up with the pair, and as had been the case all week, Daniel found himself alone with his former father-in-law. Phillip walked with him, patting him on the back.

"Don't worry son, it can't last for much longer. Eventually they will run out of topics to discuss."

He ushered Phillip into his dressing room and then slipped behind a screen to change out of his costume. "So, I'm surprised you were able to get away from work. Who's minding the shop while you're gone?"

"Well, there are a few folks that have stepped up since Charles went on leave. But, probably Vic Naumov has taken on the most responsibility. He's been with the company a while now. He's very familiar with our international divisions since he used to oversee them. And like Charles, he's a great negotiator."

Daniel emerged to find Phillip seated on the couch, holding up a picture frame.

"I remember when you had this taken," Phillip said. "Amelia was barely two."

"Kate and I argued over whether or not it should be a black and white, but in the end I gave in. It turned out OK I guess."

"It's perfect. This is my favorite photograph of the three of you."

"So, what happens if Lourdes doesn't come back? Will you stay on?"

"We fully expect him to resume as CEO. In fact, we hope to announce that before the stockholders meeting in September. However, we are working on contingency plans that may, or may not, include me at the helm. Why this sudden interest? Is this out of concern for my well-being, or more that you hope Charles will not return?"

"Both."

"Daniel, I know this business with Katharine and Charles in Russia is upsetting."

"Phillip, don't…"

"Hear me out. It may appear that something was going on between them, but I also know that Katharine loved you very much. She would never do anything to dishonor you."

"How can you say that, knowing she hid all those trips from us? What the hell was she doing over there?"

"I don't know, but I have to believe that she was helping someone in need. That's who she was and you must remember that, no matter how grim it may get." Phillip walked over to the makeup table and glanced at the photos that were attached to the mirror. "When were these taken?"

"Opening night."

He pointed to a picture of Daniel resting his cheek against Eleanor's head while she held Amelia in her arms. "This one is rather nice. You look like a family."

"Phillip, there's something I need to tell you about Ellie and me."

"No, I don't think you need to say anything. It's obvious you have feelings for her, and quite frankly, it's none of my business."

"But you don't understand."

"Yes, I do, more than you realize." Phillip motioned for Daniel to sit and then pulled up a chair next to him. "Other than the day I married Christine, I have never felt such happiness as I did when Katharine was born. The minute I held her in my arms and looked into those beautiful blue eyes, I fell in love. I had a similar experience when Amelia came along, but nothing could compare to the moment when I saw my daughter for the first time. I loved her so much, I still love her, and her presence in my life filled me up with such joy that I didn't realize how full and blessed I was. Now she is gone, and there is a cavernous space so deep within me, that I can barely fathom it."

Daniel reached into his gym bag, producing a bottle of bourbon and two plastic cups. "Sorry, but if we're going to continue this talk, I'm gonna need a drink. Do you want one?" Phillip nodded and Daniel poured two healthy shots. "I know this is going to sound strange, given I've just lost my wife a few months ago, but I can't begin to imagine what you must be going through right now, losing your only child. It must be hell."

"It is. I won't deny it. However, as wretched as I have felt, Christine's suffering has been far worse, which has compounded my misery to the point that I thought I would go mad." Phillip emptied his glass. "This brings me to the point of my morbid ramblings. I have a favor to ask. I need you to leave Christine and Eleanor alone for the remainder of our stay, and let them have this time together."

"What? You've got to be joking."

"I'm entirely serious. This bond that has formed between the two of them is literally saving my life, not to mention Christine's. And for the first time since all this madness began, I think we have a chance of crawling out of the despair that has consumed us. Now, don't think for one moment that I don't realize what is really going on here, both with Christine and Amelia, but I can live with that. Eleanor is a lovely person, who understands our suffering all too well, and unless I'm entirely mistaken she seems to be fine with that."

"Believe me, she's more than fine with it. She welcomes it," Daniel grumbled.

"Well you know the old saying: misery loves company. So, can I count on your help?"

"You know, it's not like Ellie and I are doing that great right now."

"I understand, but it's only for a week. Then we'll be gone and I will be forever in your debt."

Daniel sighed. "All right, I'll back off, but I'm going to have to send Trevor out for more bourbon or I'll never make it through the week."

✖✖

Since Bellows and Adams were not officially on the clock, she allowed him to open her car door after leaving the theater. They had spent the week together, working nonstop, and had decided to take a break to attend the final performance of *A Midsummer Night's Dream*. She did not care much for Shakespeare, but when Adams told her that it was funny and Archer's costume was almost non-existent, she just had to go. Adams turned out to be right on both accounts, and as they drove into downtown Edmond she had to work hard to push the image of Archer's naked torso from her mind before they joined him for dinner.

Originally she had planned to stay in California for only a few days. But, with the discovery of Anton Milin, and his connection to Angie Miller, everything changed. She decided to extend her trip, and that turned out to be an excellent decision as Adams opted to personally escort Miller to Los Angeles.

In between her numerous doctor visits, Angie submitted to several rounds of questioning regarding her relationship with Milin.

Bellows and Adams learned that Miller's parents had emigrated to the U.S. from Russia when she was six years old and when the family returned for a visit 10 years later, she met Anton Milin. He was introduced as a friend of the family and a businessman. He was older than her- nearly twice her age-but the attraction was immediate. She fell in love with him and on that trip lost her virginity.

A year later, after she graduated from high school, she returned to Russia and married Anton. He then sent her back to the U.S. to attend college and paid for her entire education. It was not until she was nearing the end of her final year at law school that she learned of his true occupation, and his expectation that she assist him with his business. That was when the abuse began. It lasted for the next 10 years until they divorced.

When Bellows pointed out that Angie technically had never been married in the United States, and could have left Anton at any time, Angie vehemently disagreed.

"You don't leave Anton Milin. He leaves you. Fortunately, he grew tired of me and moved on to another interest."

"Did he ever marry this other woman?" Bellows said.

"I don't know, but I did get a glimpse of her once. He was in LA and I met him in his hotel lobby. I saw her waiting in the distance. She was young enough to be his daughter and her skin and hair were as white and glowing as a pearl. I remember feeling so sorry for her."

Bellows broke from her thoughts about Angie Miller to finish her vodka martini. She was feeling tipsy and probably was sitting a bit too close to Detective Adams, but he did not seem to care. He was in the same celebratory mood as her, and he leaned into her as he rested his arm on the back of her chair. She could smell the vodka on his breath, and she noticed that despite his heavy smoking he had exceptionally white teeth.

"It's been a good week," Adams said. "The game has changed. We may actually be able to solve our cases."

Bellows laughed. "I love your optimism. Yeah, we discovered this scumbag Anton Milin exists, but the CIA has no clue where he is."

"You're right," Adams said, "but a week ago we didn't even know he existed. Look how much we've learned since then."

While Bellows and Adams spent the past week digging into Miller's past, all sorts of information regarding Anton Milin had surfaced.

As it turned out Anton Milin was of great interest to the CIA. Supposedly, he was the head of a notorious Russian crime family whose empire stretched across most of Eastern Europe. For decades the family had dealt mainly in drugs, weapons and stolen goods, but in recent years sex trafficking had been introduced.

However, even though the CIA knew of Anton Milin's existence, they could not visually identify him. There were no pictures of him, no Russian driver's license or passport. Not even a birth certificate could be found. Technically, he did not exist. But, he did possess an American passport. The identity was stolen, belonging to a Seattle resident who had been missing for 15 years, and the photo was of a man with long dark hair, a mustache and full beard. Angie Miller confirmed the picture was of Anton.

Bellows sighed as she emptied her glass. "All right, I agree we're in a much better place, hence our little soirée here tonight, but we still got a lot of work to do. We have nothing on Karl Milin other than what Angie has told us, and we still haven't been able to find Ivan Milin either."

"I agree. We need to firmly establish how all the Milins are connected."

"The Milin connection...oh, I like that." Bellows pulled out her notepad.

"Seriously, you're going to write that down?"

"Why not? It's perfect. And I believe it's the key to solving these murders."

Adams gave her a questioning look before he nodded. Suddenly his eyes shifted past her and over to a beautiful African-American woman who was approaching the table. The woman sat next to Adams, and he introduced her as Mikayla Garrison, his business partner in a dining establishment they co-owned, along with Eleanor Bouchard.

Intrigued by this new information about her scruffy partner, Bellows listened for a half hour to Adams and his southern belle drone on about their restaurant. It did not take long for her to figure out that this woman was more than a business partner. Maybe it had something to do with them holding hands underneath the table and sharing a vodka martini. Bellows was tempted to write that down on her notepad, but she decided that would really piss off Adams and slipped it back into her bag instead.

Yes, she was mildly irritated to discover he had a girlfriend, but she did not care. Adams was right; it had been a great week. Her chief was very pleased with her progress, Adams seemed less sullen, and she was definitely in a very good mood.

She ordered three shots of *Jewel of Russia* vodka, chilled, and after passing one to Mikayla, Bellows toasted to Adams and their week together. His arm was still resting on the back of her chair and for a brief moment his hand rested on her shoulder.

❈❈

It was midnight when Eleanor broke from her reading and glanced at the clock. Amelia was next to her, sleeping, while the other side of the bed remained empty. Ever since the discovery that someone was watching them, Amelia had given up all formality of sleeping in her own bed and went directly to Eleanor's room every night. Daniel took to roaming the hallway, occasionally opening the bedroom door to check on them. Finally, after two sleepless nights listening to the floors and doors creak, she suggested he bunk with them. He had slept with them every night since.

She threw off the cover and started downstairs. It had been nearly two hours since they arrived home from rehearsal and she wondered where he had gone after speaking with the deputy on duty. When she found him he was passed out on the family room couch with a glass resting on his chest. Carefully, she removed the drink from his hand, as well as the empty bourbon bottle sitting on the floor, and deposited them on the kitchen counter top. She returned with a blanket and placed it over him before turning out the light.

Settling in a chair next to the couch, she watched his impressive chest rise and fall in the darkness. He was a ruggedly attractive man, she thought, with his round, expressive eyes, square jawline and prominent nose. Now that his beard was trimmed and his hair shoulder length, he looked like some large, mythical being from one of his recent movies. No wonder every performance of the show sold out. Who would not want to sit in a dark theater for two hours and stare at his magnificent body? Yet, he was not Jeremy, whose eyes could melt her insides with just one glance.

Jeremy. How she missed him. Ever since his Fourth of July appearance in her backyard he had been constantly in her thoughts.

Jeremy was different from Daniel in so many ways. He did not require a great deal of attention, but he knew how to lavish it on others. He would do anything to help his friends and expected little in return. He could build houses, as well as cook up a storm, and most certainly he knew how to make a good cup of coffee. Yet, most importantly, no matter how tired or run down he may have been, every night he would lay next to her in bed and assured her of how much he loved her. They lived a dreamy, uncomplicated life, until two years ago when their perfect world fell apart.

Don't do it. You promised yourself not to go there.

She emerged from her thoughts to find Daniel snoring very loudly, and she decided to get some fresh air. In the refrigerator she found a bottle of her favorite Syrah rosé, poured herself a glass and wandered out onto the deck. It was a beautiful summer night, warm, with a gentle breeze blowing in from the bay. The mist had not moved in yet so the sky was still clear. She laid down on the chaise lounge, losing herself in the millions of twinkling lights above, and after several sips of the ruby colored wine her eyelids grew heavy.

It was there in that moment between consciousness and sleep that she felt him. His lips pressed against hers and she immediately recognized his kiss. She wrapped her arms around him and they shared in a lengthy embrace before she opened her eyes to find his piercing blue gaze.

"Are you really here or am I dreaming?" He said nothing as he began to work his way down her neck. "Please Jeremy, I need to know. I can't tell the difference anymore." His hands moved over her bathrobe, lingering on her breasts for a moment. He kissed her again before he stood, extending his hand. "Where are we going?"

He smiled as he descended the steps into Nina's backyard, moving towards the woods. She rushed after him. "Jeremy, I'm serious. Answer me right now or I'm going back inside." He stopped, just short of the line of trees and turned to her. "Is this all in my head?" He moved in front of her, untying her robe. He pushed the sleeves down her arms until the robe fell around her feet.

"Oh God, I don't care if you're real or not."

She threw her arms around his neck, kissing him with such force that she thought she tasted blood in her mouth. He pulled her into the woods, removing her nightgown as she frantically worked to undress him. They fell to the ground and made love. At least it felt that way to her, and when it was over they lay side by side, gazing at each other.

"I know I can't be with you. I have enough sense in me to realize that, but I don't know how to let you go, and quite honestly, I have no desire to. If I could stay here with you forever I would, even if it meant never waking again. I'm not afraid of death, not if it can be like this: you and me together." She placed her fingertips against his lips. "I wouldn't want it any other way. Except, it would be wonderful to hear your voice again. I love you my darling. I always will."

Daniel was certain it was the pounding in his head that woke him, but when he registered Eleanor and Nina's raised voices in the kitchen, he realized it was their argument that had pulled him from his stupor. It took several moments before he could sit upright and when he did the room was definitely spinning. As he pressed his fingertips to his temples, attempting to ease the throbbing, a painful yell sent him flying across the family room.

When he rushed into the kitchen he found Trevor and Nina standing alongside Eleanor, who was leaning over the sink with a bloody towel pressed against her mouth. As he approached he saw that the back of her head and nightgown were covered with pine needles and dirt.

"What the hell is going on?" he said.

Nina explained she had found Eleanor lying in the woods with blood pouring from her mouth and Trevor joined them when he heard the commotion. Eleanor straightened up and brought her hand to her visibly swollen lip. She took off, and the group followed her to the bathroom, watching from the doorway as she examined her mouth in the mirror.

"You bit on your damn tongue, didn't you?" Daniel said.

Eleanor met his eyes in the mirror and gave a reluctant nod. Then she moaned as she glanced down at her blood soaked nightgown. At that moment his head felt like it was going to explode from within, and he grabbed her hand, pulling her away from the sink.

"Come on. Let's get you cleaned up."

He helped her upstairs to his bedroom where he saw to it that she took a shower. When they emerged from the bathroom they found a clean gown lying on the bed and a glass of water with a bottle of ibuprofen on the night stand. Daniel smiled as he popped two tablets into his mouth.

"Thank God for Nina," he said. "If it wasn't for her you'd probably still be lying in the woods. I want you to take these. You're going to need it for the pain. And, in the morning I want you to call your doctor and make an appointment."

"Why?" she mumbled as she swallowed several pills.

"Why do you think? You're obviously sleepwalking again."

"No, I'm not. I had a little too much wine to drink and I must have wandered into the backyard and didn't realize that I was that close to the trees."

"That's the best you can do? I drank a quarter bottle of bourbon after we got home tonight and you know what I did? I passed out on the couch. That's what happens when you have too much to drink. You know you're lucky you didn't make it all the way down to the bay. You could have drowned."

"You're making too much of this. I'm just tired from rehearsal, not to mention I'm stressed out over the whole ordeal with this man and the pictures." Eleanor plopped down on the bed, burying her face in her hands.

"So am I, but you don't see me wandering around the woods in the middle of the night in my boxer shorts."

"No, but you are drinking a lot."

He sat on the bed next to her. "Yeah, I know I am. But it's not like before."

"Do you mean before when you and I were together, or before you came to California?"

"So that's what Christine and you have been talking about all week? That I was drinking too much before I got here?"

"Christine hasn't said a word to me and she didn't have to either. I could hear it in your voice when we talked at night and I can hear it now. I'm worried about you. You look exhausted, and I've noticed you haven't been to the gym in a while."

"I haven't had time to work out," he said. "I've been too busy entertaining Phillip while you and Christine have your little love fest."

"But I thought you couldn't miss a day between now and when you start filming."

"Well, funny you should mention that, because it looks like they're going to call off the deal, or at least postpone it for now."

"When did this happen?"

"Last week. Michael called to give me the news, something about they didn't have all the funding in place yet. And they're nervous that I may not be in the best mental shape. I guess that incident with Marco got back to them, and I'm sure all this crap about Kate isn't helping either."

"Why didn't you tell me?" she said.

"Why do you think? Besides, I was too pissed off to talk about it anyway."

"I'm sorry. I know this movie meant a lot to you."

"Eh the role is crap. It's the money that made me want to do it. It would have been the most I would have ever been paid, that's for sure, but what the hell. It's probably for the best."

"Why do you say that?" she said.

"I got two, possibly three movies in the pipeline starting in January and this just would have kept me crazy busy for the next year. Now that I got some down time, maybe I can do other things, like spend more time here or you could come to New York. Maybe we could take a vacation during your Christmas break. Paris would be a great place to spend the holidays." Daniel glanced over at Eleanor who was staring at the floor, silent. "You know, maybe you should take some time to think about it before you respond."

"I'm sorry. I'm just a little surprised."

"About what, that I want to talk about us?" he said.

"I'm just surprised that with everything that's going on in your life right now that you want to have this sort of discussion at all."

"What the hell Ellie. We only have a few more weeks left together. I want to know what's going to happen to us after I leave here."

"I understand. But it just sounds like you've been making plans."

"Yeah maybe I have," he said. "But that's what people do when they want something. I want to continue this relationship after I go back to New York and up until a few seconds ago I thought you did too. Now I'm not so sure."

"Daniel, I can't have this conversation right now."

"You can't or you won't?"

"Please, don't make me do this."

"Make you do what? Tell me how you really feel for once? Come on Ellie. There's got to be something you can say. How about you finally admit that you still love him? And you don't give a rat's ass for me."

"Why are you doing this?" she said.

"Because anything would be better than the silent treatment I'm getting right now."

"No it wouldn't. Believe me."

"Why don't you let me be the judge of that? Come on Ellie. Spit it out. Tell me the real reason why you can't talk about us?"

Eleanor stared at him for several moments before she turned on her heels and left. He figured that was it. That was her answer. She was done arguing with him and he could just go fuck himself. He thought about going after her, but he didn't want to risk waking Amelia. So, he went to brush his teeth instead.

When he emerged from the bathroom he was surprised to find her sitting on the bed holding a piece of paper. He sat next to her, glancing down at the grainy black and white image.

Suddenly he felt dead sober.

"Damn…is that you?" Eleanor nodded, and Daniel took the paper from her hand so he could examine it more closely. "The date on here says this was two years ago."

"I miscarried a few weeks before I saw you in San Francisco. I had planned to tell you that night. I really did. But, I could never find the right moment and then when things escalated between us I just didn't think it was appropriate."

"How far along were you?"

"Four months."

"Oh God Ellie, I'm so sorry."

"There's more I'm afraid. Jeremy and I separated for a while. He didn't want the baby and about six weeks into the pregnancy I moved in with Nina. I was still living with her when I saw you in San Francisco."

"So, are you telling me that we were in the same boat that night and we didn't know it?"

"Yes, it appears that way," she said.

At that moment Daniel realized Eleanor was right. The silent treatment would have been much better.

"Ellie, if you had told me about this, it would have changed everything."

"But I didn't tell you about Jeremy and you didn't tell me about Katharine. And that is the point I am trying to make. You and I made a choice that night. That choice was to return to the people we loved. We each had our reasons why we did that, and mine still holds true for me."

"So are you telling me there's no chance for us?"

"What I'm saying is that I care for you, but I can't talk about the future or make plans. I'm sorry, but I'm just not ready for that."

She retrieved the sonogram that he was holding and kissed him on the forehead before leaving. He sat there for several minutes staring at the floor, unable to move.

It had never been easy with Eleanor. As usual he had to drag things out of her, and now as a result of his badgering he was faced with the realization that she had suffered greatly and he had not been there for her. If only he had known. He would have dropped everything to be with her. He would have comforted her and told her she was not alone. He would have taken care of her and given her anything that she needed. But, most importantly, he would have gone after the damn boyfriend and given him a piece of his mind.

If only he had told her that his marriage was falling apart. But he did not. Then he was reminded of that moment when he sat in the parking lot of her school, watching her with *him*. He could have waited till the boyfriend left and confronted her. He could have told her how he really felt. But he did not.

A wave of regret washed over him as his eyes and throat began to burn. He was not sure who he was grieving for more, Eleanor or himself. It did not seem to matter. The tears came all the same, and he fell to his knees, weeping.

Chapter Twenty Three

But I have that within which passes show;
These but the trappings and the suits of woe.

Eleanor released Christine's hands and slumped back in her chair. "I'm sorry, but I just don't have it in me to do this today."

"Let's take a break. Would you like some more coffee?" Eleanor nodded as Christine reached for the pot. "I'm assuming you had another sleepless night."

"I'm afraid so."

"I would have hoped with Daniel out of the house you would finally be able to rest, but obviously this emptiness that you feel when he isn't with you is hindering you in some way. I still don't understand why your reach is limited to one person. Then again, I've never known anyone who has manifested their abilities this late in life, and you do feel different from anyone else I've ever known."

"What is it that makes me so different from Amelia or you?"

"Well, it's hard to describe exactly, but mostly I sense that there is something holding you back, that is limiting your capabilities, and it feels like you've been this way for a long time. I'm sorry to ask this again, but are you positive that your father never exhibited any sort of behavior you considered unusual? Did it ever seem like he knew what you were feeling or thinking before you had a chance to express it?"

"No, I'm absolutely sure he never was like that. If anything, he was a very quiet and reserved man, and my sister Josephine and I could barely get him to engage with us when we were young. It wasn't until we were teenagers that he took a serious interest in us. But, a lot of that had to do with Nina."

"Are you referring to Ms. St. John that lives here? Are you related to her?"

"No, not in the traditional sense, but we might as well be. Nina is a niece of my father's first wife. She died only a few years after my father married her. Dad remained in contact with the family, and the summer before my junior year of high school he announced that Nina was going to stay with us. A week later a young girl shows up on our doorstep."

"That must have caused quite a stir."

"Indeed it did. We quickly learned that despite her childlike appearance, she was in fact almost fifteen years old, the same age as my sister, Josephine. She was smart, loved literature and theater just like Jo and me, and she had lived in Europe, which my sister and I found incredibly exciting, since we had never been there. The three of us became immediate friends. Dad was quite taken with Nina as well. That's when he became friendlier towards my sister and me, almost playful at times, and the four of us began to spend an enormous amount of time together. Unfortunately, my mother did not take the same liking to Nina as the rest of us, and soon the tension started to build between my father and her. They started to quarrel- which was unheard of in our family- and eventually Mom insisted that Nina go back to San Francisco. Dad refused, and the very next day Mom left to visit her family in Boston."

"Oh my."

"I know. She was gone nearly a month, and the sad thing was that even though I missed her, the four of us were having such a wonderful time together, that I was secretly glad she wasn't there to put a damper on things. Eventually, Dad went to bring her home and when they returned, Mom accepted Nina's presence in our lives, although she really never warmed up to her. However, Dad treated Nina as if she was his own, and because of that she became a sister to us."

"So, even with this transformation in your father's behavior, you didn't notice anything else out of the ordinary?"

"Not that I can recall."

"And you are positive your mother and sister are not like you."

"Yes, but I also haven't been around them since all this craziness with Daniel started."

Christine sighed. "I'm not sure you would. You're unable to sense Amelia or me, which is also perplexing."

"Just out of curiosity, what exactly would that feel like?"

"It wouldn't be so much that you would feel our emotions, like you do with Daniel, but that you sense our energy."

"Will I know when it happens?"

"Oh yes. It's not painful, usually, but it will feel like your body is heating up from the inside and the more powerful the individual, the more intense the sensation."

"How many people are there like us?"

"I really don't know. But, what I can tell you is that our abilities are inherited. One of your parents has to have them. Now, let's get back to this emptiness that you are experiencing. You mentioned to me before that it began after your boyfriend died, correct?"

"Yes, but not right away, or at least I didn't notice it until after I recovered."

"Did you get sick after he passed away?"

"No, it was more like I went crazy… literally."

"I see. Go on."

"It started a few days after his funeral. I woke up and Jeremy was sitting on the edge of the bed, smiling at me. It only lasted a few moments before he vanished. The very next day he appeared in the kitchen while I was drinking a cup of coffee. I nearly choked when he sat across from me at the island. He stayed a little longer that time, almost fifteen minutes. The following day he showed up twice, once while I was in the shower, which was a little disconcerting, and then later that afternoon he appeared on the couch and watched television with me for almost two hours. Everyday thereafter his visitations increased both in frequency and duration until soon he was with me every minute that I was awake. Each morning he would be sitting on the bed when I opened my eyes and every night he would lie with me as I fell asleep. We did everything together."

Eleanor paused for a moment, observing Christine's thoughtful expression. "He never spoke. I did all the talking, but he listened and I could tell that he understood. I didn't leave the house for weeks. I stopped answering my phone and I didn't return messages of any kind. Mail piled up in my box, dishes in the sink, and eventually when I ran out of food I stopped eating. I'm told the day Nina and Alex found me I was so delirious that they had to transport me to the coast in an ambulance. After a brief stay in the hospital, I spent two weeks in Alex's guesthouse, and when I finally came to my senses, I realized that something was wrong with me. I figured it was depression and I found a psychologist who specialized in bereavement."

"Did you take medication?"

"Yes, for several months, but I never really felt better, or worse for that matter. I just felt nothing. Eventually I stopped taking the pills and learned to accept the emptiness."

Christine leaned forward, rubbing her chin. "Then Daniel arrives and everything changes. Why? What is it about him that has triggered this in you? Is it because he has also suffered a tragic loss, or is it because the two of you share a past? Perhaps it's both."

"Or it's something else. Maybe all of this has to do with her."

"I'm sorry, has to do with whom?"

Eleanor took a deep breath, exhaling slowly. "On the anniversary of Jeremy's death, I had a dream about him. It was a dream I had been having since he died, but this time it ended very differently. He vanished into the darkness, as he always did, and then there was this brilliant light that raced towards me. Suddenly I was overcome by a radiant, white creature. It hovered over me, like an angel. As I stared into its brilliant eyes my mind was flooded with a million thoughts and feelings, moving through me so quickly I couldn't hold on to even a one. It reached towards my face and I swear I felt it touch my skin. Then it spoke: *help him believe*. Right after that I woke up."

Christine's face was expressionless as she raised the coffee cup to her lips. "Help him believe? What does that mean?"

"Well, that has to do with Detective Adams and what happened next."

Eleanor went on to recount all the events that transpired over the next eight days, starting with the first vision of Monica Bellaso at the sight where her car had been abandoned, to the harrowing experience with Jared in Nina's town house, and ending with how they found the body in the northern woods of Birch Mountain.

"You saw how Monica died?" Christine said.

"Yes, but I ..." A pressure built in her head and she shut her eyes. "Oh my God, what is that?"

Suddenly, she heard an explicative, followed by glass breaking and she opened her eyes to find Christine staring at her, mortified.

"I'm so sorry."

"Christine, it's just a coffee cup."

"No, I'm sorry about what I just did, I didn't mean to, but I couldn't help it. I had to know what happened."

Eleanor had to think for a moment what had just transpired and her heart raced. "You can read my thoughts?"

"Yes. It won't happen again, I promise."

"Oh my God...does that mean Amelia can do that too?"

Christine grabbed her hands. "Please my dear, do not be alarmed. Yes, Amelia has the same ability. But I swear to you we do not make a habit of crawling around a person's head whenever we feel like it. Though I admit my granddaughter has a problem with that sometimes. I assure you that is not our way. Please forgive me."

Christine left, and returned moments later with a dustpan and broom. "So, Detective Adams thinks that the man from your vision is Karl Milin?"

"Yes. He matches the description that Angie Miller gave Jared."

"And now this lunatic knows that you've seen him somehow."

"You got all that from me just now?" Eleanor said.

"No. I overheard Daniel last week when Detective Adams showed the photos to the two of you. Daniel's thoughts are quite loud. So, who else knows about this?"

"Kyle was with us when we found the body, but he doesn't know what we saw during the vision. Jared insisted that we keep that between us."

"I'm assuming when you speak of Kyle, you mean Kyle Fiorelli?"

"Yes. We're close friends. I understand that you've met him before."

"I have," Christine said. "How long have you known him?"

"Eighteen years. We met at Julliard and I've been friends with him and his family ever since."

"I take it you know his father then."

"Christian? Yes, of course. Have you met him?"

"Yes. My dear I think we should suspend our session for today and have an early lunch. I don't want to exhaust you for your opening night."

"I'm sorry. I'm not a very good pupil." Eleanor said.

"Perhaps I'm a terrible teacher, but don't worry, we will figure this out. I promise you. Now, go get ready while I pop next door and rescue Trevor from my granddaughter. I'm sure she has completely exhausted him by now. Not that Daniel is any easier."

"I forgot to ask. How was Daniel this morning?"

"I wouldn't know. He locked himself in his room last night after he came back from rehearsal, and he was still there when I left. Phillip says he found another bourbon bottle in the trash this morning. I think it is best Amelia continue to stay with you until we leave on Monday."

"He barely speaks to me at rehearsal. I can feel his suffering. I want to help him, but I don't know how."

"You're not ready for that sort of thing, my dear. Besides, he's finally mourning like the rest of us. Leave him be for now. Phillip will keep an eye on him, and when we leave Trevor will take care of him, as he always does. You need to stay focused on your own battle so you are strong enough to travel. I plan to see you in New York for the Labor Day Weekend."

"I'm not so sure about that, especially with the way things are between Daniel and me."

"Rubbish. If he won't have you, then you can stay with us. One way or another, you're coming. Now run along and get ready. I'll be back shortly."

Christine was aware that Trevor could feel her fury as she marched up the walkway. The front door flew open before she reached it, and she brushed passed Daniel's baffled assistant on her way to the kitchen. Amelia, who was sitting at the island, shot her a distressed look. They both began to pummel her mind with their thoughts, and she held up her hand, silencing them.

"Trevor, please take Amelia and leave."

At that moment the deck door swung open and Kyle appeared with a glass of wine in his hand. "Well, hello there Mrs. Monroe."

"Run along now you two. I need to talk with Mr. Fiorelli in private."

Trevor helped Amelia off the barstool, and escorted her from the kitchen. She waited until she knew they were safely out of range. "A little early to be drinking, don't you think?"

"Perhaps you would like one," Kyle said.

"No, thank you. Why weren't you at Katharine's funeral?"

"I was unable to get away. Dad was there."

"Yes, I saw him. He was with Alex."

"He said that you were not able to speak with him."

"There wasn't time. What could be so important that you would miss Katharine's funeral? Certainly it couldn't be that you were here, teaching some random class at a university in the middle of nowhere. It doesn't seem very distinguished for a man of your capabilities if you ask me. And certainly Alex could have let you go. He is the head of the school now, isn't he?"

"What point are you making?"

"Why are you here and why won't you help her?"

"Help who?"

"Don't insult me. You know very well I'm talking about Eleanor. It's obvious that she is in the midst of a transformation and as you can plainly see, it's not going very well. She can't sleep, she's stopped eating and she's using alcohol to suppress her empathic abilities. I'm trying to help her, but I can't seem to break through. She needs someone with your expertise to guide her, or I fear she won't make it."

"You've certainly taken quite an interest in her."

"My granddaughter has formed an unusually strong bond with this woman and I have a vested interest in her well-being. What I don't under-stand is if you are such a good friend of hers, why are you allowing her to suffer?"

"Eleanor …is different."

"I've gathered that already. Exactly what makes her different?"

"Well, as you have already ascertained, she is quite old, which presents all sorts of complications."

"Yes, but there's more to it than that, isn't there? I can feel it. She is not like the rest of us. What is she?"

"I'm sorry Mrs. Monroe, but you know I can't answer that question."

"Just like your father. So that's it, you're not going to do anything about this?"

"You do understand the consequences if I help her."

"Let me make this perfectly clear. I don't give a damn about your organization and its superstitious tenants. I'm not going to stand by and let her suffer needlessly. Now, I will continue to help her, but if she deteriorates any further, then I will do whatever is necessary to save her. Am I understood?"

"Perfectly."

"Oh, and there's one more thing. If I ever discover that damn cult of yours had *anything* to do with Katharine's death, I promise I will use every ounce of power that I possess to come after you and your father."

Christine turned and marched towards the hallway.

"Should I tell my father you said hello?"

The front door slammed as Kyle went to the refrigerator and pulled out a bottle of white Bordeaux. He poured an ample glass and stepped out onto the deck to make a phone call. Just then Nina emerged from her lower level grotto, wearing a floral sundress and carrying a garden basket. He was surprised when the voice on the other end sounded annoyed.

"Kyle? Are you there?"

"What? Sorry, must be a bad connection."

"Did you see Christine?"

"Yes. Everything is progressing as we hoped, though she does seem concerned about Eleanor's health. Perhaps I need to look into that."

"We must be patient son. Is there any other news to report with Jared?"

Kyle watched as a gentle breeze lifted Nina's dress, revealing her slender, white thighs. "No. I'll ring you if anything happens." He ended his call with his father and watched Nina clip several stems from a rose bush, placing them in her basket. He considered calling out to her, but instead he started for the door.

"You're back."

The sound of her voice sent a shudder through his body, and he turned. "Yes, I just got in this morning. I can't miss opening night."

"I'm looking forward to hearing your music," she said.

"Well then, I hope I don't disappoint you."

As Nina glided across the backyard he noticed her tiny bare feet. She vanished into the townhouse, and he leaned against the doorway, attempting to rub away the merciless tightening in his chest.

※◉※

Daniel sat alone at his dressing room table, staring at his haggard reflection in the mirror. It was intermission, and his mind was replaying his less than stellar performance during the first half of *Hamlet*. He had dropped several of his lines, was late on one of his entrances, and his Act III confession monologue was so heartfelt that he forgot where he was, requiring one of the crew members to help him off the stage so the next scene could start. Despite all his many blunders, the audience seemed pleased with the performance and the show appeared to be going well.

He leaned forward, rubbing his temples. He wanted a drink, but he had drawn the line at alcohol consumption during performances. Additionally, he still had a nasty hangover from the previous night's binge, which was probably why he was screwing up so masterfully. Then again, a shot of liquor right now would probably relieve the incessant pounding in his head. He reached for his duffle bag, but stopped when he considered how Eleanor would react when she smelled the bourbon on his breath. He pushed the bag away and laid his head down on the table.

Eleanor. His stomach churned as he recalled the painful discussion that had driven him to move into the hotel suite of his former in-laws. They had barely talked since Sunday night, making the week of long, tedious dress rehearsals unbearable. He was miserable, and every night he could not wait to get to the hotel where he locked himself in his room and drank until he could no longer feel anything.

He figured he was consuming a half bottle or more of bourbon a night as he lay in bed watching the television with no sound, thinking. Surprisingly, his thoughts were not of Eleanor but of Kate. For the first time since the funeral, he had allowed himself to dwell on her for hours at a time. Once he got past his anger over her secret trips and the mess she had created for her parents and him, he would reminisce about the happier moments they shared together. That was when he realized how much he missed her.

Life with Kate was always exciting. She was adventurous and had an incredible zest for living, constantly exposing him to new cultural experiences he never would have sought on his own. She was friendly and outgoing and could make small talk with anyone. He had attended more than a hundred fundraisers with her over the years, and he was always amazed at how she could meet a complete stranger and within ten minutes knew everything about that person.

He missed her. He missed her generous heart and spirit that managed to raise millions of dollars for arts and women's organizations across the country. She was the most sought after celebrity in New York, possibly even the United States. She was asked to join boards or chair events, because everyone knew she could raise the money and more importantly they knew she would do it with great devotion.

Yes, he most definitely missed her. He missed her beauty-her golden hair, her crystal blues eyes, and her alluring lips. He missed her glamour and incredible sense of fashion. He missed her grace, her remarkable poise, and her uncanny ability to charm the media hounds. He missed her terribly, and as he laid there each night in his drunken stupor, he missed the sex.

When it came to lovemaking, Katharine was the opposite of Eleanor. There were no excuses, or pushing him away. There were no reasons why they should or should not. There were no arguments, or drawn out conversations, or pleading. There was just sex-wonderful, wonderful sex-and for many years, there was lots of it. Katharine exercised the same excitement in bed as she did in every other facet of her life, drawing the line only at overtly public places. She felt Daniel was too well-known to get away with his early antics, and they limited their adventures to locations where they were sure no paparazzi was lurking within shooting distance. Yes, the apartment served as their most frequent venue, but it did not matter. The sex was intense, playful, and at times a tad violent, and it was always there whenever he wanted, whenever she wanted. It was the one thing they could always count on to bring them together.

There was a gentle wrap on his dressing room door and someone entered. The smell of fresh coffee pulled him from his lusty thoughts, and when he lifted his head he was surprised to find Eleanor standing there with two carryout containers.

"Nina made a run. I thought you might want one."

"Want or need? Sorry about all the screw-ups in the first-half. I should be OK now."

"Your monologue was wonderful. I think you made all of us cry backstage."

"Tears of relief, I'm sure. Thanks for the coffee by the way."

"You're welcome. I should go. Intermission will be ending soon."

She started to leave and he reached for her hand.

"Ellie…" He never got past her name. His eyes welled up with tears and he was unable to stop the sobbing that ensued. She held him, stroking his hair until the stage manager called for places and she was forced to break their embrace. When he pulled away he saw that she was crying too. "I'm so sorry for what happened tonight…for everything."

She pressed her fingers against his lips. "Not now, all right? We have a show to do, and then we can talk."

Reluctantly, he released her and she opened the door, stopping at the threshold.

"Where's Amelia?" she said.

"What do you mean?"

"When she left my dressing room she was coming to see you. Was she here?"

"No. You're the first person I've seen since intermission started. Maybe she went back to her seat."

Eleanor lingered in the doorway for a moment before she rushed off. He sprang from his chair and watched her run down the hallway towards the scene shop. "Ellie, what is it. Where are you going?"

She vanished around the corner and he grabbed his cell phone, punching in Phillip's number. It rang several times before going to voicemail. Christine's cell produced the same results, and as he went in search of the stage manager he realized he smelled something burning. He stopped, sniffing several times, the smell growing stronger by the minute. Then a huge cloud of smoke started to form at the end of the hallway and the fire alarm went off.

"Ellie!"

The hallway instantly flooded with actors and stagehands, all pushing against him as he fought his way back to the scene shop. Soon the back area filled with smoke, limiting visibility and he forced his way over to the inside wall so he could use it to guide him. He made it to the end of the corridor before the burning fog made it impossible to see or breathe. Dropping to his knees, he crawled, calling out for Ellie and Amelia, until he realized that he had gone too far and collapsed. As he laid there choking, his skin burning from the heat, he thought of Kate and his darling baby girl before wishing his one true love farewell.

By the time Eleanor reached the scenery shop, smoke was already pouring into the hallway. She could see that the dock doors were open, allowing people to escape and continued towards the costume shop. For some reason she knew Amelia was in there, and when she burst through the swinging doors, she found the child hiding beneath a large sewing table in the center of the room. She rushed over, bending down to retrieve her.

"What are you doing here? Didn't you hear the fire alarms?"

"Shhh. It's him," Amelia said.

A large figure emerged from the shadows and Eleanor recognized the blond giant from her vision. She spotted a pair of sewing shears, snatching them off the table as she grabbed Amelia's hand. They started for the exit, but stopped when she saw the smoke pouring in through the doorframe crevices.

"We'll have to take the side exit." She spun around with her weapon extended and discovered that Karl was gone. "Where is he?"

Amelia pointed towards the dressing rooms and Eleanor ran in the opposite direction, weaving her way through the maze of rolling racks until she felt a draft on her feet. She looked up, barely able to make out the exit sign through the thickening smoke.

"He's coming," Amelia whispered.

Eleanor rushed to the doors, feverishly searching for the latch. Her hand came across a long cylinder and she felt her way down until she hit the base. She pulled upward, pushing against the heavy metal just as the giant grabbed hold of her.

Amelia screamed as Eleanor was yanked backwards. A thick arm wrapped around her waist, lifting her off the ground, and she aimed the sewing sheers where she thought there would be flesh. After three attempts, she was successful, and her captor moaned, dropping her on the concrete floor.

The doors of the costume shop burst open and she flew down the stairs with Amelia in her arms. The giant was only temporarily slowed by her attempt to wound him, and he was now chasing after them with a pair of twelve inch scissors protruding from his side. There was not enough time to make it to the front parking lot, so she ran into the woods, searching for anything she could use as a weapon. After travelling several yards, she spotted a large rock, securing it just as he appeared.

"What do you want with us?" Eleanor screamed.

When he didn't answer she repeated her question and he took a step forward, grunting.

"He can't hear us," Amelia said.

"How do you know that?"

"Because Ms. Bouchard, the little one knows that he is deaf."

A familiar voice sent her spinning around, and she saw a dark figure standing among the trees. Her belly was on fire.

"Don't be afraid," the stranger said. "I'm here to help."

"I know you from somewhere. Who are you?"

"I am a friend. And if I am to help, then you must do as I ask."

Eleanor nodded and the shadowy presence asked Amelia to use her powers to broadcast her location. Then he told Eleanor to ready her weapon.

"He is stronger than me, but I should be able to hold him long enough for you to escape."

"Please tell me who you are," Eleanor said.

A helicopter appeared overhead, shining a search light into the woods. Karl looked up, snarling, and the stranger gave her the command to strike. She hurled her weapon and took off as the rock smashed into Karl's face. As she rushed away from the teetering goliath her costume got caught, forcing her to stop. She set Amelia down and ordered her to keep running.

As she worked to dislodge her dress from a fallen tree limb, she could still hear the two men struggling. But then their grunting ceased and when she looked over she saw Karl rising. With a mighty tug she ripped free, falling on her hands and knees.

She scrambled to her feet and had only run a few yards when she noticed a white light moving towards her at such a great speed that she thought someone had driven a motorcycle into the woods. When it became apparent it was going to hit her head on, she dove from its path, covering her face as she hit the ground. A tremendous thud sounded behind her, and when she finally looked up she saw Nina standing over her, holding a combat spear.

"Are you OK?" Nina cocked her head to one side.

"I think so. Where did you come from?"

"I saw that maniac chasing after you and I followed him here."

Eleanor turned to find Karl lying face down, blood pouring from his head. "Is he dead?"

Nina walked over, kicking him in the gut. "Nah, he's still breathing. Wait a minute. Are those my good cutting shears?"

The helicopter that had been hovering overhead pinpointed their position, flooding the woods with light. Eleanor scanned the surrounding area, looking for the man who had attempted to stop Karl, but he was nowhere in sight. The fire in her belly was gone. Soon a group of deputies moved in, ordering Nina to drop her weapon, and after several moments of confusion they realized that the man lying on the ground in a pool of blood was the perpetrator, not the five foot tall woman wearing Prada jeans and Stuart Weitzman boots.

When Nina and she finally emerged from the woods, the smoke-filled parking lot was crowded with people and emergency vehicles. One of the deputies escorted them to where Amelia and her grandparents were waiting, and while she exchanged hugs with the thankful trio, she learned that Daniel and Kyle were inside a nearby ambulance receiving treatment for smoke inhalation

Inside the emergency vehicle, Eleanor found the two men conversing, covered head to toe in soot, with tubes attached to their noses. When they saw her, she was greeted with outstretched arms and she spent the next several minutes sharing in a tearful embrace with each man. Nina stood near the entrance with her arms folded.

Finally, Eleanor asked what had happened and Daniel explained how Kyle had found him and saved his life. Then Eleanor relayed her story of Nina's bravery and the men fell silent with their mouths open.

When Daniel and Kyle finished their treatment, everyone gathered in the parking lot, watching the fire. The flames had been tamed and where the scene shop had been there was now a black smoldering hole.

Amelia appeared alongside her, grasping her hand and for the first time in her long acting career, Eleanor realized that the show would not go on.

Chapter Twenty Four

What angel wakes me from my flowery bed?

Eleanor stood in the lobby of The Edmond Airport holding Amelia in her arms. The day they had both been dreading had arrived, and as anticipated it was not a pleasant one. Daniel kept his distance as they spent their final moments together.

"Can I call you tonight?" Amelia said.

"Of course, just remember the time difference."

"And we'll talk every day?"

"Yes, as long as it's all right with your grandparents. Don't worry. Everything is going to be all right."

Amelia rested her head against Eleanor's chest, sniffling. They had been up most the night packing her things, discussing how they would handle this separation. By the time they fell asleep, they had worked out how they would stay in contact, via phone calls and Skype. There was no talk of Eleanor's trip to New York as the fallout from the theater fire had put her decision on hold, and she promised to contact Amelia as soon as there was something to report.

Daniel gave her a wave, letting her know the time had come. Amelia tightened her hold as they moved towards the security check in where the Monroes were waiting.

Phillip approached first, kissing her on the cheek and expressing his hope that he would see her in New York at the end of the month. Christine embraced her next, echoing Phillip's expectation, and then took on the unenviable task of extracting her sobbing granddaughter from Eleanor's arms. Daniel kissed Amelia one last time, and then they waited until the Monroes had passed through the security line before heading for the exit.

Outside, Daniel stopped in the parking lot, his head lifted towards the sky. "God, it's perfect out today. Almost makes me want to live here."

"We don't have to go inland. We can just stay on the coast and enjoy the weather."

"We haven't been to your house in a while."

"It's going to be hot."

"You sound like you don't want to go."

"No, I should go. My gardens are probably in shambles, but it's a forty-five minute drive, we have to get groceries, and you need to be careful."

"The doctor said my lungs are fine. So I wouldn't worry about it."

"She also said you need to rest."

"So where better than your mountain home."

There was a click of a camera followed by hushed voices. Daniel rolled his eyes. "Yet another reason why we should go." He took her arm, quickly escorting her to the car.

They headed east, stopping at a local market on the way. As they passed through the front door they were met with the smell of fresh brewed coffee. Daniel wandered towards the source of the aroma while she grabbed a cart, heading for the produce section.

She threw in several selections of fresh fruits and vegetables before moving to the meat and seafood counter. After buying enough salmon and steaks to keep Daniel grilling for days, she entered the wine section, stopping when she spotted her favorite rosé bubbly from Carneros. Daniel approached, handing her a coffee cup and pulled a bottle off the shelf.

"I think it's a great idea. We got a lot to celebrate."

"Oh really, such as what?"

"Well for starters, how about that they finally caught that lunatic Karl. I think right there that's worth two bottles, and we are free of deputies and anyone else for that matter. Plus, we finally have a few days off."

"Only because the theater burnt down and we had to cancel the rest of the run. I don't think that is cause to celebrate."

"Well, yeah, that's a bummer, but there's nothing we can do about it right this minute. We spent the whole weekend salvaging what we could and now we're taking a break, just like Alex told us to. So can we stop talking about this and get moving?"

Eleanor sighed and tossed several more bottles into the cart before continuing down the aisle. Seconds later Daniel was next to her, his arm draped over her shoulder.

"Should I take that as a positive sign?"

She gave him a sideways glance as they entered the cheese section and did her best to ignore the double looks and stares they were beginning to solicit from the people around them.

Forty minutes later she was pulling her Subaru into the garage. As they opened the hatchback to retrieve the groceries, a rumble of thunder sounded in the distance. Eleanor turned towards the northwest where the sky had turned a dark blue.

"Where did that come from?"

"Looks like rain."

"My gardens are probably a disaster. I was hoping to work on them for a few hours."

"Well, at least you won't have to water. All right, don't roll your eyes at me. Go on, do your damn gardening, I'll bring in the groceries."

Eleanor rushed to her bedroom, shedding her sundress for an old T-shirt and a pair of cutoff jeans. Pulling her hair into a ponytail she entered the closet in search of a ball cap and spotted Jeremy's shotgun lying on the back shelf. Perhaps it would be a good idea to have it with her while she worked outside, she thought.

It was hot. The temperature gauge read 106 degrees and the air was humid from the approaching storm. She worked as quickly as possible and it took no time at all before her clothes were completely drenched in sweat. She spent 30 minutes weeding the flower beds before moving to the vegetable gardens, and had just filled a basket with tomatoes when the first raindrops began to fall. Determined to finish her task, she worked through the increasing droplets as she walked the rows of green beans and red bell peppers.

A streak of lightening rippled across the sky, followed by a long, loud rumble. She grabbed her gardening bag, rushing into the workshop just as the wind kicked up and the heavens let loose, sending sheets of water pounding against the earth.

She stood in the doorway amazed at the ferocity of the storm. It rarely rained this far inland and now it was coming down so hard that her house was barely visible. Deciding that it was best to wait it out, she put away her gardening tools and then wandered through the back section of the workshop, examining all the equipment that was covered in a thick layer of dust. She was reminded that she really needed to turn all these tools over to Jeremy's family. It was silly to have everything sit idle, especially when she knew they would put it to good use.

Another flash of lightening illuminated the workshop, immediately followed by a monstrous boom. She rushed to the front to see if anything had been hit and froze.

"Jeremy."

He stood in the doorway, expressionless, his eyes fixed on her, and she swore that the rain was drenching his hair and clothes. She started towards him, but he signaled for her to stop. Then he turned away, and as his body shifted she saw a woman standing on the deck, looking through the door into the kitchen.

Her heart pounding wildly, she backed away from the doorway, running into Jeremy's table saw. The woman abruptly turned and rushed down the stairs, moving past Jeremy and straight for the workshop. She squeezed her eyes shut, hoping to shake the apparitions from her mind, but when she looked again, Katharine Monroe was standing inside the workshop, dripping wet, with Jeremy behind her. If this was one of her visions, she thought, then in her opinion they had escalated to a new level, because these ghostly visitors seemed incredibly real.

"What do you want?"

She was shaking so violently that she could barely speak. Katharine appeared to struggle with her words, and after several attempts her deep voice bellowed through the workshop.

"This... was... with Monica."

Katharine held out a chain with a key attached to it, dropping it on the ground. Eleanor remembered that Monica was wearing the necklace in her vision.

"How did you get this?" Eleanor said.

A shotgun went off and Jeremy ran from the workshop. Katharine lingered, her crystal blue gaze fixed on Eleanor.

"I realize this is in my head, but why are you with Jeremy? And why won't he talk to me?"

Katharine shook her head, and again struggled to speak. "Go to New York."

There was another gunshot. Katharine let out a tremendous moan and then disappeared just as Daniel rushed towards her, brandishing Jeremy's shot gun. He fired a round in the air before barreling into the workshop.

"Ellie, are you all right?" He threw his arms around her, crushing her against him. "Thank God they didn't attack you."

The rain was pounding hard against the workshop and she was not sure she had heard him correctly. "What? Attack who?"

"The bears. Thank God they didn't hurt you. Your arm is bleeding. What happened?"

"Did you shoot them?"

She ran outside into the downpour. Anxiously she searched the woods and was greatly relieved when she spotted two dark figures moving in the distance. Maybe it was the rain relentlessly pounding against her body or the wave of exhaustion taking hold, but suddenly she did not have the strength to stand anymore and fell to her knees. She felt his strong arm around her, lifting her from the ground. Her head was heavy as it fell back, and the last thought she had before she slipped into the darkness was that Jeremy had forgotten her.

Her eyes fluttered open as a small beam of light darted back and forth. She registered several voices murmuring around her, eventually honing in on the one to her left. As she focused on the man sitting next to her, she realized she was lying in her bed, while Murphy Taylor, a county paramedic, checked her pulse. Her mouth felt dry and thick and her head was pounding.

"What happened?" her voice cracked.

"Your blood pressure got too low and you fainted," Murphy said. "It's normal now. However, you're showing signs of dehydration. When is the last time you had any water to drink?"

"I don't know. I have a tremendous headache."

"That answers my question. We're going to give you a saline solution that should help, and then Dr. Lewis will be by shortly to sew up your arm. When was your last Tetanus shot?"

Murphy tied a band around her upper arm, motioning for her to make a fist. As he inserted the needle she turned away and saw Daniel and Eric Garrison standing at the foot of the bed.

"Hey cuz," Eric said. "I heard the call come in, and I had to make sure you were all right."

Eleanor glanced over at Daniel whose expression she was unable to read, but she could definitely sense his relief. She introduced the two men.

"Yes, Mr. Archer and I acquainted ourselves. He told me you had a couple of bears up here today and that one followed you into the workshop."

"Yes, but nothing happened. It just ran away."

"Well, apparently that's because Mr. Archer scared them off with your gun. Also, I hear this isn't the first time they've been on your property. You're lucky you didn't get attacked. I'm sending someone out here to see if there is a den nearby."

"Eric, they're just looking for food. Please don't hurt them."

"I'll do whatever is necessary to keep you safe. So don't you dare argue with me missy. Well, you seem to be fine, so I'll be going. You both have a good afternoon." Eric shook hands with Daniel before leaving the room.

Murphy smiled as he removed a blood pressure device from around her arm. "I just got a page that Dr. Lewis is on the way. We should all be out of your hair in about an hour, and then you two can enjoy your afternoon. Looks like you were about to have a little celebration." He leaned over her, whispering. "If you plan on drinking whatever is chilling in that ice bucket in the kitchen, please stay hydrated. I don't want to have to come out here again."

A hot shower never felt so incredible. Eleanor rested her forehead against the tile and let the soothing water run down her back. Her thoughts turned to her vision and Jeremy's silence. Why could Katharine Monroe speak to her and not him? Had he truly forgotten her, and why was he with Daniel's wife to begin with? *She is in your thoughts, Eleanor, just like him. Eventually they would have to meet. After all, it was just a dream, right?*

Then she remembered the key.

Damn.

She left the shower, throwing on her bathrobe. When she entered the living room she spotted the bottle and ice bucket that Murphy had alluded to earlier.

"Daniel?"

There was no answer. She heard the water running upstairs and figured he was taking a shower. Now would be the time to check for the key.

As she rushed across the backyard she could see that another storm was moving in from the west. She entered the workshop, scanning the area where Katharine had dropped the chain: nothing was there. She walked around to the back, carefully examining each section of floor as she worked her way to the door. The key was nowhere to be found. A rumble sounded in the distance and with a heavy heart she returned to the house.

The downstairs was quiet and empty. She sat at the kitchen island, replaying Jeremy and Katharine's visit in her mind. She swore she saw the key drop to the floor.

This is nuts. I have no idea what is real anymore.

While she twisted her hair into a tight strand, she fumed over Jeremy's silence. She knew it was ridiculous to be upset over a possible hallucination, but she really did not care. How could he be so indifferent? Was he that enamoured with his beautiful travelling companion that he couldn't even say hello?

Stop it, Eleanor. He's dead, and obviously you're dead to him too.

Her throat tightened, and soon tears were streaming down her face. Now she felt incredibly foolish. She was crying over a vision, but she could not help it. Whether it was a dream or not, Jeremy's rejection had wounded her deeply and her heart ached with longing. She buried her face in her arms, sobbing.

Wait a minute.

She shot up in her seat, focusing on the sour feeling in her gut. She concentrated on it for quite some time until she was absolutely sure what she was experiencing was real. Then, she recounted all the emotions she had felt in the past 10 minutes, holding up a finger for each one that she listed: anger, jealousy, longing, despair.

She released the knot of hair that had now been twisted up into a tight ball.

It's me. It's all me.

The emptiness had finally left her. Throwing up her arms to the heavens, she thanked anyone who might be listening. She closed her eyes and took a deep breath, slowly exhaling, basking in the sadness swimming through her veins. Eventually the hurtful feeling subsided, and when she opened her eyes she found herself staring at the bucket of sparkling rosé. Her gaze wandered across the kitchen and up the stairwell to Daniel's bedroom door.

When she entered his room she found him in bed, reading. He peered over the rim of his glasses, frowning.

"Shouldn't you be resting?" he said.

"I'm feeling much better." She set the ice bucket on the cedar chest and held up two Champagne flutes. "Can I interest you in some?"

"Sure."

She wandered over to the bed, handing him a glass. He gave her a curious look.

"You sure you're feeling OK?" he said.

"Oh yes." She sat on the edge of the bed, facing him, and met his eyes as she drank. Then she ran her fingers across his cheek, down his neck and chest until she rested her hand on top of his heart. She pressed against his skin until she could feel the beating beneath her fingertips, reminding her that he was alive and very real. A long forgotten feeling began to swirl inside her.

"Ellie, what's going on?"

She placed her glass on the nightstand, collecting his as well, and then tossed his book to the side. She removed his reading glasses, kissing his forehead, brow and nose, before pressing against his lips. She felt him tremble and pulled away. He gave her a boyish grin, one she had not seen in years.

"What is it?" she said.

"Believe it or not I'm a little nervous."

"Ah, well if you want to wait, I certainly understand." She started to stand and he grabbed her by the shoulders.

"Oh no you don't."

He kissed her as he pulled her onto the bed. A rumble of thunder rattled the windows as a soft gray hue enveloped the room. It started to rain. Their embrace lasted for many moments before Daniel pulled away. He leaned to one side studying her face.

"I just want you to be happy Ellie."

"I am. Believe me."

He ran his hand over the silky material covering her body until he reached the tie around her waist, loosening her robe. She smiled when she heard him sigh, closing her eyes as he kissed her breasts. He continued down her stomach and then between her legs, lingering for a moment before he stood. She sat up, her robe slipping off her shoulders as she admired his naked form.

"You don't appear to be nervous anymore."

"I guess not." He wrapped his arm around her waist, pulling her up onto the bed. "Last chance to back out."

"Thank you, but I don't think so."

He shuddered as she helped guide him, and a mutual groan passed between them.

As they made love she basked in the glory of feeling both his and her emotions together. They moved in a continuous circle of passion-she gave her desire to him and he unknowingly returned it to her. Afterwards, when the remnants of his contentment had waned, she was left with a feeling of peace. For where there had been nothing, she now had everything, and could say with all certainty, that she was happier than she had been in long, long time.

✳✳✳

For four glorious days, Daniel and Eleanor did not leave her home. Occasionally, they would wander out onto the front porch or sit on the back deck in the evenings when it was cool, but mostly they kept inside where they drank wine, ate and made love.

Never in his entire life, even when he was married to Katharine, had Daniel devoted so much time to sex. There were no long conversations, barely any talk at all, just the absolute joy of Eleanor's body entangling with his. And entangled they were, utilizing almost every room of the house in ways he knew she could never have possibly imagined. He hoped after a few days with him, she would have a whole new appreciation for kitchen counters and staircases.

However, there was one place in her home where she would not go, and one night, as he pulled her off the couch towards her bedroom she stopped him. While they hovered in the doorway, he listened to her heartfelt explanation, barely able to contain his frustration. He considered ignoring her plea, but instead he yanked her up around his waist, throwing her against the wall, and did his best to drive the thoughts of the dead boyfriend from her mind. The next day he was required to re-hang several pictures that had fallen in the hallway.

By Friday morning they had run out of food and drink, forcing them to travel into town for more supplies. Their first stop was the tavern for breakfast, and Daniel sat in amazement as he watched Eleanor inhale her entire plate of food, before asking him if he was going to finish his bacon. Her brow furrowed.

"Why are you looking at me that way?" she said. "If you're not done with it, I'll just order some for myself."

"You're eating."

"Well of course I am. I'm hungry."

He slid the plate in front of her, placing an order for another side of bacon. Afterwards, they stopped by the local market where he loaded up on supplies, and for the remainder of the weekend he grilled out, providing a constant offering of food which she ate without protest.

On Monday they had to travel back to the coast so that Eleanor could attend a meeting. Daniel worried that the bliss they had shared the past week would come to an end and by the time they reached Nina's townhouse his mood had soured. When they went upstairs to drop off their bags, Eleanor followed him to his bedroom, closing the door.

"Are you not feeling well?"

"I'm just tired."

"You're depressed, aren't you?"

"Look at you all Miss Sensitive. What's up with that?"

She approached him, placing her hands against his face. "I care about you and for reasons I can't explain I haven't been able to tell you that. I'm sorry, and I hope you'll forgive me."

She pulled him onto the bed and they stayed there until it was absolutely necessary to leave for her meeting.

The days to follow continued in the same vain, aside from having to deal with the rebuilding of the theater, Eleanor and he were free to do whatever they wanted, whenever they wanted. There was never a moment when they were apart, and anytime he felt anxious over their impending separation, one kiss from her would calm him. The days flowed happily on, until one night he woke up in a panic and realized that Eleanor had not committed to the New York trip. Immediately she sensed his despairing mood and attempted to comfort him.

"We had a beautiful day together," she said. "Why are you so sad?"

She started to kiss him and he pushed her away. "You know, this new sensitivity of yours is really starting to freak me out. But since you asked, what's going to happen when I leave here next week? Are you getting on that plane with me or not?"

Eleanor rolled onto her back, sighing.

"I don't like the sound of that," he said.

"It's not what you think."

"Really, you can read my mind now?"

She gave him an odd look. "No, but I can tell you're frustrated with me."

"Sorry, I promised myself I wasn't going to do this. Forget it."

"I understand, but it's just these past few weeks have been incredible, and I've been outside myself for such a long time that I forgot what it was like to be this way. I'm a bit overwhelmed right now, but don't get me wrong, it's a good feeling. It's wonderful in fact." She placed her hand against his beard and slowly traversed his lips. "You're very handsome."

Her comment made him roar with laughter. "Oh stop with the bullshit, will you."

"I'm serious. You are. I don't think I allowed myself to admit it until now."

"You must know that I love you."

"Daniel…"

He held up his hand. "Don't. Just don't. What I said about *him* and you not sharing your feelings was wrong. I was angry, and feeling sorry for myself, and yes I was drunk. I get that you're not ready for all this, but it doesn't change the way that I feel."

"That's not why I haven't given my answer yet. I'm worried about the situation with the theater. There's still a lot to do to secure funding before we can start rebuilding, and I don't feel comfortable leaving until that's settled."

"Come on Ellie. We're talking about a few days around the Labor Day weekend when everybody else will be enjoying their last big hurrah for the summer. It's also your birthday, and I can't think of a better place to celebrate the end of your thirties."

"Thank you for reminding me, I had almost forgotten."

"So are you telling me the only reason you don't want to go to New York is because of the theater?"

"Yes."

"OK." He rolled over on his side.

"OK, what?"

"Nothing. Just OK."

The next morning he got up early to make a phone call and afterward he went down to the corner cafe to pick up two lattes. When he returned he found Eleanor sitting on the back deck reading the newspaper. She did not look up when he set her cup on the table and settled into the lounge chair next to her.

"Alex just called," she said.

"Really? Kind of early, don't you think?"

"It seems he couldn't wait to share his news with me. One of our alumni- who wishes to remain anonymous- made a huge donation to the theater project. We can move ahead now."

"That's good news, isn't it? I guess this means you can go to New York."

"I suppose that's true." Eleanor continued to read the paper in silence for several minutes. "Is there anything you would like to say Daniel?"

"Not really. Wait, there is something. This morning when I put on my shorts I found this." He fished through his pocket and pulled out a silver chain, dangling it in front of her. "I forgot I had it. I found it on the work-shop floor after the whole bear thing happened. You must have dropped it."

He placed the silver necklace with the key in the palm of her hand and was concerned when she turned white. "Ellie, you OK? You're not going to pass out on me again, are you?"

✳✺✳

Jared tossed the file of Karl Milin aside and went out to his deck for a smoke. It had been a long two weeks since the arrest of the prime suspect in the Bellaso murder case. He still could not get over the unexpected visit from Angie Miller, when she appeared at the station and told him she was going to represent Karl as his attorney.

"Are you insane? The man tried to kidnap you," Jared said.

"We both know that was a desperate act to get my attention. Karl has no family except my ex-husband, and obviously Anton has abandoned him."

"Yet another reason why you should not represent him. What happens if Anton decides to surface?"

"Then he will see that I'm trying to help his brother, which is a lot less dangerous than him finding out I could have helped Karl, and I didn't. I have no choice here. I have to do this."

"How are you going to communicate with him? He's deaf, mute, doesn't sign, and he can't understand a damn thing anyone says or writes?"

"Before, when I was married to Anton, Karl and I bonded. It was the only way to survive my ex-husband's brutality, so I'm sure I can find a way to get through to him again. I've made my decision and I would like to see my client now."

Jared leaned back in his chair, mulling over Angie's determination to represent her former brother-in-law. Over the past few days, he had been in discussions with the district attorney's office to move the trial down to Los Angeles, not so much to bow to the pressure to try the high-profile case in Bellaso's hometown, but more to provide adequate protection for Angie and Karl, just in case Anton did make an appearance.

Anton Milin.

Once they learned of Milin's sex-trafficking business, it became clear to Bellows and him that the illusive Russian gangster had captured Katherine Monroe's interest. Along with her devotion to nurturing the performing arts, Monroe was also a supporter of women's rights across the world, and had directed a significant amount of funds from The Monroe Foundation to organizations that dealt specifically with violent crimes against women. As they compared her travels through Eastern Europe to the information they received from the CIA, they concluded that Monroe had worked her way across Anton's lurid empire that stretched from Russia to Moldova.

Once they established the purpose of Monroe's travels, the next question they asked was what was the catalyst? What made Monroe start her secret investigation? Jared recalled that discussion with Bellows as they sat in The Bayside Café nursing their hangovers from the previous evening's celebration. Why he bought that second round of expensive vodka for Mikayla, Bellows and him he would never know.

"Monica Bellaso had to be the reason," Jared said as he downed his third cup of coffee. "Monroe met her at a fundraiser three years ago and within a few weeks she took her first trip to Russia. Around that same time, Monroe stepped up her visits to San Francisco and LA, and Bellaso began to travel to New York on a regular basis. That had to be it."

Bellows agreed as she popped two ibuprofens in her mouth and slid the bottle over to Jared. "Also, Bellaso accompanied Monroe when she went to Moldova. So I think now, the question we have to answer is why? What transpired between the two women that made Monroe go after Anton Milin?"

It wasn't until the following week they were able to answer that question. Bellows was back in New York and Jared was working late at the station. It was 3:00 in the morning her time when she called. He could hear the smile in her voice, despite the late hour.

"The CIA figured out where Lourdes was in the Ukraine," Bellows said. "And it looks like he spent most of his time visiting several brothels across the country. I guess he has been inquiring about Monroe and a teenage girl that Monroe had been searching for, by the name of Mariannya."

"So how did Lourdes figure that out?" Jared asked.

"Don't know, but it's really pissing off the CIA, though I really don't care because it's helping us. Dirk thinks this Mariannya person is probably a friend or relative of Bellaso's who went missing. Bellaso told Monroe about the girl, and Monroe decided to go looking for her."

"So, Monroe went in search of Mariannya, she finds out about Anton Milin and his sex trafficking operation, Milin finds out about her snooping around his whore houses and comes after both her and Bellaso. However, I still don't think that would be enough of a motive for Anton to have them killed. The CIA has known about him for a while now, right?"

"True," Bellows said. "It's not like his operation is a secret. But, whoever attacked Monroe that night searched her computer and filing cabinet. They were looking for something."

Jared stubbed out his cigarette just as the sliding glass door leading to his deck opened, and his thoughts returned to the present. Mikayla appeared with two vodka martinis and sat on his lap.

"Hey Sunshine," he said.

"Hey Shug. You ready to go to bed yet?" She swung her legs around and began to unbutton his shirt.

"I'm thinking I don't have a choice." He took a long drink from his glass while she continued to undress him. "How was the restaurant tonight?"

"Busy as usual. What's wrong honey? You don't seem very excited to see me."

"No, I'm glad you're here. But Mik, what are we doing? You're married."

"Not for much longer. Ben filed today. " She stopped undressing him and sighed.

"Are you sure this is what you want?"

"Ben doesn't want me anymore. He's been very clear about that and I'm at the point now that I'm ready to get on with my life. How about you? You still want me in yours?"

"I'll always want you with me. That will never change."

"Then there's nothing left to say now, is there Shug." Tears filled her eyes.

"Mik, I know you still love him. That's all right."

"But I love you too," she said, sniffling. "That's always been my dilemma."

They kissed, and he slipped the straps of her dress off her shoulders just as the doorbell rang. She froze, giving him a wide-eyed look.

"Were you expecting someone?"

"Hell no."

Mikayla jumped off his lap, rushing into the house. He followed, and when he arrived in the living room he found her squinting through the view finder.

"It's Eleanor," she said.

"At this time of night? Something must be wrong."

"I'm letting her in."

"Wait, she doesn't need to know that you're here," he whispered.

"Yes she does. She's my friend and yours, as well as a partner in *our* restaurant. She needs to know and more importantly I want her to know."

As Mikayla threw open the door, Jared returned to the deck to gather up their martinis. After refreshing their drinks, he joined the women in the living room.

Once Eleanor got past the shock of seeing them together, she sat and listened intently to Mikayla's story of her separation and impending divorce from Ben. Then she expressed her regret that Mikayla had not been able to confide in her, but understood why she had kept the affair with Jared a secret. Finally, she turned to Jared and asked to speak with him alone. Mikayla kissed her friend on the cheek and left without saying another word. As soon as he heard the bedroom door close, he began to explain his actions and was surprised when Eleanor cut him off. She then produced a silver chain from her purse, handing it to him.

"This is a safety deposit box key," Jared said.

"Is that what it is?" she said. I wasn't sure. Can you figure out what box it belongs to?"

"Where did you get it?"

"Well, technically Daniel gave it to me this morning, but he found it on the floor of Jeremy's workshop last Monday."

"Well, then that should be easy to find. We'll just check out all the local banks and see if Jeremy rented a safe deposit box somewhere."

"The box doesn't belong to Jeremy," Eleanor said.

"How do you know that?"

"Remember when you said to tell you if anything else unusual happened?"

Eleanor went on to explain her ghostly encounter with Katharine Monroe and Jeremy. Monroe had dropped the key on the floor of the workshop and told her it had been with Monica when she died. Jared vaguely remembered that Monica was wearing the chain in the vision.

"She said *with Monica*? Those were her exact words?" Eleanor nodded as Jared polished off his martini. "What happened after that?"

"I heard a shotgun go off, which I discovered later was Daniel trying to scare away the bears. And then Katharine told me to go to New York."

"Bears?" he said.

Eleanor explained that while she saw Katharine Monroe and Jeremy standing in her workshop, Daniel had seen two bears. Jared shot up from his seat and went into the kitchen to retrieve a bottle of Kettle One from the freezer. When he returned Eleanor was pulling her car keys from her purse.

"So I guess I should be searching for a box under Monica's name then?" Jared said.

"It sounds that way."

"Eleanor, why did you wait to tell me this?"

"It's been difficult to get away. Daniel and I are a bit attached to each other right now."

"Oh…well, nothing wrong with that. Good for you."

"Yes, but I'm losing all my friends in the process. I rarely see Kyle and Nina anymore, and obviously I wasn't there for Mikayla when she needed me."

"You're not losing anyone. Mik and I just wanted to keep it under wraps until after the tourist season ends. Then we're going to tell Ben."

"Jared, you know I care about Mik and you more than anything in the world, but you must know she loves Ben and the twins very much."

"I know. But I can't help myself when it comes to her. So, is there anything else you want to tell me? Any more visions of Amelia, or of Monica, or anyone else for that matter? What about the man that helped you when Karl was after you? Has he tried to contact you again?"

"No, there's been nothing like that. But, what if I told you I discovered I possess the ability to put people to sleep."

Jared stroked his chin. "Then I would say try it on me sometime. I haven't slept in years."

Eleanor nodded. "I better get home. I'm not sure how long Daniel will stay asleep."

271

"Wait. Mik and I are thinking of heading out of town for Labor Day. Why don't you come with us?"

"Thank you, but I think I have plans already."

"New York?"

"Yes. It sounds like I should go."

Eleanor left and he stood on the front porch watching her descend the steps to the street. As she drove away he hit speed dial on his cell phone. There was an answer after only one ring.

"And to what do I owe the honor of this call?"

"We need to talk."

ACT III

Acceptance

Chapter Twenty Five

But my true love is grown to such excess
I cannot sum up sum of half my wealth.

It was nearly 5:00 Thursday evening when Daniel's limo passed through the Lincoln Tunnel into Midtown. Eleanor felt like a tourist, her head tilted upwards as she marveled at the magnificent buildings that passed before her.

"Are you excited?" Daniel said.

"Yes, and a little nervous, I guess. It's been a while since I've been to New York."

"I know. Ten years is a long time. But, don't worry. We'll make up for that."

Daniel's grip tightened around her hand and an ocean of memories swelled inside of her. At that moment, she remembered her last night in the city, 10 years ago, when Daniel and she argued in the lobby of the Essex House hotel. They had not been a couple in several years, but they were still friends, and she had asked him to meet her there before she left for the airport.

"Ellie, come on. It's not too late to change your mind. Michael said the show would take you back in a heartbeat, not to mention there's a role surfacing he said you'd be perfect for."

"Daniel, why are you talking to my agent?"

"He's my agent too dammit, and like me he doesn't want you throwing away a promising career."

"I'm not throwing anything away. I'm going to California to teach, hopefully get my doctorate, and I'll be doing plenty of acting in the summer festival."

"That's right, Shakespeare in the sticks. I forgot. That should really help your career along. The movie deals will just pour in now."

"You know very well that's not for me. I love acting, and yes maybe I'll make another movie someday, but right now all I want is to teach and help Alex build up his program."

"You're such a liar. Leesman's stupid-ass program has nothing to do with it. You're going because of *him*."

"His name is Jeremy."

"I don't fucking care what it is, because I'm never going to say it. He's the one that convinced you to live in the middle of nowhere and I blame him for ruining your life."

Because Daniel was already famous by this time, and she had recently had her face plastered all over the city busses and billboards, their passionate debate caught the attention of the crowded lobby. Eventually, the hotel manager approached and asked if he could escort them to a private area. Eleanor said no thank you, giving Daniel a desperate hug before rushing away. A few weeks later a picture of them arguing in the lobby surfaced in the tabloids. Months would pass before the rumors stopped. It was not a pleasant way to begin her new life in California.

The limo pulled onto a quiet street that was adjacent to a small park, stopping in front of an eight story red brick building with wrought iron windows and balconies. The driver opened the door, offering Eleanor his hand. She stepped out into the warm evening air, admiring the quaint surroundings.

"It's absolutely charming," she said. "How many apartments are in here?"

"Fifteen. There are two on each floor except for the top. That one is a big space, too big if you ask me. Anyway, we live on the fifth floor. Let's go."

The doorman greeted them, tipping his hat and assisting the driver with their luggage. Daniel introduced Eleanor to the security guard before escorting her through the beautiful art deco lobby and into the elevator.

As they passed through a large, double door entrance, they were greeted with the aromas of fresh flowers and scented candles. Trevor, who had returned to New York the previous week, met them with open arms. There was the faint sound of Brazilian jazz playing and Eleanor wandered into the center of an enormous space attempting to contain her astonishment.

The living room was bigger than her entire house, richly decorated with all types of paintings, tapestries, sculptures, hand-blown glass and other mediums of art. She was amazed by the sheer volume of the collection, but what really got her attention were the photographs lining the stairwell wall leading up to the second level. As she perused the multitude of pictures, she saw almost every known celebrity she could think of, and they were all posing with Daniel and Katharine.

Daniel handed her a glass of Champagne and Trevor joined them in a toast to her return to New York. Then he gave her a tour of the lower level which included the kitchen, laundry room, dining area and master bedroom. Next, they climbed the steep, wrought iron staircase to the upper level, which overlooked the living room. He showed her Amelia's pink bedroom, passing over the office before ending at the guest bedroom where, per her instructions, her suitcase had been delivered. She started to unpack while Daniel leaned in the doorway sipping his Champagne.

"Would you like another drink?"

"No, thank you. I'm going to freshen up and I should be ready to go." She went to the bathroom to wash her face and Daniel appeared handing her a towel.

"Are you sure you're all right?" he said.

"Yes, I'm absolutely fine."

"You know, if you're uneasy about this place, we can go to a hotel."

"I told you I would be fine staying here, and I am. Please stop worrying."

"If you're OK, then how come you haven't said a word since we got here?"

Eleanor tried to mask her embarrassment, but she could not contain the smile crossing her lips. "I'm so sorry, but all of this is overwhelming me right now."

"All what?"

"All of it… the apartment, the limo, the plane. It's just a lot to take in all at once."

Daniel rubbed his eyes. "Are you still mad because of what I said about the vacation thing?"

"No."

"I'm still having a hard time understanding why *he* never took you anywhere."

"Daniel, what did I say on the plane?"

"OK, I'll drop it. Look, I get why you might be all strung out about the plane and limo, but if for any reason you start feeling weird about *this* place, and you know what I mean, we're out of here. By the way, if you're freaking out over my humble dwelling, then I would definitely reconsider that drink before we head uptown."

Despite Daniel's warning, Eleanor could not hide the shock that swept through her when she walked through the front door of the Monroes' apartment. Suddenly, she found herself in the middle of an enormous foyer with white and black marble floors, glistening white walls, floor to ceiling columns, and a huge crystal chandelier hanging overhead. In the center of the space was a large fountain, at least seven feet tall, with marble benches surrounding it. Never had she been this close to such grandeur, and she was thankful when Amelia burst into the foyer, squealing.

Christine appeared next, taking her arm. They walked through a moderate sized sitting room filled with several small chairs and loveseats, past a large, formal dining room that was set for dinner, and into a magnificent living room that offered a breathtaking view of the Manhattan skyline.

A young brunette woman appeared from an entrance near the bar wearing a chef's uniform and bearing a tray of Champagne flutes. She approached the group, offering each person a glass before presenting Amelia with a special concoction topped with fresh raspberries.

Amelia grinned. "Thank you Francesca."

"Eleanor," Christine said. "I would like you to meet Francesca Ouellette, who is gracing us with her presence tonight. She is a rising culinary star in our city, and along with her Aunt Camille is wholly responsible for the incredible meal we're about to enjoy."

"Ah, Madame is too kind. Enchanté, Mademoiselle Bouchard. Your name is French, is it not?"

Eleanor responded in French, surprising everyone.

"I have tried to teach Amelia," Francesca said, "but she does not seem that interested. Perhaps you will have better luck since she is so fond of you. We've heard nothing but your praises since she returned from her trip."

"Thank you. We had an amazing time together." Eleanor felt Amelia's arms move around her waist.

"Eleanor, I had no idea you spoke French," Christine said.

"Of course she does. The woman has three degrees," Daniel grumbled. "Look, I hate to break up this love fest but, where is Phillip?"

"He had to take a call in his study," Christine said. "But he'll be with us shortly. The weather is perfect for the balcony. We should take advantage of it and enjoy the view."

Christine took Eleanor's arm, pulling her towards the balcony. Suddenly she felt queasy.

"If you don't mind," Eleanor said, "I think I would like to use the rest-room first."

"There's one in the main foyer, right across from the sitting room. Why don't you show her, Amelia. Come Daniel, there's something I would like to discuss with you."

Amelia grabbed Eleanor's hand, pulling her towards the sitting room. She glanced back at Christine and Daniel who were staring at each other as if they were about to have a showdown. She quickened her pace, fearful if she left them alone for too long she might never get to enjoy the delicious meal that awaited them.

They entered the foyer from the sitting room, and Amelia continued across the checkered marble floor until she came to a polished black door situated next to a long, dimly lit corridor.

"What's down there?" Eleanor said.

"That's where Nana and Papa live. Papa has his office there."

"I see. Well, I'll just be a moment."

"I can go with you. Look." Amelia opened the door to reveal a small room complete with a vanity, several chairs and various magazines. Amelia pointed to Eleanor's left. "That's where the bathrooms are."

"Bathrooms?" Eleanor said.

"Yeah, it's like a restaurant."

Eleanor opened the swinging door and stepped into an elegant bronze colored room. To her right was a marble double sink and straight ahead were three enclosed stalls. Apparently, this bathroom was meant to accommodate guests when the Monroes entertained. When she returned to the powder room she found Amelia sitting, her head cocked towards the wall. Her belly felt queasy and she sat, groaning.

"I don't feel very well."

"It's because of us," Amelia said.

"What do you mean?"

"There's too many of us. It makes you feel like you have a fever."

"Oh, that explains why I felt so warm in the living room. Camille and Francesca are like us." Amelia nodded. "But, I don't think that's it. This is different. I feel dizzy and my stomach hurts. Maybe I'm coming down with something."

"Maybe it's the man with Papa."

"There's someone else here?"

"He's coming now," Amelia said.

Eleanor listened as she heard voices in the corridor that ran alongside the bathroom. Soon they were in the foyer and she recognized Phillip Monroe, but she was unable to hear the second man. Her nausea had increased substantially, and she was considering a return to the bathroom when a familiar voice boomed right outside the door.

Amelia took off, and when Eleanor entered the foyer she saw Phillip restraining Daniel while a blond- haired man marched towards the front door. Her belly was on fire and she realized she had experienced this same sensation before. Christine emerged from the kitchen entrance at the end of the foyer, her eyes widening.

"Good God Eleanor, don't move."

All eyes turned to Eleanor as Christine rushed towards her. Daniel stopped his struggle with Phillip and ran into the bathroom, while Mr. Monroe went after the stranger. Christine moved in, pinching her nose just below the bridge.

"Don't move. Just keep looking straight ahead at me."

Daniel appeared next to her, holding a towel below her nose. "Let it drain Ellie. If you blow your nose it will make it worse."

Eleanor stood still while Christine and Daniel tended to her nosebleed, as she tried to steal a glance of the stranger before he escaped through the front door.

"It appears to have slowed. Hold on to the towel, just to be on the safe side. Typically it takes a few tries before it completely stops," Christine said.

"You two seem to have experience with this sort of thing," Eleanor said, trying not to get blood on her dress.

"My daughter used to get them all the time, especially after flying. Thankfully Amelia does not suffer the same problem."

As the front door shut her discomfort ceased. Daniel left her side, and she could feel his rage as he barreled towards Phillip. Christine took her arm, pulling her in the opposite direction.

"We'll stop by the kitchen so you can rinse out your mouth," Christine said. "Don't worry about Daniel. Phillip knows how to calm him."

"Yes, but so do I."

Eleanor broke from Christine's hold, marching towards the two men. Daniel turned to her, his eyes glaring, and as he ordered her to turn back she laid her hand on his arm. Before he could say another word his eyes softened, and then the anger that was pounding in his veins subsided. His body relaxed and he grew quiet, allowing Eleanor to exchange in a proper greeting with Mr. Monroe.

Fifteen minutes later, Daniel was his usual boisterous self, and the group was able to enjoy the six course meal that Camille and Francesca had prepared. After dessert was served, Phillip convinced Daniel to join him on the balcony for a cigar, leaving Eleanor, Christine and Amelia alone in the dining room. There was a momentary exchange between grandmother and granddaughter, and Amelia sighed, reluctantly joining Camille and Francesca in the kitchen.

"I really don't trust her to not listen in. Why don't I give you a tour?"

Christine took her arm, guiding her to the south wing where they entered Phillip's study. As soon as the door shut, Christine spun around. "Clearly, your powers have matured. How long have you been able to manipulate emotions?"

"It started two weeks ago and so far it's only been with Daniel."

"Why didn't you tell me?"

"At first I didn't know I was doing it. I just thought Daniel was finally getting his temper under control, and then one night I just wanted him to stop arguing with me and he did. Right in the middle of a sentence he passed out. The next night I tried it again, and he fell asleep the minute I touched his arm. He didn't wake up until the next morning."

Christine began to pace. "You've only had your powers for a short time and already you can do this?"

"Is that cause for concern?"

"Indeed it is. Your abilities have advanced to a level that takes most of us years to achieve. Granted, Katharine was only thirteen when her powers fully matured, but that was seven years after her abilities first emerged. What is happening with you is highly unusual."

"I'm sorry. I didn't mean to upset you."

"You're not. It's just that you're moving so rapidly that I don't know how much longer I can help you. If that is the case then I will need to find you a more suitable teacher."

"But why, you just said that Katharine was powerful and you taught her, didn't you?"

"For many years I did, until she moved on to another mentor, one whose abilities surpassed all of us. I'd rather avoid that with you, but I may not have a choice." Christine's eyes glistened. "You sensed the man that was here earlier tonight, didn't you?"

"Yes. I can only assume from Daniel's reaction that he was Charles Lourdes."

Christine raised an eyebrow. "Yes, and I don't understand how you were able to sense him. He is very powerful and is able to mask his abilities from most of us, including me. He could come and go from a room and you would never know it."

"I think I felt him from the minute I entered your home. At first I thought I was sick, but it turns out it was him. You said he is powerful. What is he?"

"Ah yes, that reminds me. There is something I neglected to explain to you before. One of the rules among our kind is to never reveal another person's abilities unless it is absolutely necessary, such as an emergency or if that person grants you permission. It is up to the individual to decide whether or not they want to reveal themselves."

"Well, can't I just ask that person if I suspect them to possess abilities?"

"Yes you may, but don't be surprised if you are met with silence. You see, it is sort of a sign of trust. Even though you can sense someone is like you, you must wait until that person chooses to share the bond with you."

"You asked me about my abilities within a few hours of meeting me."

"As you know, your circumstances made it necessary. However, given you are new to all this, I will indulge you this one time. I am not certain of all of his abilities, but I know Charles is a powerful Empath, probably the most powerful one I have ever known."

"He felt familiar to me."

"That could have been Charles. I'm sure he sensed you were here. He has the ability, shall we say, to make you feel things that aren't really there."

"Why would he want me to feel that way?"

"I'm not saying that he did, but if you ever find yourself in his presence again, you need to be on your guard. These powers of ours can be used to help as well as to manipulate, which brings me to another edict. You must not use your abilities whenever you feel like it. Yes, I know it can be tempting, especially with someone as loud and obnoxious as my son-in-law, but he needs to be allowed to express his feelings freely. If you continue to calm him like you did tonight, he'll eventually become an emotionless blob. Though in Daniel's case I'm not sure that would be such a bad thing, but nevertheless, do you understand?"

"Yes, I do."

"All right then, I guess there is still much I can teach you, but not tonight. I'm afraid it's already midnight. Perhaps tomorrow we can resume our sessions."

An hour later they were back at Daniel's apartment. Amelia was asleep in her own bed and Eleanor was soaking in a warm bath, recalling her reaction to Charles Lourdes. She knew she had felt his presence somewhere before, but she could not place it. There was a knock on the door and Daniel entered.

"You mind if I join you?" Before she could answer, he stripped off his T-shirt and boxers and slipped in at the opposite side of the tub. "I'm sorry about what happened tonight, this was not the kind of homecoming I had planned."

"Are you going to be all right?"

"I don't know. When we were out on the balcony Phillip told me that Lourdes was back and the board wants to reinstate him as CEO." Daniel leaned his head against the wall, staring at the ceiling. "Screw it. I don't care if the cops ever find out if he knows something about Kate's murder. I really don't give a damn anymore. I just want it to all go away. In fact, now that I'm back, I'm considering selling this apartment and getting a place where Amelia and I can start fresh."

"It's very beautiful here. It would be a shame to let it go, but I understand."

"I don't know how you do it. Why do you stay in that house?"

"I guess because I cherish the memories that are there. They've helped me through some pretty tough times."

"Memories are exactly why I don't want to be here. Never mind me. I'm just tired."

He stepped out of the water, grabbing a towel on the way out the door. She remained in the bathtub, wondering if she should go after him when she heard the television in the next room. A few seconds later she was standing in the doorway, dripping wet.

"What are you doing?" she asked.

"I'm watching TV before we go to bed."

"Don't play dumb, Daniel. We discussed this-separate rooms when Amelia is with us."

"Not necessary. I talked with her and she knows we'll be sleeping together while you're here. I told her she can't come in the bedroom unless she knocks first."

"But what kind of message does that send her? We're not married. To her I'm just…"

"You're just what?"

"I'm really not sure," she said.

Daniel turned off the TV, tossing the remote on the nightstand before crossing the room to lock the door. On the way back he grabbed her hand.

"Ellie, I don't know what you think is going on here, but as far as Amelia and I are concerned, you're the woman that I love. You do remember me telling you that a few weeks ago that I loved you, right?"

Eleanor nodded.

"Good. So you can call yourself whatever you like-girlfriend, lover, part-ner-I really don't care, just as long as we're together. We can stay up here or go to my room, your choice. Either way, we're sleeping together tonight. Now, I'm going to crawl into bed and hope that in the next few minutes you'll join me."

Daniel dropped his towel to the floor and moved under the covers, turning out the light. She had no desire to argue with him, especially with Amelia sleeping nearby, so she decided it was best to keep the peace for now. Besides, she had a more pressing issue to deal with at the moment: to figure out a response to his proclamation of love before he forced one out of her.

Chapter Twenty Six

My only love, sprung from my only hate!
Too early seen unknown, and known too late!

Bellows smiled as she answered her cell phone. "Don't you ever sleep Adams?"

"Sorry, did I wake you?"

"No. I was waiting on a call from the CIA."

"Are you still at the precinct?"

"Yeah, I slept here. We're on round two of the security recordings from the hotel in Moscow. This time we have the lobby and elevator camera from the floor Lourdes was on. Still no sign of Katharine Monroe, but we've only covered the first twelve hours."

"Sheila, I don't get it. Why do you care if they were together in that hotel? We got proof they were both in Moscow at the same time. We know something was going on between them."

"Lourdes has lied about his relationship with Monroe from the beginning. I'm sure he'll figure out a way to explain his way around a tourist picture, but he can't talk his way out of a security camera catching him going into a hotel room with her. Why did you call so early?"

"Angie Miller's residence and office in LA were vandalized last night. I'm looking at the police report right now. They went through her files in both locations and stole her laptop."

"Is she all right?" she said.

"No, that's why I am calling. She is very upset and now on her way to New York to join Walker while he visits his kid. I've got her flight information."

"All right, we'll send someone to pick her up. What's going on with Karl Milin's trial? Is it moving to LA?"

"I should have the official word after the holiday, but it looks like it's going to happen. I for one will be glad to get him out of here. So are you still questioning Lourdes today?"

"Yes, this afternoon. I can't wait. It should be loads of fun with him and his cache of lawyers. Wish you could be here for it."

"Well," he said, "I can't make it in time for that, but I could be there tomorrow. Maybe I could lend a hand with those security recordings and help you keep an eye on Miller."

"Now why would you want to do that? Surely you have plans."

"They got cancelled. So what do you say? You owe me a visit."

"Sure, I can always use the help. Are you all right?"

"Yes, of course I am. I'll text you when I have everything shored up."

As the call ended, Jared opened the sliding glass door to his house and went into his office, searching for Daniel Archer's cell number. It took about a half-dozen rings before the sleepy actor picked up. "Sorry, it sounds like I may have called too early."

"No, I just didn't get much sleep last night. I'm actually reading the paper. What's up?"

"I had a change in plans and wanted to see if your offer was still open?"

"Of course, do you have Trevor's number? He can give you all the info."

"Yes I do. Thanks again."

"So, what's going on?" Daniel said. "I thought Ellie said you had plans with your girl?"

"Something came up with her kids and she had to cancel. So, how are things going with Eleanor? Is she excited to be back on the East Coast again?"

"It's hard to tell. We sorta got into it last night. Look man, I gotta go. Talk to you later."

Daniel hung up just as Eleanor entered the kitchen. She was wearing her white cotton sundress from the previous evening, and her long red hair was flowing over her bare shoulders. She stood in front of the coffee maker, her arms folded.

"Don't worry. Trevor preset the machine last night and then you can make the next pot. I'm over learning how to do it." He buried his face in his newspaper, listening as she poured the coffee and rummaged through the refrigerator. "There's creamer on the top shelf."

The door shut and he heard her walk across the tile floor, sitting on the stool next to him.

"Thank you for remembering I drink soy milk," she said.

"You can thank Trevor. He's the one that does the shopping. I guess he knows what you want. I certainly don't."

"Daniel, please don't do that. If you're upset with me, we should just talk about it."

"What's there to talk about? You said it last night. You don't want to sleep with me anymore."

Eleanor groaned. "That is not true."

"Ok, then how come you didn't want to make love last night and don't give me all that crap about sending the wrong message to Amelia, because you know that's just an excuse."

"It's not. I feel very strongly about how our relationship affects her, and I believe when she is staying with us, we should not sleep in the same bed."

"Is this because we're not married?"

"Well, yes. That's one reason, I guess."

"OK. I can fix that. Marry me."

"Stop it," she said. "That's not funny."

"I'm dead serious Ellie. Look, I'll even get on my knee."

"I'm going upstairs to get ready."

"No way." He pulled her off the stool, grasping her hands. "Marry me. Say yes and we'll go down to city hall right now and get a license. Then with Trevor's help we could probably pull off a pretty nice wedding by next weekend. The honeymoon would have to be short because of school, but we could work around that. Hawaii is nice and that's close to California."

Eleanor's expression had gone from one of shock to contemplation, and for a moment he thought she might be seriously considering his impromptu proposal.

"Why are you doing this?" she said. "You know very well we can't get married."

"Why? Because my wife just died and the media will have a field day with me?"

"I can't believe we're having this conversation. Yes, because of that and a whole host of reasons I could list."

"Like what?"

Eleanor cocked her head to one side, her eyes narrowing. "Daniel William Archer. Is your head really that far up your ass that you can't see what it would do to this family?"

"What did you just say?"

"You heard me."

He stood, studying her face. Her eyes were bluer than usual. "Who told you to say that?"

"No one did."

"Kate used to say that when she was really pissed off. Are you wearing contact lenses?"

"No, of course I'm not. Look, the point I was trying to make last night is that I don't want to do anything to hurt or confuse Amelia. If it came across as anything more, then I'm sorry."

"Well, if you won't marry me, do you at least want to sleep with me?"

"Yes, just not while Amelia is down the hallway."

"She's not down the hallway now."

Eleanor was silent as the corners of her mouth turned upward. He took her hand and started to leave the kitchen.

"No. Not your bedroom," she said.

"Where then?"

Her eyes darted back and forth for a moment. Then she smiled as she pulled him towards the opposite end of the kitchen.

"Whoa, someone's feeling adventurous this morning." Daniel picked her up, and she wrapped her legs around his waist. Her eyes were now a bright blue. "Are you sure you aren't wearing lenses?" She kissed him and he carried her into the laundry room, shutting the door with his foot.

❈❈

During breakfast Eleanor learned that Daniel had taken the liberty of planning her agenda for her visit, and an hour later they were travelling uptown in his limo to The Metropolitan Museum of Art. They spent two wonderful hours visiting the various exhibits, until Daniel gave her a look that said he was done and heading to the museum store. When Amelia and she finally joined him, they found him holding several items in his hands while surrounded by eager fans.

Despite the multitude of emotions flooding her body, she could clearly feel Daniel's frustration mounting. Sensing he was about to snap, she leaned down, asking Amelia for help. Hand in hand they approached him. As they cast out their signal, the crowd that had swelled around him slowly peeled way, until there were just a handful of wide-eyed children and their parents left. Eleanor suggested that he sign a few autographs, which he did, and then she led him to the checkout counter.

While she stood in line she could not say exactly what possessed her to try such a bold move in a public place, but a part of her felt like she had done this many times before.

Next they travelled to Monroe Industries to meet Phillip and Christine for lunch. After checking in with building security, they rode the elevator to the top floor, where they were met at the front desk by Phillip's assistant, Alice Mead.

The matronly woman led them down a long wood paneled hallway, filled with numerous portraits of past CEO's of the 150 year old multi-national company, and into a large, open space, filled with several sets of sleek chairs, couches and coffee tables. Alice crossed to the right side of the floor, passing several large offices, each with an assistant posted outside the door, and she turned down a secluded hallway.

Phillip was finishing a phone call when they were ushered into his sprawling office. He greeted them with his usual warm embrace and then offered to give everyone a tour before they went to the executive dining room for lunch.

Daniel passed on the offer, opting to head down to the dining room with Amelia while Eleanor stayed on. He kissed her on the cheek and whispered something playful in her ear, causing her to smile. Phillip gave her a curious look, patting her hand as they began their walk. She often wondered what he really thought about Daniel and her diving into a relationship so soon after his daughter's death, but she probably would never know. Phillip had been nothing but gracious to her, and as she was introduced to a long succession of darkly clad business executives, she felt like she had been a part of his family for years.

Eventually, they finished with the introductions and cut across an area that looked like a hotel lobby. They arrived on the opposite side of the floor where there were two large glass doors.

"What's back here?" Eleanor asked.

Phillip smiled as he pushed against the chrome handle, motioning for her to pass.

The décor instantly changed, and she noticed the walls were now constructed of shiny, cream-colored bricks that glimmered in the soft light. They took a right down a curved hallway that opened into a round room with a vaulted ceiling. Lining the perimeter were several sleek arm chairs, tables and floral arrangements, but in the middle was a life-size marble statue of a woman in a Grecian gown.

"Oh my goodness." Eleanor approached the white, opulent beauty and stared into her colorless eyes.

"It's Aphrodite, the Goddess of beauty and love," Phillip said as he stood alongside her.

"She looks familiar," Eleanor said.

"It's Katharine."

Eleanor held her breath when she heard the familiar baritone voice echoing through the marble room. Suddenly, her entire body was on fire.

"It's from a movie that she starred in," Lourdes said. "When it was over, the director gave it to her. As soon as Phillip found out about it, he had it placed here."

Phillip laughed. "Yes, and she never forgave me for doing it either. Charles, I had no idea you would be in today. Let me introduce you to Eleanor Bouchard."

Slowly she turned towards the blond-haired man standing next to her. He took her hand in his, and when his lips touched her skin everything grew quiet. All she could hear was the sound of her heart beating in her ears. Just then Phillip's assistant rushed into the room, informing him of an important call that had just come through. He looked at his watch and took Eleanor by the arm, explaining they would need to cut their tour short.

"Phillip, you can't let Ms. Bouchard leave without seeing the art collection. Please, let me take over for you and I'll bring her back as soon as we're finished."

Phillip hesitated for a moment, but then his assistant reminded him of his call. Hastily he agreed and abandoned her in front of Katharine's shrine. Within seconds, she could feel Lourdes brushing up against her.

"What are you afraid of Ms. Bouchard?" he said. "Did Christine warn you about me?"

"Yes she did. Should I be worried?"

"No, but I'm beginning to think I should be."

Eleanor turned and met his bright, blue eyes. He stood motionless, searching her face. Her heart was racing and every fiber of her body was consumed with his energy.

"You can sense me. How is that?" he said.

The desire to feel his touch swelled up inside her. She reached for his hand and he flinched. Then a look of recognition spread across his face. He moved in so close that she could feel his breath on her cheek.

"Dear God," he whispered.

He grabbed her hand, rushing her down a dimly lit hallway. They passed an empty desk that sat outside an office, and he pulled her inside, slamming the door shut. He took her face in his hands.

"I can sense her inside you," he said.

"What are you talking about?"

"Katharine. She's here, with you. How is this possible?"

"Katharine Monroe?"

"Yes. She's pouring out of you." Lourdes brought his face within an inch of hers. "Can you not feel it?"

"I feel the need to be with you. Are you doing this to me?"

"No. I assure you I am not."

Her eyes closed as his arms encircled her waist. They shared a passionate kiss, and her last thought before she drifted away was that Katharine Monroe had a profound love for Charles Lourdes.

When Eleanor emerged from her daze, she was standing in a bathroom and Lourdes was placing her purse on the vanity in front of her.

"I thought you might want to touch up your lipstick," he said.

His look was apologetic. Then she noticed several light pink blotches that were circling his mouth. She spun around, examining his face.

"What did we do?" she said.

"We kissed, that was all. Don't you remember?"

Eleanor struggled to recall anything past the feeling of his lips pressed against hers and drew a complete blank. "I have to go." She backed away from him, grabbing her purse as she rushed from the bathroom.

"Ms. Bouchard, please don't leave."

"Daniel is waiting for me."

"Can we just talk for a moment?" he said.

"If I don't join him soon he'll come looking for me."

"Obviously you're upset. Wouldn't it be better to collect your thoughts first before you leave here, so as to not arouse any suspicion?"

Eleanor stopped. He was right. Christine and Amelia would immediately suspect that something was wrong. She turned to him, unsure what to say next.

"Please, have a seat. Can I get you something to drink, some water perhaps?"

She nodded, walking to the couch while he retrieved a bottle of Perrier from a full size bar. She began to look around the office, marveling at its size.

"It's rather big for just one person," he said. "But it's good for conducting business."

"I noticed a door at the other end of the bathroom. Where does that go?"

"It's a bedroom. Occasionally I work late, or have very early meetings and it's just easier to stay here. Don't worry Ms. Bouchard. We were never in there."

"How would I know? I can't remember a thing."

"You'll have to trust me."

"What about Katharine Monroe?" she said.

"She and I have not been together in years."

"She was in love with you."

Lourdes nodded. "That was a long time ago, before she married Archer."

"What about the incident in Daniel's apartment last year? He said you made a pass at her and she was quite upset."

"We were arguing over a business matter, and it was easier to have Archer believe I had behaved like a cad." He joined her on the couch, handing her a glass. "What are you?"

"I thought we weren't supposed to ask that question."

"I'm afraid we don't have time for formalities. What powers do you possess?"

"All I know is that I am an Empath."

"Clearly, you are much more than that, or how else could I feel Katharine's presence so strongly within you. What does Christine say? Surely she has felt it too?"

"Christine has never said anything about that, but she has said that I am different."

"Indeed you are. The powers within you burn bright and I am strangely drawn to it."

Lourdes turned sullen, and she found herself mesmerized by his bright blue eyes. Her gaze wandered up to his soft blond hair and down to his perfectly shaped ears. He was boyishly handsome, and as she continued down the line of his muscular neck she could feel that he was very strong. Their eyes met and suddenly she knew where she had heard his voice before.

"You were in the woods the night of the fire. You were the stranger that saved Amelia and me. Why were you there?"

Lourdes sighed. "My travels brought me to you, just as fate brings us together now."

"I have heard your voice in my dreams. I know you from somewhere. We have been together before. You, me…and Amelia."

"I should take you back to Alice now."

Lourdes shot up from his seat and suddenly she saw a black mark appear at the base of his wrist.

"What is that on your hand?" she said.

"What do you mean?"

"It looks like a tattoo of some kind."

Lourdes gave her a perplexed look and pushed back the cuff of his right sleeve, revealing unblemished skin.

"But, I know I saw something there." Eleanor grabbed his wrist to examine it and the room went dark.

She was on her hands and knees, looking down, blood dripping down her arms. She saw a pair of dark shoes appear in her view and then someone gripped her hair, pulling her face upward until she was looking into a blinding light. Something swung at her, smashing against the side of her skull and when she was able to raise her head again, she saw a large silver flashlight dangling from a hand with a black tattoo.

The vision ended when Lourdes fell to the floor. Eleanor came out of her daze to find him lying on his back, red-faced and clutching at his chest. She sprang for the phone on his desk and when she picked up the receiver it rang Alice Meade, who then called 911.

Twenty minutes after Daniel took Amelia to the executive dining room, he received a call from Mrs. Meade, informing him that there had been an incident involving Eleanor. He raced up the stairwell to the lobby where she was waiting for him, and he was escorted to the CEO suite. As he stormed past the statue of Katharine-which still creeped him out to this day- he could feel his fists clenching. If it was not for the two paramedics strapping a semi-conscious Lourdes onto a gurney, Daniel would have strangled him right there. However, what really unnerved him was finding Eleanor at his side. Later he learned that Lourdes had suffered a cardiac arrest and Eleanor had saved his life by administering CPR.

After Lourdes was rolled away, it was obvious that Eleanor was distraught, and he recommended that they cancel their plans for the afternoon. However, she insisted that they proceed, and after lunch they travelled to the

Empire State Building where he surprised Amelia and her with a private ride to the observation deck. Eleanor clung to him during their hour long stay, and occasionally he could feel her trembling.

When they returned home, she went directly to her bedroom. He allowed her some time alone while he made sure Amelia took her bath and picked out a dress for their evening at the theater. Then he grabbed a bottle of Pinot Gris out of the refrigerator, along with two glasses from the cabinet and made his way to her room. When he joined her in the shower, she was leaning her head against the wall. The moment he touched her she wrapped her arms around him.

"Listen," he said. "I just talked to Phillip and Lourdes is going to be fine. He didn't require surgery and he'll probably be released over the weekend. Phillip wanted me to thank you again."

Eleanor remained silent as she held him, and eventually he had to pull away so he could see her face.

"I'm not upset. What you did was amazing and I just hope if my time ever comes you're there to save me. So don't worry about it, OK?" She continued her silence as she looked up at him. "Ellie, for God's sake, please say something, you're starting to freak me out."

"I love you."

He heard her, but asked anyway. "What did you say?"

"I love you Daniel. I love you very much."

He did not expect for his life to suddenly change in the shower of his guest bedroom, but it did. He lifted Eleanor off her feet and kissed her so hard that he thought he might have bruised her lips. When he lowered her to the ground he thought of the many questions he wanted to ask her, mainly why she had picked this particular moment to put him out of his misery, but he thought it was best to wait. Instead, he held her close, returning her words of love, and thanking her for making him the happiest man alive.

Chapter Twenty Seven

One woe doth tread upon another's heel.
So fast they follow.

Eleanor stood in the doorway of Daniel's office, staring into the darkness. It was the only room in the apartment she had not seen yet, as he had purposely skipped over it during her tour.

Slowly she crossed the threshold and wandered around the perimeter of the room. Much like the space alongside the staircase, the walls were filled with pictures of Katharine and Daniel, mostly in evening attire, smiling for the camera. There was a poster of the movie they made together, several plaques and awards with Katharine's name on it, and a small glass case filled with several statuettes. She sighed when she examined the Oscar he had won for Best Actor. He received the award almost 10 years ago, not long after she left for California. Katharine was at his side that night, and for the first time in her life, she wondered what would have happened if she had stayed in New York.

She continued around the room, running her hands over the mahogany bookcases that lined the walls. On one side of the office was an oak, roll-top desk which she figured to be Daniel's. A handful of movie scripts were stacked to one side and his laptop was open. In the center of the room was an oblong black lacquer table with curved legs. She approached the nearly barren desk and picked up a lone picture frame that was sitting on the corner.

The photo was of Daniel, Katharine and Amelia. She recognized the Monroes' white living room furniture in the background and guessed that it had been shot around the time that Daniel and Katharine were first married. She studied their smiling faces; they seemed so happy, so in love, yet Eleanor knew better. She did not know whose feelings were moving through her veins at that moment, but her heart swelled up with an unbearable sadness, and she held the picture to her chest, crying.

Katharine Monroe had loved Charles Lourdes her entire life. Eleanor discovered this yesterday when she hovered over the paling CEO's body attempting to save him. Feelings of love and regret flowed through her as she pumped away at his heart. When Lourdes lost consciousness she was not sure who was trying harder to save him, Katharine or her, but in the end it did not matter. Eleanor brought her fist down on his chest with a mighty thump and his eyes popped open as he gasped for air.

In that moment, Katharine took over and when Lourdes recovered enough to give her a smile, she kissed him as a lover would. Thankfully, the door burst open and Phillip pulled her away so the medics could take over.

As Lourdes was lifted onto the gurney his gaze never left her. They spoke no words while the medics strapped him in, but she knew his feelings. An oxygen tube was placed in his nose and one of the paramedics asked if she would like to travel in the ambulance with her husband.

The room went silent.

There were a few uncomfortable moments as Eleanor tried to explain the situation, but Lourdes saved her with some clever remark that made everyone laugh. The medics rolled him away and when she turned to watch, she saw Daniel standing in the doorway with a stunned look on his face.

She broke from her thoughts and sat at the window seat, looking out on the quiet street below. Her mood had darkened considerably since entering the office, and she realized she was feeling an emotion she rarely experienced on her own: anger. Yes, she was angry- angry with Katharine Monroe for loving Lourdes and for deceiving Daniel all those years. To her it was truly heartbreaking, and it drove her to tell Daniel that she loved him when she was not ready. Now she had lied to him just like Katharine had, and he deserved so much better than that.

She felt Amelia approaching and quickly wiped the tears from her eyes. "You're up early."

"Daddy was snoring," Amelia yawned.

"He stayed with you last night?"

"He fell asleep while we were talking."

"I guess it was late when we got home. I had a wonderful time, by the way. I can see why *Wicked* is your favorite musical."

Amelia sat next to her. "Why are you sad?"

"Oh honey, it's complicated. But, I'll be fine now that you're here."

"Mommy used to say that when she was sad."

"Did she?" Eleanor's gaze fell on Amelia's necklace, and she picked up the tiny key, examining it. "Do you remember the first day we met? When we were at the airport?"

Amelia nodded.

"It was a wonderful moment for me, magical really. When you wrapped your arms around my neck I felt as if I had known you since the day you were born. Since then, I have dreamt of that day and many other days in your life, and I'm beginning to believe that you and I are meant to be together."

"It's because Mommy is inside you."

Eleanor looked into Amelia's crystal blue eyes. "So you have felt it too?"

"Yes."

"Since that very first day?"

Amelia nodded. "Can you be my mommy now?"

She took Amelia's face in her hands. "Someday my darling, when the time is right for all of us, but until then I will do everything I can to be a part of your life. I love you Amelia Monroe. You most definitely hold the key to my heart."

"I love you too." They embraced, and Eleanor held Amelia for quite some time before she grew weary of the dark and gloomy office. "Come on. Let's see what we can scrounge up for breakfast."

They walked into the hallway, passing a long wall of photographs, and she stopped at one that caught her attention. It was a picture of Katharine with her arm around Monica Bellaso, and Katharine was wearing the heart-shaped pendant that Amelia had been coveting all summer. Eleanor leaned in, examining the picture.

"Amelia, what is that on the front of your mother's necklace?"

"It's a tree."

"What sort of tree?"

Amelia shrugged her shoulders and then pointed to the pictures that filled the hallway. As Eleanor scanned the wall she realized that Katharine was wearing the same necklace in all of them. She returned her focus to the photo in front of her, staring at the engraving. "This image seems familiar to me. I know I've seen it somewhere before."

"Daddy's coming," Amelia whispered.

Daniel entered the hallway, still wearing his clothes from the previous evening. He stood next to them, yawning, and when he saw what had captured their attention, he groaned.

"OK, let's go downstairs. Daddy really needs some coffee." He reached for Amelia and she protested. "No baby girl, I'm not doing it."

"But Daddy you can take it to that jewelry man. He'll fix it."

"And I told you no. Now you know what we have planned today, so let's not spoil it." Daniel winked at Amelia, and she smiled. "That's a good girl. Go get ready. We're eating out for breakfast."

Amelia ran into her bedroom, giggling, and Eleanor grimaced. "I can't believe you're making me do this."

"Look, you're in New York and you can't visit here and not go shopping. It's just not right. Besides, you need to pick out an outfit for tonight."

"Oh no, dare I ask?"

"I was going to take you to the opera, but the season hasn't started yet. So, I found something else that I think you'll like."

"What is it?"

"It's a surprise. But you need a dress. So no more arguing about anything, including that damn necklace."

"Daniel, she just wants it because she misses her mother."

"Yeah, I get that. But I said it was broken and she can't have it. So I would like you to stop bugging me about it. OK?"

"I'm sorry. I'll get ready."

She closed her bedroom door, fighting the tears rimming her eyes. Her abilities had now advanced enough that she was able to block out Daniel's anger while she focused on her own bruised feelings. It was still unsettling to have all of her emotions back, and she knew with just one thought she could make the sadness float away. However, that wasn't the purpose of this madness that had been thrust upon her. The purpose was to feel.

So when Daniel came into the bathroom to apologize, she did not resist him. He moved behind her, and for a moment she caught his longing gaze in the mirror before he kissed her neck. Then she closed her eyes as his hands moved beneath her robe and she gladly accepted the desire that was now flowing through her veins.

※※

Bellows returned from the bathroom to find a large coffee sitting on her desk and Chen leaning over her computer. "Did you get my message?"

"Yes, did you spend the night again?" Chen said.

"Yeah, I was so pissed about Lourdes bailing on us yesterday, that I had to do something."

"The man had a heart attack. I don't think he had much choice. You should have gone to the game with us."

"I wasn't in the mood to be a third wheel with you and your boyfriend. Anyway, take a look at this. Tell me what you think." She clicked on a video that was paused on her computer and watched as Charles Lourdes entered a hotel lobby with a dark-haired woman on his arm.

"Who is that?" Chen said.

"Unfortunately, it's not Katharine Monroe. She has appeared a handful of times with Lourdes in the hotel lobby, but so far we haven't seen her going into his room. Betsy is starting to look at all the elevator recordings next to see if we can get a shot of them getting on together. It's possible she was staying on a different floor."

So what's next with Lourdes?" Chen said.

"He's going to be in the hospital for another day at least. That gives us time to finish the recordings. I'd rather have this kind of ammunition before we try and bring him in for questioning again."

"I saw that Cameron from Barney's left a message," Chen said.

"I swear if he's calling to hit on me again, I'm going to have him arrested."

"You should go out with him. He seems like a nice guy."

"He wears pink socks," Bellows grumbled. "Besides, he's not my type."

"All right, I'll see what he wants then. What about Detective Adams?"

"He has a girlfriend already."

Chen laughed. "I meant does he need to be picked up at the airport?"

"Oh…no, he said he has a ride. Listen, I was thinking of heading home to freshen up."

"Go ahead, I'll check on Betsy. And maybe you could change into something a little more casual."

"Is something wrong with my suit?" she said.

"I was just thinking its Saturday and you might want to loosen up a bit." Chen winked as his cell phone buzzed. "Why is Morgan calling? Isn't he supposed to be on surveillance?"

While Chen answered his phone, Bellows grabbed her purse, starting for the exit. She tried to recall where she had stored her only pair of jeans when suddenly Chen grabbed her arm, rushing her towards the elevator.

"It's the Fifty-Seventh Street building," he said. "Angie Miller and Zach Walker just entered the lobby."

�֎֎

Eleanor stood in the dressing room of some designer clothing store in SoHo, unable to try on another item. The extremely persistent salesperson named Gabrielle knocked on her door and presented her with three more dresses.

"Mr. Archer would like you to take a look at these as well. He was wondering when you would be out to model them."

Eleanor collapsed onto a cushioned bench, burying her face in her hands.

"Are you all right Ellie?"

"Actually, I prefer to be called Eleanor. Daniel calls me Ellie."

Gabrielle blushed. "How long have you and Mr. Archer been dating?"

"We're not dating. I'm just an old friend visiting for the holiday weekend."

Gabrielle hung the dresses side by side, telling Eleanor how lovely she would look in all of them and then scurried away, leaving her to deal with the dozen or so garments lining the wall. She checked her cell phone, wondering why Jared had not returned any of her calls, and slumped down on the bench.

Katharine Monroe was haunting her. The realization she had shared with Amelia earlier that morning sent a shudder rippling through her body. Daniel's wife had sought her out from the beyond, and like Monica Bellaso, she had a message to convey.

Then her mind went to the moment with Lourdes when she grabbed his hand and was thrown into her harrowing vision. She was certain it was Katharine's murder she had seen, and based on what happened to Lourdes, he had experienced it as well. Obviously, Katherine wanted her to come to New York in order to find Lourdes. Now that Eleanor had done that, what was to happen next?

Gabrielle knocked on the dressing room door. Eleanor threw on the first dress and went out to show Daniel. He made her turn around several times, soliciting comments from Amelia, as well as Gabrielle and the other sales people. After all that, he liked the dress, but wanted to see more. Reluctantly she returned to the dressing room, checking her cell phone. There was still no call from Jared. Gabrielle knocked again, asking if she needed assistance. Sighing, she changed into the second of the dozen dresses that were still hanging in the room.

It was going to be a long morning.

✖✖

Jared stepped out of the limo and crossed 57th Street to where Bellows was talking with a smartly dressed Asian man. As he approached she lowered her sunglasses.

"Looks like you got the message." Bellows introduced him to Detective Chen, who then left to take a phone call.

"What happened?" Jared said.

"About an hour ago Walker and Miller entered the building supposedly to pick up a package that was left for her by her ex-husband."

"What?"

"Yeah, that's right. Milin has an apartment in this building. His name was left off the tenant list we got back in July. I am sure we'll find out that it's his place where Gus Fenton did his electrical work. Chen is working on a warrant and already we are running into resistance. I had to call my chief in for help."

She motioned him to follow her into the building. "Anyway, while the front desk guard was searching for the package, a man dressed in black, wearing a ski mask and carrying a gun, emerged from the elevator. Chen and I had just arrived as he was heading for the front desk. By the time we entered the lobby we found Walker on the floor with a bullet in his shoulder, and Angie Miller was gone. I guess there was a car waiting in back and the security camera got most of the plate. We're running a check now."

She walked him through the entire lower level where the incident had taken place and then they moved into the back area where they met with building security. By this time Chen had returned announcing they had acquired all the necessary warrants to enter Milin's apartment. Bellows instructed Chen to work with the security manager to review the recordings while she prepared the team to go up to the 46th floor.

"But ma'am," the security manager interrupted her, "we saw who entered Mr. Milin's apartment. He used the access code thirty minutes prior to the shooting. Take a look."

Jared, Bellows and Chen watched as the security manager brought up the 46th floor camera. It showed a man of medium build, dressed in black, with long dark hair, a full beard and mustache, walk down the hall to apartment 46A. He punched in a four digit number on the keypad and went inside.

"That's Milin," Bellows said. "That's what he looks like on his American passport."

"We're not sure who that is ma'am. The apartment has been vacant for the past three years. The last person to access it was on March 25."

The three detectives were quiet for several moments. Finally Bellows spoke. "Do you have the recordings for that day?"

As the security manager searched, Bellows paced. Jared could see she was shaking.

"Are you all right?" Jared said.

"March 25 was the day Katharine Monroe was attacked."

"I know. We're getting closer."

"Closer to what?" Bellows whispered. "Angie Miller has been kidnapped and we still have no idea where Anton Milin is or how he got back into the country. He certainly didn't use his American passport. We would have known."

"Or, he's been in the country the entire time, using another identity," Jared said.

The security manager announced he had found the recording. They stood silent as they saw a woman with long black hair exit the elevator and walk down the hall to Anton Milin's apartment. Seconds later she opened and shut the door.

Chen left the room and Jared glanced at Bellows who was smiling.

"Obviously I'm missing something here," Jared said. "Do you recognize this woman?"

"Yes," Bellows said. "We stumbled on her late last night when we were reviewing the security recordings from The Inter-Continental Hotel in Moscow. She was seen entering the hotel with Lourdes."

Bellows was now grinning. Jared shook his head. "Sheila, you can't be serious. There is no way Lourdes kidnapped Miller. He's lying in a hospital bed right now."

"No he isn't," Chen said as he returned to the room. "Lourdes was released early this morning. And I just got the trace back on the van and you're gonna love this. It's owned by Monroe Industries."

Bellows turned to him, her eyes narrowing. "Think about it Adams. His family lived in Russia and now he has been seen with a woman who entered Anton Milin's apartment on the same day Katharine Monroe was attacked."

"Sheila, he was beaten nearly to death by these people?"

"Maybe that was a warning. Maybe he was there to take care of Bellaso and he backed out at the last minute. Karl, or whoever beat the hell out of him, decided they still needed him and dumped him in a hospital parking lot. It would explain why he refuses to tell us what happened to him. They could be blackmailing him." She moved closer, her voice lowered. "Look, we have no record of Anton entering the country with his passport. Now maybe you are right and Milin has been here all along, but also couldn't it be that Lourdes is doing his bidding for him?"

Jared stared into her round brown eyes. He had to admit there was some logic to her statement, and he reluctantly nodded. She smiled, and then took his arm leading him back into the lobby, introducing him to the rest of her team.

When Daniel received the call from Detective Bellows that Zach Walker had been shot, he had just purchased Eleanor's dress for the evening and they were heading uptown. By the time they arrived at the hospital Walker was already in surgery and his prognosis was good. Daniel gave his cell phone number to the nurse on duty, and convinced Amelia and Eleanor to continue with their plans to have brunch at David Morgan.

The mood during the meal was subdued, both Eleanor and Amelia barely spoke. Finally, after tiring of having to carry the entire conversation, he recommended that they return to the hospital. He was surprised when Amelia said she did not want to go.

"But honey, wouldn't you feel better if you were there when Zach comes out of surgery?"

"He's not my daddy. You are."

"Oh baby girl, don't get me wrong, I love to hear you say that, but technically he is your father and he wants to be a part of your life. Right now that may not be a big deal, but when you get older you'll probably wish he had been around."

"He's not like me." Amelia pushed away her plate. "Can we go shopping now?"

"Honey, did something happen between you and Zach?"

"No."

"Then why don't you want to go to the hospital and see him?"

"I told you. He's not my daddy."

"All right, I get it. But the poor guy just got seriously hurt and his girlfriend is missing. I think he could stand to see a few friendly faces right now."

"I don't like her very much."

"You mean Angie? Why do you say that?"

"She's got something wrong with her head."

"Amelia, where is this coming from?"

"Can I stay with you tonight?"

"Oh, now I get it. No, you can't. Ellie and I are going to be out late. Now I'm sorry your plans with Zach aren't going to happen, but you'll be with your grandparents and I'm sure you'll be fine. So let's just stop with the theatrics."

Amelia turned silent and scooted over to Eleanor, crawling into her lap. Soon her eyes closed. Daniel ordered a cup of coffee and watched Eleanor rock his daughter while peering down at her cell phone.

"You've been checking that damn thing every ten minutes. Is something wrong?" he said.

"I've been texting Nina all morning and she's not responding for some reason."

"Maybe she has her phone off. Listen, what do you think is up with Amelia and Zach?"

"Honestly, this isn't the first time she's said this about him. When he visited her in Edmond she seemed disappointed by their differences."

"I can see why. The guy is just nothing like her, but what am I going to do? He's been great about the adoption and he saved Amelia's life, not to mention this whole thing with Angie must have him scared to death. Hell, it scares me to death. The police think this Anton person is behind Katharine and Monica's murders and then there's that whole business with Angie having property only a few miles from your home and Monica staying there all the time. I still find that incredibly weird, don't you?"

"Daniel, are you sure that Katharine didn't know about me? Surely, after all those pictures of us surfaced in the celebrity magazines, she would have figured it out."

"Maybe, but if she did she never would have admitted it. That was sort of an unspoken rule we had between us. I didn't tell Kate about you, and she didn't tell me about *him*."

"Are you talking about Zach?"

Daniel shook his head while Eleanor gave him a blank stare "We'll talk about it later. In the meantime, I have a surprise for you, well I hope you think it's a surprise, of course knowing how you are, it's hard to say."

"What did you do now?"

Daniel signaled for the check, unsure as to how he would handle Eleanor if she reacted negatively to their next destination. But, when they arrived at Eiji and he explained that she would be there for the remainder of the afternoon to receive a haircut, manicure and pedicure, he was shocked when she did not offer up one word of protest. He told her he would return at 5:00 and then took Amelia shopping for Eleanor's birthday presents.

⁂

Anton Milin sat sipping a glass of vodka as he watched Angie Miller sleep. Behind him a door slid open, and his beautiful paramour appeared wearing a silk robe. She spoke to him in Russian.

"How long will she be like this?"

"Until the sedative wears off," Anton said. "Then we can begin."

"What happens if we can't get her to remember?"

"She stays in this room until she does. It's soundproof and secure. No one will come looking for her here."

His pearly white goddess moved in front of him, letting her robe fall to the ground. She was Ukrainian born, but her mother moved back to Russia after her father died. Anton met her when she was 13, and although he was 30 years her senior, he knew he had to possess her. Patiently he waited, and when she turned 16 she willingly became his lover.

"She is strong. Can this room hold her?" she said.

"That is one advantage of her memory loss. She doesn't remember her powers, but no worries, I am stronger."

"I know."

She moved onto his lap, loosening the tie on his robe. As she straddled him, Anton kept a watchful eye on Angie, who was now stirring in her sleep. His blond-haired temptress took his face in her hands, forcing him to look into her lavender eyes.

"First me… then her."

"For now my dear, but soon it will be the three of us together, again."

He set his glass on the floor and grasped her slender hips.

Chapter Twenty Eight

Be thou assured, if words be made of breath,
And breath of life, I have no life to breathe
What thou hast said to me.

Eleanor woke early Sunday morning to find Daniel's body curled around her like a protective cocoon. Slowly, as her mind emerged from its slumber, she remembered where she was, and recalled the events of the previous evening.

Daniel's surprise turned out to be a benefit concert for The New York City Opera. It was an amazing event, and as they left the theater and walked out into the warm night air, Daniel was unusually cheerful. He wrapped his arm around her, guiding her away from the long line of limos parked outside Lincoln Center.

"Let's take a little walk first."

Immediately she knew where he was leading her, and within a few minutes they were in front of The Julliard School. Suddenly, she was transported back 20 years to the first day she arrived in New York. Closing her eyes, she imagined her younger self standing there, so full of hope and possibilities. She glanced over at Daniel who had the same reflective look on his face.

"Thank you," she said.

"For what?"

"For tonight and for bringing me here."

"I wasn't sure how you would feel about seeing this place. There are a lot of memories floating around here, some good, some not so good, for us at least."

"I'll take them…all of them."

"I will too." He checked his watch and turned to her. "Happy Birthday, Ellie."

They shared in a long kiss that made her tremble. "Thank you for remembering."

"Have I forgotten your birthday once since we met? I remember everything about us, including our wedding date."

He paused, donning a hopeful look. She had not thought about that day for a long time. "March 7."

"We would have been married seventeen years."

Eleanor saw a camera flash from a few feet away. "Daniel…"

"Yeah, I know. We should head back. I'm not up for a confrontation tonight."

The first few minutes of the ride home were quiet. Daniel held her hand, nervously caressing her fingers while he stared out the window. His mood had turned sullen, and finally she had to ask what was troubling him. He gave her an apprehensive look and then instructed the driver to shut the privacy divider.

"I hope you'll forgive me for doing this on your birthday, but I'd like to get this off my chest. It has to do with Kate and what I was talking about earlier today."

She nodded for him to continue, and he took a deep breath before speaking.

"When Kate and I met, I was a mess. You had just left for California and I was still in love with you. As it turned out, Kate was in the same boat. She had just ended a long term relationship and was desperately in love with the guy. Anyway, despite all that, we started seeing each other while we were filming our movie and became friends. A few months later, after the movie was finished, we began showing up in public together. I took her to the Oscar's and she dragged me out to some of her fundraisers and we sort of got each other through a tough time. We were on again, off again for a few years and then she had that stupid fling with Walker and got pregnant. That's when everything changed for me."

Daniel leaned back in his seat and looked out the window. It took him a while before he could continue. "I went to the hospital to visit her after the baby was born and it was love at first site. Kate put Amelia in my arms and an hour later the nurse had to pry her out. After that I found every excuse I could to be around Amelia. Kate and I started dating again and we went everywhere with her. I know for a long time everyone thought she was my kid, but I didn't care. I realized that I desperately wanted a family and suddenly there was one right in front of me that needed a father to step in. So, I made a proposal to Kate, we both agreed we cared enough for each other to make a commitment, and we got married."

"You weren't in love with each other?"

"Not in the beginning. We sort of had an arranged marriage, one that we arranged ourselves, but don't get me wrong, we took it very seriously. We agreed from the very start that if one of us couldn't handle it, we would let the other one know right away. The first few years were interesting. We accepted that we loved other people while we played couple. We actually had a lot of fun together, and I became Amelia's father, which made me insanely happy. Then sometime during our third year of marriage things changed between us. We started to let go of our previous loves-a little-and we fell in love."

"That's the saddest story I've ever heard."

"Maybe in the beginning it was, but in the end we were all right. Though, that whole thing with Lourdes almost took us down. Look, you have to believe me. Kate and I loved each other. We really did. It's just we got there in an unconventional way. I'm sorry I didn't tell you about this before."

"Don't be. That was between Katharine and you."

"Maybe, but I want you to know everything."

"There is a question I would like to ask you though."

"Sure."

"You said that when you met Katharine, you were still in love with me. What did you mean by that?"

Daniel shrugged his shoulders. "Just what I said. I had been in love with you since the moment we met."

"Even after our annulment?"

"Especially after that, look, you had to have known. Why do you think I did everything in my power to keep you here in New York?"

"But you forced me to move out of our apartment. You told me to leave."

"I know. I just didn't want you making a mistake because of us, and I knew if we stayed together you'd go to England with me and not finish school."

"Of course I would have gone with you. I loved you and I would have found a way back to Julliard eventually."

"Let's face it Ellie. I was making you miserable with my demands, and if you had gone with me how long would it have lasted? Six months, a year at best? Then your entire last year at school would have been screwed up for nothing. I couldn't let that happen. I loved you too much for that."

"Neither one of us knows how long we would have lasted."

"*He* came along three months later. I think we know the answer to that."

"You leave Jeremy out of this. I married you because I loved you. If we had stayed together I would have made it work. You have to believe that."

He sighed and pulled a handkerchief from his pocket, handing it to her. "Your mascara is running. Take a look." He leaned over and flipped open a panel on the door, revealing a mirror. "Are you going to be OK?"

"Yes, it's just a lot to take in all at once."

"Sorry. Please tell me I haven't spoiled your birthday."

"No, but you do have me thinking."

"About what?"

"About what might have been."

"Don't do it. It will only drive you nuts, believe me."

"Yes, I suppose you're right." She finished drying her eyes. "You look rather handsome in your tuxedo by the way."

"Oh yeah, well you look incredibly hot in that dress. I nearly went crazy tonight lusting after you."

"Then I guess it's a good thing you didn't know that I wasn't wearing any underwear."

"What? No way." Daniel laid her back on the leather seat as he pushed her dress up her thighs. "Oh my, what has gotten into you Dr. Bouchard?"

She ran her hands down his chest, feeling his muscles tense as she tugged on his belt. "I've never had sex in a limo before."

"Believe it or not, me neither."

She smiled as she undid his buckle and unclasped his pants. His round hazel eyes reached deep inside her as he pulled her closer, reminding her of that August afternoon when she finally found her way to him.

"Do we have enough time?" she whispered.

"Darling, we can spend the entire night in here if we want."

Darling. The word lingered in her head as she wrapped her arms around his neck, her body arching beneath his. She considered what would have happened if they had stayed together all these years-where they would be living, how many children they would have- but soon his movements brought her back to him, allowing only one singular thought to occupy her mind.

Twenty minutes later he was pulling her into the elevator of his apartment building, kissing her as if the limousine ride had never occurred. He pinned her against the wall, pressing the length of his body against her, so she would know he wanted her again. To her surprise, as they rushed across the hallway to his apartment, she was as willing and wanting as him.

The heavy metal door flew open and they moved across the living room, shedding their clothes along the way. They were near his bedroom when she stopped him.

"We should go upstairs."

"No," he said.

"Then the couch... the floor... anywhere but in there." She tried to coax him away, but he continued to push her towards the doorway. "Please Daniel, I don't belong in there."

He grabbed her shoulders, pulling her to him. "Listen to me Ellie. Kate is gone, so is he, and no amount of grieving or suffering is ever going to bring them back. I loved her. I still do, but God help me, I'm in love with you." He took her face in his hands. "I've never stopped loving you."

He swept her up in his arms and carried her to the bed. There were no more words after that. Daniel lay her body down and in the darkness proceeded to convince her that the land of flesh and blood was where she needed to be.

He stirred behind her. His warm breath brushed against her cheek, and she wondered how she could ever sleep alone again. She glanced at the clock on the nightstand and noticed the picture of Katherine, the same photo that he had kept next to his bed in Edmond. She had to avert her eyes. She could hardly look at the deceased actress without thinking of Lourdes.

"How did you sleep?" Daniel ran his hand over her shoulder and down her arm until their fingers intertwined.

"Well, since we only went to sleep a few hours ago, not that much."

"Sorry about that. I should go turn on the coffee maker."

"Wait, don't go yet."

He chuckled when she moved beneath him. "Ellie, I don't think I have anything left to give."

"That's all right, I'm probably spent too, but I just wanted to feel you against me."

"Where is all this coming from?"

She could not understand his surprise as she kissed him. Her body started to writhe and he responded by moving his mouth down to her breast. She groaned and uttered words that were not hers and he continued down her stomach until his mouth rested between her legs.

That was when she realized she was not entirely alone inside her body. Thoughts and feelings of Daniel started to move through her that were not her own, and she attempted to reconcile them as her mind began to drift. Soon, she was experiencing visions of making love to him throughout his apartment. They were passionate, almost violent moments, as if they were desperate lovers that had been denied each other for years. The scenes grew more and more intense as Daniel's movements increased, and Eleanor gave herself over to all of it. She grabbed his hair, moaning.

Then Katharine Monroe appeared at the foot of the bed.

When she screamed her body jolted backwards, causing Daniel to pull away. She could not hear his voice over the pounding in her chest, and it took her a few moments before she could open her eyes.

"Ellie, did you hear me? Are you OK?"

She glanced at the end of the bed. Katharine was gone. "Yes. Sorry. I'm fine."

Daniel fell back on the bed and pulled her to him. "Don't take this the wrong way, but since the limo ride home you've been acting like a different person. You even feel different."

He was right; she did feel different, entirely different about him. Katharine Monroe had evened the playing field, flooding her mind with fiery memories of Daniel. Turns out they were a rather lustful couple.

Eventually they rolled out of bed and showered together. She went upstairs to get dressed and when she joined him in the kitchen he had a cup of coffee waiting on the island, along with a beautiful arrangement of fresh flowers. He motioned for her to sit, and then asked her to close her eyes. When she opened them, there was a small box from Tiffany's on the table in front of her. Her heart skipped a beat. Daniel leaned over her shoulder as he embraced her from behind.

"Don't worry. It's not what you think."

She suppressed her sigh of relief and eagerly opened the light blue box. Inside was a pair of diamond stud earrings. She gasped, and instead of arguing with him over the expense, or telling him he should not have bought her such a lavish gift, she kissed him. He was the one who finally had to end their embrace.

"Whoa. Whatever Ellie showed up for your birthday, will you please ask her to come back tomorrow?"

"These are wonderful, but I hope this is it. You've bought me enough already."

Daniel laughed. "Now, there's the girl I've come to know and love. Look, I told you I was going to spoil you while you were here, but yes, that is the last of the gifts, except for Amelia's. So, are you hungry?" Daniel went to the refrigerator and pulled out a casserole dish.

"What are you doing?" she said.

"Making breakfast, well, actually I'm going to put this egg dish in the oven that Trevor made and then attempt to fry some bacon."

"Here, let me help you."

He held up his hand. "No, I am going to do this on my own. However, if you want, you can pull a bottle of Champagne out of the fridge."

Eleanor watched as he dumped the entire package of bacon in the pan. "Daniel honey, you need to spread all that out a bit."

"What did you just call me?"

"I guess… I just called you honey. Is that all right?"

He wrapped his arm around her, kissing the top of her head. "You can call me that anytime you like. What should I call you?"

"Well, last night you referred to me as darling, so I guess we could go with that."

Daniel cringed. "Sorry, that's what I used to call you when we were together before. You sure that's still OK?"

"Yes." She wrapped her arms around his waist and could sense he was struggling with his thoughts. She waited a few moments before probing.

He laughed. "There you go again, Miss Sensitivity."

"Would you rather I ignore you?"

"Are you kidding? I love the attention, I just have to get used to it, but yeah, there is something I want to talk about." The door buzzer rang and he turned down the skillet, setting aside the tongs. "Look, I promise we'll do this later, but right now I know a little girl that can't wait to surprise you."

❧

The afternoon of Eleanor's 39th birthday was spent walking The High Line with Daniel and Amelia, eventually meeting Trevor for a late lunch at the Chelsea Market. Despite having kept his long hair and beard he had grown for the summer, Daniel was approached numerous times to sign autographs, and when he had reached the limit of his patience, he called for his car. Back at his apartment, Eleanor spent the remainder of the afternoon learning how to use her new iPhone-her birthday gift from Amelia.

Eventually, they travelled uptown to drop Amelia off at the Monroes' and joined them for a glass of bubbly. Phillip was unusually quiet, offering only a brief update on Lourdes, and that he was home, resting comfortably. Eleanor appeared relieved when she heard the news.

Next, Daniel and Eleanor travelled to New York Presbyterian, where they visited with Zach Walker. They learned Walker would be released by mid-week and that he would return to Los Angeles while he waited out the search for Angie. Zach expressed his disappointment that Amelia had not accompanied them and hoped to visit with her before leaving New York.

Finally, they arrived at the St. Regis where Daniel had booked a suite for the night. After a relaxing soak in the Jacuzzi, he went into the bedroom to get dressed. When Eleanor emerged from the bathroom, hair and makeup complete, she was surprised to find a dress box lying on the bed. Daniel had just finished straightening his tie when he caught her scolding gaze.

"I thought we were done with the presents," she said.

"I know, but I think you'll be happy with this one."

He was right. When she opened the box from Bloomingdale's and pulled out the black satin dress, she gave him a tremendous smile. After all the colorful and revealing outfits he had bought her during their shopping spree, he had managed to find one he knew she would enjoy. It was an elegant dress that suited her perfectly, with a slightly low-cut neckline, a fitted waist bodice and a flared skirt that hit her at mid-calf.

As she held up her dress in the full length mirror, he approached her from behind. "I'm sorry Ellie, but you really need something to go with those earrings." Before she could react, he slipped the diamond necklace around her neck and clasped it in place. He wrapped his arms around her waist and waited for the tirade to begin. It did not. She just stood there, quiet, staring at him in the mirror. Her sea-green eyes sent chills down his spine. "I promise that is the last one."

"You said the same thing when you gave me the dress. It has to stop. This is too much for me. What happens if I get robbed wearing these?"

"I don't think anyone is going to steal your jewels in Edmond, especially with Nina around. Come on Ellie, I have seventeen years of gifts to make up for."

She turned to him, her eyes rimmed with tears. "No you don't."

"Hey, what's wrong?"

She led him over to a small loveseat located near the window and motioned for him to sit. It took her several moments before she could speak.

"I've been thinking about our discussion in the limousine last night, and what you said about our marriage. You have taken on way too much blame and not given enough to me. I may have been young and naive at the time, but I was still an adult. When you asked me to leave, I didn't put up much of a fight. I left, despite my feelings for you. I guess the point that I'm trying to make is that we separated, that's our reality. Then we went on to have other lives and other loves, and that's our reality too. Let's just accept it as our history and get on with the life we have now. No more regrets."

Daniel took a moment to study her face while he considered her words. "Where is this coming from?"

"What do you mean?"

"I'm talking about your change in attitude about us. Where did it come from?"

"I'm ready to move on to whatever is next for us. Isn't that what you want too?"

"Yeah, but up until a few days ago, you could hardly talk about the future. I'm just wondering what got you to this place."

She smiled. "You, and Amelia, that's what got me to this place. I can no longer imagine my life without the two of you in it."

"Well, I was going to wait to discuss this with you tomorrow, but what the hell." He stood and went to his overnight bag, retrieving a large envelope. He returned, removing a lease agreement and handing it to her. "I haven't signed anything yet. The realtor gave me the paperwork before I left California and I put down a deposit so she would hold it for me. Anyway, I found a house in Edmond we can use while I'm visiting. Its s right on the bay and I figured during the weekdays it would be convenient since it would be closer to your work. This is not meant to replace your house, it just gives us a place we can call our own. Of course, that's if you want something we can call ours." He held his breath as he watched her flip through the document. "So, what do you think?"

"I think the rent they are asking is outrageous, and it's going to be expensive furnishing another house, but... I have to say that this is truly the best birthday gift of all."

Daniel squeezed her till her bones cracked. "God, you just made my whole life. I'll leave a message while you get dressed. We need to get going in a few minutes."

"What is your hurry? I thought you said our dinner reservation was at 8:30?"

"Yeah, but we have a stop to make first."

"Oh really, and where is that?"

"Sorry, that's a surprise."

"Well then, I guess then there's no time for this." Eleanor stood and let her robe fall to the ground, revealing a red lace push-up bra and French-cut panties.

"Where the hell did you get that?"

"It's a birthday present from my sister Josephine. She bought it for me in Paris. She said you might like it."

"Like it?"

Twenty minutes later he was pulling her into the limo, his hair disheveled and his body still shaking from their passionate exchange on the loveseat. As his thoughts were flooded with images of her scantily clad body, something occurred to him. He pulled her close, whispering in her ear.

"I don't want you to take this the wrong way, but since we're together again I want you to know that if you were ever to get pregnant, I would be fine with that."

She gave him a questioning look, shaking her head. "Daniel, I'm taking birth control pills. There's no need to be concerned."

"I'm not. I'm just saying I never want you to worry about that with me, ever. OK?" He brought her hand to his lips, waiting for an answer. Eleanor studied his eyes before nodding her head. "And no more regrets. Like you said, it's time to get on with what's next in our lives, and we start *here*."

The limo stopped in front of the Essex House.

"Here? You must be joking." The door opened and Eleanor pulled on his arm. "In case you've forgotten, the last time we were here it didn't end well."

"I know. And tonight I plan to undo all that."

He helped her out of the car and led her into the lobby. Inside, the manager, who 10 years earlier had asked them if he could find them a private room to continue their argument, greeted them with a bottle of Champagne and two glasses. Onlookers started to gather as Eleanor and he toasted to each other, then he gave the manager a signal and Eleanor's friends-Kyle, Nina and Jared- entered the lobby with open arms.

Chapter Twenty Nine

Farewell! God knows when we shall meet again.

∞

Jared arrived at the precinct with three large coffees and stopped in his tracks when he saw an attractive man in a business suit leaning into Bellows.

"Sorry."

He spun around heading back towards the elevators and Bellows called out to him to stop. He turned, forcing a smile and she introduced him to Cameron, the general manager from Barney's. Chen arrived a few moments later, and soon it became apparent that Cameron's early morning visit was an official one. Bellows then tacked two pictures of a blond woman up on the white board behind her desk. When Jared moved in to examine them, he could see that one was of Angie Miller. The other woman looked like Angie Miller and was wearing large sunglasses that masked the upper portion of her face.

"Where were these taken?" Jared asked.

"A security camera from Barney's in Soho. That's the same sales associate in each one. The picture on the right was from this past Friday night, not long after Angie arrived in New York. She was there buying a designer handbag. The picture on the left is also Angie Miller buying a handbag the night Katharine Monroe was attacked."

"It looks like her," Jared said.

"Yes it does," Bellows said. "And when we interviewed the sales associate in March, she confirmed it was Angie as well. However, there is one little problem. The woman that purchased the handbag this past Friday night was significantly taller than the woman that was in the store on March 25. The sales associate who noticed the height difference on Friday night, checked to see if Angie was wearing heels. She was wearing flats."

Jared glanced over at Cameron who was beaming at Bellows, looking pleased that he had done the right thing by bringing the discrepancy to her attention. Bellows on the other hand did not look pleased at all. In fact, she looked like she was ready to implode. Eventually, she thanked Cameron, escorting him to the elevator. Jared watched as the man whispered something in her ear that made her smile.

When she returned to the whiteboard she was all business. "What about the van? Have we heard back from Monroe Industries yet?"

Chen shook his head. "I told the security manager he has until noon. The warrant is ready if we need it."

"What about the evidence we found in Anton Milin's apartment?"

Yesterday's sweep of the 57th Street apartment had produced very little, only a few strands of dark hair and a sticky residue found in the bathroom sink of the master bedroom. A preliminary analysis showed the hairs to be synthetic and the residue some sort of glue.

"I think we need to assume that Anton Milin has been disguising himself from the beginning," Chen said. "It would also support the theory that Milin has been here all along and using another identity."

Bellows folded her arms, staring at the white board, her face void of any expression. Jared allowed her a few moments to collect her thoughts before he broke the silence.

"If Angie lied about her alibi, then we have to assume she was with Katharine Monroe when she was attacked. We just need to figure out how she got into the building without security seeing her."

"I know exactly how she got in," Bellows grumbled. "David, where is the Lutsenko file?"

Chen rushed over to his desk, searching through a bin of manila folders. He returned a few moments later holding a newspaper clipping with a picture of Daphne Lutsenko and Victor Naumov posing for the camera. He pinned it up next to the security shot from Barney's and Jared felt the hairs on his arms rise.

"Their faces are almost exactly the same," Jared said.

"Daphne Lutsenko was in her penthouse apartment the night Monroe was attacked," Bellows said. "She entered the building about fifteen minutes before Zach Walker left. The front desk guard remembered her, but he must not have been paying attention to her height. And of course the cameras weren't working because the electricity was out in the building. I don't know, it's feasible, but it doesn't explain how Angie could pass all those lie detector tests we gave her."

"The doctors in LA did say she is suffering from memory loss," Jared said. "It's possible she forgot what happened that night."

"Well, Angie didn't forget everything. She remembered buying a purse." Bellows groaned, folding her arms. "If it really was Daphne Lutsenko who was in Barney's on March 25, I would need a lot more proof than just some sales person noticing a height difference. What I need to do is connect Daphne Lutsenko to Anton Milin."

"There is Ivan Milin." Jared said.

"I can't even connect Ivan Milin to Anna Lutsenko. All of the Ivan Milin's that the CIA found are not related to her. I'm beginning to think he doesn't exist except in Mrs. Lutsenko's dementia ridden mind."

"Out of curiosity, is the CIA only looking among the living? It's possible our Ivan Milin could be dead. Mrs. Lutsenko hasn't seen her son in decades, right?"

"Well, that's what Daphne told us, but I see your point. Let me check with Dirk on that. I knew there was a reason why I invited you here."

"You didn't. I invited myself," Jared said.

Chen's cell phone rang and he stepped away.

"So, you're not missing out on any special plans back home?" Bellows said.

"I told you they got cancelled. So the guy that just left here, is he a friend of yours?"

"Not really," she said, smiling. "Did you have fun at your little soiree last night?"

"Yes, I'm still full from all the seafood."

"I bet. I wish someone would take me to Le Bernardin for dinner."

Chen cleared his throat. Jared realized that Bellows and he were leaning in close enough that their shoulders were touching. After a moment they backed away from each other and turned.

"There's been a development with Monroe Industries," Chen said. "We're going to need that warrant after all."

※※

After enjoying breakfast in bed, Eleanor and Daniel wandered outside the St. Regis, attempting a stroll through Central Park. For the first time since she arrived in New York she felt at home and began to imagine what it would be like to live here again. Daniel draped his arm over her shoulder and she was catapulted back to her 21st birthday, when they took a similar walk. On that day he asked her to move in with him and before the afternoon was over he had convinced her to say yes.

They found a secluded bench beneath a tree and sat.

"What time do we need to check out?" she said.

"We don't. Fiorelli is keeping the suite through Tuesday, so we can do whatever we want-stay, go, it doesn't matter."

"I don't think I've officially thanked you yet for bringing everyone here. That was an amazing surprise and incredibly generous of you."

"Yeah…well, I think the lingerie that your sister sent you was thank you enough. I'm still not over that second number you tried on after we got back from dinner. When we go to Paris we're going to have to make sure we find that store and stock up."

"I'm sorry, did I miss something? When are we going to Paris?"

"At Christmas, I told you I wanted to go to Europe during your holiday break. We'll take Amelia and if the Monroes want to come along they can. Maybe we can find a house to rent."

"We should do something less involved. I'd be more than happy to come to New York if that is better for everyone."

"I don't think you understand Ellie. I want to get the hell away from here, so we can just be us for a while."

"Us?"

326

"You, me and Amelia."

Eleanor was about to comment when she noticed a man lingering nearby with a camera. She suggested they leave.

"Yeah," Daniel said. "I saw him follow us from the hotel, though I don't see what difference it's going to make now. He saw me with my arm around you. Might as well give him what he came for." Daniel gave her a long kiss. "Let's go back to the room."

Eventually they left The St. Regis and travelled to the Monroes' penthouse. They found Phillip leaving the apartment as they were arriving, and he gave them an apologetic greeting as he hurried out the door.

Inside they found Christine and Amelia waiting for them on the balcony. Daniel inquired as to where Phillip was off to on a holiday, and Christine gave a vague answer about a work issue that required his attention. Lunch was served, and they had a quiet meal as they peered out over Central Park. Afterward, Daniel took Amelia inside to review her homework, and Christine finally spoke.

"Charles is in trouble. That's why Phillip left. I think the police are going to arrest him."

"For what?" Eleanor said.

"I believe for Angie Miller's kidnapping. Phillip got a call yesterday from Detective Bellows. Apparently the car that was used to kidnap Ms. Miller was traced back to Monroe Industries. When the security department checked to see who had the vehicle last, they discovered that the employee had been a personal driver for Charles. This morning the police went to this man's house and discovered from the neighbors he had not been seen since Friday."

"Do you think that Lourdes had something to do with Katharine's death?"

"Honestly, I can't be certain anymore. Katharine kept so much from all of us. It's hard to know what to believe."

Christine's eyes rimmed with tears, and for the first time since they met, Eleanor felt the guarded matriarch's emotions. She squeezed Christine's hand. "I know about Katharine and Lourdes."

"Did Charles tell you?"

"No, he did not. Katharine did."

Christine pulled her hand away. "You haven't touched a bit of your food my dear. Aren't you hungry?"

"You know Katharine is with me, don't you?"

Christine laid down her fork, wiping the corners of her mouth with her napkin before neatly folding it and placing it on her plate. "I wasn't entirely sure at first, but yes I know."

"Why haven't you said something?"

"I didn't want to frighten you away. I just couldn't bear the thought of losing you or Katherine again."

"How is this happening to me?" Eleanor said.

"I don't know. I've never actually met a true medium before. They are much rarer than one would think. But, clearly the dead speak to you."

"It's more than just speaking to me. I share in Katharine's memories."

Christine's eyes narrowed. "Exactly what has she shared with you?"

"Mostly memories of Amelia and her feelings for Lourdes, and then there has been a few about Daniel."

"Have there been any of me?" Eleanor shook her head and Christine gave her an apprehensive look. "Remember the other night when I told you that my daughter had a mentor?"

"Yes, you said you found one for her because you felt you could no longer teach her."

"Unfortunately, that's correct. Katharine was seventeen when they first met, but he didn't officially become her mentor until she was in her late twenties. For the first few years he helped her I guess, but then he started to expose her to some methods that I questioned and I became concerned. Eventually, she and I clashed over it and I asked her to break her association with this person. She refused and for many years thereafter our relationship suffered greatly. It wasn't until Amelia was born that we reconciled. We were never close like we were before our fallout, but at least we were talking and I was a part of my granddaughter's life." She produced a tissue from her skirt pocket, drying her eyes. "I hope you understand now why I didn't say anything before."

Eleanor held Christine's hand. "I won't leave you. I promise. And in fact, I believe Katharine meant for us to be together. That is why I have felt such a strong connection to both Amelia and you."

Christine sighed. "Perhaps Daniel and you could spend the night here. I have a feeling that Phillip and I are going to be in need of company."

"Yes, of course. We would just need to stop by Daniel's apartment to pick up a few things."

"You should hurry. There's a storm coming."

"But the sky is clear."

"Not for long I think."

❈❈

Daniel and Eleanor entered his apartment just as a soft rumble of thunder sounded in the distance. He went into the kitchen while she went upstairs to find an outfit for the next day. A few minutes later he appeared with a garment bag and two glasses of Prosecco.

"I thought you might need this for the dresses I bought you," he said. "They'll never fit in that little suitcase of yours."

"That was thoughtful of you, thanks. So, who was that we just met in the hallway?"

Daniel laughed. "Victor Naumov, he works for Monroe Industries. I forget what he does, but he's pretty high up there. Did he weird you out a bit?""

"No. He's just different."

"Yeah he looks strange with all that bright red hair and those thick glasses, but he seems like a nice guy. I think you made him nervous."

"Why do you say that?"

"Well, he could hardly speak at first and then he started sweating like crazy. Maybe he's not used to looking up at a woman."

"Stop it. We were the same height," she laughed.

"Barely. So what's with all the clothes on the bed? Are you in a hurry to get out of here?"

"No, I just thought I would get organized. I fly out day after tomorrow."

"About that, do you really have to go Wednesday? Can't you wait till the weekend?"

"Alex is already covering my classes for two days and I also have the Napa trip with Nina this weekend."

"That reminds me," he said. "What was going on with Fiorelli and her last night? They seemed pretty chummy."

"Yes, they do appear to be getting along, though it's hard to tell with Nina. She never talks to me about that sort of thing."

"I thought she was your best friend."

"She is, but it's a bit of a one-sided relationship. I talk about me and she listens."

"That doesn't sound like much of a friendship."

"Believe me," Eleanor sighed, "I've tried numerous times to get her to open up, but she just can't bring herself to talk about her feelings. Yet she insists on being there for me. She knows everything about me. Well, except for San Francisco. I told no one about that night."

"Would you like some more Prosecco?"

Daniel hurried from the room, leaving behind a distinct feeling of guilt. She left her packing to go after him, and was halfway down the stairs when he appeared holding a bottle.

"Are you done?" he said.

"I've stopped for now. Is something wrong?"

"No. Why are you asking?"

"Because you left the room rather quickly after I mentioned San Francisco and I got the impression that you were not telling me something."

A flash of lightening illuminated the living room and Eleanor waited patiently as he emptied his glass.

"You know, this sixth sense of yours is starting to annoy me. All right, you got me. I sorta told Alex about what happened between us."

"Alex knows? When did you tell him?"

"That night. I was really upset and I wasn't sure what to do, so I asked him for advice. All I told him was that we had a fight, nothing else."

"So that explains his strange expression when I gave him the letter. Obviously he figured out something else was going on."

Eleanor sank down on the steps, sighing. Daniel filled his glass, handing it to her.

"So what," he said. "Maybe that's why Alex invited me to California. He realized I was still hopelessly in love with you and he felt sorry for me."

"I thought we weren't going to do this anymore. We're supposed to be moving on. Not dwelling on the past."

"You started it. Besides, I don't think we're done with this quite yet. I still don't get how both of our relationships could have been in that much trouble at the same time, and we said nothing that night."

"I asked you what was wrong. You didn't want to talk about it."

"I know," Daniel said. "I still don't get why I did that. But think about what would have happened if I had said something? You would have told me about your problems and everything would have been different."

"We don't know that."

"I do. If I had known about your separation I wouldn't have stopped us that night."

"But I would have."

"Why?"

She polished off her glass. "I wasn't using any birth control at the time, and I wouldn't have done that to you."

He knelt in front of her. She could smell the wine on his breath and his intoxication was mixing with hers. He rested his forehead against hers.

"I want you to remember that night my darling. I wanted you so badly, just like I do now. We started out like this, but now we're going to finish it."

He carried her to the couch. The rain was streaming against the glass as he unbuttoned her dress and kissed her breasts. She was not sure how it was happening, but she was feeling the same yearning and apprehension she experienced that night in his hotel suite. It had to be him she thought, as she helped to remove his T-shirt. He must have been reliving every emotional moment, because she could feel the tension burning inside her as he asked permission to continue. She nodded, and he slipped off her panties while she unzipped his jeans. He paused, his feelings of guilt and desire swirling together. For a moment she thought they would stop, just like they did that night, but when he looked into her eyes this time, his guilt vanished. His desire carried no shame and as they rolled off the couch and onto the coffee table, they sent a vase of silk flowers crashing to the floor.

They elected to take a shower before attending to the mess in the living room. Afterward, while they were on their hands and knees picking up pieces of broken glass, he announced that he would be travelling with her to California in order to finalize the lease.

"I could fly Nina and you down to San Francisco so we could look at furniture."

"We have furniture stores in Edmond," she said.

"We'll have more to choose from in a bigger city."

"This is really going to happen, isn't it?"

"Well yeah Ellie, this is us moving ahead, remember? You're looking a little pale. Maybe you should eat something."

"We're having dinner with the Monroes. I can wait."

"That's three hours from now and after the workout we just had, I'm sure you're starving. I know I am. There's a Thai place right around the corner that delivers."

They finished cleaning the debris from off the floor, and then Daniel called in a carryout order while she went upstairs to continue her packing. As she passed the office she noticed that the door was ajar, and a breeze sent her hair blowing across her face.

"Daniel, did you leave a window open?"

The moment she entered the office she felt Katharine Monroe emerge in full force. She went to close the window and Lourdes slipped his arms around her waist. Her body heated up with his presence.

"You know why I am here," he said.

"Yes. Katharine has a message for us." Eleanor turned to him and stared into his bright, blue eyes. "Do you still love her?"

"I never stopped." They kissed. When it was over, he brushed the hair from her face. "I would do anything for her, so that is why you need to understand that whatever happens next between Katharine and me, it was done for love. I hope you will forgive me."

"Forgive you for what?" she said.

Lourdes pulled out a gun and pointed it at her, forcing her to emit a scream. He pulled her to him, spinning her around so that when Daniel flew into the room it looked like he was holding her hostage.

"Come a step further and I'll be forced to shoot." Lourdes said.

"What the hell are you doing?" Daniel said. "She saved your life."

"Please, step over to the filing cabinet. I have no wish to hurt you."

"No fucking way. Let her go."

"I am going to ask you one more time. Step over to the cabinet."

"Or what?"

Daniel lunged forward. Lourdes barely flinched as his fist met Daniel's jaw, sending him sailing across the room and into the metal cabinet. Eleanor screamed as Lourdes pulled her across the room. He produced a pair of handcuffs from his pocket, quickly snapping one end around Daniel's left wrist, before attaching the other end to the lowest drawer. He assured the cabinet was locked.

"Give me your phone." Appearing disoriented, Daniel fished his cell from his pocket, tossing it on the floor and Lourdes kicked it away. "Are you all right?"

Daniel stared up at him in disbelief. "Are you fucking kidding me?"

"I'll take that as a yes. Now, if you'll excuse us, Ms. Bouchard and I have business to attend to." He pulled her to the middle of the room, gripping both her arms.

"I'm begging you, don't do this to him. Don't make him see this," Eleanor whispered.

"He must. This is what Katharine wanted."

Daniel had managed to sit up, leaning against the filing cabinet. "Ellie, what the hell is he talking about?"

Lourdes shook his head. "If you would shut it and allow her to concentrate you'll see."

"See what?" Daniel growled.

Eleanor started to answer and Lourdes placed his hand over her mouth, silencing her. Then he walked over to Daniel and knelt in front of him, whispering. He spoke for only a moment before returning to her. Daniel appeared to be in shock.

"Now, to show I mean no harm, I'm giving Ms. Bouchard the key to the handcuffs. When we're done she can set you free." He slipped the key into her dress pocket. "We are running out of time Ms. Bouchard."

Eleanor met Daniel's terrified eyes and apologized. Then she turned to Lourdes. "Once this begins, I have no control over what I say or do."

"I understand. I will not let any harm come to you."

"It's not me I'm worried about."

Eleanor and Lourdes joined hands and a surge of energy passed between them, forcing them to their knees. She heard him gasp for air and then the room went dark.

She was standing in the office. The oblong desk in the middle of the room was decorated with a fresh vase of flowers and there was a laptop and a file folder on top. The sun had set and the room was dark. She had a flashlight in her hand and was searching through the closet for batteries. Finally, she discovered a fresh package only to struggle with the thick plastic covering. Eventually she was able to tear apart the container, sending the batteries scattering across the floor. She was on her hands and knees retrieving the spilt contents, when she caught a light in her peripheral vision. She took a deep breath and turned as a bright beam rushed towards her.

The blow hit the right side of her skull, throwing her against the desk. Before she could turn to face her attacker, there was another blow to the back of her head and she fell to the ground. As she lay immobilized she could hear low voices murmuring as they moved around the office. Minutes passed and she heard the sound of a computer keyboard clicking. Then someone grabbed her arm, forcing her up onto her hands and knees.

"Where are the files?"

She did not answer. She could see blood dripping onto her arms and hands. Someone approached, and a pair of men's shoes came into her view. He gripped the back of her hair, pulling her up to the bright beam of light.

Blinded, she could not see his face. When she tried to cover her eyes he smashed the flashlight against the side of her head. She crumbled to the ground. When she was able to raise her head again, she saw the silver flashlight dangling from a hand with a black tattoo of a tree.

The man grabbed her hair, dragging her to the safe and commanded her to open it. She gave him the combination and watched as he sifted through her expensive jewelry and various legal documents. A cell phone went off and she could hear a woman speaking in Russian.

"The whore is dead," the man said. "It's just you and your lover for the time being. Of course, there is also the child. Ah, you're surprised I know about her. She's very beautiful. I would imagine very powerful too."

Katharine spat, spreading droplets of blood everywhere. He removed a handkerchief from his pocket, blotting his face and hands.

"You have spirit Ms. Monroe. I like that in a woman. Just think what power we could wield together if you would join us."

"You still don't understand," she said. "This was all meant to be."

"Spare me your superstitions. I have no use for the old ways. For the last time, where are the files?"

She remained silent.

"You are a fool Ms. Monroe."

He stepped away and a woman with long black hair came into view. Her eyes were bright blue, and she grasped Katharine's head in her hands. There was a moment of mental struggle. Eleanor could feel the tugging in her own brain, and then suddenly an electrical surge swelled inside her head that was directed towards the woman.

The black-haired woman shrieked, grabbing the sides of her head as she doubled over in pain. The man rushed to her side and Katharine managed to rise to her knees, stumbling towards the doorway. She had just entered the hallway when he grabbed her.

"Stop it," he said. "Stop it now."

"It's too late."

Katharine struggled against him, knowing he was more powerful and could end her with one more blow. She latched onto the railing, holding on with all her strength. He grabbed her hair, yanking her back to him so her tip toes were balanced at the edge of the first step. She could see straight down the steep staircase.

"End her suffering or I let go," he said.

The screaming ceased, followed by silence.

"What did you do to my Vera?"

"You told me to end her suffering."

He pushed her, sending her full force down the stairs. Her body sailed through the darkness, weightless, eventually making contact with the staircase. She bounced against the metal steps and then tumbled several times before landing on the lower level floor. She had enough strength to roll onto her back, so she could make out the silhouette of the man carrying a limp body from the office. Darkness moved in as she heard him descend the steps.

"Is she dead?" he said.

"She lives. But you are dead to her."

"Don't leave her this way."

"Make your peace with the world Anton, before it is too late. It has begun. The Passer comes."

"O, here will I set up my everlasting rest and shake the yoke of inauspicious stars from this world-wearied flesh," Lourdes said.

Eleanor had given only minimal thought as to what would happen to her when she died. She believed in some sort of afterlife, but she had never really visualized what that might be. So when she found herself standing next to Lourdes, watching a medic attempting to revive her, she wondered if that moment of visualization had arrived.

"Are we dead?" she asked.

"We're in the Twilight," he said, "that peaceful place between the living and the other world. If you concentrate, you can make all these people vanish."

Eleanor followed his suggestion and immediately Daniel's apartment was empty except for Lourdes and her. "I take it you've been to this place before?"

"Yes, on Friday. Though this time I would have to say it's much more pleasant having you with me instead of watching you slam your fist down on my chest. Come, Ms. Bouchard."

He took her hand, leading her down the hallway into Amelia's room and over to the window seat. "This view was always my favorite. I can see why Katharine loved it here. It's in the middle of everything, yet it's so quiet and charming."

"You told me that Katharine and you weren't together after she married Daniel."

"In the very beginning of her marriage we would meet occasionally. It was entirely my fault. I couldn't stay away. She indulged me, for a little while at least. Don't worry. She was always faithful to Archer. Our encounters were strictly platonic."

"I've felt her love for you. I don't understand why you couldn't be together."

"There were complications that kept us apart. Initially I fought against it, but in the end Katharine convinced me that we didn't have a choice."

"What sort of complications?" she said.

"Perhaps another time Ms. Bouchard, right now we have more urgent matters to discuss. First there is the matter of Katharine's files."

"She didn't tell us where to find them."

"I know. She is waiting to release them."

"Why?"

"As she was digging into Milin's organization she made a terrifying discovery. One I'm afraid that links back to Monroe Industries."

"What is it?"

"That must stay with me until her files are exposed. In the meantime the wheels have been set in motion to hopefully spare the company, but I must ask for your help."

"Of course, tell me what I can do?"

"You must promise that whatever Archer claims happened here today, that you do not dispute it. For now, his story must be accepted as the truth."

"Is that why you forced him to watch us?"

"It was one of the reasons. Please, our time together grows short. Do I have your word that you will do as I ask?"

"Yes."

"Good. Now there is the matter of your safety." He took her arm, guiding her from the room. "That night Karl came after you, Anton sent him. He wants something from you and I fear he will come for you again. You must be ready to use the power that burns within you."

"But I've only had my abilities a short time."

"You are stronger than you realize. All of Katharine's powers rest with you now. Do not be afraid to summon them when the time comes."

"Katharine spoke of The Passer. Just like Monica. What do you know about it?"

Lourdes stopped and met her gaze. His bright blue eyes seemed to fade. "That's what started me on my journey. Monica said those words to me and I sensed that I was a part of all this madness, yet I didn't know why." He took her arm and continued walking. "So I went in search of an answer, and I quickly learned I wasn't alone. It seems this Passer has captured the interest of many of our kind, and as I followed Katharine's trail across Eastern Europe, I discovered she had been searching for it as well."

They arrived on the landing and Eleanor heard a noise in the office. She spun around to see a vision of Lourdes and her rushing into the hallway. They were struggling with each other.

"What am I seeing? Are we still alive?" Eleanor said.

"It's time for you to go Ms. Bouchard."

She turned to face him. "What? No. What about you?"

He brought his hand to her face, caressing it. "Perhaps someday we will meet again."

"But what about The Passer? Did you ever find it?" A sharp pain shot through her belly, pulling her away from Lourdes. "Wait, the child that Anton mentioned. Was he talking about Amelia?"

Another surge brought her to her knees. Lourdes knelt in front of her grasping her face in his hands. His eyes were now a pale blue and she realized he would not be leaving this place. She ran her fingertips over his cheek, and she was certain she felt tears.

"Amelia is your daughter."

He vanished, and she turned to see a vision of herself gripping the railing while she fought viciously against Lourdes. He pulled on her hard, sending her sailing across the landing. Her head slammed against the doorframe and she slid to the floor, blood pouring down her neck. At that moment Daniel came barreling into the hallway with a gun, a handcuff dangling from his bloody wrist. He forced Lourdes to the edge of the stairs. She rose to her feet, attempting to come between the two men, but Lourdes lunged at her, pushing her away. Daniel fired, and Lourdes fell backwards as everything faded to black.

An electrical shock blasted through her limbs. Her eyes shot open as her body sprang upward, screaming for air. For a moment she saw the stunned faces of Daniel and a uniformed woman that was hovering over her before she fell into the darkness again.

Chapter Thirty

To die, to sleep—
No more—and by a sleep to say we end
The heartache, and the thousand natural shocks
That flesh is heir to!

"Lourdes is dead."

Jared opened his eyes to find Bellows sitting next to him with two carryout coffees.

"One of the nurses saw me on the way back from the cafeteria," she said. "The preliminary assessment is cardiac arrest. You like yours black, right?"

Jared nodded as she handed him a cup. He peered across the ICU waiting room to find Fiorelli and Nina St. John asleep.

"Oh, Bouchard is awake now. The nurse said she appears to be out of danger."

Jared gulped down his coffee before he spoke. "Are you going to charge Archer?"

"We'll see what the final autopsy says, but I don't think so. The emergency doc said the bullet wasn't fatal. Besides, he could easily claim self-defense."

"So I take it you're good with his story then?"

"Yes. I believe Lourdes knew all along who killed Monroe. I'm just not sure why he attacked Bouchard, or why he thought she could help him find

Monroe's files that supposedly are hidden somewhere. It will be interesting to hear Bouchard's side of the story."

"I doubt we'll get to talk to her today. I'm sure the doctors won't let us near her."

"Well, maybe they won't let *me* near her, but you are technically her friend."

"Are you taking advantage of my relationship with Eleanor?" he said.

"No, I'm taking advantage of my friendship with you."

"I see, so that's what we are now. Good to know."

She smiled. "So when do you think you'll head back to California?"

"When Eleanor's ready to travel. Why?"

"It would be great if you could stay on for a few more days. I could use your help."

"Well, I got a lot going on back home, but let me see what I can do. I was going to go out for a smoke. Want to join me?"

They left the waiting room and started for the elevators.

"Does your smoking bother your girlfriend?" Bellows said.

"Not that I know of."

"So she doesn't mind that smelly breath of yours."

"No, but it sounds like you do."

"Well, a piece of gum now and then would be helpful."

"I'll be sure to make a note of that," he said. "So, why don't you ask me the question that's really on your mind?"

"Am I being that transparent?"

"No, actually I think you're just being polite. But since you and I are friends now, you might as well just say it."

"Fine," Bellows said. "I've noticed that you haven't been talking with your girlfriend since you've been here, and I was wondering if everything was all right?"

"Thanks for asking and no, everything is not all right." The elevator doors opened and they stepped into the crowded car, facing front. "I have a question for you."

"All right, go ahead," she said.

"By any chance do you have some chewing gum on you?"

He swore he saw Bellows blush, and then she pulled a package from her skirt pocket, handing it to him.

Eleanor slowly opened her eyes to find a bright light dancing across the ceiling. When she glanced down she saw that Amelia was curled up alongside her and the sun was reflecting off her silver key necklace.

"You're awake." Amelia smiled.

"Yes. Why aren't you in school?"

"Nana said I didn't have to go. Are you better now?"

Eleanor didn't know the answer to that question since she had not stayed awake long enough to know how she was doing. She thought it might be Tuesday, but she could not be sure. Her head did not hurt at all, but there was this sound that was beginning to annoy her. Daniel came into view, kissing her on the forehead and she could feel his relief flooding her body.

"The doctor said you're going to be sleepy for the next few days, but that's normal. Are you hungry? Can I get you something to eat?"

"What's that noise I hear?"

"It's just the nurse's station. We're right outside. Kyle and Nina are anxious to see you, would you like me to get them?"

Eleanor glanced over at Amelia who gave her a curious look. The sound grew louder and she rubbed her ears, attempting to stop it.

"Ellie, what is it? Do you want me to get the nurse?" Daniel said.

She nodded and he rushed from the room. Amelia moved to her knees, pressing her fingertips against Eleanor's temples.

"This is what Mommy did when I first started to hear," Amelia said.

"Hear what?"

The noise grew into a powerful rumble and when Daniel returned with the nurse she had to indicate she could no longer hear anything. Amelia was pulled from the bed, the nurse disappeared and Daniel squeezed her hand until she thought it would break.

Suddenly there was silence that was followed by the sound of a voice: Daniel's voice. He was speaking, but his lips were not moving. She listened to his words and shot up in bed.

"Charles Lourdes is dead?"

The moment that Christine Monroe heard her granddaughter's mental plea she left her husband's side and rushed down the corridor toward Eleanor's room. When she entered she found Eleanor and Daniel staring silently at each other. Slowly she approached the bed and immediately recognized Eleanor's terrified expression. It was the same look she had seen on Katharine's face the day her telepathic powers emerged.

A female doctor breezed into the room, prodding and probing Eleanor, asking questions that would inevitably lead to a useless round of tests. Sure enough, a CT scan was ordered, which would then be followed by a hearing examination and an MRI. A part of her just wanted to plant the thought in the doctor's mind that Eleanor was perfectly fine, but Christine knew that would be irresponsible given Eleanor's head injury. How she wished one of their own was working the ICU today. Finally, the doctor left and Christine was determined to get Daniel to leave the room. She was about to force a suggestion when Eleanor spoke.

"Daniel, would you mind taking Amelia for a few minutes while I visit with Christine. Maybe you could both get lunch."

Amelia helped things along by grabbing her father's hand, pleading with him to take her to the cafeteria. Daniel refused at first, but Christine got him to agree when she promised to stay with Eleanor until he returned. He went to find the nurse to inform her of his plans, and they were finally alone.

"Please tell me you didn't hear my thoughts just now," Christine said.

"No. Amelia told me to say that."

"Smart girl…how are you feeling?"

Eleanor's eyes rimmed with tears. "It's very overwhelming at the moment."

"I have to get you out of here and I think I know someone who can help, but in the meantime the best thing you can do is to sleep. It's the only option you have to stop the noise."

"Is Lourdes really dead?"

"Yes, about thirty minutes ago. That's where I was before I came here. Please my dear, close your eyes and rest. I can help you if you like."

"What did Daniel tell the police?"

"I'm not entirely sure," Christine said. "I wasn't here when they questioned him, but I sense that Charles is now a suspect. What happened in Daniel's apartment?"

"I saw how Katharine died."

"Just like you did with Monica?"

"No, this was entirely different. With Monica it was as if I was watching a movie of her, but with Katharine I saw everything through her eyes. I felt what she felt. I was Katharine." Eleanor met Christine's eyes. *-I know about Amelia. I know Lourdes is her father.*

Christine moved closer, grasping the sides of Eleanor's face. "Now listen to me my dear. You have to find a way to stop these thoughts. Now is not the time for this."

"Amelia already knows that Zach is not her father, and she has already been searching."

"How do you know this?"

"I heard her thoughts before she left with Daniel."

"Oh God, that means she heard yours."

Christine ran from the room and found Daniel at the nurse's station speaking with a doctor. When she asked him where Amelia was he pointed her to the restroom. She knew better and started towards the opposite end of the ICU. When she arrived at her destination a nurse was just leaving the room.

"There you are Mrs. Monroe. Your granddaughter said you would be joining her. She's inside paying her respects. She's very brave for such a little girl. Was she close to Mr. Lourdes?"

"Apparently." Christine entered the room and stood next to her granddaughter. "Why are you here?"

"I'm saying goodbye."

"But you hardly knew the man."

Amelia placed her hand over his heart, closing her eyes. Her tiny arms began to tremble.

"What are you doing?" Christine whispered.

Her granddaughter remained silent as Lourdes began to move. Christine gripped Amelia's shoulders and could feel the vibrations pulsing through her limbs.

"Darling, the nurse will be returning soon."

The vibrations increased, causing his body to shake violently from head to toe.

"Amelia, I'm serious. The nurse is on her way."

Her own body was trembling uncontrollably, causing her teeth to chatter. Lourdes began to rise from the bed and for the first time in her life, Christine Monroe felt genuinely frightened. "Amelia Isabella Monroe, I command you to stop this very instant!"

The shaking ceased and Lourdes fell onto the bed with a thud. The nurse returned and Amelia took off, pausing briefly to say thank you before leaving.

"Is she going to be all right?" the woman said.

"I think so." Christine forced a smile as she passed through the doorway and grabbed Amelia's hand. They had travelled only a few feet when the nurse burst into the hallway.

"Oh my God, did you just see him?"

Christine stopped and exchanged glances with Amelia before turning to face the wide-eyed woman "Did we see whom my dear?"

"The man you were just visiting in this room, Charles Lourdes?"

"Well, if you are referring to the body that was lying on the bed, then no, we have not seen it since we left. Why, is something wrong?"

"Yes something is wrong. He's missing!"

The nurse raced down the long corridor, disappearing around the corner. Christine locked eyes with Amelia, trying to determine if she should be incredibly angry with her or scared to death. She decided that neither emotion was appropriate at the moment and that she should focus on leaving the building as quickly as possible.

※※※

Eleanor was released from the hospital Wednesday morning with instructions to rest and not travel for 48 hours. Daniel and she spent a silent ride in the limo, and when they arrived at the Monroes' apartment, they were surprised to find Jared and Detective Bellows waiting in the sitting room with Phillip and Christine. They were asked to join the group and by the time Eleanor sat, she knew from the thoughts in the room what information had been shared with the Monroes. It was heartbreaking. Eventually she had to excuse herself, escaping into the foyer where she sat at the fountain. It was not long before Jared joined her.

"I'm sorry," he said.

"Lourdes knew this was going to happen. He knew the police would think he was behind Katharine's murder." She started to cry and Jared wrapped his arm around her shoulder. "I feel sorry for Phillip. He loves Lourdes like a son and this is killing him inside."

"Are you positive you didn't see Anton's face during your vision?"

"Yes. Katharine didn't show us what he looked like, just like she didn't tell us where the files are hidden. Were you able to make use of the other information I shared with you?"

"Your description of the woman in your vision, the one you said was named Vera. She matches the description of a woman that was seen with Lourdes in a hotel in Moscow. I don't think that will help him at all, if anything it will further incriminate him."

"What about the tattoo I saw on Anton's wrist?"

"Archer didn't mention it in his statement, but I'll see what I can do about it."

"He saved my life, Jared. If he hadn't pulled me off that staircase I would have fallen. Just like Katharine Monroe. Now he's dead, or missing, or whatever he is, because of me."

The sound of voices echoed in the foyer and they turned to find Bellows signaling for Jared.

"What about The Passer?" she said.

"Eleanor, I told you. There's nothing I can do about that right now."

"But Katharine used the same words as Monica. She warned Anton, and I'm beginning to think that The Passer is part of the reason they got killed."

"Listen to me." He grasped both her hands, squeezing them. "The reason Monroe and Bellaso were murdered was because they had something Milin wanted. Most likely it was information that seriously threatened his organization. Now either that information was locked up in their heads or it is hiding somewhere, waiting to be found. What concerns me now is that *you* may be the repository for that information, not some hidden files. I think Lourdes knew that when he came to you. He was trying to get to that information."

"Didn't you listen to a word that I said yesterday? He already knew what Katharine discovered. He was there to take the blame so he could help protect the company. He's innocent."

"No, he's not, Eleanor. We have proof he is connected to these people. He very well was lying to you, just like the rest of these bastards who think they can fuck with people's lives."

"What are you talking about?"

Jared released her hands and pulled a cigarette pack from his pocket. "Sorry, I didn't mean to say that."

Eleanor attempted to read Jared's thoughts and was met with silence. He turned to her, his dark eyes looking more tired than usual.

"Jared, what's going on?"

"I am not like you, if that is what you're asking?" he whispered.

"I can't feel or hear anything. It's like you're not even here."

"I know."

"What are you?"

"Eleanor, please. I can't get into it right now. Listen to me. You have to be careful. Some of these people cannot be trusted."

"You mean people like *me?*"

"Again, I'm sorry. I don't mean to offend you, but yes, I mean people like you. Unfortunately I've had firsthand experience with how manipulative and underhanded some of them can be."

"Lourdes is not that way. He loves Katharine and she loves him. I know he would never do anything to hurt us."

Jared's eyes narrowed. "I hope you're right, because other than using conventional means, I really have no real way to protect you from Milin or anyone else like him."

Bellows appeared, clearing her throat. Jared asked her to give them a few more minutes and she studied them for a moment before starting for the front door.

"Look," he said, "I will do what I can to help Lourdes. However, before I go there's something I need to tell you. Mik is going to call you shortly, but I want you to hear it from me first. There's a problem with the restaurant."

❊❊

Eleanor had packed the last of her belongings when Daniel entered the bedroom.

"OK, everything is set. My driver will pick you up at 5:00 tomorrow morning. What about Kyle and Nina, should I have him swing by their hotel first?"

"They're staying here tonight so we can leave together."

"Really, Fiorelli is giving up his suite at the St. Regis? God tell him to hold on to it and we'll use it. It would be nice to have some privacy for a few hours."

"What are you talking about? We have an entire wing to ourselves."

"You know what I mean, privacy from the Monroes, the cops, everything. I just want this whole fucking thing to be over so we can get on with our lives." Daniel plopped down in the chaise lounge near the window and held out his hand. "Come here."

"I need to finish packing."

"You can do that later. Come sit with me."

He held out both arms, motioning for her to join him and reluctantly she left her task and sat on the lounge. He pulled her alongside him so that her head was resting against his chest.

"Where are the dresses I bought you?" he said.

"They're inside the hanging bag you gave me."

"You should lay it out so you don't forget it. What about the jewelry?"

"They are already in my suitcase."

"Good. It'd be just like you to leave them behind."

"They were a gift from you. I won't leave them. Can I get back to my packing?"

"No, I'm not done yet. You shouldn't be travelling tomorrow. You know that. Your head is full of staples and you have a concussion."

"Kyle and Nina will be with me. I'll be fine."

"And then what? You'll go to River Mist and work all day when you should be resting. Why are you doing this?"

"I told you. Ben walked out on the restaurant last night and left Mikayla to deal with everything. She knows nothing about running that place and she needs someone who knows what to do. I helped Jeremy manage that business for years and I know what it takes."

"Can't you wait two more days? At least see the doctor and make sure your head is all right."

"I said I would check in with my own doctor when I get home. You have to understand, Friday and Saturday are our busiest days and the weather is going to be nice, so I'm sure it will be packed all weekend. I'm going and that's all there is to it."

She stood up and returned to her suitcase.

"OK, if you're going to be an ass about this, then I'm going with you."

"We've been through this already. You need to stay here with Amelia and be around in case something comes up with Katharine's case."

"The Monroes can watch Amelia, and if Bellows has a damn question she can call me. I promised the doc I would take care of you and that's what I'm going to do."

"I don't need you to take care of me."

"Yes you do. You look like hell Ellie. When's the last time you ate something?"

"An hour ago, remember? You were with me in the kitchen."

"That was a bowl of soup. When's the last time you had a real meal?"

"I really can't recall."

"It was your birthday dinner, Sunday night. The next day you hardly ate any breakfast and you didn't touch your lunch. And of course we never got to eat the Thai food that I ordered."

"I didn't realize you were keeping a record of my eating habits."

"Well I am, and I know you've lost weight the past few days. You look sick."

"Daniel, if you think this approach is going to convince me that you need to travel back with me, it's not. Amelia needs you to be here. This is where you belong."

"I belong with you. We belong together."

"No we don't, not like this."

Daniel sat up in the chaise and leaned forward. "Not like what?"

"You know what I mean."

"This is about *him*, isn't it?"

Eleanor zipped her suitcase shut. "For the love of God, Danny, this has nothing to do with Jeremy. This is about us and what happened in your apartment on Monday."

He lowered his head, seemingly preoccupied with the pattern on the rug. A moment later he was biting away at his thumb and Eleanor sat next to him.

"I understand why you can't talk about it right now, but eventually we need to, and I think until you're ready, until *we're* ready to discuss it, we should just spend some time apart."

"Are you breaking up with me?"

"No, I am not. I'm trying to give us space while we process what happened to us."

"I don't need to process a damn thing."

"Yes you do. You are filled with so much anger right now that it's frightening."

"No I'm not."

"Yes you are. I hear it in your voice and see it in your face. You are angry, very angry at what happened between Lourdes and me. Don't say that you aren't because I can feel it in every muscle in my body and I can hear your raging thoughts pounding in my head."

"OK, enough with the drama. Yeah I'm angry, who wouldn't be? That bastard chained me to the floor and forced me to watch you with him. It was horrifying, and then when he took you into the hallway and I couldn't see you anymore and you screamed, I lost it. I blanked out. I don't remember pulling the handle off the filing cabinet or hurting my wrist. I just picked up that gun and aimed."

Daniel slumped forward, burying his hands in his face. Soon his body began to quiver and she held him while he cried. When she was certain he was done, she pulled a tissue from her pocket and dried his eyes.

"How's that for processing. I hope you're happy," he said.

"I wish I could say we were finished, but I can't."

"I don't want to talk about this anymore."

"You need to understand what really happened that day."

"I don't need to understand anything," he said. "I know what I saw and I don't have to hear your version. Can't we just be done with it so we can get on with our lives?"

"It's not a version Daniel. It's what I believe, and I won't be able to move on from here if I don't do this. What transpired between Lourdes and me in your apartment had nothing to do with him. Yes he restrained you, but everything else was me. Whatever you may have seen him do or say was because of what was happening to me."

"Stop it Ellie."

"If you think about it for a moment, you know I'm right. You saw it with your own eyes. You heard everything I said. I saw how Katharine died that night."

He gave her a blank stare. "That's just fucking nuts. I think your concussion has really screwed with your head."

"You heard me recount every detail of her attack down to the combination of your safe. You can't deny that."

"What I saw was an insane man terrorizing you into doing something against your will and as far as I'm concerned when he dragged you into that hallway he was trying to kill you."

"That's what you believe?" she said.

"Yeah, that's what I fucking believe and I would suggest you stop with the crazy talk, or I'm going to take you back to the hospital and demand they give you a brain scan."

Daniel walked over to the window, leaving her alone on the chair. His thoughts were exploding inside her head and she fought against them as she struggled with a response. Finally, unable to shut out the noise she decided to leave the room. She had barely made it to the doorway when his words flew into her mind. At first she was not sure if she had heard him correctly, but after a few moments of concentration she understood him perfectly.

She realized that fear was driving his hurtful thoughts, and if she would just accept it for what it was, an angry, frightened rambling, then she could just walk out now and he would never know that he had wounded her. By the time she summoned up the courage to speak she was in tears.

"How could you possibly think I would ever do anything to harm Amelia?"

"What?" he said.

"You're questioning if it's safe for her to be around me. How can you think that when you know I love her? How could you think such a terrible thing?"

Daniel did not have time to reach her. As he bounded across the floor Christine appeared, pulling Eleanor into the hallway. Phillip and Trevor rushed past them, pushing Daniel back into the bedroom as the door slam shut.

Chapter Thirty One

Good night, good night! Parting is such sweet sorrow
That I shall say good night till it be morrow.

Eleanor and Amelia spent their final moments together sitting in the Monroes' living room, watching the first signs of the sunrise appear over Central Park. Phillip joined them, announcing that the car had arrived, and that Nina and Kyle had gone ahead to meet the driver. He escorted them to the elevator, kissing her on the cheek before returning to the apartment. She knelt down, soaking in Amelia's crystal blue gaze.

"You'll call me tonight?" Amelia said.

"Yes, as soon as I am home and settled in." Eleanor kissed her on the forehead, reaching for the call button.

"Wait, take this with you."

Amelia started to remove the key necklace from around her neck and Eleanor stopped her. "No, that was a gift from your mother. It should stay with you."

Amelia frowned, and then reached into her dress pocket, producing the silver heart pendant that Katherine was wearing when she died. Eleanor held her breath as Amelia placed the chain in her palm. There was no use in refusing it. The child had no intention of letting her leave without it.

"You should go before the elevator gets here," Eleanor said.

Amelia embraced her one final time before returning to the apartment. The doors opened, and she had just stepped inside when she heard a deep voice echoing in the hallway. She turned as Daniel stopped the doors from closing.

"Ellie, I'm sorry. The last thing I want is to hurt you, but I don't know what else to do."

"And I don't know what I can say to make you believe me, so please just let me go before we both say something *else* that we're going to regret." She pressed the button for the garage level as he stepped away, allowing the elevator to close. "Wait!" His arm came between the doors, forcing them open. She held out Katharine's necklace. "There is something you can do."

"How did you get this?"

"How do you think? It was meant to be hers, Daniel. Fix it for her."

She handed him the pendant and moved to the back of the elevator. For a moment their eyes met before she forced her gaze to the floor. Then the doors closed, and she was alone.

When she entered the garage she was surprised to find The Monroes' car parked outside the elevators. The driver quickly emerged from his front seat perch, opening the back door. Christine leaned forward handing her a carryout coffee.

"You didn't think I would let you leave without saying goodbye?"

"Thank you. Where are Kyle and Nina?"

"I told Daniel's driver to take them on to the airport. Would you like a tissue my dear, it looks like you've been crying."

She sat next to Christine, drying her eyes. "Oh God, Daniel thinks I'm some sort of freak."

"My son-in-law is a damn fool. I could never understand how someone with his limited imagination could be such a talented actor."

"I really don't blame him. I have a hard time believing all this and I'm living it."

-Yes, but you certainly believe in all this now, don't you?

Eleanor nodded as Christine's silent words lingered in her mind.

"Don't worry my dear, he loves you. Eventually, he'll find a way to get past this."

"I don't want him to get past it. I want him to understand what is happening to me."

"Why? I've never told Phillip about my abilities and we've lived a happy life together. Katharine did the same with Daniel, though I know she struggled with it, but in the end she knew it was the only way. Once a mortal knows you can read their thoughts or feelings, it's just a matter of time before the paranoia and the accusations begin."

"But how can you have a trusting relationship based on lies? I can't be like this- whatever I am- and not have him share in it. I want him to believe in all this. I want him to *believe* in me." Eleanor drank her coffee. "Oh my God, that's what she meant."

"Who meant what, my dear?" Christine said.

"You remember when I told you about the ghostly being who came to me on the anniversary of Jeremy's death? She said *help him believe*. All this time I thought her message was about Jared and finding Monica Bellaso, but that wasn't it at all. She meant for me to help Daniel. She wants *him to believe*."

"Well, if that is the case then you certainly did your best to convince him yesterday. Though you see where that got you. I don't understand why it would be necessary for him to know anything. He's been blissfully ignorant his entire life, why spoil it for him now?"

"Everything has changed because of what happened between Lourdes and me. He handcuffed Daniel to that filling cabinet so he would see us. He said that is what Katharine wanted."

Christine gave her a bewildered look. "Good God child. What on earth has happened to your eyes?"

Christine took a compact from her purse, passing it to her. Eleanor looked into the mirror and saw the same crystalline gaze she had seen in her dream.

"They're Katharine's eyes," Christine whispered.

"I know." A lump formed in Eleanor's throat and she could hardly speak. "It's her. It's been her all along. Katharine came to me that night."

Christine held her, and while she wept she felt Katharine stirring inside her once again. Her eyes felt heavy, and as her world faded to black she heard the words pass through her lips.

"Mother, I need your help."

When she woke, several minutes later, Christine was drying her face with a tissue and the limo was parked near the front entrance of Atlantic Aviation. Mrs. Monroe instructed the driver to give them a few moments before opening the door.

"What happened to me just now… is that what Charles experienced?" Christine said

"I don't know. Katharine chose not to share her message with me. Whatever it was, it was only meant for you."

Christine squeezed her hand. "This is madness. You shouldn't be travelling in your condition and if I had any sense in my head, I would take you back to New York with me this very minute."

"We both know I need to go home. It's where I belong."

"I would strongly argue that you belong here, with Amelia and me. But, since you insist on returning, I have had to make the necessary arrangements to get you the help that you need. And after that experience I just had, I am thanking the heavens that I did."

"I beg your pardon?" Eleanor said.

"In all my time on this earth I have not once had to force the hand of one of my own kind, until now. I don't particularly feel good about it and most likely it will come back to haunt me, but it had to be done. You lifted me from my despair when I thought no one could and you gave me a reason to hope for better days. I love you like a daughter, and therefore I will do anything to ensure your safety and well-being. You are different than anyone I have ever encountered, and although I believe I have been able to help you come into your own, your abilities are such that you need someone with a certain kind of experience to guide you. Believe me, it caused me considerable pain to have to do this, but I had no choice."

Christine signaled her driver to open the door and Kyle slid onto the seat opposite them.

"Before you say anything my dear, please listen carefully. We are going to begin this revelation here, with the three of us, so I know that Mr. Fiorelli honors our agreement per my expectations. Then, the two of you will continue this conversation on the plane and when you arrive in California I expect a full report on how you plan to proceed. I don't care how angry or dismayed you become with him. That makes not a bit of difference to me. All I care is that you have the guidance in place to help you fully realize your powers. Have I made myself perfectly clear? I'll assume by the stunned look on your face that is a *yes*. Mr. Fiorelli, you may proceed."

Chapter Thirty Two

I would my father looked but with my eyes.

The office door flew open and Mikayla sank into a chair next to the desk, groaning. "Honey, I have not seen it this busy since before the recession hit. What is going on?"

Eleanor glanced up from her paperwork, bleary eyed. "I told you the nice weather would bring them in town. How is it out there, do you need me back on the floor?"

"No, we're steady for now. How's the scheduling going?"

"Good. It's done through the end of the month and tomorrow I'll write up the beverage order. Jonah is doing a great job. He really has that kitchen in shape."

"I know. It's the best it's ever been, well, since Jeremy passed away. Your friends are real gems helping us out. Kyle is a natural. I don't think I've ever seen the bar this busy before."

"Yes, and it's packed with women," Eleanor said.

"True, but they're paying customers who are drinking lots of alcohol and are happy to have him serve them. What's wrong honey, you seem irritated. Did you two have a little tiff?"

"It was more like a huge misunderstanding about our entire friendship since the moment we met."

"That sounds serious."

"It is. Speaking of which, when are we going to talk about what happened with Ben?"

"Oh darlin' now is not the time to get into that mess. I need a quiet room and a bottle of vodka for that conversation."

"Come on Mik, that's why I'm here. I'm your friend and I want to help you through all of it, not just the restaurant."

"Well, if you must know. Ben was in here doing his paperwork and I guess my phone was going off every few seconds. He went to turn down the volume and that's when he saw the messages from Jared. There were several. One in particular was rather amorous," Mikayla winked. "And I guess Ben saw them, got pissed off and left."

"What do you mean you guess? He didn't tell you that he read them?"

"Well, not exactly. He just walked out of the office, told me he was done with the restaurant for good and that my boyfriend and me could run it from now on."

"That sounds like he read them."

"Yes, but that's not exactly why he was upset honey."

"What do you mean?" Eleanor said.

"Ben isn't mad because Jared sent those texts. Ben is mad that I didn't tell Jared about *him*."

"Pardon?"

"Oh God sweetie, I really wanted to wait until we had time, but now that you got me started you might as well know the whole story. About three weeks ago Ben and I were at one of the kid's games, can't even remember which one, they have so many. Anyway, we were sitting together having a good time when he suggested that we all go out to dinner afterwards. So we did. I can't even remember the last time we all had a meal together. It was nice. The kids spent the entire time texting and Ben and I just talked. When we were ready to go I asked him if he wanted to come over to the house for a drink. He did. And then he spent the night."

"Oh boy," Eleanor said.

"The next morning I wasn't too concerned. I figured it was our way of bringing closure to everything. I didn't make a big deal of it and neither did he. I went to work at the coffee house he came here. Then later, after the lunch rush was over and we were cleaning up, something happened between us. I'm not sure what it was, but a minute later we were going at it on this desk like there was no tomorrow."

Eleanor quickly pushed her chair away while Mikayla grabbed a menu, fanning herself.

"Oh don't worry honey I cleaned up this entire office afterward. Now where was I?"

"I don't know, but I could use a drink right about now," Eleanor said.

"I tried to warn you. Anyway, after our episode in the office, Ben suggested we get together and talk about it, which we did. That's when I told him about Jared. I thought for sure that would make him put on the breaks, but it didn't. He ended up staying the night again. After that he started sleeping over pretty regularly."

"Where was Jared during all this?"

"By that time your theater had burnt down and he was caught up in all that. Business here was nuts with the summer season coming to an end, so we didn't see much of each other."

"Is that why you cancelled your trip, so you could be with Ben?"

"Well, sort of," Mikayla said. "We did want to spend some time with the kids, and at the same time see where all this was taking us."

"So, what now, what are you going to do about Jared?"

"Ben has said good riddance to me. I guess Jared and I will continue if he'll have me."

"But Mik, it's obvious that Ben was attempting to reconcile. Don't you want to at least find out if there is still a chance for the two of you? Maybe you should go talk to him."

"And tell him what? I didn't say anything to Jared because I wasn't ready to break it off. I still don't want to break it off. I love Jared and that's the truth."

"I know you love him. But you also love Ben too, right?"

"Yes, of course. But Ben was the one that left me, remember? I tried to reason with him. But he refused to talk about it, refused to get counseling and then he just moved out and filed for a divorce."

"I know," Eleanor said. "And you have every reason to be cautious as to his motives right now, but it seems to me that he's having second thoughts and perhaps you are as well. Talk to him. If anything just to give Ben and you the closure you deserve."

Mikayla leaned back in her chair, her eyes watering. "Damn, honey. Look what you've gone and done. Now I'm going to have to reapply more of that fancy mascara I bought online."

"Yes, I saw the Sephora box in the desk drawer."

"It helps me relax when I'm upset. There's a real pretty nail polish in there you might like. It kind of matches what you have on now."

"I forgot about that. Manicure. It was a birthday present from Daniel."

"I was going to say. You would never do that on your own. So how is that hunky man of yours? You haven't said a word about him since you've been back."

"I've been home less than a day. There really isn't time to talk about that sort of thing."

"And yet you managed to find out plenty about Ben and me. What's wrong honey? Did something happen between you two?"

"Yes, and it's difficult for me to discuss right now, but when I'm ready I promise I'll tell you. In the meantime, I'm here for you. We will get through this. Jeremy's Tavern will survive."

"Oh honey, the restaurant is gonna be fine." Mikayla said. "The summer season saved us. Jonah's amazing cuisine is bringing in all sorts of people, and once we get through the holiday season we can start remodeling."

"I still don't think it's necessary to change everything. The customers appear to be fine with the current décor."

"I think they tolerate it because the food is so good, but I've seen people's reactions and I've heard the comments. Our new clientele is not so enamored with the mountain man thing and quite frankly, neither am I."

"But this is Jeremy's place." Eleanor said. "People come here because of him."

"Honey they *came* here when he was alive. And in case you haven't noticed a lot of those folks don't hang around here anymore. That's why our business started to suffer- that and we couldn't find a decent cook. But all that has changed now. We have turned things around. And of course that famous boyfriend of yours certainly helped. Jeremy is gone, and keeping everything the same isn't going to bring him back. It's time to make this place our own."

Eleanor stared down at the desk, her vision slowly clouding.

"Well there you go," Mikayla said. "Now I've made you cry. I guess we're even. Here honey, have a tissue. I'm gonna fix my mascara and then go out there and see if the women are still salivating over your poor friend Kyle."

"I'm sure he is just fine."

"My, my, I guess you aren't too smitten with the men in your life right now, are you? Well, me neither. I can't believe Jared stayed on in New York with that detective woman."

"He's busy with this case, but I'm sure he'll be home soon."

"He's always busy with a case. It's the story of his life. Honey, what is that sound?"

Eleanor opened her bag and saw an incoming video call flashing on her phone. "It's Amelia!"

"I can't believe you got your cell phone to work in here. Well, at least you're happy to see her. I'm gonna leave so you two can chat."

Eleanor accepted the call as Mikayla closed the office door and Amelia's beaming face appeared on the screen. "Hey sweetie, how are you?"

"I'm good. How is the restaurant?' Amelia said.

"Fine. We seem to have everything under control for now. How was school? Did you do well on your spelling test?"

"I didn't go. Daddy let me stay home. Guess what? Nana and I are coming to see you."

"When is that?"

"Soon," Amelia said. "Daddy is going away to make a movie."

"Oh...when did this happen?"

"Last night. He was on the phone a long time. He said he had to sleep on it. What does that mean?"

"Well, that he wanted the night to think about it first before he gave an answer."

"He didn't sleep."

"It sounds like he said yes. Though, I'm sorry you two will be apart. Perhaps you should ask him to take you with him. I'm sure he could find you a tutor."

"I don't want to go," Amelia said. "I want to see you."

"Oh honey, believe me I want to see you too, but Daniel is your father and you should be with him."

"You could be my mommy and we could all be together."

Eleanor smiled through the tears that were rimming her eyes. She thanked God that Amelia could not read her mind at the moment. Just then Nina appeared in the office doorway.

"You need to come out here. Mikayla got a phone call and had to leave and a busload of tourists just pulled up. Also, I think Fiorelli may be in trouble. Some woman climbed over the bar and refuses to let go of him."

"I have to go honey. I'll call you later."

"Eleanor, wait." Amelia kissed the screen of her phone. "I love you."

"I love you too honey. I love you very much."

When Amelia ended her call with Eleanor she knew her father was standing outside her bedroom door. He was angry and he was about to tell her something she did not want to hear. She thought about calling out to her grandmother for help, but instead she closed her eyes, drowning out his thoughts. He had to shake her to get her attention.

"Did you hear me Amelia?" he said. "Who was that on the phone?"

"You know who it was Daddy."

"Excuse me?"

"You know it was Eleanor."

"I have no clue who you were talking to, and by the way when I ask you something I expect an answer, not some smart assed comment."

"That's not a very nice word."

"Sorry, you're right. That wasn't very nice." Daniel sat on the bed. "So what have you been doing all afternoon, baby girl?"

"Listening to my new music and I did my reading homework."

"And talking to Eleanor, but I knew that already, didn't I?"

"Nana showed me where New Zealand is. It's far away."

"I know. I'm going to get you out of school right before Thanksgiving, so you can stay with me until I'm done filming. It will be summertime there."

"When will you see Eleanor?"

"I probably won't see Ellie. She has her job and the restaurant and she won't be able to get away."

"You should ask her. Maybe she'll say yes."

Daniel pulled her into his lap, hugging her. "Listen honey, Ellie and I are having some problems right now and it's possible we won't see her for a while."

"Is that because you think she's crazy?"

"What? I never said that. Amelia, look at me. Did Ellie tell you that I said that?"

"No."

"Then where did you hear it, because I know I didn't say it."

"You're thinking it."

Daniel removed her from his lap and sat her on the bed, facing him. "How could you possibly know what I'm thinking?"

"I just do."

"OK, then if that's true, tell me what I'm thinking now?"

"You won't be mad at me?"

Daniel chuckled. "No, I promise. Go ahead."

"You think I'm doing something to your head? What does screwing mean?"

Daniel's smile left him and his eyes narrowed. "Keep going."

"Now you think I'm saying this because of Eleanor and…"

"And what?"

"You don't want me to talk to her anymore."

Her father shot up from the bed, rushing towards the door. She ran after him, standing in the doorway so he could not leave. "I'm like Eleanor."

"No you're not."

"Daddy, listen to me. Eleanor and me are the same."

He knelt down in front of her, grasping her shoulders. "Stop saying that. You are not like her, do you hear me? Eleanor is not well in the head right now. She needs help and until she is better I don't think you should talk to her anymore. Do you understand me?"

Her father was scaring her now, not because he was angry, but because of what he was about to do. She ran to the bed, grabbing her cell phone on the way to the bathroom. While he pounded on the door she made one last call to Eleanor.

Christine closed the door to Amelia's bedroom and sat on the rose-colored loveseat near the window, with her hands folded in her lap. Quietly, she waited. A moment later the bathroom door opened. Amelia emerged with her cell phone in hand and sat next to her.

"Daddy is in the hallway," Amelia whispered.

Christine pointed to her head.

-*What were you thinking child? You scared the man to death. Now he is contemplating whether or not he should leave you with us.*

-*I was trying to help Eleanor.*

-*Well, unfortunately, you made things worse for her and for you. Now he doesn't want you to have any contact with her at all.*

-*I just want Daddy to believe in us.*

-*Just like Eleanor. Haven't you seen what your attempts have done to him? The man is seriously thinking about taking you to the doctor. Not to mention that if he does decide to leave you here I'll have to sneak you out to California. Then I'll need to make up some lie to tell your grandfather, or worse. What a mess you have created.*

-*Daddy is different. We just have to help him. That's what Mommy said.*

-*How do you know that?*

-*Mommy's thoughts are inside Eleanor.*

-*What else did your mother tell you?*

-*To help that man in the hospital.*

Christine rubbed her eyes. -*And exactly how did you help him?*

-*I made his heart feel better.*

Christine shot up, smoothing the creases from her skirt. "Give me your phone, please. I am complying with your father's wishes."

"No."

-*Amelia, I need your cooperation until I can figure this out. In the meantime, I'll find a way for you to talk to Eleanor. Now, your father is about to come through that door and I want you to be extremely apologetic to him. And stop rolling your eyes at me. You're an actress child. For God's sake act.*

Daniel entered the room and Christine stood, handing him Amelia's cell phone. He slipped it into his jean pocket.

"I believe Amelia has something she wants to say to you," Christine said.

Amelia approached Daniel with clenched hands, and Christine suddenly realized that her granddaughter had no intention of obeying her commands.

The child was about to speak when a familiar tune began to play. Daniel gave Amelia a quizzical look as she pointed to his pocket.

His panic shot through her veins. Christine listened to the barrage of thoughts that were racing through his mind, praying that he would not land on the one that would cause Amelia to lunge for him. Unfortunately he did, and Christine had to latch onto her screaming granddaughter while Daniel rushed from the bedroom with Amelia's phone to his ear.

❈❈

Eleanor knelt next to Jeremy's tombstone, clearing away the debris before placing a bouquet of flowers on his grave. Her eye caught a metal object on the ground and she reached across the plot to retrieve it. As she brushed the loose dirt off the surface, she realized it was the ring that Jared had left there on the anniversary of Jeremy's death. Unable to read the markings through the encrusted mud, she worked with her fingernail to clean it but was interrupted when her stomach started to burn. Quickly, she slipped the ring into her jean skirt pocket before the powerful presence made it to the top of the hill.

"I thought I would find you here," Kyle said. "I tried your cell several times."

"I turned it off. Too many unwanted calls."

"Nina and I were worried. Mikayla said you were crying and you nearly hit another car leaving the parking lot. Did something happen?"

"Funny, I thought you would have known already."

"It doesn't work that way Eleanor. I just don't listen in whenever I feel like it."

"Then you need to explain to me how it does work, because I am having a hard time grasping how someone can be my friend for eighteen years and not tell me who they are."

"I tried to tell you on the plane, but you wouldn't listen."

"I was a little upset at the time. Can you blame me?"

"No, I can't." Kyle knelt next to her. "The flowers are beautiful."

"Thank you. I didn't mean to alarm everyone. Should I call Mikayla?"

"When I saw your car I let her know that I had found you. So, the three of us figured you must have talked to Archer. What happened?"

"I guess he is having some issues with Amelia and he asked me to stop communicating with her until he can get them resolved."

"What sort of issues?"

"I wouldn't know," she said. "I ended the call before he could say anything else."

"I'm sorry. I know how much you care for her."

"If I never see Amelia again, I don't know what I'll do. It will be like losing Jeremy all over again and you can't imagine how that feels."

"Well, as a matter-of-fact, I don't have to imagine," he said.

Eleanor turned to him, studying his luminous brown eyes. "Why didn't you tell me?"

"Believe me, there were many times over the years that I wanted to, but I couldn't."

"Were you afraid I would think you were crazy?"

Kyle laughed. "Somehow, I think you of all people would have understood, but it was more than that. I wasn't in a position to tell you."

"I don't understand."

"Eleanor, I think you have already learned that we don't go around telling people about our abilities whenever we feel like it. You've seen what kind of heartache that can bring. But, I also happen to belong to a group that is very private. We do not reveal ourselves to anyone, not even our own kind, unless that individual is invited to join us."

"So, the only reason you told me now is because Christine forced you?"

"Let's just say Mrs. Monroe garners great respect in our community and when she came to me with her request, I took it very seriously. If you're asking would I have made a move without her influence, I believe I would have. The incident with Lourdes made it necessary."

"Will you be in some sort of trouble with your group, now that you've told me?"

"Right now I am only concerned about you. Tell me. Have you accepted your abilities?"

"I thought I didn't have a choice," she said.

"You always have a choice to ignore them, but that has its drawbacks as you know. There is also a way to suppress the powers. However, it takes as much effort to do that as it does to develop them, and I would recommend against that."

"Why?"

"Eleanor, you are different. I've never known anyone who came into their abilities at such a late age and with such velocity. From what I understand, you've grown very strong in a brief amount of time. What normally takes most of us years to develop you are accomplishing in a matter of months. And it appears you are manifesting new abilities at a very rapid rate."

"Do you think something is wrong with me?"

"No, I do not. If anything, I would say you are very special. Please, let me help you realize your talents and maybe I can finally repay you for saving me those many years ago."

"I hardly think salvaging your college career can be compared to this," she said.

"No, but meeting you had a profound influence on my life."

"You can be so dramatic sometimes."

"Well, I am Italian. So, what do you say Dr. Bouchard? Will you grant me the privilege of becoming your mentor?"

"On one condition. Tell me what's going on between Nina and you?"

He stood, brushing the dirt from his jeans. "First, tell me that you and I are all right."

-For now we are.

Kyle smiled at her silent message and started to leave.

"Not so fast," she said. "Answer my question."

Kyle stopped and sighed. "I like her very much. In fact, I adore her."

"Does she know how you feel?"

Kyle shook his head. "Are you ready to head back?"

"I need a few more minutes." She turned to Jeremy's grave. "Kyle, wait."

"Yes?

"Do you think we continue to exist after we die?"

The burning feeling inside her belly suddenly vanished, and she was filled with joy. When she turned to Kyle he was smiling.

"Promise me you will ask that question at our first session," he said.

He disappeared down the hill and she returned to her task. When she finished arranging the flowers, she leaned back to examine her handiwork, her gaze slowly moving up the tombstone.

"I shall forget, to have thee still stand there, rememb'ring how I love thy company."

She brought her fingers to her lips and pressed them against the marble surface just above Jeremy's name.

Chapter Thirty Three

More light and light—more dark and dark our woes.

Jared flicked his cigarette to the ground as Bellows pulled up to the curb. She released the trunk and he tossed in his suitcase before joining her in the front seat.

"Whoa, are you wearing jeans?" he said.

"I got a surprise for you."

Bellows pulled up in front of the precinct where Detective Chen was standing with three coffees and a large envelope tucked under his arm. He motioned for Jared to roll down the window, passing him two cups before jumping in the back seat. The two men exchanged a few pleasantries while Bellows inhaled her coffee.

"All right boys, enough chit-chat. Let's get to it."

Chen reached into the envelope, handing Jared a CIA report titled: *The Milin Connection.* Jared turned to Bellows who was grinning. "Seriously, the CIA gave the report this name?"

"I sort of told Dirk about our little joke. He couldn't resist. But Adams, your hunch was right. Ivan Milin was among the dead. In fact, he has been dead for over forty years. Finally, they were able to connect him to Anna Lutsenko."

Jared scanned several pages of the report. "Ivan was from Dmitrov. That's the same town where Charles Lourdes had his accident."

"I know. After you dug up that information on Edward Lourdes I asked the CIA if they could find anything. That's how they stumbled on Ivan. All of the Milin clan is in that report: Ivan, Karl and Vera. But don't let me spoil it for you. Go ahead David, take him through it. This is a story I can't wait to hear again."

❊❋❊

Daniel woke as he had every morning since he watched Eleanor disappear behind the elevator doors. He wiped the tears from his eyes and sat up in bed, tired and miserable. Today he would have been in San Francisco with her picking out furniture for their new home in Edmond. But, instead he was alone in bed, hungover, wondering why the buzzer was ringing and no one was answering it. Then he realized that it was Sunday and Trevor was off.

He pulled on his robe and stumbled into a living room filled with moving boxes. After the incident with Lourdes he decided to sell the apartment. The hope was to be out by Friday and have the condo on the market before he left for New Zealand. As he lumbered towards the foyer he heard the door latch engage and was surprised to see Phillip and Amelia enter.

"Sorry," Phillip said, "but when you didn't answer I had to use the key. We were on our way to church and Amelia needed something from her room."

Daniel watched as his daughter rushed up the stairs, purposely avoiding his gaze. Ever since he confiscated her cell phone and forbade her to communicate with Eleanor, she had not spoken to him. He glanced over at Phillip who appeared unusually sullen.

"You're welcome to join us," Phillip said.

"No thanks. I've got plenty to do here. Plus I need to run an errand."

"You seem lost, son."

"I am very lost."

"Then I can't think of a better place for you to be."

"You know the church thing is not for me."

"I know. But I think you could stand a little self-reflection right now, whether you believe in God or not. Get dressed. We'll pick up some coffee on the way."

※❂※

By the time Bellows had entered the Lincoln Tunnel, Chen had reviewed the entire CIA report. Jared was still processing all the information that had been shared, but one detail lingered in his thoughts.

Ivan Milin died the same day that Charles Lourdes had nearly drowned.

Jared turned to Detective Chen. "If I read this report right, it suggests that Ivan was with Edward and Charles Lourdes when they had their boating accident. Edward Lourdes may have been responsible for Ivan's death."

"You're right," Chen said. "But the report never states that Edward was at fault. However, it does give us a connection between Lourdes and the Milin family. More importantly, it gives us a connection between Charles Lourdes and Anton Milin."

"So," Jared said. "Anna Lutsenko was married to Vladimir Milin, the eldest son of Boris Milin who at that time was the head of the Milin family crime organization."

Chen nodded. "Correct. A month after Ivan Milin died, his father, Vladimir, was killed in a hunting accident. Then Anna left the town of Dmitrov and moved to Moscow, where she lived with her father-in-law, Boris. Within a year she gave birth to Karl and then two years later she had Vera."

"I don't get it. The CIA ran a check on Karl Milin, how come we couldn't find him?"

"Well, there are several reasons. First off, Anna's last name at the time was Vasilly. She never took her husband Vladimir's name, so that's why we could never make a match to Anna Lutsenko or Anna Milin. Secondly, there is no father listed on the birth certificate for Karl or Vera, and the last name given to both children is Vasilly, not Milin. Anna's children have her last name.

"So David, where is Anton Milin in all this?" Jared said.

"Well, as you know, there is no documentation or records of Anton Milin ever being born. However, based on what Angie Miller has told us about Anton's age he would have been approximately ten years old around the time Anna Lutsenko, rather Anna Vasilly, moved in with Boris Milin. Anton would have been living with Boris at the time, which means Anna would have known him."

"What happened to the girl, Vera?"

"Basically, she disappeared," Chen said. "If you read the report you will see at around age five she vanishes. As far as we can tell she doesn't hold a Russian driver's license or passport under the name of Vera Vasilly or Vera Milin."

They arrived at Teteboro and Bellows parked the car in front of Atlantic Aviation where they continued their conversation.

"So what next?" Jared said. "I'm assuming you are going after Daphne Lutsenko?"

"With everything I've got," Bellows said. "She is my best hope of finding Angie Miller and hopefully the rest of the Milin clan. I'll let you boys have a moment."

Bellows left the car while Jared shook hands with Chen. When he joined her she had removed his suitcase from the trunk. He lit a cigarette and she gave him an annoyed look.

"Really Adams, do you have to do that now?"

"It's going to be my last smoke for a while. What's wrong? Are you mad about last night?"

"No, and be quiet. Chen will hear you."

Jared tossed his cigarette and then motioned for her to follow him into the terminal. After he checked in, they went to a quiet corner of the waiting area.

"So what's up?" he said.

"Do you think Angie is still alive?"

"I don't know. I hope so."

"If I am able to prove that Daphne Lutsenko bought that purse the night Katharine Monroe was murdered, that means Angie no longer has an alibi. If I find Angie, I'm going to have to arrest her."

"I'm sorry Sheila. I know you like her. I do too."

"Why do you have to go? Can't you stay and help me figure this damn mess out."

"I need to get Karl Milin, or whatever his name is, out of Edmond and down to LA."

"And you need to figure things out at home," she said.

"Yes. Are you sure you're all right?"

"Of course, I'm not some teenager you know. Look, you love her. I get that. She's lucky to have an honorable sap like you."

Jared chuckled. "Boy, you are not going to make this easy on me, are you?"

Daniel Archer's pilot appeared in the lobby, signaling for Jared. He and Bellows could only stare at each other, sharing in an awkward moment. Neither was sure what to do. Finally, she just backed away. She had only taken a few steps when he pulled out the package of gum she had given him earlier in the week and popped a piece in his mouth.

A moment later they shared in a proper goodbye.

✄✄

When the service had ended, Daniel and the Monroes returned to the Flatiron District where they went out for lunch. Afterwards, he attempted to leave the group so he could run his errand, but Phillip insisted on accompanying him while Christine and Amelia returned to his apartment.

It was a quiet walk to his destination and as they approached the jeweler where Katharine had purchased her heart pendant, Phillip broke the silence.

"I was wondering if this was where you were going. What made you change your mind?"

"It's a long story," Daniel grumbled. "And I really don't want to talk about it."

"If this is about what happened in your apartment, you should just spit it out. I assure you after the week I've had, there is nothing you could say right now that would shock me."

"Phillip, what happened to Ellie and me was unexplainable. I'm not sure if I'll ever be able to talk about it."

Phillip nodded his head and smiled. "She spooked you son, didn't she?"

"Well... yeah, you could say that."

"Daniel, I don't know how you've been a part of this family for all these years and not have noticed this before, but there are a whole lot of unexplainable things going on around you."

"What do you mean?"

"Let's drop off Katharine's necklace first. Then you and I need to have a little chat about the women in this family."

Phillip opened the door, motioning for Daniel to enter and they walked into the tiny shop where a bald man was sitting behind the counter, busy at work. A tiny bell rang as the door opened and the man peered over the rim of his glasses, smiling.

"Well hello there Mr. Archer. I'm glad you were able to find us."

Daniel had spent the previous day searching through Katharine's collection of business cards and had located the name of the jeweler that had made her necklace. He had called ahead to explain the situation and that he would be stopping by today. He produced the pendant from his jacket pocket and anxiously watched as the jeweler examined it.

"So Mr. Bolles, do you think you can repair it?" he said.

"Please, call me Mike and I am happy to say that the necklace is perfectly fine. By any chance did you bring the key with you?"

"What key?"

"Why the key that goes into the heart to open it. It's silver, about three fourths of an inch long, and if you insert it at the base of the heart it will release the bottom portion."

Daniel glanced over at Phillip who appeared to be as stunned as him. "Release it? Are you telling me there is something in the necklace?"

"Well yes, of course. That's where she kept her files for the book she was writing?"

Daniel was not sure if his father-in-law would be able to keep up with him as they ran the two blocks from the jeweler to his building, but he did. They raced up five flights of stairs, and when they burst through the front door of his apartment they had to pause for a moment in order to catch their breath. Christine and Amelia rushed into the entryway, surprised by all the commotion, and in between gasps Daniel threw out his hand, asking Amelia for her key necklace.

Everyone was silent as he produced Katharine's pendant from his pocket. His hand was shaking so much that Phillip had to steady him while he inserted the silver key into the heart. There was a click, the bottom of the pendant released, and Daniel held up a tiny metal object so that Phillip and he could examine it together.

Seconds later he was inserting the miniature flash drive into the USB port of his laptop and dozens of folders appeared in a pop-up window. He expanded to full screen, clicking on the first folder titled 01_Russia_ Mariyanna. His heart was pounding so fiercely that he could hardly breathe.

When he opened the first folder and scanned it, Christine was asked to remove Amelia from the office. After skimming through several folders, Phillip placed his hand on Daniel's shoulder, asking him to stop. He then pulled out a handkerchief to wipe his eyes before placing a call to Detective Bellows. Daniel removed the USB from the computer and then went downstairs to polish off what was left of his last bottle of Woodford Reserve.

✖✖

Daniel entered his apartment to find the movers busy at work. He made his way to the kitchen where he pulled out a fresh bottle of bourbon from the cabinet and poured a hefty shot. Trevor appeared a few minutes later.

"How did it go with the police?"

"I'll let you know after I'm numb enough." Daniel emptied his glass.

"Goodness, that bad?"

Daniel sat at the island, rubbing his eyes. "I can't get into the details, but Katharine was involved in such disturbing shit, I don't think I'll ever understand it. But, in the end she did a remarkable thing. It was a fucking dangerous thing, obviously. But it was a good thing."

"Can I at least ask if this had to do with Monica Bellaso?"

"Yeah, mostly it did. But there is other stuff that cropped up that has made it worse, a lot worse, especially for Monroe Industries. Phillip has a real shit storm ahead of him."

"Is there anything I can do to help?"

"Just get us packed up in time to leave for New Zealand."

"Daniel, there is something I need to discuss with you."

Daniel looked up to find Trevor sitting across from him, his hands folded with an unusually grim expression on his face. "What is it?"

"I can't go with you to New Zealand."

"Trev, we talked about this. You are going with us. You only have to stay a few weeks until Amelia and I get settled. Then you can come home."

"You don't understand. I can't go with you, because I'm leaving New York and moving to San Francisco. I'm officially giving you my thirty-day notice."

Trevor sat silent while he waited for a response. When it was evident that none was forthcoming, his assistant went to the cabinet to retrieve a glass. He returned to the island and poured both of them a hefty shot of bourbon.

"Please don't get angry with Michael," Trevor said. "But, we've started a search for a new assistant. We have several highly-qualified candidates already. You could interview them next week and I could have someone trained and on a plane with you by the time you leave."

Daniel felt his chest tightening and he went to the sink to splash cold water on his face. Trevor approached, handing him a towel.

"Are you going to be all right?"

"Hell, I don't know," Daniel said. "I think I just lost all the feeling in my legs."

Trevor took his arm, leading him back to the island. They sat in silence and it took Daniel a while before he could speak again.

"You picked a hell of a lousy time to do this."

"Yes, and I'm deeply sorry for that," Trevor said.

"Well, I'm not going to ask you if you were unhappy working for me. Or if I did anything to piss you off. So just tell me what I have to do to convince you to stay."

"I have enjoyed every moment working for you, and you have been nothing but generous to me. But, the truth is I've never been truly comfortable living in New York. And when I visited San Francisco this summer, well, I felt like I belonged there."

"Did Fiorelli have something to do with this?"

"Only that he introduced me to some people while I was there, and I was able to make a few connections. Eventually that led me to a job opportunity."

"Look, I know you work for me and basically run my entire life, but it's more than that. I consider you my friend, Trev. Hell, sometimes I think you're my only friend. I'm really going to miss you."

"I'm going to miss you too, but I hope we can remain friends."

"Yeah, of course we will. Once I stop being pissed off."

Trevor nodded as the doorbell rang and he disappeared. A moment later he returned, announcing that Victor Naumov was waiting in the foyer. When Daniel arrived he found the COO of Monroe Industries standing with his arms behind his back, his expression grim.

"I'm sorry to bother you Mr. Archer. I didn't realize you had company."

"No, that's OK. Come on in. Can I get you something?"

"I would love a drink."

"Then you came to the right place." Daniel led him into the kitchen and pulled a glass from the cabinet. Naumov sat at the island while Daniel poured.

"Thank you. I wasn't ready to go upstairs and face my Daphne just yet. This business with Charles and her family is very disturbing, not to mention the implications for Monroe Industries. I have to say I'm completely overwhelmed at the moment."

"So obviously Phillip told you everything. What's going to happen next?"

"Thankfully, the police need more time to review the information that you found. It will be a while longer before anything is announced. We're going to need to call an emergency board meeting of course. Thank God the annual shareholder meeting took place already. I guess in a way your timing was impeccable. How on earth did you figure out that there was something in Ms. Monroe's necklace?"

"Long story," Daniel said. "So what's the deal now? Will you take over as CEO?"

"It's one of the options on the table. Phillip will need to make the recommendation and of course the board will need to vote on it. Then there is the issue of Daphne and her mother's connection to all this sad business. I'm not sure how that will play out."

"It's not your fault. You didn't know that this Milin person had infiltrated the company."

"No, but I am the COO and my girlfriend is possibly related to this gangster. That sort of thing does not bode well with shareholders. Not to mention this man is still out there and may not be done with any of us yet. It's a good thing you are moving from this building, though it's unfortunate that you have to give up such a nice space. Will you be moving in with Phillip and Christine?"

"Yes, until Amelia and I find a place."

"And will Ms. Bouchard be joining you eventually?"

"I can't say."

"I'm sorry. That was rude of me. Your relationship with Ms. Bouchard is none of my business. I should really get going. Good luck in New Zealand." Naumov hopped off the barstool and started for the foyer. Daniel followed, opening the front door.

"How did you know I was going to New Zealand?"

"Phillip mentioned it to me. He said you are leaving soon."

"Yes. I have to be on location by the end of the month."

"Well then, it explains why you are in such a hurry to vacate the apartment. Will you be able to see Ms. Bouchard before you leave?"

"Doubtful," Daniel said.

"Ah, then it is too bad that you will not be able to say goodbye."

Naumov's bright blue eyes met his. He bowed his head as he backed away towards the elevator. Daniel moved into the hallway.

"Why are you so curious about Ellie? You only met her just the other day."

Naumov pressed the call button. "Yes, that is true. But just that one time was enough to make an everlasting impression on me."

"What does that mean?" Daniel said.

Naumov smiled, and his teeth glowed through his thick red beard. "Let's just say there is something about her that is special. Goodbye Mr. Archer."

Daniel watched Naumov disappear as the elevator seemed to swallow him up. A chill came over him. He pulled out his cell and was dialing Ellie's number when the intercom rang. He returned to the apartment to answer it, and was informed that Detective Bellows had just entered the building. By the time he opened the door she was already on the landing.

"Sorry to bother you, but I noticed the truck outside, and thought I would stop by. I didn't realize when we talked this morning that you were moving out so quickly?"

"First off, *we* didn't talk. You asked questions and Phillip and I answered them."

"Well Mr. Archer, it's my job to ask questions."

"Yep, I get that, but I didn't appreciate the tone. I felt like Phillip and I were on the witness stand. Haven't we been through enough with this bullshit investigation? You've spent the last five months making it look like Katharine was up to no good. You drug her name and her family's name through the wringer. And then when you finally get the information that everyone has been searching for, you go after me and Phillip like we're the guilty ones. What the hell. Katharine gave you enough evidence to put this Milin family away forever. That's if you can ever find them."

"Mr. Archer, I can understand your frustration, but will you please keep your voice down. The information we shared with you today is strictly confidential and it would also be in the best interest of you and your family to keep it that way. As you know there are serious implications for Monroe Industries and we are trying to help Mr. Monroe the best we can."

"And what about Monica and what happened to her? What is still happening to people like her? It's disgusting."

"Mr. Archer, can we please move inside where we can have a private conversation?" Bellows said.

Daniel motioned for her to follow him, and marched into the kitchen, grabbing the bourbon bottle off the table. As he filled his glass, his thoughts travelled back to earlier that morning, when Bellows and Chen revealed the true purpose of Katharine's trips.

Her name was Mariyanna Besleaga. She was born in Moldova to a teenage mother who died in childbirth, after which she was shuffled between family members. When she was twelve, one of her uncles, a local thug, sold her off to Anton Milin's organization to pay off his gambling debts. From there she was absorbed into the sex slave trade in Moldova and eventually was moved to the Ukraine where she remained until she was fourteen. Then she was transported to Russia; however, during that trip she managed to escape her captors. A few months later she surfaced in Italy, where she took on a new identity and started her life as Monica Bellaso.

Daniel pounded back his drink. "So what are you going to do about Monica? Are you going to let the story get out?"

"Eventually we will," Bellows said. "But for now we need to keep it confidential. As you know Ms. Monroe gathered a considerable amount of information over the past three years, and it is going to take us, as well as the CIA and the FBI, some time to go through it all."

"Monica was just a child when she was forced into prostitution. How do you have a normal life after something like that happens to you?"

"I don't know. But obviously Ms. Bellaso was resilient and determined to go after these people and she found a kindred soul in your wife. They were both incredibly brave."

"And she's dead, and the people who killed her are still out there."

"We'll find them. In the meantime I need you to keep what you have learned today to yourself and not discuss it with anyone. Can I have your word on that?"

Daniel nodded and Bellows started for the foyer. He followed after her. "If you're heading up to the Lutsenko apartment then I suggest you tell Naumov to shut his trap."

Bellows turned to face him. "What do you mean?"

"He was just here and was jabbering on about what we learned this morning."

"How would he know anything about it?"

"He said Phillip told him."

"That's impossible. Mr. Monroe is still at the precinct with Detective Chen. He wouldn't have had an opportunity to talk to Naumov. Is he upstairs now?" Bellows pulled out her phone, punching in a number.

"Yeah, he said he was going to talk to his girlfriend. Hey, what's going on?"

Bellows sprinted up the stairs and he could hear her speaking with Detective Chen as he closed his apartment door. Suddenly he had an uneasy feeling about the conversation that had just transpired and he called Eleanor.

❋❋

Anton was washing his face when he heard the bedroom door open. A moment later a pair of white silky arms wrapped around his chest. He continued as she moved slowly down his stomach to his groin. He had to stop momentarily so as to not splash water all over his white shirt. She laughed as she glanced at him in the mirror.

"Anton, you have such a handsome face. I wish you didn't have to wear that disguise."

Daphne Lutsenko turned him around, unbuttoning his shirt. Slowly she worked her way down his chest until she was on her knees, removing his belt. He leaned against the sink, looking up at the ceiling as he felt his trousers give away. The warmth of her mouth enveloped him and he closed his eyes, remembering the first time he experienced this exotic creature. He reached down and caressed the back of her soft, curly hair, allowing another moment of pleasure before pushing her away.

"Anton, what's wrong?" she said.

"It's time to leave."

"Why, has something happened?"

"Yes. This place is no longer safe for us. I must get Vera away from here."

"It's still too dangerous to move her. She doesn't know who we are."

"She will. Once I take her to the woman."

"I thought you didn't believe in her. You said that Katharine Monroe was lying to you."

"I've since changed my mind." Anton walked into the bedroom, removing his shirt.

"What about our plans? What about Victor? Isn't he supposed to run the company?"

"Our plans have changed. I'm sending mother home today and you will accompany her."

"I don't want to go back to Russia, not without you."

Anton turned to her. "Are you disobeying me?"

"No, I just don't want you to be alone…with *her*."

"Vera is our family. We are meant to be together. That is our way."

"But for a long time it has been only you and me," she said.

"You have always known this was a temporary situation and that Vera would join us eventually. That time has come. Stop with your childish nonsense and do as I command."

"I won't leave you alone with her. In her current condition she's a danger to all of us and you know it."

"You can't go with me Daphne, you have to take mother. The portal is not safe for her and time is short. I have to get to the woman while she is still vulnerable."

"Listen to you. I thought you didn't believe in our family's superstitions."

"You weren't there Daphne. You didn't feel the power that this woman possesses. And she doesn't even know it. She is beyond all of us. Just imagine what it would mean to our family if we possessed that power."

"You are a fool. You want power?" She moved towards the bed, unbuttoning her blouse.

"Stop it Daphne. It won't work this time."

"It always works. You think you control me, but we both know it's always been me."

"I said stop."

She pushed her leather skirt down past her hips, revealing the expensive lingerie he had bought her in Italy. "I've given you pleasure you will never know with her." She removed her bra and panties and lay down on the bed, naked. "And I will love you Anton. Vera never will."

She was right. He was unable to resist her seductions. It was the power she had always held over him. He moved on top of her and ran his hands over her breasts. Her pale skin radiated against his slightly darker complexion and for a moment he tried to forget that she had become a liability to the family. His loins ached for her, but he knew in the end he had to be stronger.

She pulled him down onto the bed and moved on top of him. Slowly he moved his hands up to her beautiful white neck. He waited until the moment when her focus shifted away from him. Then with one quick movement Daphne Lutsenko's head snapped, and Anton Milin's half-sister was dead.

※※

Detective Bellows had just finished her call with Chen when she arrived at the Lutsenko's apartment. She rang the buzzer several times and was surprised when Mrs. Lutsenko answered the door. The old woman invited her in and motioned her towards the living room. Bellows scanned the area, eyeing the long corridor that lined the north side of the apartment. "Is anyone home?"

Mrs. Lutsenko did not respond and Bellows followed her into the living room, sitting on the couch next to her. On the coffee table was a tray with a steaming tea pot and three cups.

"It looks like someone is here. Ma'am, do you know where Daphne or Mr. Naumov might be?"

The woman's eyes lit up. "Daphne and Ivan are in bedroom."

"Mrs. Lutsenko, I know you can barely understand a word I say, but your daughter is probably not with Ivan. He died a long, time ago ma'am, when you were living in Russia."

Mrs. Lutsenko gave her a vacant stare. "Tea?"

"No thank you. You know, perhaps I will have a look around and see what might be keeping your daughter and Mr. Naumov."

Removing her handgun from her holster, Bellows moved down the north corridor. She paused, listening for any movement before rounding the corner. The hallway was empty and dark with the exception of a light shining through an open doorway. Her phone vibrated in her jacket pocket and she saw that it was Chen.

"Where is my back-up?" she said.

"We're on the way. What's going on?"

"So far I've found Mrs. Lutsenko wandering around telling me her dead son Ivan is here. I'm heading back to the bedrooms now."

Bellows inched along the wall, stopping before she reached the doorway. Slowly, she moved her head past the frame and saw that it was a small sitting area with a set of open double doors on the opposite end. She took two long strides and stopped when she heard the sound of muted voices. Poking her head around the corner, she discovered a woman sitting in a wheel chair, her head slumped over. Bellows darted into the room, moving in front of the woman.

"Chen, call an ambulance. I just found Angie Miller and she appears to be drugged."

"Where are Lutsenko and Naumov?" he said.

"No sign of them yet, but I can hear people talking nearby."

Bellows turned towards the sound of the voices and saw a door, slightly ajar. She moved quietly across the room, peering through the doorway to discover that the sound was coming from a television that was on. Slowly she opened the door and walked into the room.

"It's nothing, "she said. "No one is here."

A creaking noise sent her spinning around and for a brief moment she came face to face with Charles Lourdes before he swung a silver metal object at her head. She fell to her knees and his arm snapped around her neck in a chokehold. With lightning speed he pulled her from the bedroom. They travelled so fast that her feet left the ground, and as she clawed at his arm, she noticed a black mark at the base of his right hand. Suddenly they stopped, and she realized they were in the kitchen, next to a deep freezer.

"You've got to be kidding," she screamed.

He responded in Russian as he tossed her inside. She only had a second to realize she had landed on the naked body of Daphne Lutsenko before everything went dark.

Chapter Thirty Four

Eyes, look you last!
Arms, take your last embrace!

Bellows was about to lose consciousness when she heard a loud banging noise above her. The freezer door opened, a bright light blinding her as she gasped for air. Then a large, dark figure reached towards her, grabbing her by the shoulders lifting her up. When she was able to focus she realized Daniel Archer was carrying her across the kitchen. By the time they reached the living room the police had arrived and Chen was rushing towards her, relieved that she was still alive.

"Get someone into that back bedroom, now!" she yelled.

As Chen led several officers down the hallway, Archer remained with her while she attempted to regulate her breathing.

"How the hell did you know I was in the freezer?" she said.

"Chen called me. I guess your phone was still on when you were attacked and he knew you had just left my apartment. I ran up here as fast as I could."

"Did you see anyone else?"

"No," he said.

"Are you all right? You must have seen Daphne Lutsenko in there."

"I did. I think I'm going to go get Amelia out of school and take her to the Monroes."

"That's a good idea. I'll have someone take you." She laid a hand on his shoulder. "Thanks for what you did back there. You saved my life."

"You should thank Chen. I just provided the muscle power."

"Now I see why they hire you for those action movies."

After Bellows arranged for a police escort for Archer, she went to the back bedroom where she had been attacked. She retrieved her gun and noticed a set of wheelchair tracks leading back to the far end of the room, ending at a thick metal door. Summoning an officer to assist her, he readied his gun while she slowly opened it.

Inside they found a sound proof room with a bed and four metal shackles secured to the walls and floor. On the nightstand there were several empty syringes. Chen entered the room, standing next to her.

"Well, it looks like this is where they were keeping Miller. What the hell were they doing to her in here? These chains are made of iron." Bellows moved around the bed, examining the restraints. "Take a look at this. Where the metal plates are secured, it's almost completely pulled out from the wall. I can't believe Miller would be strong enough to do this."

"I think you better come take a look at something we found in the kitchen." Chen said.

Bellows and Chen walked to the opposite end of the corridor and entered a room full of police and technicians. The medical examiner had already arrived and was aiming her camera down into the deep freezer. They walked to the far end of the kitchen where part of the wall was now missing, exposing a space the size of a telephone booth with steel walls.

"Check this out." Chen stuck his hand inside the closet and a sudden bolt of lightning shot from one side to the other.

"What the hell was that?" Bellows repeated Chen's action, garnering the same result. She felt a tiny vibration pass through her hand. "What is this thing?"

"Don't know. We've got someone coming in from the lab to take a look at it."

"Any idea how they got out of here?" Bellows said.

"Not yet. The front desk security never saw them leave, and there's nothing on the recordings. We've contacted the transportation authorities and we're watching the airport, train stations, busses, everything."

"Who did you tell them to look for?" she said.

"Charles Lourdes, Angie Miller and Anna Lutsenko, should there be someone else?"

"Add Naumov to that list," Bellows said. "Supposedly he was here." Her phone rang and she was happy to see it was Adams. "Your timing is amazing."

"Chen just called me. How are you?"

"I'm fine. Listen, the man who attacked me looked like Lourdes, but there was something on his right wrist. It looked like a tattoo."

"Lourdes doesn't have any tattoos," Adams said.

"I know," Bellows moaned.

"All right, calm down. Who is over at your precinct right now that can help me access the recordings from that hotel in Moscow?"

"Morgan should be there. Adams, if you find a tattoo on Lourdes, we have a whole new problem."

"Yep, I know. Let me get working on it."

Bellows ended the call as Betsy Cartwright, her evidence technician, approached, holding up a baggie with several hairs in it.

"Ma'am I just discovered these in the bathroom sink that was adjacent to the room where you were attacked. There's a sticky residue on them. I want to wait for preliminary analysis, but this may be the same type of synthetic hair and glue that we found in Anton Milin's Fifty-Seventh Street apartment."

※⊛※

Zach Walker unlocked the front door of Angie Miller's house and stepped into the dark foyer. This was the first time he had been home since he returned from New York, choosing to stay with a friend while Angie was still missing. Already he was feeling uneasy in the empty house and quickly set to his task to retrieve some equipment he required for his recording sessions. Empty box in hand, he shuffled across the house to the music room.

Several minutes later he emerged, and on the way to the front door he thought he noticed a movement in the hallway leading to Angie's office suite. He called out to see if anyone was there. When there was no response he continued through the living room and it was not until he was in the foyer that he heard the distinct sound of a cat's meow.

"Snowflake."

Zach set the box down and sauntered into the office. He scanned the room and eventually located Angie's white Persian cat, perched on top of a bookcase. As he approached, she moved to greet him, allowing him to pick her up. She appeared to be well fed and groomed, and he figured Angie's assistant had seen to her needs.

As he stroked Snowflake, he noticed a pile of photographs strewn across the top of Angie's desk. One in particular caught his attention. It was an eight by ten photo of Eleanor Bouchard standing in the front yard of Angie's vacation home with Detectives Adams and Reyes. Then he glanced down at the other photos and was surprised to find one of Angie and him. He heard a sound behind him and spun around.

"Angie, oh my God, you're here."

He let the cat go, giving his girlfriend a long hug. She did not reciprocate and when he pulled away, he could see that her pupils were dilated. "Hey baby, you don't look so well. Maybe you should sit down?" She collapsed against him and he helped her to the couch. "Honey, I don't know what you took, but I'm gonna call for help." As he dialed 911 Angie began to mumble. He leaned in, asking her to speak up. "What do you mean I should get out now?"

Something sharp pierced his neck and he fell into her lap, paralyzed. Angie muttered something in a language he did not understand and a cloth was placed over his mouth, forcing him to breathe in the burning fumes.

❊❊

Christine was smoothing her hair when Phillip entered their bedroom carrying two martini glasses. He placed one on the vanity next to her and then sat on a nearby loveseat. She glanced at him in the mirror and watched as he crossed his legs, sipping his drink.

"My, my, whatever is the occasion? Certainly we are not celebrating anything."

"No my dear, we are not. In fact, I can say with all certainty that today will probably go down as one of the worst days of my life."

"Are we drinking to forget our sorrows then?"

"Heavens no, I'm not going to turn into a drunk like our son-in-law. If you must know, I figured you would need one of these lovely libations, and I didn't want you to drink alone."

Christine turned to him, meeting his pale blue gaze. "And why would I need a drink?"

"Come my dear and sit with me. We need to talk."

Christine picked up her glass and took a seat on the couch next to him.

"Have I been a good husband?" he said.

"Of course you have."

"And for the most part I've stayed out of your way. I haven't asked many questions and rarely demanded that you comply with my wishes."

"Yes darling, you've been an absolute saint," she said.

"You're a lot to deal with my love. No question about that. Most mortal men wouldn't have lasted more than a few years with you, but I defied all the odds. I'm still here. And I realize today, of all the worst days I could imagine, that all this rubbish around me means nothing. It could all go away tomorrow, and I wouldn't care, just as long as I have you in my life."

"Now I need a drink."

"Not so fast, I'm not finished yet. Christine, I've asked very little of you over the years, but now I'm afraid our current situation is requiring you to step in and lend a hand."

"Good heavens Phillip, please don't tell me you want me to help you run the company."

"Well, that's a thought given that Naumov has disappeared and these criminals have infiltrated our supply chain, but no. I'm thinking more along the lines of how you can utilize your special talents to help our family through this crisis."

"What on earth are you talking about?"

"I want you to do something about Daniel."

"I beg your pardon?"

"I want you to do something about his current problem with Eleanor. For some reason, that woman has been able to rattle his cage in a way that Katharine was never able to achieve. I realize a few more years with Amelia will probably force the issue, but we don't have time to wait for that. I need everyone in this family, which includes Daniel and Eleanor, to put up a united front. We are about to go to war with everyone. Now I'm prepared to take a hit financially, but my family's reputation is a whole other matter."

"I ... have to admit I'm in shock at the moment. I'm not entirely sure how to respond."

"Yes, would do just fine," he said as he sipped his drink.

"But... how did you know?"

"Really darling, I've lived with you for forty years. How could I not know? So, what's it to be? Will you talk to Daniel?"

"Phillip, you may be an enlightened soul, but you know what he is like. What happens if it backfires and he thinks we're all crazy? That could have implications for Amelia and for the family as well."

"I don't think so. I had rather an interesting chat with our passionate son-in-law after we discovered Katharine's files, and I believe I've laid the groundwork. I just need you to come in to seal the deal. Oh, and see if Trevor would like to join us as well. I'm sure the boy would like to tidy things up before he takes off for his new life."

"Good God Phillip. Why didn't you say something to me before?"

"For the same reason as you I guess. It was easier to act blissfully ignorant. So what do you say darling, can I count on you to do this?"

"Yes, against my better judgment."

"Excellent. I would like it to be tonight." He kissed her and started for the door.

"Phillip, wait. You must have questions."

"Of course I do, but you've gone this long without telling me, I figured I can wait a little longer. Let's take care of Daniel first. Then we can talk."

"I hope you know that I love you."

"Yes, I do. Oh, and I think now would be a good time for you to have that drink."

※◈※

His months of silence were over. Soon a guard came to his cell and took him to where his sister was waiting. She wrote words on paper he did not understand, but he could hear her thoughts and she told him how he should escape.

Later that night he sat on his bed, remembering everything she had said. There would be an explosion and smoke would fill the air. Then, he was to use his gift of strength to rip the door off its hinges. She told him the path he should take from his cell, and the number of guards he would encounter. He was to kill anyone that got in his way, acquiring as many weapons as possible. She said the smoke would be thick, but to not be afraid for that would mean he was close.

Follow the sound of my voice until you see light. We will be waiting for you there.

That is what his sister said for him to do. And when he saw the black van that was waiting for him, Karl Milin knew he was finally free.

※※

Eleanor retreated to one of the more comfortable booths in the restaurant and sank into the seat. Nina followed, bearing a bottle of Pinot Noir and two glasses.

"I don't understand why it's so crazy in here," Eleanor said. "Labor Day weekend was over a week ago. It should be slowing down by now."

Nina slid a glass in front of her and poured. "I thought you wanted it to be busy."

"I do, but I've never seen it like this so late in the season. We need to hire more people."

"You need to get rid of Fiorelli," Nina said.

"I don't know. He's been great for wine sales since he's been working behind the bar."

"So, have you decided what you're going to do when Ben and Mik pull out?"

Eleanor grimaced. On Sunday, when she arrived with Kyle and Nina to open the restaurant, they found Ben Garrison working behind the bar. He greeted them as if nothing had ever happened. When Eleanor confronted Mikayla, she discovered that they had reconciled, but they no longer wished to be business partners in the tavern. After Eleanor got past the initial shock, she pleaded with Mikayla to reconsider.

"We're Jeremy's family," Eleanor said. "We can't let his restaurant go."

"Jeremy's dead honey and Ben can't do this anymore. If he and I are going to have any sort of future together, then we have to be done with this place."

"What about Jared? Have you told him yet?"

"I haven't gotten that far in my thinking. But don't you worry honey, I'll talk to him."

Eleanor's thoughts returned to Nina's question as she emptied her glass of wine. "Jared and I discussed it, and we're going to buy them out. Jeremy's Tavern will live on."

"I know you don't want to fix up this dump, but can you at least do something about the bathrooms?"

Eleanor laughed. "I admit we have a problem there, and I promise we'll spruce them up."

"I'm starving. I'm going to ask Jonah to put in an order for us."

"Wait. I want to talk about rescheduling our Napa trip. How does mid-October sound?"

"Yeah, about that," Nina said. "What do you think about going down to LA instead?"

"And do what?"

"We could hang out at Fiorelli's and visit Santa Barbara. I heard the wine is good there."

"I thought you hated LA."

"Maybe I don't anymore."

"Nina, what is going on? We've done our Napa trip every year since I moved here."

"I want to do something different this time. I'm going to put in our order."

Eleanor watched as Nina walked to the bar, stopping to chat with Kyle on the way to the kitchen. At some point Kyle looked over at her, waving, and she wondered if the Los Angeles trip was already a done deal. Dismayed at Nina's eagerness to jettison their traditional autumn sojourn, she was convinced more than ever that something was cooking between her two friends-something that they had no interest in sharing with her. At that moment she felt incredibly alone.

A chill passed over her and she left the table to retrieve her jean jacket from the office. As she grabbed it off the back of the desk chair, she paused momentarily to check her cell phone. It was dead, and she would have to wait until she was home to check her messages. She wondered if Daniel had called. They had not talked since last Saturday when he asked her to cease all contact with Amelia. The thought of their last conversation made her throat burn, and she decided to go outside for some fresh air.

September in River Mist was an amazing time of year. During the day it could be over 100 degrees, but at night the temperature could easily drop into the lower 50s. As she stepped onto the long narrow porch that encircled the building, she filled her lungs with the cool air. It felt good, and she strolled around the side of the tavern, sitting on one of the long benches that lined the outside wall.

Jeremy. She still missed him so much. Since her return he had not once appeared to her, not that she had not tried to make herself available. Every night she would sit on her deck watching the woods, hoping he would come to her. Even the bears had not appeared, though occasionally she would see a dark figure moving through the trees. Tears filled her eyes and she searched her pockets in vain for a tissue, eventually forced to use her sleeve. She stood and continued towards the back of the restaurant.

One of the kitchen windows was propped open and she could hear the sounds of pots and pans clanging. It was a comforting reminder that his restaurant was still alive. That he was still alive, even if only within the confines of the tavern walls. Perhaps it was a blessing that Ben and Mikayla wanted out of the business. Jared would never push her to make changes, which suited her just fine.

She walked through the back parking lot until she reached a small overlook. The valley and surrounding mountains were still glowing with the last remnants of the sunset. In a few minutes it would be pitch black and the stars would form a thick blanket overhead.

Jeremy. She wondered if he had sensed her feelings for Daniel, and if that was the reason why he had not appeared. Like Mikayla, she loved two men, and it took her recent separation from Daniel to realize it. She missed him, and it pained her to think she might never see him again. However, despite her love for Daniel, Jeremy had to know that she would never abandon him. What would she need to do to prove that she would never let him go?

She peered down into the valley below and recalled the moment when Monica jumped to her death. Perhaps that was the way to show him her devotion. She knew there was some sort of afterlife, her time in the Twilight with Lourdes had convinced her of that. She stepped onto the lower rung of the railing, leaning as far forward as she could, her arms outstretched. How hard could it be to just let go? She closed her eyes.

"Eleanor."

Her eyes opened and she stared into the darkness, the sound of a voice echoing in her head. She waited a moment to see if it was just her imagination and closed her eyes again. A strong breeze blew against her back and she thought now would be a perfect time to soar.

"Eleanor."

This time she was certain she heard the voice. She stepped off the railing and turned around, scanning the parking lot.

"Who is that?"

The wind stopped and everything around her became quiet. She cleared her mind of any thoughts, waiting for the voice to call to her again. It was then she felt a burning sensation forming inside her. Someone with powers was approaching, and she opened her eyes to discover that no one was there.

She started across the parking lot towards the front of the restaurant, the presence moving with her. The burning continued to build, but as she reached the entrance something changed and a feeling of longing overcame her. Instantly she knew who it was. She ran back into the parking lot and watched as a black SUV passed by her before heading east on Route 6.

Moments later she retrieved the spare key from the visor of her car and turned right onto Route 6, heading east towards her mountain home.

�ం✖

After dinner, Daniel had been instructed by Phillip to join him in his study. When he arrived he found his father-in-law, along with Christine, Amelia and Trevor gathered in the small sitting area that was located on the opposite side of the room. He was asked to have a seat in a large leather chair that appeared to have been left empty for him.

"Son, I'll get right to the point," Phillip said. "We're here to help you."

"Just stop right there. I don't need help. I've already decided to quit drinking."

"We're not here to discuss your drinking problem, though I guess you could call this an intervention in a way. We are here to change your view of the world and to tell you the truth about the people that you love."

"Oh God, does this have to do with Ellie and what happened in my apartment?"

"Ultimately, yes. But we need to start further back, with Katharine and Christine."

"And me too," Amelia said.

Daniel shifted in his seat, crossing his arms. "OK, you got my attention. What the hell are you talking about?"

"I think now would be a good time for Christine to take over."

Phillip leaned back in his chair and everyone's attention turned to Mrs. Monroe. She sat silent for several moments, appearing to struggle with how to begin. Finally she smoothed the creases in her skirt and cleared her throat.

"First off, I need to go on record and say that I am firmly against this, but my husband has convinced me that this is the right thing to do for the sake of our family's future. Secondly, whatever you learn here today, whether you choose to believe it or not, cannot be shared with anyone outside of this group. Is that understood?"

"Yeah, I got it," Daniel said.

"All right then. How do I begin? Katharine and I, *and* Amelia, have certain abilities that allow us to experience the world in a wholly different way than other people. We can sense and hear things that others cannot. For example, right now I can feel that you are nervous and very uncomfortable with this conversation."

Daniel let out an abrupt laugh. "That goes without saying."

"And I know what you're thinking as well."

Daniel felt a lump forming in his throat, and sat silent, staring at Christine. Suddenly she gave him a smile that sent a chill down his spine.

"That's absolutely right," she said. "Amelia and I can read your thoughts."

All the blood in his body rushed to his head, and he shot up from his seat. "I'm done." He bolted for the door and by the time he threw it open, Christine was in front of him. He recoiled and was surprised when Phillip made no effort to stop her. She moved into him, whispering.

"I know what Charles said to you in your apartment as you were chained to that filing cabinet. He said that this moment would happen, and I would be the one to tell you. Is that not true?"

It took him a while, but Daniel finally nodded.

"He said *that I would help you believe.*"

He could no longer speak and the hairs on his arms were pointing straight up.

"I know you are incredibly frightened right now, but allow me to do this little demonstration," she said, "if anything but for Amelia's sake."

She motioned him towards the chair and waited until he had sat before she continued.

"All right then. Daniel, think of a number. Thank you. Amelia, you may go first."

"Five," Amelia said, grinning.

"Think of another one, please."

Tears filled his eyes. He sat there dumbfounded, allowing a random number to pop into his head.

"Twelve," Christine said.

"Come on Daddy, you can do better than that. Give me a really long one."

His entire body was shaking, and he was unsure if he wanted to complete this surreal exercise. Finally, Daniel closed his eyes and slowly allowed the number to build in his mind. He could barely hear his daughter's voice over the pounding in his chest.

"Sixty-three thousand, two hundred and fifty-one, that's a good one Daddy!" Amelia clapped her hands in excitement.

A glass of water was placed in his hand and he drank it down in one gulp. He was not sure how long he sat there staring at the carpet, but eventually he made eye contact with Christine.

"Does this mean that you two can hear every thought that I have?"

Christine shook her head. "Well yes, we are certainly able to hear everything, but we choose not to do that. Quite frankly, it can be very distressing to listen in to another person's thoughts. However, my granddaughter is not very good about staying out of your head as you've probably figured out by now. So you do need to be careful around her."

Daniel glanced at Amelia, who gave him a sheepish grin and then turned to Trevor. "Why are you here? Do you already know about all this?"

Trevor nodded and then explained that he shared in the same abilities as Christine and Amelia. It took Daniel a while before he could respond.

"Oh God, I was right. You can read my mind. Phillip, please tell me I'm not the odd man out here."

"No son, you aren't," Phillips said. "You and I are the mere mortals amongst this little clan of ours. I just happened to be a lot more observant than you are."

"That goes without saying," Christine quipped. "All right, so what happens next? What do we need to do to help you process this?"

He had no idea where to begin and when he looked up at Christine, he was surprised to see her smiling. "What is it?"

"At least you have questions," she said. "That is a good sign."

Amelia sprang from her seat and stood in front of him. "Mommy was just like us. I can say that Nana, right?" Christine nodded. "What else do you want to know Daddy?"

As fast as the thoughts could form in his mind, Amelia answered his questions, and when she could not, Trevor assisted her. With each revelation his brain went down a new path until he thought his head would explode. Finally after 10 minutes of not uttering a single word he had to make it stop.

"Dammit, will you all shut the hell up so I can say something." He slumped back in his chair, exhausted. "Sorry Amelia. Daddy's feeling a little crazy right now. What about Ellie?" Silence fell over the room, and he noticed that both Amelia and Trevor were now looking at Christine. "What? I can't ask that question?"

Christine folded her arms. "One of the rules among our kind is to never reveal the abilities of another, not unless we are given permission to do so. That's why Trevor is with us today. He personally wanted to tell you. I'm afraid Eleanor must answer that question for you, but what I will tell you is this. Whereas Katharine, Amelia, Trevor and I came into our abilities when we were children, Eleanor is just now realizing hers. She is different than all of us, and she has had quite a tough time of it I'm afraid."

His mind sifted through the past several months, recalling all the odd, unexplained moments he had experienced with Eleanor, and he began to comprehend why she had been so cautious about their relationship. Obviously, he thought, she was fearful of the day when he would learn the truth, for what did he do at the first sign of trouble, but abandon her.

"God, she must hate me," he said.

"She'll get over it. We all do," Christine said.

Daniel slumped back in his chair and looked at Amelia who was smiling at him. Suddenly he was overcome with guilt. "Oh my baby girl, I'm so sorry for what I've said to you over the past few days." Before he could speak another word she threw her arms around his neck, hugging him. "Now I know what you meant when you said Ellie and you are the same."

Phillip's cell phone rang and he stepped away from the group to answer it. Trevor moved next to him, asking if he could do anything to help. Daniel laughed through his tears.

"Hell Trev, you can read my mind. You already know what I need."

Trevor smiled and pulled out his laptop from his messenger bag. Phillip ended his call and the room grew quiet as everyone turned their attention towards him. Amelia started to speak, but Christine held up her hand, silencing her.

"What is it Phillip?" Daniel said.

"That was Detective Adams. There was an attack on the county jail and Karl Milin escaped. There's a concern that he and the people that helped him might go after Eleanor."

"She's probably at the restaurant right now. Are they sending someone to protect her?"

"Well, you see that's the problem. They don't know where Eleanor is at the moment. I guess she is missing."

※❂※

Kyle did not realize that Eleanor was gone until he felt her presence suddenly leave him. At that same moment the kitchen door flew open and Nina stood before him, her emerald eyes glowing. She paused to scan the crowded restaurant before taking off for the front door. Kyle followed, and when they reached the parking lot, she stopped.

"What is it?" he said.

"She's heading up the mountain to her house." Nina turned to him. "She's not alone."

A deputy cruiser came barreling into the parking lot, gravel flying as it stopped. The driver's side door flew open and Eric Garrison emerged, barking orders into his radio as he rushed inside the restaurant. Kyle caught his thoughts as he passed through the door.

"We should take my car. It will be faster," he said.

"You won't make it in time. Go ahead, I'll meet you there."

Nina was across the parking lot before he could even speak her name, and as he ran to his car she disappeared into the woods. Seconds later he saw a stream of light burst through the treetops, shooting up the side of Birch Mountain. For a moment he could not breathe, and then he pushed the gas pedal to the floor, his heart pounding wildly. It had been lifetimes since he had felt the exhilaration that was now pumping through his veins, and he wondered how he could have been so incredibly blind.

Chapter Thirty Five

And, lips, O you
The doors of breath, seal with a righteous kiss
A dateless bargain to engrossing death!

∞

Eleanor pulled in front of her house, stopping next to the deputy cruiser that was parked outside. It was empty, and as she emerged from her car she could feel a presence rushing towards her. She stepped onto the porch just as Deputy Vargas rounded the corner. After a brief exchange she learned that Karl Milin had escaped and she was instructed to stay in her home while he contacted Detective Adams.

Inside, she rushed to the deck doors, searching the backyard for him. He was near, and as she attempted to reach him with her thoughts, her body heated up. She spun around, recognizing his form in the shadows.

"I knew you were here."

She went to Lourdes, throwing her arms around him. He felt strong, much stronger than she remembered, and as he increased his hold on her, it became difficult for her to breathe. With effort she pushed him away in order to see his face.

"Something has changed with you," she said.

His fingers trailed across her lips and down her throat. "No, Ms. Bouchard, I assure you I am the same man I've always been."

It was not Lourdes' voice, and when he pressed her against the wall, she realized that Katharine's love for him had left her completely.

"Who are you?"

"I think you already know the answer to that." He held up his right wrist, brandishing the black tattoo she had seen in her vision. "Now it's time to find out who *you* really are."

❉❉❉

Bellows and Chen rushed into the precinct, stopping at Betsy Cartwright's desk. The young evidence technician and Detective Morgan were attaching several enlarged photos of Charles Lourdes on the white board. Each image had a red circle around his right wrist.

"Damn, that looks like the same tattoo I saw today. And where is the one of him checking into the hotel?"

Morgan pointed to the picture of Lourdes that was separate from the others. There was no tattoo on either wrist.

"Who the hell is this person?" The room was silent as Bellows thought. "Betsy, you're positive those hairs you found in the Lutsenko's bathroom are synthetic?"

"Yes ma'am."

"And they were black, like before?" Bellows said.

"Well, actually there were several colors ma'am." Betsy searched for the report on her desk. "It says here there were black, blond…and red."

Bellows did not have to say another word. Chen ordered Betsy to bring up the front desk camera recordings from the Inter-Continental Hotel and search for Victor Naumov. Everyone gathered around the computer. While Bellows waited for her to locate Naumov checking into the hotel, she called Adams. When he answered she could barely hear him over his car siren.

"I'm on the way to Eleanor's. What's going on?" he said.

"Is she all right?" Bellows said.

"Don't know yet. The deputy watching her house is no longer responding."

"Morgan showed me what you found. Lourdes has a damn twin."

Betsy announced she had found Naumov. Bellows asked her to slow-down the playback speed, watching for the moment when he reached for his room key.

"Stop right there. Can you enlarge it?" Bellows said.

Betsy captured the shot and Bellows held her breath as the technician zoomed in on Naumov's right hand.

"Sheila, what's going on?" Jared said.

The image was grainy, and she had to move in close to the computer screen in order to see his wrist. After a few moments of examining the photo, she exhaled.

"It's Naumov," Bellows said. "The man who attacked me was Victor Naumov."

❧

"You're Anton Milin," Eleanor said.

The words had barely escaped her lips when the man who looked like Lourdes clamped his hands against her head, flooding her mind with his thoughts. She tried to push him away but he slammed her up against the wall.

-Vladimir Milin, the eldest son of Boris Milin, was a drunk and impotent. Two years after Vladimir married Anna Vasilly there were no children. This was unacceptable to Boris. Anna Vasilly came from a long line of powerful Empaths and Boris was counting on his equally powerful son to produce heirs. When Vladimir was unable to procreate, Boris took matters into his own hands, and bedded his daughter-in-law. Twin boys were born. As part of the agreement with Anna, Boris took the first born back to Moscow with him, while she kept the other boy. Vladimir, who was on a drinking binge, was not present for the birth and was never told about the other child. Anna named her son Ivan.

"Charles Lourdes is Ivan," Eleanor whispered.

"Yes," Anton said. "For the first ten years of my life, I didn't know my mother or twin brother existed. Then one day Vladimir discovered the truth about Ivan's paternity. Instead of confronting his father, he beat Anna nearly to death and disappeared with Ivan. A few weeks later Vladimir surfaced and Anna learned that he had sold Ivan off to a Canadian couple whose son had

405

recently died. Vladimir didn't live long after that. Boris had him killed, and then he moved Anna in with us."

"Why did Ivan stay with the Canadian couple?"

"Father thought it would be advantageous to the family someday. For a while that was true, until that bitch Monroe discovered us and ruined everything."

Anton grabbed her arm, pulling her into the darkly lit family room. As they entered she could make out two figures on the couch, and when he turned on a lamp she saw Angie Miller holding a bloody and unconscious Zach Walker in her arms.

"What happened?" Eleanor started towards Zach and Angie, but Anton held her back.

"An unfortunate misjudgment on Mr. Walker's part, isn't that right Vera?" Angie looked up, her right cheek bruised, blood dripping from her nose. "Of course, she came to his rescue Now that you are here Ms. Bouchard, Walker is no longer needed."

The double doors leading to her deck opened and Karl Milin appeared. The blond giant lumbered across the kitchen and into the family room, stopping in front of Angie.

"Let him go Vera," Anton said. "There's nothing you can do for him now."

Angie glared at Anton for several moments before tightening her hold around Zach. She cried as Karl pulled Walker's limp body from her arms.

"Where are you taking him?" Eleanor said.

"That's none of your concern Ms. Bouchard. You are here to help my sister." He yanked her over to the couch, forcing her to sit next to Angie.

"Angie is your sister?"

"Yes. When she was five I arranged for a Russian family to adopt her and take her to the U.S., mainly to protect her from our father, who was a brutal man. Years later she returned to me, and we were reunited. She has been my partner ever since, until Katharine Monroe stole her from me. But now you are going to get her back."

"What is it I am supposed to do?"

"Fix whatever it is Monroe did to her head and restore her memories."

"I can't do that. I've only had my abilities a few months and I can barely control them."

"You are lying, Ms. Bouchard. I have felt your power. You burn inside me, like the sun. I'm starting to believe Monroe was right. You just might be this Passer that all these superstitious fools are dying for."

"You know about The Passer?"

"Unfortunately, yes. I come from a long line of simple-minded people who believed in the old ways. They all talked of the great power this being would possess-the most powerful of our kind. I never paid attention to my mother and father's nonsensical ravings. I had a modern world to live in and conquer, but then that demon Monroe came along and started a crusade against me and my family. First she destroyed my mother's mind to where she remembered nothing but my dead brother Ivan. Then she erased me from Vera's memories and now she has exposed my empire to the world, all because of that whore Bellaso and her idiotic beliefs. It will take me years to undo the damage she has caused, but none of it matters, unless my Vera is with me."

"I swear to you. I don't know how to help her."

He grabbed her throat. "Then perhaps you need a little persuasion."

"Anton, stop. Let her go," Angie moaned.

Anton released his hold on Eleanor and knelt before Angie, cradling her face in his hands. "Vera what is it? Do you remember something?"

Angie pushed him away. "No. I still think you are a heartless bastard, but I can't fight you anymore, and I can't bear to see you kill another person. Come Ms. Bouchard. I believe in you. He is right. You have the power to do this thing that he asks. You just need to focus."

Eleanor took Angie's hand and sat next to her. "What if I hurt you?"

"Supposedly, I was a soulless killer once, just like Anton. I don't think there is anything you could do to me that I don't deserve."

"Silence, Vera." Anton pressed his gun to Eleanor's head. "It's time, Ms. Bouchard."

When Nina landed near Eleanor's house, she recognized the blond giant moving across the backyard. *Karl Milin. I should have ended you when I had the chance.* She slipped into Jeremy's workshop in search of a weapon, and emerged just as Karl moved into the woods.

Slowly, she crept up on the unsuspecting human, and with one swift movement swung the shovel against his thick head. Milin teetered for a moment, before falling forward with a thud. It was not until she walked around to survey the damage, that she saw Zach Walker's ashen face, crushed between Karl's massive frame and the ground. She kicked Milin's body sending it rolling further into the forest and grabbed onto Walker's leg, dragging him. She had nearly reached the deck when she registered another presence behind her.

"You know you can't leave him like that. When he wakes he'll come after you."

Nina dropped Walker's leg and turned, her weapon raised. "Would you like to join him?"

"Karl is stronger than you think, as are the two inside. You will need help."

"Why should I believe you?"

"I am here for the same reason as you, to protect our friend Ms. Bouchard. Please, let me help you."

At that moment Karl Milin began to stir, rising to his knees. Nina shook her head as she headed back towards the woods. "I saw a pile of chains inside the workshop. Make yourself useful and grab them."

Eleanor emerged from her trance to find Anton kneeling before Angie Miller. He asked his sister if she remembered him and Angie nodded. Then Anton took her face in his hands, pressing his lips against her forehead and cheek, before kissing her on the mouth. In Eleanor's opinion it was a rather passionate kiss for a sibling, and she was not surprised when Angie pushed him away, screaming.

"What are you doing? You are my brother," Angie said, wiping her mouth.

"We have always been this way. You've been my lover since you were sixteen."

"Not any more. Get the hell away from me, now."

Anton stared at Angie, a look of horror on his face. He turned to Eleanor, grabbing her by the throat. "What did you do to her?"

"I did as you asked. I gave her back her memories."

"Not the most important one. She has to remember everything or she's no good to me."

Anton's grip tightened. Eleanor attempted to pry his fingers away, but he squeezed harder, until she could barely breathe. She began to think about returning to the Twilight when she heard a thud. Anton's hands slipped from her neck as his head fell into her lap. She stared down at the blood pouring from his skull and then looked up to find Angie holding a fireplace poker.

"We should go." Eleanor shoved Anton onto the floor and started for the front door.

"I wouldn't bother Ms. Bouchard. The deputy outside is dead. Karl killed him after you arrived. We need to stop Anton before he wakes."

"You just put a sizeable gash in his head. I don't think he'll be up anytime soon."

"He's already healing, look."

Eleanor glanced down and saw that Anton had stopped bleeding. "Let's go then. We can call for help in town."

"They can't stop him, "Angie said. "No one can, not even me. You are our only hope."

"What is it you propose I do?"

"Take away his memories. Make him forget who he is."

"Are you insane? I'm not sure what I just did to you, and apparently it didn't work. I am leaving here now, with or without you."

Eleanor continued for the front door and Angie moved in front of her, pressing the bloody poker into her chest. "If you don't do this, we will never be free. Why do you think he came here? It wasn't just to make me remember. It's you he wants. He intends to take you with him."

"I don't believe you."

"She speaks the truth Ms. Bouchard."

His familiar baritone voice sent a shockwave through her body and she turned to find Lourdes standing in her kitchen, his clothes covered in dirt and blood. Angie dropped her weapon to her side and Eleanor ran to Lourdes, throwing her arms around him.

"I knew that was your presence I felt in the restaurant parking lot." She met his bright blue eyes and Katharine's love swelled inside her.

Angie appeared next to them, interrupting their embrace. "After all these years I finally am close enough to look into your eyes. I always wanted to meet you my brother, but Anton would never let me near you."

"I'm sorry Ms. Miller, but I don't remember anything," Lourdes said.

"I know. When Mother learned what Vladimir had done, she went to Moscow and found you. She made sure you would forget everything, so you would be happy with your new family."

"How did she do that?" Lourdes said.

"Your accident never happened. Mother made you believe that you nearly drowned and she erased your memories so you wouldn't remember us. You were no longer Ivan. You were Charles Lourdes."

"But, I remember there was a Russian boy that drowned. The police questioned my father about it. They thought he might be responsible."

"Edward Lourdes was responsible for drowning a boy, but the boy was *his son*. There was a cover-up. Money exchanged hands and you exchanged places with the real Charles Lourdes."

Lourdes swooned momentarily while Anton stirred behind them. They turned to find that his head wound had almost completely healed.

"I want both of you to leave now," Lourdes said.

Angie grasped his arm. "Anton is much stronger than you. You cannot defeat him alone."

"Don't worry," Lourdes said. "I have help."

At that moment Nina emerged through the open deck doors carrying a large garden shovel. Her white gloves were bloody shreds on her hands and she walked with a slight limp.

"This is your help? She looks like a child?" Angie said.

Eleanor swore she heard Nina growl.

"She will wield more damage than you and I combined. Please, take Ms. Bouchard away from here. She is not ready for this."

"If we don't kill him now, he'll come after her anyway. You need me, and if we can't do it, then Ms. Bouchard is our only hope."

Eleanor felt his arm tighten around her as he considered Angie's words. Finally Lourdes turned to her, his bright blue gaze fixed on hers. "She is right, Ms. Bouchard. Remember what I told you before, about the power that lives within you?"

Anton groaned and they turned to find him moving onto his hands and knees. Lourdes pushed her behind him, and the unlikely trio of warriors formed a line in front of her. For a moment she felt slightly insulted by his chivalrous move, but then she realized she was the only one who was not holding a weapon.

Anton stood, smiling. "Brother and sister. At long last you meet. How sad your little reunion will be so short lived. Look at her Charles, isn't our darling Vera beautiful? She loved me once, before your lover ruined her. Now she is no good to me. I would let you have her, but I'm afraid I can't let you live either. If I were you, I would say my goodbyes, now."

Anton raised his gun, firing several shots into Angie's stomach and chest. Blood spewed from her mouth as she fell to the ground. Next Anton emptied his gun into Lourdes, but he was unaffected by the bullets. Again, Anton smiled.

"I'm impressed. Your resurrection has made you stronger, my brother. I guess we will have to do this the old-fashioned way."

He tossed aside his gun and flung open a large pocket knife. Lourdes and Nina sprang forward, sending her couch toppling backwards and her coffee table smashing against the fireplace. She felt completely helpless as she watched Anton sink his dagger into Lourdes, and it occurred to her at that moment that Angie was right. There was no stopping this monster, certainly not with conventional methods. If she did not do something now, there would only be more bloodshed, more people dead, more of her loved ones gone. She took off through the front door, tripping over the body of Deputy Vargas as she rounded the side porch to her bedroom.

When she entered the family room, her shotgun readied, she found Lourdes lying on the ground in a bloody heap and Nina in a chokehold with Anton. She knew her bullets would only slow him momentarily, but that was all she needed. She marched forward, firing as many rounds into his back as she could. Before he could turn, she was on him.

Summoning the powers of Katharine Monroe to rise up within her, she slammed her hand against his head and delivered the first blow to his mind. He released his grip on Nina, and her tiny friend fell to the ground. The next attack sent Anton reeling backwards. He was clearly stunned, and she could feel his memories begin to slip away. She came at him again, but this time he latched onto her wrist, attempting to dislodge her hand. She pushed against him as hard as she could, sending another surge of power through his brain before he knocked her to the floor.

Her last attempt appeared to have done the most damage. Anton stumbled, staring at her with lost eyes. His defenses had been weakened and she could hear his jumbled thoughts, searching for anything he could recognize. Then his gaze caught the black tattoo at the base of his right hand. He stared at it for several seconds before locking eyes with her. A look of recognition crossed his face. She smiled at him, and suddenly she realized that Katharine Monroe felt compassion for this madman.

"It's not too late Anton. Join us now, while you still have a chance." The voice was hers, but the words belonged to Katharine Monroe.

Anton teetered, his eyes narrowing. "I killed you once before, bitch. I can kill you again."

As Anton swooped down on her, she could feel Katharine's powers emerging in full force. It did not matter that he was attempting to squeeze the life from her body, for she knew she possessed the ability to end him. She took a moment to search his fading blue eyes, perhaps as a last attempt to save his soul, but there was only darkness. She lifted her hand to his face, clearing her mind of all thoughts except one.

Anton released her and began screaming as he clasped his hands against his head. She scrambled to her feet as he thrashed around the room, attempting to stop the rapid disintegration of his identity. Then a tremendous roar sounded and she turned to see two black bears flying through the open deck doors.

She backed away, allowing the creatures to move in. Anton found his knife and began to lash out at them, wildly. They kept their distance, growling as they moved around him, forcing him to turn in circles. Soon he grew dizzy, stumbling, and the small bear moved in, clamping down on his calf. Anton howled as he sank his knife into her black fur, but the animal maintained its hold, despite the blood pouring from its backside.

The larger bear moved closer, rising to its hind legs. It let out a tremendous roar that shook the rafters and then he slashed a mighty claw across his victim's neck. Anton's head hit the floor with a thud and Eleanor had to close her eyes as a spray of blood splattered across her body.

Exhausted, she fell to her knees and the large bear nestled against her for a moment, before moving to Nina. The small bear was with Lourdes, licking the blood from his face until he finally opened his eyes and sat up. Nina stirred, and yelled at the large bear to get away from her. Eleanor smiled, greatly relieved that her best friend was all right.

The sound of sirens could be heard in the distance, and Lourdes rose to his feet, removing the knife from the small bear.

"I must leave," he said.

"Where will you go?"

He moved in front of her, kneeling. "It is best you don't know."

"What Anton said about me, is it true? Am I The Passer?"

"Katharine believed you to be, and now a part of her is with you. There must be truth in it."

"But what does it mean? What am I supposed to do?"

"I don't know. But Katharine's quest has brought us together and I promise you I will continue to search for the answer." He brought his hand to her face. "Thank you for saving my life, for saving all our lives."

Eleanor smiled. "Well, I guess that makes us even for now."

Lourdes laughed, kissing her on the forehead. Then he stood and gathered Angie in his arms. He started towards the open deck doors, the small bear alongside him.

"If you do find the answer," she said, "how will I know where to find you?"

"You will know. Goodbye Ms. Bouchard."

"Goodbye Mr. Lourdes."

He carried Angie Miller into the night. A siren was blaring out front and she could hear the sound of tires rolling against the gravel. The smaller bear let out a moan and rushed towards the deck while the large bear approached her.

"You should go." She wrapped her arms around the bear's neck, pressing her lips against his fur. Suddenly she felt skin against her face and when she pulled away she was looking into Jeremy's eyes. He leaned in to kiss her. It was not until she heard the slide of a shotgun engaging, that she broke from her spell. A man's voice called out to her and she turned.

"Dammit Eleanor, I told you not to move."

It took her a moment to realize that Eric Garrison was standing in the entryway with his shotgun aimed at the bear.

"Eric, what are you doing?"

"What the hell do you think?" he said. "Cover your ears."

She screamed for him to stop, but he would not listen. The bear roared at Eric and then turned, bounding for the kitchen. He fired, and Eleanor watched in horror as the large, black creature fell to the ground.

Eric tried to stop her from crawling to the wounded bear, and she had to push him away several times before he finally let her go. By the time she reached the animal, a pool of blood had formed beneath his body and his breathing was barely noticeable. She knelt next to him, laying her hands on his fur. He lifted his head for a moment, groaning softly, before lowering it again. Eleanor glanced outside and could see the glowing eyes of the other bear.

Nina stumbled into the kitchen and pointed towards the deck doors. "Karl Milin is out there. So is Zach Walker." Eric ran out as Nina made her way over to the bear, kneeling next to him. "Zach is dead. I'm sorry."

"I know. What happened to Karl?" Eleanor said.

"He's dead too. Your friend Lourdes helped me."

"Nina, I…"

"I don't want to talk about it right now."

"I understand," Eleanor said. "I just wanted to thank you."

Nina shrugged. "Are there any more of these crazy people coming after you?"

"I sincerely hope not."

Just then Kyle rushed through the front door, with a phone to his ear. He stopped in his tracks, wide-eyed, and then turned his head towards the family room. His mouth dropped open when he saw Anton's decapitated body. Nina took a deep breath.

"I'll take care of Fiorelli. You should stay. His time is near."

Nina rose to her feet, ordering Kyle to follow her so Eleanor could be alone with the bear. Kyle seemed to understand and left without saying a word.

Eleanor turned her attention to the dying creature, stroking him until he took his final breath. Then when his large form grew still, she laid her cheek against his snout and said her silent goodbye. Finally, she sat up, wiping the tears from her eyes and froze when she saw Jeremy standing there.

He was leaning in the doorway with his arms crossed, smiling. She started to stand, but he held up his hand, signaling for her to stay. As she sat there soaking in his handsome form she realized he was saying goodbye. He had saved her and now it was time to go. He brought his hand to his heart, and then his lips and sent her a kiss. She did the same, and watched through tearful eyes as he backed away and melded with the darkness.

Eventually she went outside to where Zach Walker's crumbled body lay and fell to her knees crying.

As Kyle followed Nina onto the porch, he ended his conversation with Daniel Archer, promising to call back when he knew more.

"How are your hands?" he said.

"They're fine."

"Come here, I want to see them." They moved away from the door and she held out her palms. "They're already healing. That's remarkable."

Several deputy cruisers arrived. Jared emerged from his car and stopped momentarily to check on them before heading inside. They walked to the end of the porch and sat on the swing.

"You know I'm not like all of you," Nina said.

Kyle laughed. "Well, I gathered that when I saw you fly up the side of Birch Mountain."

"Eleanor is different too, isn't she?" Nina said.

"Yes."

"Are you here to help her?"

"I am. You must know I have a million questions."

"Me too, but not now."

"Let me at least ask you this. When I met you at Jeremy's party and I touched you. I felt something amazing pass through me. Is that why you've been so hard on me all this time?"

She turned to him, her green eyes glistening, and nodded. Suddenly he felt something brush against his hand, sending a vibration flowing through his arm. He glanced down to discover that her little finger was touching his. Slowly, he moved his hand on top of hers, and their fingers intertwined. Then they leaned back in the swing, as they gazed at the night sky.

Chapter Thirty Six

My bounty is as boundless as the sea,
My love as deep; the more I give to thee,
The more I have, for both are infinite.

By 8:00 the following morning, Eric Garrison and the last of Jared's team left Eleanor's home. Jared stayed on, and along with Kyle and Nina helped to clean up what was left of her family room. When they were finished, Jared suggested they go into town for breakfast and discuss how they were going to handle the events of the previous evening.

When they arrived at the restaurant, Mikayla was so relieved to see Eleanor that she dropped everything, embracing her for what seemed an eternity. Then she stood back, her dark eyes glistening, and listed all the mindless offenses that Eleanor was guilty of, including driving off without any identification or her cell phone.

"Thank God Jared let me know you were all right. Oh, and that boy-friend of yours must have called here a dozen times."

Eventually Mikayla gave up on her scolding session, grabbed a pot of coffee from behind the bar and seated them. Then Jared began the process of working through the story that they would agree to going forward. Eleanor had to laugh, recalling the time when they sat in Nina's kitchen, having a similar discussion about how to handle her vision of Monica. She wondered if all this madness had finally come to an end and was slightly alarmed when no one responded.

Two hours later, they finished breakfast, shaking hands on their story. Kyle and Nina opted to return to the coast while Jared and she stayed back to discuss the restaurant. She surprised him when she said she wanted to go ahead with the renovations.

"Seriously, what changed your mind?" he said.

"Jeremy's gone, and he's not coming back. I finally understand that now."

She watched as Jared's gaze moved beyond her shoulder towards the bar where Mikayla was working, and he suggested they move the conversation outside so he could have a smoke. In the parking lot they leaned against his car, looking up at the neon sign towering over the restaurant.

"So what about the name, should we change it?" he said.

Eleanor sighed. "I think so. It's the only way we're ever going to be able to move on."

"We could call it Eleanor's."

"No, that's a horrible name for a restaurant."

"Well it's not going to be my name."

"Maybe we should just call it Jonah's," she said. "That way your cousin will stay with us. He's the reason for our success."

"Yeah, but don't forget Archer. We could call it Daniel's."

"You know, that would be a nice name for a restaurant. But I don't think so."

"You really should call him," Jared said.

"Kyle talked with him several times. He knows what happened."

"Come on Eleanor. Give the poor guy a break. Yeah, he screwed up, but it sounds like he's trying to make amends."

"So I take it you and Mikayla worked everything out?"

Jared shrugged his shoulders. "I think so. We've been down this road before."

"You still love her, don't you?"

"That will never change. But, maybe it's time I started to explore other options during this life of mine."

"I know a detective in New York who would be happy to hear that."

Jared turned to her, grinning. "You figured that out, did you?"

"Let's just say her thoughts are rather preoccupied with you. Jared, what you said to me in New York about why I can't sense you…"

"Yeah, I know I owe you an explanation."

"No you don't. I never should have asked."

"You had every right to. I don't prescribe to that bullshit code of ethics. I meant what I said. I'm not like you. I can't read minds, or emotions, or anything else for that matter. However, I'm also not like the rest of the souls walking around, and right now that is the only explanation I can offer you."

"It's all right, I understand."

"Look, I promise someday I will tell you. Until then, just know that I am your friend and you can trust me, always. Which reminds me, what do you want to do about this business with The Passer? Do you want my help with figuring it out?"

Eleanor took a deep breath. "I don't see why you should. You know why Katharine and Monica were murdered. The killers are dead. You should just let it go."

"Well, unfortunately it's not over. Angie Miller and Charles Lourdes are still out there, and even if Lourdes isn't a suspect anymore, he's still a person of interest and he's now harboring a fugitive. Also, Anton came after you because he believed you might be this thing…whatever it is. I think it's time we found out what it means."

"And how do you propose we do that?" she said.

"We make contact with this woman in Berlin, Dr. Manning and see if she can help us."

"Us?"

"Yes. I've been as much a part of this as you have. I want to know what this all means."

Eleanor gazed into his dark eyes for several moments, before leaning over and kissing him on the cheek. He smiled and then they turned their attention to the Jeremy's Tavern sign.

"You know," she said, "let's just call it The River Mist Tavern. That way we don't have to worry about changing the name ever again."

Jared agreed and they continued to talk about the restaurant until Detective Bellows called and he had to leave.

When she returned home, the thick scent of pine was still lingering in the air, and she opened up the windows to alleviate the smell. Next she plugged in her cell phone, before heading out to the garage in search of boxes. After several minutes she located a stack behind a set of golf clubs, carted them into the bedroom and began the task of removing Jeremy's clothes.

An hour later she had filled every empty box available. Sweaty from her work, she took a quick shower and then passed over the many summer dresses that Daniel had bought her, for a T-shirt and her favorite jean skirt. When she pulled the comfortable stretch denim over her hips she noticed there was something in the right pocket, and discovered it was the dirt encrusted ring she had found at Jeremy's grave.

Curious as to the marking on top, she cleaned it and was surprised to find that it was a tree, the same tree she had seen on Katharine Monroe's heart pendant. She grabbed her phone that was still charging and started to call Jared. Then she saw the 20 missed calls from Daniel. Perhaps she would try Jared later and she grabbed her car keys, heading for the door.

※❈

When Jared arrived on the coast he stopped at his home to shower and change clothes before he went into work. As he walked out onto the deck for a smoke, he found an envelope lying in front of the sliding glass door. His name was on it and there were no other markings. He opened it, and found a note along with the safe deposit box key that Eleanor had given him after her ghostly visit from Jeremy and Katharine Monroe. He read the note.

Found the box, but it was not in LA or at a bank. Please see enclosed
card for location.

Jared removed the thick white business card from the envelope and stared at the tree that was embossed on the front. He sighed. Sadly, he was very familiar with the San Francisco address.

His cell phone rang and it was Bellows.

"Hey," she said. "We found Anna Lutsenko. The man who stole the car from Monroe Industries, Lourdes' former driver, was trying to get both him and Anna on a flight to Moscow."

"What's going to happen to Anna?" he said.

"Don't know yet. We're trying to figure that out. Also, have you talked with the LAPD today?"

"No, I haven't been back to the office yet. Why do you sound out of breath?"

"I'm climbing a ridiculously steep set of stairs," she said.

"So what's going on with the LAPD?"

"Well, they wrapped up the evidence gathered at Angie Miller's house and guess what they found? Inside one of the closets was a faux wall, and behind it was a small telephone booth like space, completely lined with metal. One of the detectives sent me a picture of it and it looks exactly like the room we found in the Lutsenko's apartment. I was thinking of going down to LA tomorrow to take a look at it. Want to go with me?"

"I need to check my schedule, but sure why not. Except, don't you mean you'll go out to LA?"

"Hold on a second," she said, panting.

He could hear her heels clicking loudly as she breathed heavily into the receiver. "Sheila, just call me back when you get to your destination."

"No need," she said. "I'm here, now."

The call ended as his buzzer rang. When he opened the door he found Bellows standing on his landing attempting to catch her breath.

"No," she said. "I actually meant go down to LA."

"I see that. Why are you here?"

"Well, you do have the decapitated body of the key suspect in the Monroe murder case sitting in your morgue. I figured I needed to see it firsthand."

"Uh-huh. Weren't you just in New York a few hours ago?"

"I hitched a ride. So, look if you're busy, I can go ahead to the station and meet you there."

Jared pulled Bellows in, closing the door. "I have a better idea. Why don't we just take the next few hours off and celebrate. It's been a long five months and I think we deserve it."

"So, I take it you got things settled here?"

"Yes, although I have seemed to misplace my gum."

Bellows smiled, opening up her purse. "I stocked up, just in case."

A moment later her bag dropped to the ground, scattering the dozen packets of chewing gum across the floor.

✳✳

Eleanor made a generous donation to the local Goodwill center and then went to the restaurant to scrounge up more boxes. While she was there she asked Ben if he wanted the golf clubs. He gladly accepted them and then gave her a curious look.

"You talk to Daniel yet?"

"Did he call here again?" Ben nodded. "I'm sorry. Look, I promise I'll contact him as soon as I get home."

"So, we'll see you here for dinner then?" Ben said.

"Sure. Where else would I be?"

On the way home she stopped at the market to pick-up flowers and groceries. When she got to the wine section, she was annoyed to find the sparkling row completely empty. At the checkout aisle she told the two girls assisting her that they were out of bubbly, but they were so busy giggling over some man they had just met that they completely ignored her. She caught one of their racy ramblings while they bagged her items and was thankful to get out of there.

The ride up the mountain was a peaceful one. She emptied her mind of all thoughts, reveling in the clear blue skies above her. As she pulled into the gravel drive she thought perhaps she could spend the rest of the day on the back deck just staring into the heavens. Then she saw him sitting on the front porch and her body froze. It took a while for her to relax her grip on the steering wheel and open the door. When he approached she was too stunned to speak.

"I guess you didn't get my message I was coming," Daniel said.

She shook her head and opened the back door, removing her groceries and flowers.

"What's with the boxes? Are you going somewhere?"

"No. How's Amelia? Does she know about Zach?"

"Yeah," he said. "We need to call her in a little bit. Beautiful flowers."

"I should get them in water."

"Why don't I get the boxes for you?"

He followed her into the house and she pointed him towards the bed-room. Halfway through the family room he stopped.

"Ellie, what happened to your coffee table?"

"Long story."

He nodded and disappeared into the bedroom. She opened up the refrigerator to put away the cheese and fruit she had bought and saw three bottles of sparkling sitting on the shelf. She stood there for quite some time before slamming the door. When she entered the bedroom she found him surveying the half-empty closet.

"What happened to all of Jeremy's clothes?" he said.

"I gave them away. Wait a minute. What did you just call him?"

"Jeremy. That's his name isn't it?"

"Yes, but you told me that you would never speak his name."

"Yeah, I did say that."

"So, what happened? Why did you just call him Jeremy?"

"Why are you giving away his clothes and golf clubs?"

"How did you know about that?"

"I talked to Ben. He told me you were on the way over."

"I saw the bottles in my refrigerator. How long were you here before I arrived?"

"About thirty minutes. Sorry, I had to let myself in. I didn't want the wine to get warm. Hey, where are you going?"

Eleanor marched to the front door, throwing it open. "I want you to leave."

"I just got here."

"I don't care. Look, I am assuming Kyle told you what happened last night and if you think the incident in your apartment was unnerving, I can guarantee you that the experience I had here was far more terrifying. It's probably going to take me weeks, if not months to sort it all out and I don't need you belittling Jeremy's memory, or telling me I'm crazy. So just go now before we have even more regrets between us."

"Whoa, hold on a minute. You're not even giving me a chance to explain."

"Why are you here?"

"Well if you would stop trying to throw me out and listen, you would know."

"Listen to what, Daniel? I'm not going to do this with you. Nothing has changed with me since I left New York and if you think I was nuts then, I assure you after last night I've reached a whole new level of craziness. So please, please…just go, before…"

She was unable to finish her sentence. The tears started flowing and there was nothing she could do to stop them. Daniel tried to comfort her, but she pushed him away and went into her bedroom to continue packing up Jeremy's clothes. He appeared several minutes later carrying two glasses and a bottle of sparkling.

"I'm not in the mood for a drink," she said.

"OK, that means more for me."

"Why are you here?"

"I want to be with you."

"Why?"

"Because I love you," he said.

"No you don't, not really. You love some version of me from eighteen years ago. Well I've got news for you my friend. She doesn't exist anymore. That young, naive girl is gone."

"Give me a break Ellie. I know that. I may be an insensitive jerk, but I'm not an idiot."

Eleanor laughed as she stuffed several shirts into a box.

"Finally," he said. "I get a smile."

"Sorry. I just had a really long night and I haven't slept."

"Well, that makes two of us. I just spent the last twenty-four hours wondering if I would ever see you again. And when I finally do, I have to spend the first fifteen minutes bullshitting with you about our screwed up relationship, when all I really want is to hold you."

Eleanor stood there with an armful of Jeremy's clothing and realized at that moment that Daniel and she had come full circle. 18 years ago he had rejected her and despite her feelings for him she had never attempted to fight back. He asked her to leave and she went. Now, 18 years later they were in the very same place, except this time *he* was fighting back. She tossed the pile of pants in the box and left the closet.

When he joined her she was sitting on the bed. He poured two glasses of sparkling, handing her one, and they drank in silence. Her eye caught Jeremy's picture sitting on the nightstand and she recalled the moment last night when he stood in her doorway and said goodbye. She took a deep breath and emptied the contents of her glass.

"You asked me why I was giving away his clothes and my answer is that it's time to move on."

"Moving on is a good thing," he said.

"Yes. That's what I hear."

Daniel placed his glass on the nightstand and knelt in front of her. "It's time for you and me to move on."

She peered into his tired hazel eyes. "I have a confession to make."

"What?"

"I was still in love with you after we broke up. Even after I met Jeremy. And that day I left you standing in the Essex House lobby, you don't know how close I came to turning around. But that night in San Francisco, that was the worst because I discovered that I still loved you and if I had slept with you, I would have ended it with Jeremy. I ran out of there that night not because of him, but because of you, because I loved you. I have never stopped loving you."

"Why didn't you tell me this before?"

"I don't know. Probably because I just now finally figured it out. But also, I realize that's what I do when I'm with you. I run away."

"Well, you had a good reason to leave this time."

"Daniel, you're right. It is time for you and me to move on, but not together."

"Oh God Ellie, don't do this."

"You know I'm right. You just don't want to admit it."

"You just said that you loved me."

"I do. I love you very much, which is why I have to let you go."

"What about Amelia? Are you ready to give her up too?"

"You should leave now."

"Yeah, I thought as much. OK, I've been patient long enough. It's time for you to listen."

"Daniel, there isn't anything you can say that will change my mind."

"I don't want you to listen to what I'm saying." He took her hands, placing them against his face. " I want you to listen to what I'm *thinking*. Please Ellie, just shut the hell up and listen."

She did as he asked.

The world around her grew silent and all she could hear were his thoughts. She carefully listened as he recalled the past 24 hours: how he was uneasy when Victor Naumov made his strange comment about her, how he bust open the lock off a deep freezer and saved Bellows, how he nearly went mad when he could not reach her, and how Christine Monroe changed his view of the world forever. He told her all this with his surprisingly lucid thoughts, and then he conjured up a rather lusty image that made her laugh.

"Oh, you thought that was funny, huh?" he said.

"Embarrassing is more like it. I think I need to stop, if you don't mind."

"See. There's plenty of the old Ellie still in there. Can I hold you now?"

She nodded and they embraced. "Daniel, it's not going to be easy for us. There is still so much more I need to tell you and some of it I barely understand myself."

"I know. We got a lot to sort out and it doesn't help much that I'll be away for three months. But it's OK, because this is what I want." He stood, offering her his hand.

"Where are we going?"

"If you don't mind, I'd like to finish this conversation in the guest room."

"It's all right. There's no need to leave." She pulled him onto the bed.

"Are you sure?"

"Yes, I am. As I said before, it's time to move on."

Epilogue

∞

The first week of October, Eleanor moved into the ocean view house that Daniel had leased in Edmond, and officially made her River Mist property a vacation home.

Daniel was not there for the occasion as he had already left for New Zealand to begin filming, but he had spent the two weeks prior to his departure assuring that the two-story Victorian style house would be fully furnished and ready for occupation. Every evening they Skyped so he could see how the move was progressing and he would make a list of items he thought she still required, but she felt were wholly unnecessary. Then they would talk about their days, which eventually led to how miserable and lonely he was, and him inquiring as to how soon could she come to visit.

The weeks following the deaths of Anton and Karl Milin, the investigations into Katharine Monroe and Monica Bellaso's murders were officially concluded; however the search for Angie Miller continued. Phillip Monroe cooperated with the authorities, and along with the NYPD, the CIA and the FBI they were able to apprehend many of the Milin family operatives who had infiltrated Monroe Industries. After a significant number of arrests were made, the story of Katharine Monroe's findings was carefully leaked to the public, and Phillip Monroe began the arduous task of saving his family's reputation and his company.

Although Kyle returned to Los Angeles to begin a new project, he continued to help Eleanor develop her telepathic abilities. Eventually, Nina and she went to visit him, spending a long weekend in his home, doing nothing but eating, drinking wine and laying by the pool. There was no talk of the night Anton and Karl Milin died, in fact there was no discussion at all, and Eleanor found Kyle to be unusually reserved.

Eleanor and Nina agreed between them that neither was ready to discuss what they had witnessed that night in her River Mist home. However, Nina admitted that she was not like everyone else, which caused Eleanor to burst into laughter. When Nina took offense to Eleanor's reaction she apologized and promised her best friend that when the time was right for the both of them, they would sit down and have *the talk*. Until then, Eleanor was perfectly fine to continue as they had always been, as long as Nina did not require her to go clothes shopping.

After the anonymous donor made a sizeable donation to the university, construction began on the new theater. The current plan was aggressive, but the hope was to have the facility ready by the following May, in time for the summer season.

In mid-October Christine and Amelia visited for a long weekend, and Eleanor entertained her first guests in her new home. Amelia was overjoyed with her bedroom, as well as the charming park that was located at the end of the street, and every night they would sit in the backyard and watch the sun set over the Pacific Ocean. Aside from missing Daniel very much, it was the most content she had been in quite some time.

As the month progressed, the town prepared for its Halloween celebration and Eleanor found herself once again struggling to find a costume for Alex Leesman's annual masquerade ball. Eventually, Nina stepped in and decided to recreate a less revealing version of her gown from *A Midsummer Night's Dream*. She spent the prior week sewing garments and constructing wings so that Eleanor, her sister Josephine and Nina could all go as fairies.

The month drew to its close and the day of the party arrived. Josephine flew in from Paris, and the three women spent the afternoon trying on costumes, drinking wine and reminiscing. Then they donned their gowns and fairy wings and went out into the streets of Edmond to enjoy the festivities before making their way to the masquerade.

When they arrived at the party they were happy to discover that Kyle had made a last minute decision to fly up and surprise them. He looked stunning in his toreador costume, and he spent the night at their sides, laughing and being his usual charming self. At one point, when he was talking with Nina, they stood so close that Eleanor thought she saw their hands touch.

Then, near midnight, Kyle asked if he could speak to her in private. He took her arm, leading her out into the gardens and down a long, narrow stone path. As they neared the edge of Leesman's property she realized they were about to enter the public park. She suggested they turn back.

"Actually, there is something I want to show you," Kyle said.

They continued down a set of slate steps and found the grounds were filled with several costumed revelers enjoying a midnight stroll. They wandered for a few moments before settling on a stone bench.

"So what is it you wanted to show me?" she said.

"Well, it's not so much me that I need to show you, as it is something you need to see." Kyle looked at his watch and then took her hands in his. "Eleanor, I need you to open up your mind in a way you haven't before and consider the possibility that what is before you may not be all there is to see."

"All right, what is it you want me to see?"

"It's not so much a what, as it is a where. You need to see *where* you are."

The park grew silent. Eleanor stood up, and as she turned to take in her surroundings, she saw that it was empty. "What happened to all the people?"

Kyle smiled. "They're still here. Now, you just have to let go."

She continued to look around her, but the park remained vacant.

"Open your mind Eleanor," Kyle whispered, "and allow yourself to see."

She closed her eyes, releasing all thoughts of constraint and imagined them floating away. Suddenly she heard voices humming around her and when she opened her eyes she found the park filled with dozens of people. There were all sorts of gatherings from couples strolling to families playing with their children, which she found odd given the late hour. Many were in costume, just like her, and as she watched them pass by, she began to notice that these late night strollers were wearing all manner of dress from present time to centuries gone by.

Then she started to recognize people that had died in Edmond over the past 10 years.

"Kyle….where are we?"

"We are still sitting on the park bench."

"So, this is all happening in my mind."

"Yes and no. Your mind allows you to be here, but you are truly in another place."

"What am I seeing?"

"That which you have been asking me about for weeks… this is the other world."

"But, how am I able to do this?"

"You have the gift Eleanor. I will tell you all about it, but first, there is someone who has been waiting for you." Kyle pointed ahead to a man that was moving towards them.

Immediately she recognized his confident gait, and as he drew near, she could see his golden skin and his well-defined form. He was wearing his work clothes, a dark T-shirt, jeans and boots, and when he approached he flashed that sweet smile she had fallen in love with years ago. He held out his hand and she could feel their fingers intertwine. Then she heard the most beautiful sound in the world.

"Hello Ellie."

"Jeremy."